Praise for FALLEN GODS:

Beneath the fantasy and horror, a simmering love story brews. One that left me uneasy and completely unsure how to feel. Not because Ms. Simper failed, but because she succeeded so very, very well.
-Evie Drae, author of Beauregard and the Beast

Simper has created a brilliant combination of gruesomely dark fantasy and scorching romance. The protagonists are both so flawed, you are at once drawn to and repelled by them. Simper takes the idea of grey morality and writes it to perfection.
-The Lesbian Review

Simper has created a complex, immersive world for the series and that's not even touching on the well-developed characters or the complicated, fucked up relationship you can't help but ship anyway.
-Manic Femme Reviews

Praise for SEA AND STARS:

"If you like your fantasy with an extra dark twist, exceptional world building and deeply complex characters then reel this book in fast. You'll be hooked."
-The Lesbian Review

"The Fate of Stars, the first book in the Sea and Stars trilogy, is delightfully dark and sexy, full of lush imagery, vibrant characterization, and enough adrenaline to keep me up way past my bedtime."
-Anna Burke, award winning author of THORN and COMPASS ROSE

Praise for Carmilla and Laura:

A beautiful retelling . . . perfect for anyone who likes darker-themed romance, horror stories, or plain ol' lesbian vampires.
-The Lesbian 52

THE Sting OF Victory

THE *Sting* OF *Victory*

S D SIMPER

The Sting of Victory | Fallen Gods Book One

Cover art by Jade Merien

Cover design and interior by Jerah Moss

Map by Mars Simper

ISBN (Paperback): 978-1-7324611-2-3

Visit the author at www.sdsimper.com

TikTok: @sdsimper
Facebook: sdsimper
Twitter: @sdsimper
Instagram: sdsimper

For Veronica

Publisher's Note: The Sting of Victory is a fantasy horror novel intended for adults and may contain material upsetting to some readers. Please visit sdsimper.com to view a list of spoiler-free content warnings.

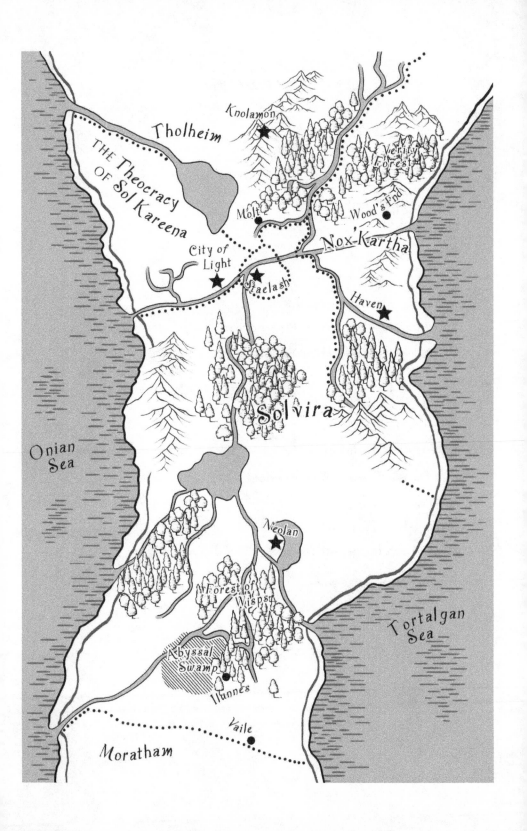

Names

THE ROYAL COUNCIL OF STAELASH

Marielle Vors—Mair-ee-el Vohrs

Etolié—Eh-toh-lee-ey

Khastra—Kas-truh

Thalmus—Thah-muhs

Flowridia—Floh-rid-ee-uh

Sora Fireborn—Sohr-ruh Fire-bohrn

Meira deShamira—Mee-ruh Dey-sha-mee-ruh

FOREIGN DIGNITARIES

Xoran—Zoh-ran

Lunestra—Loon-es-truh

Ayla Darkleaf—Ai-luh Dahrk-leef

Zorlaeus—Zor-ley-uhs

Casvir—Kas-veer

Alauriel Solviraes—Ah-law-ree-ehl Sohl-veer-es

OTHER PLAYERS

Odessa—Oh-**des**-uh

Soliel—Suh-**lil**

Demitri—Dih-**mee**-tree

VARIOUS GODS, ANGELIC AND DEMONIC

Sol Kareena—Sohl Kuh-**ree**-nuh

Eionei—**Eye**-uhn-eye

Alystra—Ah-**lees**-truh

Staella—**Stey**-luh

Neoma—Ney-**oh**-muh

Izthuni—Iz-**thoo**-nee

Ku'Shya—Koo-**shy**-uh

Onias—Uhn-**eye**-uhs

Moonlight brushed the air in silver wisps, barely perceptible through the thick cover of trees. But enough shone through to cast a shadow upon the secluded cottage, that of a wolf coated in mud and grime.

From within, Flowridia ripped the door open. "Aura!" she cried, weeping as her arms tangled in the damp fur of her beloved companion—Aura the wolf, her lost friend and familiar, had come for her at last.

Noxious odors from the swamp mixed with the earthy, rotting scent of mushrooms and the horrors that fed them. Aura's golden eyes shone bright, reflecting the filtered celestial light and the phosphorescent glow of fungi dotting the walls and moist garden plots. More garden than room, the fungal forest grew in patches, some of the mushrooms taller than Flowridia herself.

Aura had grown during their three years apart, standing nearly at Flowridia's shoulder in height. Even matted in swamp filth, her silver fur matched the dim moonlight.

Despite the joy at their reunion, urgency tugged at Flowridia's panicked heart. "Aura, we have to leave. If she hears us—"

Shattered glass broke the fragile peace. Flowridia, her arms tight around Aura's neck, saw a dark silhouette in the doorframe of the bedroom and the remains of a ruined potion on the floor. "Flower Child, what is this?" The woman spoke gently, the eye of a storm Flowridia knew capable of tearing them both to oblivion. Odessa the Swamp Witch stepped into view, beautiful despite her sneer, a distorted, matured mirror of her cowering daughter. Eerie green shone from within her eyes, her mouth, even the pores of her skin.

1

"All of my love, and this is how it's returned? Slinking off in the middle of the night?"

Growling from Aura's throat vibrated against Flowridia's arms. Mother merely chuckled. "Your familiar is every bit the hero that you are the coward." She turned her gaze onto Aura directly, stepping forward as that same green began to swirl at her feet, smoke before a raging fire. "Stay with us. She'll be better with you and I both to guide her."

A snarl tore from Aura's throat. Flowridia's grip on her neck tightened.

"No? A pity," Mother said, and as she stepped, Flowridia watched her form shift and elongate. "So much wasted potential."

Flowridia had seen hints of Mother's shadow, one that never quite matched her sultry figure. Now the woman twisted and grew, her hands gnarling into vicious claws, her skin shriveling and turning grey. Those eyes, still illuminated by sickly green, grew large, bird-like. The woman, once beautiful, became hunched.

Flowridia tugged on Aura's neck, pulling her to the door, but green fire—the same shade as the smoke swirling around Mother's grotesque form—blocked their exit.

Aura tore herself from Flowridia's grip, a beastly roar at her throat as she bolted forward. Leaping, the wolf tackled the monster and ripped at the woman's face with her teeth. A swipe of Mother's mutated hand threw Aura aside. Bleeding, cackling, Mother pulled herself to her feet in time for Aura to pounce.

This time, Mother braced herself. Her hands dug into the wolf's fur and skin, blood seeping from her nails as Aura struggled in her grasp.

The light shining from Mother's eyes changed from green to deep purple, and the smoke swirled to match. Aura released a pained howl, and Flowridia screamed as the wolf's body began to shrivel, withering away as though starved.

On the table, a knife—encrusted with dried blood— caught her eye. Heart pounding, Flowridia didn't think; she grabbed the knife and threw.

Blood sprayed. The knife embedded into Mother's throat, soaking Flowridia and the limp wolf in the monster's vital fluids.

Mother shrieked, that same purple glow bursting from the wound, the hilt protruding from beneath her chin. The smoke, once peaceful, spun into a violent torrent. Aura fell motionless to the ground as Mother's cry grew higher, louder. Her clawed hands shook as she reached toward the knife.

All at once, the light ceased. Smoke dissipated. Mother fell to the ground, her monstrous form dissolving into the air. A woman's corpse, a knife jutting from her throat, lay in a pool of her own seeping blood.

Silence.

Flowridia's sob cut the taut string of peace. She fell to her knees, giving no mind to how her skirts absorbed Mother's blood. Silver fur, stained red, met Flowridia's fingers as she desperately pulled Aura's emaciated form to her lap. The wolf's coat, once soft, had become coarse, aged by Mother's dark magic.

No light in those golden, clouded eyes. Already, Aura had gone cold. With that came an awareness of the hollow in Flowridia's soul. Her familiar, the animal companion granting her mysterious power, lay dead, and with it her connection to the world of magic. Muted, all she had worked for; the power she had gained gone away.

Three years trapped in hell, but never had she felt so lost. She held Aura's body to her chest and wept.

Here lies Aura—a friend.

The words shone pristine, carved in stone, the last gift she could give her dearest companion. Content to lie down and starve to death, Flowridia might have lain on the grave forever had red eyes not shone from the woods.

The demon began to hunt her then.

For weeks, it followed. Flowridia left the swamp but saw it on distant hills and in the shadow of trees. A blight upon her vision, it had come to haunt her sleep—nightmares, more often than not—and at times she heard metallic steps emerge from her dreams and infiltrate whatever dark woods she slept in. It followed; she fled.

Was it punishment for her sins? A demon come to personally escort her to her seat in hell?

It cornered her on a moonless night. Alone and half-starved, she collapsed.

The demon emerged as a silhouette, his horns a crown atop his head. Metal met earth with each step upon the forest floor. Mist swirled about, and no stars could penetrate the cover of trees—only the shadow of a monster leering before her as she sobbed.

Tears and dirt had mixed to become a sticky mess upon Flowridia's face and body. She shrunk before the armored figure, falling to the ground, cowering as he stood before her. To meet her end now would be best. To forget the horror of these past few years and meet a swift demise was far more than she deserved.

Flowridia dared to speak. "Please kill me quickly."

The demon offered an enormous, clawed hand. Trembling, she reached out with her own, surprised at the cold touch, but also the gentle way he helped her to rise. Once her feet were stable, she wrenched her hand back.

Closer now, she saw the rich detail of his armor, blackened and dented, worn and well-used. He stood several heads taller than she, more so with the horns jutting from his head. Darkness obscured the rest, but she could faintly see the bold red of his eyes.

In the crook of his arm, she realized he cradled a small, bundled creature. He offered it forward—a sleeping wolf pup. Flowridia carefully took it into her arms.

They touched, she and the wolf, and a network of energy suddenly spiked her senses. The very essence of the universe, the threads that wove the tapestry of the world were hers to touch, to pluck and weave.

Her head grew light at the sudden influx of awareness. Magic coursed through her veins. Surprised, she kept a protective hold on the baby creature, daring to tear her eyes away from the demon and instead look at the soft form.

It breathed peacefully, innocently. She held the wolf and felt a piece of her soul—the one brutally ripped away only weeks prior—begin to mend and heal.

"You have one more chance." The demon's words resonated deep and soft, a terrible threat to the power lying behind them; an underground rumble, a volcano brewing beneath the earth. "Do not disappoint me."

He stepped away, disappearing into the swirling mist.

Flowridia held the bundled, sleeping form close to her chest, stroking the fine puppy fur. Tears continued streaming, but of relief; no more fear.

At her feet, a dying patch of clovers raised a curious thought, and without hesitation she fell to her knees and touched the leaves. Like veins, she felt what energy the plant used, the life it stubbornly clung to, and felt what it craved.

A healing spell slid from her fingers. The clovers grew, and were the night not so dark, she knew she would have seen vibrant shades of green. Whatever horrors she had witnessed and committed, the joy of the moment blinded the shadows.

The small wolf stirred, roused perhaps by the slight draining of energy she knew they had both felt. Golden eyes met her own. A voice, young and childish, wove through her mind.

Hello.

Chapter 1

Flowridia's own blood would feed the roses today. With a wince, she took her hand back, giving no regard to the dirt as she stuck her finger into her mouth. But the damage was done; blood had dripped onto the stem, the petals, and her white sleeve.

Grimacing, Flowridia released her finger and frowned at the deep puncture. Such carelessness should have been beyond her. Instead, she breathed out a sigh, letting her senses expand and touch upon the torn flesh, the welling blood. She released a silent spell, one that welled from her core. A bit of heat and discomfort, but only slight, and before she could blink the wound had knit together, leaving only a shined scar.

A slight weight on Flowridia's thigh caused her to turn. Her hair covered her face as a child's voice, as small as the wolf padding at her leg, wove words into her mind. *I smell Marielle. She has someone with her.*

Wide-eyed, Flowridia lifted the wolf into her arms, hiding her bloodied sleeve as another spell drained her of energy. "Stay quiet, Demitri," she whispered, and before she had finished her sentence, both their forms had faded from view. Not quite invisibility, but living with Mother had taught Flowridia that if she gave herself no regard, people often looked directly through her. It hadn't failed her yet.

She stepped beyond the garden path and stood beside a tree, just as a familiar voice danced along the faint breeze.

"... garden is new, and it's the safest place in the manor. We won't be overheard here. Flowridia has protection spells everywhere."

Not quite spells, Flowridia corrected internally. Spells were spoken, silently or not; wards were written, and writing ancient words with the roots of plants and trees wove them into the earth itself. But she remained silent as Princess Marielle Vors appeared at the center of the shaded path, accompanied by a woman Flowridia had never seen. Diminutive and regally dressed, the woman's soft eyes were as silver as the tiara atop her head. Curious, Flowridia watched as the unknown woman's unique gaze traced over every part of the greenery and floral bushes.

"This is impressive," she said. "Wards are a difficult thing to place." Flowridia found herself quietly surprised by the woman's ability to differentiate the two. "Who did you say did this?"

"Flowridia, Etolié's apprentice," Marielle replied. "She's a witch; isn't that something? I think Etolié's finally snapped and picked someone to train as Magister for when she's out scouting. She found Flowridia in the woods not six months ago."

"Etolié found a witch in the woods and brought her home as an apprentice?"

"Odd, I know, but I trust Etolié's judgement of people." The young monarch frowned suddenly. "I was hoping Flowridia would be here, that shy little thing. She spends all her free time gardening."

The woman glanced down, pursing her lips. When she looked back up, she stared directly at Flowridia. Their eyes made contact. Flowridia shrunk back, but a slow smile spread across the other woman's face. "Oh, I'm sure she's hiding around here somewhere. Do you trust her?"

"Very much so."

Her gaze lingered, then she turned back to Marielle as the two continued walking. The woman's disposition changed, pleasantries fading into something ascetic.

"My father always said that your own father's idealism was why this kingdom ever had a hope to survive," the woman said, and she stopped as she stared at a bush of vibrant hyacinths. "Be careful, Marielle. We aren't our fathers, even if it's their shoes we have to step into, prematurely or not."

Marielle's frown threatened to wilt the flowers in her gaze. "What do you mean?"

The woman steeled her jaw, and behind her back, away from Marielle's view, her hands began to fidget. "The news will be announced to the citizens of my empire upon my return, but my father is dead."

Marielle's face paled. The young monarch-to-be brought a hand to cover her mouth. "No, no, he can't be. I received a letter not two weeks ago congratulating me on–"

"It was three days ago," the woman interrupted, breathing in deep. Her voice caught, but she gave no other sign of emotional compromise. Flowridia knew of only one empire, and for this woman's father to have ruled it meant she was a famous name—Alauriel Solviraes, heir to the long-lived dynasty of legendary sorcerers and cousin to Princess Marielle.

"I'm here for your coronation," the empress continued, amidst Marielle's visible disbelief, "but also to keep the peace at your party afterward. Whatever concoction of political kindling we stand on, it will not combust so long as we tread lightly, even with your tempestuous guest list— not while my father's shadow lords over it all. But with his death comes uncertain future. Be careful, Marielle."

"But how?" Marielle finally managed to sputter. "If he was sick–"

"He wasn't sick. The investigation is ongoing, so there's nothing more to say. Not yet." Empress Alauriel placed a hand on Marielle's back. She summoned a smile, though Flowridia saw it flicker and threaten to fade. "Today is your day. You'll want to focus on your own political cesspool." A slight push, and she began to lead Marielle down the path, out of the garden. "The coronation is soon. Perhaps we'll find Etolié's gardener somewhere else."

This time, the empress didn't acknowledge her. When they left the garden, Flowridia reappeared, her heart beating rapidly.

The coronation was for royals and for Marielle's guests. Flowridia had come up with several excuses to not attend: *"Oh, Demitri would be lonely without me–" "I wouldn't know what to say–" "I would only embarrass you–"*

Etolié had accepted none of them but agreed to compromise: Flowridia would be excused from the coronation if she would attend the ball instead. Content to join in the small celebration, Flowridia had agreed.

Marielle had then vastly expanded her guest list. The ball would be the more social of events.

Now, standing before the mirror of her bedroom, Flowridia wove flowers into her long, thick hair. The residue of wards permeated the floral life, granting protection, though at a much smaller scale.

A knock at the door startled her, and with it came a voice. "Rise and shine, Flowers. Nox'Kartha's late, and so are you."

With some reticence, Flowridia peeked out the bedroom door, unsurprised to see Etolié at the other side. "I'm awake, Etolié," she said, letting the door swing open. "Why do we care if Nox'Kartha is late?"

Etolié stepped in, her dress a galaxy as it swirled and glittered in varying shades of purple and black—fitting, given her luminous, silver hair and her tendency to stare off into space. Some might mistake the sway of her steps as some ethereal quirk, but Flowridia had learned to blame her indulgent drinking habits.

Still, Etolié was stunning, ageless. Flowridia thought her the most beautiful creature she had ever seen. Celestials—those with the blood of angels from Celestière—often held an otherworldly sort of beauty, and Etolié was second generation.

"Representatives from many kingdoms were at the coronation, but Nox'Kartha has yet to show." Etolié's frown pulled her entire face into a pout as she surveyed Flowridia's appearance. "You look terrible," she continued, and she immediately pushed Flowridia in front of the mirror and began pinning her hair away from her face.

Flowridia flinched at the gesture. She studied her hair, her dress—one of Marielle's, from her youth. "Demitri said I looked beautiful."

"You're always beautiful, Flowers. But how old was Marielle when she wore this? Twelve?" With a wave of Etolié's hand, the buttons all came undone at once. The dress crumpled to the floor. Flowridia instinctively covered her exposed form, but Etolié gave no care to her near nudity. "You will not look twelve at Marielle's ball."

"I don't own anything fancy."

"Well, I do. And fortunately for you, we're the same size. I, too, have the body of a twelve-year-old." Chuckling,

9

Etolié grasped the empty air. In her hand, a perfect duet of yellow and lace appeared. "I'll help you put it on."

From the bed, Demitri's voice mingled with her thoughts. *I still think you look beautiful.*

A blush darkened Flowridia's cheeks. "Thank you, Demitri," she said, glancing at his reflection in the mirror. The tiny wolf watched the scene from the bed, his golden eyes shining from within a pile of blankets.

Etolié glanced between the two of them. "I've never met a girl and her familiar quite so attached. I still think it's odd he can talk to you."

Etolié finished adjusting the gown around Flowridia's thin shoulders. Truly, the modest gown did look better, casting her aura in warm autumn shades, the dress and her hair a sunrise upon her earth-toned skin.

"See? It even covers your feet. Now you almost look your age," Etolié teased as she inspected Flowridia's hair. "The flowers are cute. Keep 'em."

Tiny white buds dotted the sea of her sepia hair, ships along the waves. Picked only an hour before, the white gardenias all followed a large yellow blossom stuck behind her ear. "I do this every day, Etolié."

"Keep doing it. All the Theocracy boys come running for a head full of flowers."

Flowridia grimaced at the jest. "Even if I look twelve?"

"You look at least fifteen. Now, come on. No one will even notice your feet."

Instead of following her to the door, Flowridia stepped toward her bed and pulled the lump of blankets into her arms. She kissed the tiny head peeking out. "You're sure you don't want to come?"

I would get squished and die.

Slipping her hands inside the blanket, she managed to pluck Demitri out and cradle him in her arms. "I won't be gone too late, dearest Demitri." She kissed his nose and set him back down, smiling as he burrowed his way back under the blankets.

Etolié immediately began plucking grey hairs from the lacy gown. "You're not in the woods anymore, Flowers."

"And you're not liberating slave camps."

Etolié's dramatic sigh held resignation. "For now, we play the political game. When I decide to run for good, I'll take you with me. Fortunately, Marielle is eighteen now, and I don't have to be the only one making decisions."

In the oligarchy that was Staelash, there were three council members who made decisions, and it seemed Etolié had dismissed one entirely. "What about Khastra?"

"Lady General agrees to everything I do. She hardly counts." She beckoned Flowridia forward, and they traveled down the stone hallway and toward the stairs.

Sconces attached to the walls held glowing crystals, bright enough to provide ample light even in the early evening. "What did you mean by 'Theocracy boys?'" Flowridia asked as they skirted down the deserted hallway.

"Representatives from the Theocracy of Sol Kareena are here, and most look about your age. With the size of their envoy, they're definitely trying to kiss up to Marielle."

Flowridia's feet barely touched the stairs as they stepped down, the motions smooth and well-rehearsed. "Why, though?"

"Because Nox'Kartha will surely do the same," Etolié replied, resignation apparent as she rolled her eyes. "Especially after Marielle insisted they send Zorlaeus to her party."

The thought pulled a smile to Flowridia's face. "Those two are awfully cute."

"I expect wedding bells within the year." On the first floor, Etolié paused and inspected Flowridia one last time. "Don't tell anyone I let you out of your room without shoes," she said, straightening the gown around Flowridia's shoulders yet again. "But have fun. And don't talk to anyone with a title higher than your own."

Flowridia frowned. "And how will I know?"

"You won't. Don't speak unless spoken to." Etolié looped her arm through Flowridia's. "Now come, Lady Flowridia of Staelash. The ball awaits."

Nervous, she followed Etolié's lead, knowing the eccentric Celestial had her best interest at heart.

The enormous double doors opened at their approach, and Flowridia grew faint at the crowd of people. Many races—human, Celestial, dwarves, and others—met her eyes, and she might have backed away had Etolié not held an iron grip around her arm. Instead, they moved forward, the crowd parting at Etolié's passage.

Etolié had been born for rich crowds and majestic halls, whereas Flowridia often felt she would be better suited to be transformed into her namesake. Flowers were pretty, but no one expected them to interact with people.

At the back stood the newly crowned Queen Marielle. Tall and curvaceous, clearly visible in the queen's ample cleavage was an odd gem, one that glowed in the same fiery shades as her hair. She looked every part the young monarch, decadent and heavily made-up, but she frowned as she searched the crowd.

She smiled wide when she spotted Flowridia and Etolié and ran forward at their approach. "Flowridia, I'm so glad you came!"

"Etolié dragged me out–" Cut off by Marielle's crushing hug, Flowridia held her breath, smothered by the queen's plunging neckline.

A looming shadow covered the trio as Marielle released her. Thalmus, nearly twice Flowridia's height, stared down, wearing as rich of attire as Marielle would have been able to force on him. Upon their first meeting, Flowridia had recognized giant's blood in his hulking figure, but he was as quiet and gentle a man as she had ever met. He served as the financial advisor to their kingdom and unofficial bodyguard to Marielle, though his knowledge of healing arts had intrigued Flowridia since their introduction.

Flowridia looked up, smiling at her reserved friend. "You look as miserable as I feel."

Thalmus simply nodded. "But I am here for Marielle."

"Where is Nox'Kartha?" Marielle asked as she nudged Etolié with her hip.

Etolié's lip twisted into a mischievous grin. "I didn't think they could come out before dark."

"Oh, hush," Marielle said, still surveying the crowd. "They aren't all undead and nasty things."

"Not if you hear the Theocracy talk," Etolié muttered, watching with amusement as a well-dressed gentleman approached.

The representative from the Theocracy of Sol Kareena– an elf, Flowridia realized, from his lithe physique and pointed ears—bowed low in Marielle's presence, an empty wineglass balanced in one hand. "Queen Marielle, the archbishop sends his regards to you and your kingdom. Your father's legacy is a heavy one to bear, but he believes you will carry it with grace."

Flowridia watched as Marielle stood taller, regal as she spoke words to match her title. "Thank you, Lord Ashwood. Your presence is a delight to my kingdom."

"I'm to offer an apology as well—there has been an uproar in my kingdom, with the recent news of the Goddess giving birth. Plans for the celebration are already underway, and the archbishop heads the celebratory planning."

"Oh, of course," Marielle replied, unoffended. "Magister Etolié says Celestière is radiating with joy. The child is a good omen to both the worlds."

"Numerous priests have announced their intention to pledge to Sol Kareena's child during the celebration. Should any of yours wish to join them, we would be happy to accommodate," he said, gesturing with the glass. "Such a delightful group of allies you keep."

"Unfortunately, not everyone is here," Marielle replied with some regret. "Nox'Kartha has yet to arrive."

Perhaps Flowridia only saw it because she was looking, but a slight frown pulled at Lord Ashwood's lips. "It certainly would be an insult for Imperator Casvir to arrive late."

"I only hope they haven't run into trouble," Marielle said, keeping her pleasant smile.

"You are young, Queen Marielle, so a piece of advice," Lord Ashwood said, and then he lowered his voice. "Nox'Kartha is often the aforementioned trouble."

Marielle simply nodded. "Your words are well-received."

He nodded in return and stepped away.

Once gone, Marielle turned around, enraged. "I want spies on the Theocracy's trail." Her eyes narrowed. "Wouldn't want there to be any trouble."

Thalmus nodded and waded into the crowd. An impressive space parted around him, his size matched only by his daunting aura.

Marielle stepped back up and toward her throne. Etolié placed a hand on the newly crowned monarch's shoulder. "First lesson in diplomacy, Marielle: smile sweetly and always keep a dagger behind your back." Straight out of the air, Etolié pulled out a tiny silver flask. She tipped it back and swallowed, grinning. "And never be sober." Then, she made her way into the crowd.

Marielle leaned in toward Flowridia. "Is that her first drink of the night?"

"I can never tell," Flowridia admitted. "Now what?"

"Go socialize! Even though Lord Ashwood is unpleasant, it doesn't mean the rest of them are."

13

"But Etolié said–"

"Go, little wallflower. Make up a title and find some friends." Marielle shoved her forward.

Unfortunately, Flowridia stumbled directly into a nondescript young man, one who wore a servant's garb. Horrified, she said, "I am *so* sorry."

But the young man's face was sheet white, his eyes wide and wary. Ignoring her, he said, "Queen Marielle, Nox'Kartha has arrived."

The breath Marielle sucked in hitched, and she covered her mouth with her hands. "All right, breathe. Marielle, breathe." She turned to Flowridia. "Pinch my cheeks."

Flowridia obeyed, gently pulling at the skin to make a faint blush appear.

"Is Zorlaeus with them?"

"I-I admit, my queen, if he was, I didn't notice. Would you like me to find out?"

"No, no," Marielle said, flustered. "I'll know it soon, if he's here. You're excused."

Flowridia took that as her cue to step away as well, but Marielle stole her hand. "Stay," the young queen said. "Be strong with me."

Flowridia offered a shy nod, unwilling to explain to Marielle that strength was hardly transferable, but then fought the urge to squeak when the grip suddenly tightened. The double doors opened, and Marielle nearly toppled over.

Flowridia had met Zorlaeus a time or two, the deep maroon of his skin in comparable tones with the boyish mop of hair curling around his horns. Humanoid by appearances, yet his ancestry was unmistakable—the demons of Sha'Demoni had bred with humanity in the same way angels had countless generations ago, any demonic talents diluted over time by human influence. They made up an entire race—De'Sindai—and most lived under the benevolent tyranny of Imperator Casvir.

The man's stance betrayed nothing but palpable anxiety. Flowridia found Zorlaeus endearing at best.

But the elven woman who led him, pale and bone-thin, radiated a presence as wide as the walls of the ballroom. Her black dress, painted on by appearances, slit down to her navel, though her small cleavage barely cast a shadow. Tiny in every dimension, the woman surveyed the crowd with a predatory glint in her vivid, icy blue eyes.

The sea of people parted, and Flowridia found herself utterly enthralled as the elf moved gracefully through the crowd, her feet as silent as the hushed onlookers. Three earrings, stone specks embedded into her pointed ear, flashed in the artificial light and matching stones glittered in her black hair.

Was it rude to stare at someone who so clearly reveled in the attention? Marielle seemed focused on Zorlaeus, but all others watched the intoxicating woman he trailed behind.

She bowed, and he followed in synch. "I am Lady Ayla Darkleaf, Grand Diplomat of Nox'Kartha," she said, teeth flashing as she grinned. Wide and beguiling, Ayla's smile reminded Flowridia of a wolf before it devoured its prey. "I come on behalf of Casvir."

Zorlaeus kept his gaze to the ground, but Flowridia saw the flash of panic in his wide eyes. "*Imperator* Casvir, First and Last of his name, Tyrant of Nox'Kartha, and Marshall of the Deathless Army, sends his regards, Queen Marielle," he said, straightening his posture. His expression softened as he met Marielle's eyes, and when the grip on Flowridia's hand suddenly tightened, she thought it might lose all blood flow. "He wishes you the best and offers a small gift." From his pocket, he procured a small box. Within shone a vibrant pendant: the Nox'Karthan seal, a skull embedded within a gold coin.

Marielle kept her smile for Zorlaeus. She released Flowridia's hand to accept the gift. "Tell Imperator Casvir 'thank you.'"

Flowridia took a step back, uneasy in Ayla's presence. The woman loomed like a storm cloud behind the brilliant sun of Marielle and Zorlaeus. Even in the bright lights, her cheekbones looked capable of cutting diamonds, especially when she smiled at Lord Ashwood's approach.

"Lady Darkleaf," the man said. "Appropriately late for one of your kind."

Ayla laughed at the slight. "Didn't you know? We Nox'Karthans can only come out after dark."

Etolié had made the same joke—so it was merely a joke, right? Flowridia watched as Ayla's laughter increased at Lord Ashwood's obvious discomfort.

Marielle, however, resumed her regal aura, though Flowridia knew her heart palpitated in Zorlaeus' presence. "Lord Ashwood, I wasn't aware you and Lady Ayla had met."

"I have not had the honor until now," the ambassador said, "but her reputation precedes her."

"My reputation?" Ayla said, placing a hand against her visible sternum. "Oh, you flatter."

"We Sun Elves never forget one of our own." His stare held no humor, but he took a small sip from his drink.

Ayla chuckled yet again, this time with less sincerity. "A pity. I have not considered myself a Sun Elf in a long time."

"Then it is good a country of monsters so benevolently accepted one of their own," Lord Ashwood said, and before Ayla could respond he returned his attention to Marielle. Flowridia, however, kept her stare on Ayla, watching her amusement rapidly fade into anger. "My country extends their best wishes, and I hope it will be no insult to you if we leave tonight."

Marielle's gaze tore away from Zorlaeus. "No insult. But if we can fix your accommodations in any way–"

"Your accommodations have been more than adequate and more than kind. But I do not wish to subject my people to share a roof with something I would not sleep within a hundred miles of." Lord Ashwood bowed low, maintaining eye contact with Marielle. "Congratulations, Queen Marielle."

As he walked away, Ayla's spiteful glare followed. She turned to Marielle and smiled, though her eyes stayed the same. "Another gift, Queen Marielle. I hope you shall enjoy it." With purpose, she strode toward the center of the room, all attention shifting to her.

Marielle stepped closer to Zorlaeus and whispered, "She won't eat my guests, right?"

"Not with as short a leash as Imperator Casvir keeps on her," he replied, and Flowridia watched Zorlaeus lean closer, letting their arms brush.

"Attention, guests of Queen Marielle," Ayla said, her voice ringing out to every corner of the room. Slowly moving, she turned in a circle, letting her gaze rest on each face—including Flowridia's. Their eyes met, and she felt a chill travel down her spine and farther still, warming and settling somewhere deep. "Keep your music, but dim the lights," Ayla continued, her gaze finally shifting away. "I have a gift for the queen."

The lights grew low, and Ayla's eyes fluttered shut, a certain grace in the pose she assumed. The music continued,

16

and Ayla let her movements match in time, dancing on silent feet upon the polished stone floor. Flowridia knew little of dance, only enough to watch couples move and sway, but unquestionable talent lay in every minute motion of Ayla's body. An artist, with how she twirled and bent, each lithe muscle of her body held in absolute control.

Ayla wove nearer to the crowd, approaching a shadow cast by one of the guests, and vanished when her foot touched the darkness. A hushed gasp filled the room, and Flowridia's hand reached up to cover her mouth when Ayla reappeared, but several feet away, emerging from the shadow and skipping into the next. She disappeared, flickering in and out like a candle. A beautiful display, yes, but Flowridia sensed a purpose behind it; a warning to those who would dare insult her.

At the conclusion of the song, Ayla stood with poise, bowing and shutting her eyes to bask in the rousing applause. Captivated, Flowridia found she could not even join in the ovation.

"Incredible," she heard Marielle mutter.

Ayla's stance relaxed, and Flowridia joined in the rich applause. "That was beautiful," she said, to no one in particular.

"She thinks very highly of her talents," she heard a man say; she realized Zorlaeus had spoken. "But she is quite accomplished, yes."

For a fleeting moment, Flowridia wondered what it might be like to share a dance with Ayla, realizing she blushed at the idea.

Ayla herself bowed again to Marielle, not a hair out of place and no hurry to her breath. "I hope you enjoyed the performance," she said, charm in her smile. But when she looked to Zorlaeus and saw their touch, ire marred that splendid grin.

Marielle nodded, as mesmerized as the rest. "Absolutely stunning."

"Thank you," she replied, words curt. She lingered a moment, staring between Zorlaeus and Marielle. "Now if you'll excuse me, I've heard that your kingdom is famous for its specialty alcohol."

"Oh, yes! Our Magister, Etolié, is a descendent of the Drinking God himself. Her brews are here for sampling. And, of course, I have my vineyard. There is a selection of wine from my personal stores."

"How generous of you," Ayla said, standing tall. "Excuse me, then. I would love a sample." She turned, dress swaying with each minute, haughty motion of her body.

"Lady Ayla is somewhat of a connoisseur of alcohol," Zorlaeus whispered, once she had disappeared into the crowd.

"Good to know," Marielle said, "if I need to strike up a conversation with her."

Flowridia watched the crowd, hoping to catch a glimpse of the entrancing diplomat. Compelled by a force she could not quite name, she stepped forward, the quiet fear that she might speak to Ayla overshadowed by pure intrigue.

Distracted, she gasped when Etolié suddenly grabbed her arm. "Now that was some sorcery! Did you see that stunt, Flowers?" A half-full stein threatened to spill from Etolié's hands, but the frothy liquid did not splash out even once. Instead, Etolié grabbed the collar of a well-dressed woman beside her. "Flowers, meet Lara."

The Lara in question was, in fact, Alauriel Solviraes, Empress of Solvira, heir to the Silver Fire, benefactor of their territory, and the same woman Flowridia had seen in the garden.

She remembered, then, that she wasn't even wearing shoes.

The woman offered her hand along with a knowing smile. The other held an empty wine glass. "So, you're Etolié's gardener?"

The words slurred slightly. Flowridia accepted the hand, quest forgotten as Lara's soft, silver eyes glanced down her form. "I am," she said, and she bowed, still holding Lara's hand. "Flowridia–" She stopped, a blush filling her cheeks. "I don't have a title."

Lara laughed, her volume amplified by the presence of alcohol. "Etolié dressed you, didn't she."

"I don't own many nice things of my own." Then, realizing she still held hands with a woman capable of leveling the building with a mere thought—or so rumor said—Flowridia wrenched her arm back.

"I've known Lara since she was a tiny little moonbeam," Etolié said, affection in her drunken stare. She ruffled Lara's immaculately braided hair, and Flowridia wondered what degree of insanity one had to reach to touch an empress without permission, much less ruin her hair. "Practically raised her."

18

The empress in question simply smiled, her gaze set to Flowridia. "For Etolié to show interest tells me you're something special."

With her hands held behind her back, Flowridia smiled curtly. "All I really do is hold books for her."

"Lies, Flowers," Etolié spat. "That's like saying Khastra sometimes punches things with her personality, or that her hoity-toity diplomat of Nox'Kartha-ness avoids tanning."

"Speaking of whom," Flowridia said, uncaring of her wistful tone, "did you see where she went? I wanted to compliment her."

Etolié shook her head. "And good luck finding her."

Flowridia felt her cheeks color. "Etolié, do you know if Nox'Kartha is staying in our kingdom for long?"

"I know Marielle certainly hopes so. And I know they're invited to the royal hunt tomorrow." She nudged Flowridia with her elbow. "Are you coming?"

Flowridia frowned and shyly shook her head. "I told you–"

"You think it's awful—I remember. But the rest of the castle will be there. And Demitri might enjoy himself."

There mere thought turned her stomach. Instead of responding, she glanced at the crowd. "Where is the alcohol?"

Etolié pointed to a table at the wall. "Off to try a sip?"

"Looking for a friend," she said, and before Etolié could question her, she turned to the intoxicated Empress. The wine glass had mysteriously refilled. "It was a pleasure to meet you."

"Likewise," Lara replied, and Flowridia darted away before they could say more.

Guests crowded the tables, but the elf was nowhere to be seen. Even with her diminutive size, Ayla would be difficult to miss.

But there was no sign of the elven woman among the party revelers. Flowridia stood invisible among the sea of important strangers.

She could socialize, as Marielle had suggested, find the so-called 'Theocracy boys,' but instead she glanced back to where she had left Etolié. The Celestial woman would hardly notice if she disappeared, drunk and content among her royal companions. Perhaps the party was over.

Relieved at the thought, Flowridia quietly slipped through the double doors and into the hallway.

In her bedroom, Demitri burst from the bed sheets. His voice mingled in her thoughts as the door clicked shut. *How was the party?*

"I'm not a fan of crowds," Flowridia said, but a smile spread wide across her face. "I met someone. Sort of."

Demitri crawled over to the edge of the bed and licked her hand. *Sort of?*

"I didn't talk to her. I couldn't find her." Demitri began sniffing at her dress. Flowridia collapsed on the bed next to him, shutting her eyes as she replayed the scene inside her head, that of Lady Ayla and her dance. "But she was something."

What was her name?

"Ayla," she whispered, the name a pleasure on her tongue. "Lady Ayla Darkleaf, Grand Diplomat of Nox'Kartha. And she could dance."

Why didn't you talk to her?

"I doubt I would be of any interest to her," Flowridia said, but still her smile remained wide. "But I might be able to introduce myself, at least."

Bring me along. I think I'm a great conversation starter. Demitri's tiny claws caught themselves in the lace of her dress as he attempted to climb up her torso.

Flowridia freed his paws and settled him onto her chest. "Perhaps Ayla likes wolves," she said, and she planted a kiss onto his nose.

Chapter 2

W ere actual smoke rising from Marielle's footsteps, it might give justice to the anger visibly stirring within the newly crowned queen. Flowridia and Demitri, descending from their room to find breakfast, slowed when the seething queen stopped her pacing and said, "You haven't heard, have you?"

Flowridia shook her head.

"My wine cellar has been ravaged!" Marielle said, and Flowridia did not presume to imagine the heat radiating from her form. At her bosom, the orb glowed to match her fury.

Nervous, Flowridia's posture caved as she mumbled, "I'm sorry. Do we know who did it?"

"Ayla Darkleaf. That's what Zorlaeus said. And now she's too hung-over to join the hunt. The audacity!"

"Ayla is hung-over?"

"Zorlaeus said she was impulsive. But how does a person that size drink an entire wine cellar?"

Gears began turning in Flowridia's mind. "Ayla isn't going on the hunt?"

"No, she is not." Marielle folded her arms, a 'huff' escaping her lips. "But maybe that's for the best. Zorlaeus seems nervous around her."

Flowridia nodded, slipping past as Marielle continued her ranting. Instead of entering the kitchen, she took a detour outside, running across the stone steps until she reached the small patch of land she had claimed for her own—her garden.

The stone steps led to a grassy path, decorated at each side by expansive, colorful greenery. Trees shaded the entrance, patches of flowers and bushes creating a pathway. Flowridia slowed her steps as she entered her space, the only sounds the faint singing of birds in the trees and Demitri's soft steps beside her. Her senses lit as she breathed in the clean air, the sweet scent of flowers filling her nose. A gift from Etolié and Marielle upon being brought to Staelash, the plot of land had been meant to help her feel welcome in the strange kingdom. Flowridia had turned their gift into a sanctuary.

A particular root drove her quest—a common one, but infused with energy beyond its natural state. Mother's advice given long ago wove through the tangle of knowledge in her head: *"Soak the listrous root, Flower Child. Seems I drank a bottle more than I'd intended last night."*

So many herbs and medicines grew within the plot of land, and Flowridia knelt in the dirt by the listrous flower—a jagged, orange-colored blossom—and carefully plucked three, roots intact. She removed the buds and wove them into her hair, practiced fingers easily braiding them into her thick curls.

The protective wards written into the ground permeated the blooming petals. Every morning, she wove fresh ones into her hair and stole a few for her pockets. Near the listrous flowers, a patch of bluebells flourished, and Flowridia stole a tiny bud, one that had barely poked its head from the ground. With care to preserve the roots—ones that bore sigils of protection—she braided it into her hair.

Moon lilies, nearly in full bloom, pulled her attention. Such a vibrant blue, she thought. Icy, almost like—

A mar on the petal caused her to frown. She reached out and let her fingers gently rub against it, breathing out a sigh and allowing a healing spell to pass through. Demitri placed his head against her knee, and she knew he felt it too—the draining of energy, and with it the course of adrenaline that came from using magic.

When she removed her hand, the petal shone pristine and no blemish met her eye. Smiling, she stood, taking the listrous roots and heading back toward the castle. The noise of the world bombarded her as she left the protective wards.

With Demitri close behind, she darted straight to the kitchen.

The small kitchen, reserved for the royal council and, due to Marielle's affection, herself, kept a decent stock of ingredients for all Flowridia's purposes. The kitchen itself held countertops and an iron stove near a large window to prevent the room from becoming a boiler. Beside the kitchen area, separated by a half wall, a plain table and several chairs sat. Typically, Thalmus would be found reading as he ate his breakfast, or Etolié might wander up, in a rare appearance, before continuing her typical pattern of sleepless days and nights.

This morning, however, all were assembling for the hunt. It begged the question—had Lady Ayla eaten breakfast? Flowridia sparked the fire within the great iron stove and set a kettle of water on top to boil.

From the cupboards, she withdrew ingredients for baking, and soon a concoction of flour, water, seeds, and more filled her bowl. Demitri stood on his haunches, barely reaching above her knee. *Do I get some tea?*

"Would you like some?" she asked, motherly affection in her smile. In her arms, she mixed the bowl with practiced movements. "I have enough water boiling."

Yes, please.

Flowridia beamed, his peculiar tastes a joy to her heart, before setting down the bowl and rummaging through the pantry to find dried raspberry leaves.

She withdrew three tea cups, two of which bore lavender buds painted onto the glass. Soon, they sat in a row, one with listrous root and the others with raspberry leaves.

Once the muffins were in the oven, Flowridia slid down the side of the counter and sat beside Demitri. "Is this a bad idea?"

Why would it be bad? The tiny creature climbed onto her thigh, and Flowridia stole him into her arms to cradle him.

"I don't want to bother her. What if she doesn't like tea?" The mere idea pulled a frown to her face. "Who doesn't like tea?"

Even I like tea.

"Etolié said I shouldn't speak to anyone with a title higher than my own." She had no title, unless 'Ward to the Magister of Staelash' counted for a title. 'Flowridia, Daughter of Odessa' was a name she had resolved to let die, a secret she kept to herself.

As merely 'Flowridia,' her name meant nothing, but better to be thought of as nothing than to inherit a legacy of fear.

"Everyone is gone, though," Flowridia mused, "I might have the highest title of anyone in the manor."

Flowridia stroked the fine hairs along Demitri's neck. "And it would be rude to leave a guest all alone."

Very rude.

Footsteps from the hallway gave her pause. She pulled Demitri closer to her chest. Hadn't everyone left?

"Smells good in here," said a voice, and then a half-elf rounded the corner into the kitchen. Flowridia recognized the stablemaster in passing and had always found her lovely, her stark blond hair difficult to miss. It fell in long, matted ropes down her back, always pulled into a tail, and beautifully juxtaposed with her darker, earth-toned skin. Whatever blending of heritages had culminated in Sora spoke of comradery between the two of them, for while Flowridia claimed a human bloodline, their skin shone in comparable shades of ochre and amber, neither dark nor light.

"Hello, Sora," Flowridia said, relaxing slightly. "I thought everyone had left for the hunt already."

"We're assembling the stragglers," Sora said, glancing between Flowridia and the oven. "Are those going to be done soon?"

Flowridia peeked at the stove. "Twenty minutes. Maybe more."

"I'll be gone by then." Sora stepped through the kitchen and to the pantry. "Were you at the ball last night?"

"I was," she replied, shy at the thought. "Were you?"

"No interest," said the voice behind the pantry door. "Meira and I were visiting the Temple of Sol Kareena." Sora reemerged with a bag of dried meat. "Marielle mentioned that the representatives from the Theocracy didn't stay the night."

Flowridia gave her a small nod. "Lord Ashwood said he didn't want to sleep within a hundred miles of..." Her? "...Nox'Kartha."

"If they're going to cause trouble, let them go." Sora stopped at the doorframe. "I'll wait until your muffins are done, if you want to come."

Flowridia shook her head. "Thank you, but no thank you."

"You don't eat meat. Right." Sora's quirked eyebrow conveyed some judgement, something Flowridia found odd, considering elves were often vegetarian. But it made no difference to her—Sora was visibly only half-elven, with her

24

softly pointed ears, and Flowridia had long ago stopped taking such scrutiny personally. "Have you ever eaten meat?"

"It's been a long time," Flowridia replied truthfully, and she hoped Sora couldn't sense her discomfort at the query.

"Why did you give it up?"

Mother had pushed her similarly, as testy as any parent granted a child with a picky palate. *"Oh, try another bite, Flower Child. Elves are a delicacy, difficult to come by in a swamp."*

Flowridia kept her plastered smile. "I don't like it."

"Whatever you say. I'm off to begin the hunt." Before Sora rounded the corner, she pointed her finger directly at Flowridia. "Save me a muffin."

Flowridia nodded as Sora disappeared.

Soon, with a plate of muffins in one hand and a platter of teacups balanced on the other, Flowridia made her way to the guest quarters, where she knew Nox'Kartha would be staying. If she listened carefully, she could hear the crowds outside; soon, the hunt would begin.

Lady Ayla's room waited at the far end of the hall, nestled between Zorlaeus' quarters and the window. Court gossip was hardly Flowridia's business, but she did wonder whether or not Marielle's affection had actually spent the night in his room.

Flowridia balanced the plate of muffins on her forearm—the same one holding the tea—and quietly turned the doorknob.

The curtains were drawn, but Flowridia could easily make out the details of the guest suite. Guest rooms had been built to be the same, with a mirror, a wardrobe, and a large bed in the center—a bed Ayla herself sat at the side of, watching. She wore the same dress from the previous night, but her hair fell in gentle waves, like an ocean on the darkest night.

To have those blue eyes turned directly onto her nearly caused Flowridia to falter. But she forced a smile and took the plate of muffins back into her free hand. "Lady Ayla, I . . ." She stepped forward, her courage steadily depleting. "I heard you were unwell."

Ayla tilted her head, her eyes fluttering, sensuously half-veiled. "Oh, yes," she said, slowly sliding back down into the perfectly made bed. The pillows propped her up, even as she lounged. "I have the most terrible headache."

Though diminutive in size, Ayla's voice held luxurious depth, dark waters Flowridia could have soaked in for hours. "I made tea for that," Flowridia said, perhaps brighter than Ayla appreciated. She stepped toward the bedside table next to Ayla and set the platter of teacups down. Demitri's tiny feet disappeared into the plush carpet as he walked. "It's a bitter tea, but it will help your hangover." Supported by the saucer, Flowridia picked up the specially-brewed tea and offered it to Ayla.

The woman sat up to accept the teacup, fingers brushing against Flowridia's. The sudden temperature shift gave her pause; those lithe fingers were ice.

Ayla held eye contact as she sipped the steaming tea. Her demeanor made no change as the bitter liquid traveled down her throat. "And what is your name?" she said, the words impossibly smooth as they slid off her tongue.

Lady Ayla Darkleaf, with her illustrious titles and responsibilities, would not be impressed by someone who hardly merited a 'lady' in front of her name. Flowridia took a breath to speak, but instead she grabbed her own teacup and brought it to her lips. The water burned her tongue, but she swallowed her pain as she recalled Marielle's words from the previous night.

"Make up a title and find some friends."

This might end poorly.

"Flowridia," she said. "I am . . ." She smiled wide as she brought the teacup to her lips again, miming a sip to buy herself time. ". . . the Grand Diplomat of Staelash."

Later, alone, she would kick herself for being a sore liar.

"Grand Diplomat?" Ayla said, sounding impressed, but Flowridia sensed a bit of force behind it. "You're awfully young to be a Grand Diplomat."

"I'm older than I look," she said quickly. Hopefully not too quickly.

But Ayla chuckled, and a vicious grin spread across her lips. That smile, directed at Flowridia alone, pulled a blush to her cheeks. "Age is simply a number, Lady Flowridia, Grand Diplomat of Staelash."

Ayla's voice made the title sound so much more notable. Words became a difficult thing, but Flowridia managed a shy smile.

"I must ask, Lady Flowridia," Ayla continued, each word absolute pleasure to Flowridia's ears, "why is there a wolf in my room?"

She had entirely forgotten about Demitri. Ignoring the question, Flowridia took the third teacup and saucer and placed them onto the carpet. "Here you are, dearest Demitri."

Demitri licked her hand as she pulled away. *I didn't want to bother you.*

"You're always so thoughtful," she said, and when she stood back up, Ayla watched with a grin too wide to be sincere—and understandably so, given that a girl who talked to her pets had invaded her space. "Demitri is my familiar." At those words, Flowridia hesitated, watching Ayla's reaction carefully. "I apologize. Are you bothered?"

"No, I'm not," Ayla said, and her expression grew less severe. Talk of familiars often ended conversations; Flowridia fought to hide her relief. "Never apologize for what you are. Though I wouldn't have picked you out as a witch."

Ayla had guessed the logical conclusion—that no acolyte to an angelic being would have a wolfish familiar. "It's a path that picked me," she said, and when her hand brushed against the plate of muffins, she nearly jumped. "I made these." She picked up the plate and offered it to Ayla. "I figured you didn't make it to breakfast if you were unwell."

To watch Ayla inspect the pastries tied her stomach into knots, but the woman smiled and accepted one nearest to her. Instead of taking a bite, she sipped her tea, immune, it seemed, to the burning water.

"I'm feeling much better already," she said, practiced charm in every syllable. "Must be the tea."

"Oh, wonderful," Flowridia said as she set the plate back down. "Can I get you anything else? Water?"

Ayla raised an eyebrow, and Flowridia's words died on her lips. "Most diplomats don't wait on their guests."

Flowridia spoke slowly, choosing her words with care. "It's my duty to foster relationships between kingdoms," she began, "and since you're staying behind, I've been instructed to entertain you." Another lie, and still she couldn't tell if Ayla accepted any of it.

"I have no wish to impose."

"It's no trouble at all!" Too eager, Flowridia realized, and she snapped her mouth shut. "I'm happy to entertain you. I do know a few games."

She hoped Ayla couldn't see her blush. But the way Ayla licked her lips as she sat up certainly darkened it. "Games?"

Flowridia nodded slowly, mesmerized as Ayla leaned forward. "I could show you some."

Ayla's eyes looked down to Flowridia's lips, sliding closer. Seduction bled into her hungry gaze, lashes fluttering when she met her eye. "Then entertain me, Lady Flowridia."

"You played chess for eight hours?"

An enormous skylight lit Etolié's underground library, a convenience given that the Celestial required only starlight to live. At night, when she was most active, various crystals hung from the walls and ceiling illuminated her reading and research. Shelves lined the walls of the hexagonal room, most with books sequestered into every corner, but a few were devoted to odd little inventions Flowridia had dared to investigate once or twice. Miniature trebuchets, forever spinning tops—most crafted from some sort of gemstone— and when she asked where Etolié had stumbled upon such a strange collection of trinkets, Flowridia was told they were gifts.

The shelves layered each other as they progressed toward the center of the hexagonal room. There, blankets and scarves lay in a pile, where Etolié could collapse once the sun began to rise.

Flowridia nodded, her back to a shelf as she sat near the center.

"And what in Eionei's Asshole causes a self-respecting woman to play chess for eight hours?"

"It was nice," Flowridia said with a shy smile. Demitri lay cradled in her arms, her fingers idly stroking his soft puppy fur.

Quick as lightning, Etolié suddenly knelt beside her and stared. "Eight hours?"

The bookshelf cushioning Flowridia's back now betrayed her an escape. She nodded as she sunk into the floor.

"Multiple games, or one long session?"

"Multiple."

Etolié leaned forward, the faint lavender of her eyes oddly penetrating. Flowridia somehow managed to create distance between them. "Were your, uh, victories balanced?"

She brought Demitri up to cover her face. "I only won once."

Etolié began to cackle, standing as her laughter echoed across the high ceilings. "That's just not fair," she said, and from the air she pulled out a flask. After taking a sip, she handed it to Flowridia. "You've earned it, Flowers. Nice work."

Confused, Flowridia made a show of tipping the flask but blocked the entrance with her tongue. She handed it back, the tip of her tongue burning slightly from whatever devil-brewed concoction Etolié had offered her.

"I do have a problem, though," Flowridia said, preparing for another assault on her personal space.

"Was she weird down there?"

"What?"

Etolié waved a hand, dismissing her own comment. "Nothing. Go on."

"Well, I may not have mentioned I was your ward," she began nervously. "Instead, I may have said I was the Grand Diplomat of Staelash."

Etolié's good humor suddenly vanished. "You said what?"

"I panicked! I wanted to impress her."

"So, your method of impressing her involved lying to the representative from the scary undead superpower–" Etolié cut herself off, looking pained as she said, "Can't be caught in a lie if it's not a lie."

"Etolié–"

"There's a meeting with Nox'Kartha once Marielle is done with the Tholheimer ambassadors," Etolié said, but then an exasperated grin spread across her face. "You'd better come, since you're the new diplomat."

To her horror, Etolié offered a hand to help her stand. With Demitri secure under her arm, she accepted, and when

Etolié pulled her out of the library, Flowridia wondered how far this joke would go before they kicked her out of the manor for good.

The ruling council chambers held a circle of small thrones. Marielle was queen, but Staelash had been founded as an oligarchy, with three council members reigning above the rest. Marielle sat at the head, face in her hands, but she perked up when the door opened. To her right, an empty seat, one meant for Etolié.

To Marielle's left, General Khastra lounged against the strong wood of her own throne, inspecting one of the many elaborate, silver tattoos embedded into her skin. A shining beacon in gem-carved armor, with her sweeping horns she made a comparable match in size to Thalmus, but the enormous weapon propped beside the chair made for an imposing sight—a crystal hammer, one Flowridia had not yet seen in action.

She bore unquestionable femininity in her high cheekbones and coy smile, her lavender hair always aloft in some elaborate tail. Beautiful, in a different, striking sort of way, and with her blue-tinged skin and hulking physique, Flowridia had always presumed she was demon-descended, with her hooves and tail. But she cast a different aura, nothing human in her glowing, blue eyes.

Thalmus sat beside Khastra, his own chair rivaling her throne in size. He slouched, pouring over a document. Meira deShamira, the High Priestess, sat to his left, surveying the scene with pupil-less eyes. A human by appearances, she rarely spoke, but her words were often condescending at best. She had visions of Sol Kareena herself, or so they said, and Flowridia wondered if she truly were a speaker for the Goddess or simply mad.

Sora, the stablemaster, stood by the High Priestess' throne. Not a council member but taken under Meira's wing as an acolyte for Sol Kareena, she followed wherever the eerie High Priestess went.

"Etolié!" Khastra said, glancing up at the magister's entrance, though it sounded much more like 'Eh-toe-lay,' rather than 'Eh-toe-lee-ay.' She bore an odd lilt to every phrase, her deep, throaty accent more suited for Nox'Karthan territories than Staelash.

Still, every word she spoke held the hint of a laugh. "Late as usual. Come and listen while Marielle tries to sell my soldiers off to the highest bidder." Then, with one eyebrow quirked, she stared at Flowridia. "Why did you bring the tiny one?"

Khastra's accent also prevented her from properly pronouncing Flowridia's name, the first syllable always catching like a frog in her throat. Flowridia typically avoided the bombastic woman, knowing she was pleasant but petrified in her presence nonetheless.

"Apparently being ward to one of godly lineage wasn't good enough," Etolié replied as she pushed Flowridia forward. "Flowers, here, told Lady Ayla Darkleaf she was our Grand Diplomat. We can't make a liar out of the tiny one."

Marielle glanced at Etolié, then at Thalmus, and finally to Flowridia. "We'll make it official."

Flowridia's limbs seemed to inexplicably lose all feeling. "Marielle, you don't have to–"

"Oh, please," Marielle said, waving off the objection. "It's practically what you're training for anyway. You'll be our official representative for Nox'Karthan affairs."

Flowridia turned toward Etolié. "Etolié, I can't–"

"There are consequences to lying, Flowers. Fortunately, we don't have to find out what they are, because now you aren't lying."

"People have been promoted in stranger ways," Khastra interjected, looking bored as she inspected her nails. "Meira took Sora from one of Etolié's rescued slave parties."

At Meira's side, the half-elf blushed fiercely, forcing her stare to the floor.

Etolié placed her hand on her chair, a bit of glitter shimmering from her form. Beneath her opposite hand, an identical chair appeared. "Your throne awaits, Lady Flowridia of Staelash."

With each passing moment that they didn't reveal the jest, Flowridia inched closer to the chair. When she sat and they said nothing, she hugged Demitri tight to her chest.

The wolf licked her hand. *You've been promoted.*

"Not my intention," she whispered.

"Khastra, my most tactful friend," Etolié said, "did you scare off the Tholheimer ambassador?"

Marielle cut in instead. "No, but she refuses to even consider helping them."

Khastra scoffed. "I train soldiers for Solvira. Not for dwarves."

"You also train them for me, and if we sign a treaty with them, you'll have to send a few."

Etolié held up a hand. "Someone reasonable explain to me what happened in the meeting."

When no one immediately responded, Meira shifted in her seat. "The ambassador offered a warning about attacks near our shared northern border." Deep and near monotone, as she spoke, Thalmus offered the paper to Etolié. "King Thovir sent an envoy of soldiers led by his own son, but they've disappeared."

"And Marielle offered to send a battalion of my soldiers to aid in the search party," Khastra said. "They can have them, if they pay for them."

Etolié, with her eyes on the paper, frowned slightly. "Marielle, this is a letter. Not a treaty. Did he ask for help?"

"No," Marielle replied, fingernails clicking nervously on the arm of the chair. "But it was kind of him to warn us of danger."

"Not kind," Etolié said, still studying the letter. "Intelligent, perhaps. He's saving his own skin if anything does happen to one of our own. He's denying all involvement in advance."

Marielle frowned. "Be that as it may, he appreciated the offer and wants to discuss it more in the morning, before his envoy leaves. And after what happened to the ambassadors from the Theocracy, we'll also need plausible deniability."

Flowridia wondered at the statement, especially when Etolié grimaced and let her hand fall. She looked to Flowridia, still curled in her doppelganger throne, and said, "I think you heard that the representatives from the Theocracy of Sol Kareena left last night after the ball. During the hunt, their remains were found in the woods, as were the spies sent to follow them."

Marielle had asked for such, for spies to keep on the Theocracy's trail. But for them to be killed with the rest meant they, too, had been spotted.

"There are no survivors and no witnesses," Marielle added. Etolié moved to sit beside Flowridia as the queen spoke. "I have plans to personally pay a visit to the archbishop of the Theocracy and pay my respects. But if there's any connection to this and the disappearance of the Tholheimer Dwarves, this might mean something bigger."

Something bigger. Flowridia hadn't thought of the prospect of 'something bigger' in months, focusing all her energy on enjoying her freedom, content to ignore the greater evils of the world.

"That's all," Marielle said, turning Flowridia's attention back to the present. "The investigation continues. Maybe Nox'Kartha will have something to add. We're meeting with them next."

Nox'Kartha? A blush rose to Flowridia's cheeks. She braced herself when she heard the door open and sat up straight, smoothed her hair, but froze when she realized Sora had been watching her primp.

With her head held high and haughty, Ayla entered, Zorlaeus trailing demurely behind. She stepped right past Flowridia, hair free and flowing, her dress tight where it mattered, loose enough to tease, and long enough to cover her shoes. She stopped in the center of the room, her unsettling stare fixed on Flowridia as an amused grin twisted her lip. "Hello, everyone," she said, her tongue drawing out each syllable. "I come with a gift for your queen."

Flowridia watched as those lithe fingers reached into Zorlaeus' trouser pocket and withdrew a letter. Only then did Ayla tear her eyes away, and Flowridia felt as though a piece of her were ripped away with it.

With Ayla's focus now on Marielle, Flowridia could see the thinly-veiled rage brewing within her queen as she watched those fingers—fingers that had all but groped Zorlaeus—offer her the letter. A wax seal closed the front, bearing the official seal of Nox'Kartha. Marielle ripped it open and began to read.

"The letter dictates his terms," Zorlaeus said stiffly. Did Ayla really make him so nervous? Or was it Imperator Casvir? "But his Highness, Imperator Casvir, wishes to establish trade in your kingdom. He offers the construction of a Nox'Karthan Embassy on the outskirts of your city and requests use of your waterways. You'll receive ten percent of all the gold that passes through your kingdom for his use."

"Your imperator wants our waterways?" The question came from Thalmus, and Flowridia could already see him calculating the increased income in his head.

Nox'Kartha's trade empire dominated the land, but the small river running through Staelash connected the seas.

"Casvir requests use of them," Ayla said, charm lacing every word that tumbled from her lips, "and offers an alliance in return. The embassy would be an offering of friendship. And Zorlaeus would be your representative." At the mention of his name, Ayla let her hand rest a moment on his back before pushing him forward. He stumbled, nearly falling at Marielle's feet.

Marielle stood and offered a hand to steady him. "You would be stationed in our city?"

Sincerity crossed his features for the first time since entering. "I would," he said softly. All eyes rested on him, and perhaps he realized it. "For business, but you and I could still . . ." He hesitated, fighting the smile that pulled at his lips. ". . . have meetings."

"I would love to have meetings," Marielle said, regal in every way. "Tell Imperator Casvir that I accept."

Etolié whirled her head around. *"You* accept?"

Thalmus stole the letter from Marielle's hand and began to read.

"I'm certain we can discuss the details later," Marielle said. "Our diplomat and I can meet with you once the embassy begins construction."

Flowridia perked up at her newly bestowed title. "Yes, we can meet again," she said, eyes wide. "But tell Imperator Casvir that Queen Marielle accepts his offer."

Ayla stared at her again, leering like a snake about to strike. "I will tell him. Personally." Flowridia prayed she misunderstood the lecherous undertone. "Come, Lae Lae," Ayla continued, grabbing his forearm. She nearly wrenched him back. For as small as she was, she stood as though twice his height. "Our carriage awaits. We return home tonight."

"So soon?" Marielle said. Flowridia wondered if the queen purposefully avoided looking at Ayla.

Zorlaeus nodded, disappointment clear on his face. "Tragically, yes. Imperator Casvir will want to hear the news immediately." He made no attempt to hide his longing. "Farewell for now, Queen Marielle."

He bowed, and Marielle said, "Safe travels."

Perhaps he would have said more, but Flowridia saw Ayla's nails dig into his arm as she dragged him away. With a nod, he turned to leave, Ayla by his side.

But Ayla lingered when she passed Flowridia's chair, her hand flicking out and dropping something into her lap.

A chess piece. The black queen.

"It seems I nearly walked out with that," Ayla said as Flowridia picked up the small, stone figure. "A pity to have nearly lost it." Flowridia met her gaze, intoxicated when Ayla smiled, wicked as it was. But she made no further comment, though her fingers caressed the wooden chair as she passed.

The door clicked shut. Flowridia realized she still hadn't breathed.

"So, Flowridia," Marielle began, suspicion lacing each word, "where exactly did Lady Ayla lose the chess piece?"

"We couldn't find it anywhere," Flowridia said, picking the queen up from her lap. She ran her fingers along the cold figurine—colder, it seemed, in Ayla's possession. "After one of our sessions, we had to pause so I could dig around for it. Ayla proposed we stop, but we ended up using a candlestick instead."

Marielle raised an eyebrow and sat back in her chair. "Oh, did you?"

Flowridia nodded. "We went for a couple more hours, until the rest of you came home from the hunt."

"And, dear Flowridia," Marielle continued, "is this the first time you've . . . played chess?"

"You know Thalmus was the one who taught me how," Flowridia said, her tone growing wistful at the memory of her day with the sultry elf. "But it was Ayla's first time. I don't have much experience, but she performed excellently by the end. Beat me almost every time."

Then, she looked out and noticed the horrified stares that met her own. The only exception was Marielle; her slack-jawed expression was aimed solely at Thalmus.

And then it hit her.

"I did not have sex with her!" Flowridia exclaimed, jumping to her feet. "You can ask Demitri; he was there the whole time."

"Demitri isn't really suited to testify on your behalf," Marielle said, grinning wide as she chuckled.

"No, we played chess!" Flowridia held the black queen forward, increasingly flustered. "She knocked it off the table after I captured it, and we couldn't find it." Her eyes met Thalmus', her reserved, horror-stricken friend, and Flowridia wished she would be struck down by whatever god she might pray to for lightning.

Khastra stood, laughing with her deep, feminine voice. "Rather than watch the tiny one suffer, I will adjourn this meeting." She continued to chuckle as she left, followed by Meira and Sora.

Marielle stood and approached Flowridia. "Next time say so."

"You want me to tell you every time I don't sleep with a diplomat rather than take my words at face value?" Flustered, Flowridia pouted, then noticed Thalmus attempting to sneak out. She brushed past Marielle and blocked the door. "Thalmus," she began, biting her lip, "I–" Embarrassment choked her words.

Thalmus smiled faintly. "I know. And it's all right." She stepped aside so he could leave and stared at the ground until his steps were out of earshot.

Marielle followed, and soon only Etolié remained. "You really only played chess?" she asked, disbelief clear in her tone.

Fresh exasperation pulled an angry groan from Flowridia's throat.

"And you expect me to believe that Lady Ayla Darkleaf, high-class, hoity-toity elven asshole of Nox'Kartha, had never played chess?"

"That's what she said–"

"Do you know the rules of chess?"

"I, an elf raised in high society?" Ayla remarked, raising an eyebrow. "Chess, a game lauded for centuries as a simulation for warfare? Never heard of it."

"Oh, it isn't too difficult," Flowridia said as she set up each piece. The glass pieces, each one lovingly molded by Thalmus, brought with every tap on the stone board a memory. "Thalmus taught me to play when I first came to live here. He and I would play for hours . . ."

Flowridia, standing in the council chamber, brought a hand up to cover her mouth. Her eyes widened in horror. "She knew how to play chess," she whispered. "Oh, I am such a fool."

Etolié began to snicker. Soft fur against Flowridia's legs caused her to jump. *Is that why she beat you every time?*

"I did win!" Flowridia let her hand drop as she pouted. "Once."

"What I'm hearing," Etolié said, visibly struggling to not cackle, "is that Ayla took pity on you and let you win the first game."

"It was a few hours in, actually. The mood took a strange turn . . ."

"If you'll excuse me, I need to relieve myself."

Flowridia smiled brightly, already reassembling the board for their next game. "I'll be waiting!" The door shut, and she released a long sigh. "Oh, Demitri," she whispered, breathless, and she lifted the little wolf onto her lap. "I don't think I've ever had such fun playing chess."

She keeps beating you.

"That doesn't mean I'm not having fun. It means I'm a good teacher."

When Ayla returned, hardly a minute later, she slinked inside without a sound. Her eyes held a vicious glint, like a lion about to rip out the throat of its prey, but her grin—oh, that grin—made Flowridia's cheeks grow warm. "I appreciate you waiting," Ayla said, the slight drawl of each word utterly mesmerizing. Her long hair seemed . . . different. Disheveled slightly, in a way that made Flowridia's heart flutter.

Flowridia adjusted her posture as Ayla sat, crossing her legs to squelch the discomfort brewing between them. Demitri jumped off and settled by her foot. "Think nothing of it. We have been here a while."

"Yes, we have," Ayla said, and Flowridia sensed a certain menace behind the statement. But Ayla's smile widened, and she turned her attention to the board. "So, another game, is it? I'll start this round." Her fingers caressed the black queen's pawn as she lifted it, biting her lip when she set it down.

That was different.

With a shy smile, Flowridia moved her king's pawn two spaces forward.

"Have you been a diplomat for long?" Ayla asked, leaning forward. Her white teeth gleamed in the natural light.

Ayla hadn't been quite so talkative before. "I haven't," Flowridia admitted and prayed she wouldn't pry. "Have you?"

"Five years now, so no. Hardly a blink in my lifespan."

Ayla, being an elf, had probably outlived Flowridia's natural lifespan already, perhaps twice over. Her face held sharp lines, but nothing marred her pale skin—no wrinkles, no scars, nothing to signify her age. Not even a blush colored her chiseled cheeks. "How old are you?"

Ayla's grin turned awfully coy. "Age is simply a number, Lady Flowridia," she said, echoing her previous sentiment.

Flowridia turned her attention back to the board, determining her strategy until a brush against her leg caused her to stiffen. Demitri snoozed at her feet. That meant it was Ayla's foot leisurely dragging down her bare leg.

Theoretically, the gesture held a specific and undeniable implication, but Flowridia's shy heart shut down the thought immediately. She quickly moved her piece—the rook—and pulled her leg back, crossing her ankles underneath her chair. "Your move."

Victory etched itself across Ayla's face as she casually lifted her queen and moved it across to capture Flowridia's piece. "Check," she cooed, her eyes never leaving Flowridia's.

The knight moved to defend its king, sacrificed in the onslaught of the black queen. Watching Ayla's calculated smirk drew heat to Flowridia's cheeks, and she silently thanked the gods that Demitri was asleep. Next fell the bishop, and Flowridia braced herself for disappointment when Ayla inevitably slaughtered her pieces yet again.

But when Ayla's queen moved back, Flowridia's moved forward, and she studied the board, realizing she might have a chance if—

"Have you had to spread your legs for Marielle yet?"

Ayla asked with the same nonchalance you might ask someone about the clouds, or if you wanted sugar with your tea. Flowridia reasoned she must have misheard. Hesitant, she glanced up as she moved her pawn forward. "I beg your pardon?"

"Oh, my apologies; on her behalf, I mean," Ayla clarified, her demeanor the same as she moved her queen forward. "Though if that's your taste ..." When Flowridia didn't immediately answer—too stunned to form words—Ayla tilted her head. "No? Oh, but it's practically the job description–"

"Hold on," Etolié interrupted, leaning back in her chair. In the council chambers, Etolié lounged as Flowridia paced. "Ayla spent the afternoon bragging about how many ways she had spread her legs for Casvir?"

"Not quite."

38

"Oh, but it's practically the job description. I'm prepared to offer a few favors here in Staelash, if it comes to it. All for my kingdom, of course."

Flowridia stared, praying that the horror she felt didn't convey quite so obviously on her face. And, of course, any intrigue that came with it. Against her better judgement, she spoke. "Is Nox'Kartha wanting something from us?"

Ayla pursed her lips. "I have a letter from Casvir for your queen. Not much more to say than that, not without some . . ." The way her hand wrapped around her king was nothing less than obscene. ". . . convincing."

Flowridia watched as she set the king down, one space forward, and realized Ayla had left her queen vulnerable to the attack of an otherwise forgettable pawn. "I'm not sure what I could offer you, not without Marielle's approval."

Ayla hardly seemed to notice the assault on her queen; she merely laughed and tossed it aside as she said, "Who says Marielle needs to know?" She didn't even look at the board as she idly moved to steal a pawn. "Oh, but I jest, I jest, Lady Flowridia. I have never slept with anyone for Casvir."

Flowridia eyed the board, realizing Ayla had failed to notice the pawn not a space away from becoming queen. She reached to steal it, prepared for eminent victory, when Ayla's grin twisted into something murderous. "I only do that for me."

Tap. Ceramic on stone. "Checkmate."

"She stopped being quite so friendly after that," Flowridia said. "I also never won another round."

"What I'm hearing, is that after an inspirationally aggressive attempt to seduce you, you used her own attempt to distract you as a distraction to her and managed to thwart her?" Etolié rested her head on her fist as she leaned to the side. "Clever," she said, and she held out her flask.

Flowridia hardly noticed, too aghast at her own blatant denial. "So, she *was* trying to seduce me?" Etolié dangled the flask like a carrot for a donkey, but Flowridia waved away the offer, horror settling at her own idiocy . . . along with disappointment.

"That, or trying to make you royally uncomfortable so you would leave," Etolié said. "Either option is viable.

After a few hours of chess, I'd whore myself out to get a break too."

Glass seemed to shatter in the back of Flowridia's mind. "Was I annoying her?"

"No one plays chess for eight hours willingly, Flowers."

"When Thalmus and I first started–"

"Let me stop you right there," Etolié said, holding out a hand. "Thalmus watches the sunrise. Every morning. For fun. He's a statistical outlier and should not be counted."

"Oh, gods . . ." Flowridia covered her face with her hands as she collapsed into Khastra's seat. "I am such a fool."

After some dramatic moaning, she felt Etolié's hand pat her on the back. "First dates often go poorly, Flowers. I would let it, and any hope you have of sweeping Ayla Darkleaf off her feet, go."

This time, when offered the flask, Flowridia didn't say no.

Chapter 3

When not weighed down by a mountain of paperwork, Thalmus could be found at his kiln, working silently among molten glass. Separate from the manor, the kiln kept its distance from everything surrounding it, much like the man who worked there. The entrance faced Flowridia's garden, and she would often wave if she caught a glimpse of the man working inside.

Today, with her satchel hung over her shoulder, and Thalmus' own on the other, she came with a purpose. She steadied it with her arms, aware of the fragile contents, all the while dodging Demitri as he stepped under her feet. She peered inside the stone building and knocked on the doorframe when she saw Thalmus near the back, standing beside the furnace.

Thalmus smiled when he saw her. "Give me a moment," he said, and with care he withdrew a rod of glass, the far end a violent, luminous red. She watched him place the fiery end within a designated mold—one designed to come apart when coaxed—and gently blow at the hollow top. In his infinite patience, he had once explained the process, that the glass would expand to fill the ceramic mold and take on the pattern within. She'd seen the results of his craftsmanship countless times, as shown in the half-finished projects lined across the walls and the chess set she kept in her bedroom.

The withered lines of his face and quiet disposition spoke of maturity, more than the fraying grey lines growing through his hair, like silver streaks through onyx. Often, they would dwell in silence together as he created and she read, or as she gardened and he watched and learned. Something heavy, even beyond his size, rested behind those kind eyes, and while he served as an advisor to the queen, his devotion to healing and art set him apart from the others in her service. He would lift an axe in defense of his loved ones, but Flowridia suspected a violent history colored his view, the scars on his body writing a story more poignant than words could tell.

Thalmus looked up from his work and beckoned her forward. As she approached, she watched him kneel—though he was still nearly her height—and carefully removed the mold, revealing what Flowridia suspected was the beginnings of a vase. "I brought you healing salves," Flowridia said, holding out the open bag.

His hands could have easily engulfed her entire head, but with as much care as one might use to hold an infant, Thalmus withdrew a single, clear container, all while gently rotating the glass rod in his opposite hand. "Perfect as always," he said, inspecting the innocuous paste. His voice rumbled softly, deceptive of his size, like a thunderstorm miles away. "Someday I'll have you teach me to do this myself."

Flowridia took the vial back, and Thalmus set the shaped glass into the kiln. "You have so many responsibilities," Flowridia said, shaking her head. "I don't mind helping. Synthesizing my plants into something useful isn't difficult for me."

"You said your mother taught you?"

Flowridia nodded, unwilling to elaborate. From her other bag, she withdrew a small bowl filled with muffins. "I also thought you might be hungry."

Hardly a surprise—Flowridia made an effort to deliver pastries as often as she could to the residents of the manor—but Thalmus smiled, and Flowridia sat on a bench— far enough away to avoid being scorched with molten glass— with the bowl and Demitri in her lap. Thalmus withdrew the glass rod from the kiln, and Flowridia watched in rapt amazement as he stole an innocuous tool from the wall—like an oversized piece of surgical equipment; something her mother might've used—and let the blown glass rotate around it, creating a lip.

It took time, but she never grew bored in his companionable silence. She steadily gathered her courage and finally dared to voice what haunted her thoughts. "Thalmus, am I selfish to say I don't want to be a diplomat?"

"I don't think you're selfish."

"I've only lived here a few months. I don't know anything about politics or diplomacy." Flowridia let her head fall into her hand. "Is this really only because I lied? Or is there something I don't know?"

"The risks of promoting someone young and under-qualified are still far lower than the threat of being caught lying to Nox'Kartha, even innocently," Thalmus said. Satisfied with his work, it seemed, he returned the cooling glass to the kiln, all while steadily turning it over and over. "You won't be left to the wolves." He cracked a smile, glancing down at Demitri. "So to speak. What I mean to say is Marielle and Etolié handle most diplomatic endeavors, and you will merely be accompanying them from now on."

When Demitri leaned up to steal a muffin from her bowl, she let him. The pastry filled his entire mouth. "I've spent more time living in a swamp than in a city–" She shut her mouth, having never spoken openly of her life before Staelash before.

Perhaps her panic showed. Thalmus did not press for details. "Every day you've been here, you've worked to better yourself," he said. "You've more than proven your worth to me."

Touched by the compliment, Flowridia felt a blush blossom onto her cheeks. She cursed her open heart, but of all the residents in the manor, it was Thalmus she trusted above the rest. "You think I'll do well?"

"I do. They know nothing about you. Keep it that way, and they'll have nothing to hold against you." Thalmus' expression hardened into something thoughtful. "A bit of history for you. Nox'Kartha and the Theocracy of Sol Kareena have been at odds for as long as they've been established. Staelash lies in the middle, and both would have us as their allies. We have a complicated relationship with Solvira, given that we're funded by their treasury but technically our own territory. Marielle's father elected to stay neutral and remain close to Solvira, but this hasn't been the first attempt to initiate a treaty between our kingdom and Nox'Kartha."

The pieces settled into a messy but coherent puzzle in Flowridia's mind. "So, you think Marielle was unwise to accept Nox'Kartha's proposal for an embassy?"

"Only because she has not considered the consequences of insulting the Theocracy. Allying ourselves with Nox'Kartha could be beneficial, but she hasn't weighted the implications. She accepted out of hand, without consulting Etolié or Khastra, because they offered her Zorlaeus on a silver platter."

"They did give her a rather 'handsome' proposal." Flowridia quirked a smile at her own jest.

Thalmus gave a grave nod, however. He had withdrawn the vase and now she watched him dab a second, smaller, searing rod onto the artwork of the first. "They manipulated her. An engagement between Zorlaeus and Marielle would be a happy one, but Nox'Kartha will now have a piece of themselves in our kingdom." He turned his scrutiny directly on her. "You'll be accompanying Marielle to the Theocracy tomorrow. Keep this in mind."

Flowridia's fingers stroked against the soft fur of Demitri's neck as she considered this. "I will."

With his tools, Thalmus turned the dab of molten glass into a loop, creating a handle on his piece. "And in the future, be careful you don't fall for such manipulations yourself."

A frown pulled at Flowridia's mouth. "What do you mean?"

Thalmus' gaze stayed on her as he considered his next words. "You'll be meeting with Nox'Kartha often." On instinct, Flowridia bit her lip, and Thalmus nodded knowingly. "She's beautiful. And she looks fully capable of ripping your heart from your chest."

Was that a statement to be taken literally? Sensuous words could turn biting, but when she thought of Ayla, how she danced in the darkness, moved with the grace of a knife, perhaps there was a warning to be had. "There's nothing between us," she said, cursing the heat rising in her cheeks. "We played chess. I brought her tea."

"And that's all?" Thalmus asked, suspicion weighing each word.

She nodded nervously, more skittish than an unearthed crab. If Ayla had once held intentions for her, it was best for Thalmus not to know.

Relief filled his features. "I had wondered. Forgive me; I find myself protective of you. Perhaps it tainted my perception. Lady Ayla watches us all like some sort of snack."

To be eaten alive by Ayla . . . A macabre thought, but metaphorically speaking, the idea caused her heart to race. However, Thalmus had spoken a warning. She whispered, "I'll be careful."

When he approached, his rod held straight up into the air, forever spinning, she held a muffin forward, one he accepted with his enormous hand. Calloused fingers brushed hers; stone-like skin covered the man's frame. An entire muffin would have been merely half a bite to the enormous man, but Thalmus ate slowly, eating what might have equated to crumbs for someone of his size. "Please, join me," he said, gesturing to the bowl, and they returned to companionable silence as Flowridia began to eat.

"Have you ever met the Goddess, Sol Kareena?"

The carriage rolled along the worn road between Staelash and the Theocracy of Sol Kareena. Marielle, Meira, and Sora all sat inside, but Etolié had insisted on sitting at the back of the carriage on a smell bench meant for servants. Flowridia preferred the outdoors, so the sun beating down upon her skin felt like a blessing as she enjoyed the quiet company of Etolié—quiet only because Etolié was engrossed in a book.

Angelic writings, the same language as the wards written into the plants of Flowridia's garden, caught her eye, but Flowridia respected Etolié's privacy enough to not read over her shoulder. Demitri snoozed between them, jostled slightly when Etolié shut her book. "Once or twice. Technically, she's my aunt."

Whatever Etolié's eccentricities, Flowridia forget that true power flowed through the Celestial's veins. "You're related?"

"By marriage."

"Sol Kareena is married?"

At that, Etolié chuckled. "No. Marriage is generally a mortal concept. The only angels who engage in something so sentimental are the hopeless romantics, such as my mother, who was married to Sol Kareena's sister."

Etolié took a sip from her flask, but the story still bespoke a few questions. Sol Kareena was the Sun, and her sister was the Moon; that much Flowridia knew. "Forgive me for asking, but if your mother is married to a woman, how were you conceived?"

"Neoma's been dead a thousand years. My father is the half-angel son of Eionei, hence, the god of drunken debauchery is my grandfather. I was an accident–" Etolié held up a hand, her words more subdued. "'The sweetest accident in the realms,' as my mom put it. She loves me very much."

The carriage hit a bump, and Flowridia instinctively scooped Demitri into her arms. The sleeping puppy melted into her embrace. "Is your mom a goddess?"

"Goddess of Stars. But Staella doesn't talk to mortals anymore. I'd call her a demi-goddess now, at best."

Flowridia said, "I'd never heard her name."

"She hasn't touched your world in a thousand years; her memory has largely died out among mortals. Sailors will pray to her, with hopes the constellations will keep their paths clear. I'm told the sky was once her palette. Eionei says she used to grow stars in a garden, like you grow flowers, and that she'd devote constellations to great heroes of the era. But . . ." Etolié's radiating light faded to a mere glimmer. From the air, she pulled her flask and took a long sip. "I never knew that side of her."

Flowridia had always thought Etolié's godhood came from her grandfather; it seemed it was an even shorter rope. Still, Flowridia realized she had stumbled across some private thing and chose to not press.

The idea that gods could procreate was not an unprecedented concept, and it made Flowridia wonder about the news regarding Sol Kareena and the child she bore. So instead, she asked, "Has Meira deShamira really spoken to Sol Kareena, then?"

Etolié glanced toward the carriage, conspiracy written all over her face. "Between you and me," she whispered, "Meira *Schmeira* is loose a few screws. Sol Kareena is kind of the big cheese among angelic gods. Maybe she's spoken to an oracle of Sol Kareena—they'll speak to mortals. But Sol Kareena hasn't appeared on the mortal plane in thousands of years." Etolié frowned, her words fading away. "That said, Meira creeps me the hell out."

Meira was perfectly normal by appearances, though perhaps a bit stout, except for her eyes; white as milk and glowing faintly, holding no pupils yet missing absolutely nothing. "I suppose she can be a bit off-putting."

"A bit? Oh, Flowers, you are precious beyond all reason." Etolié kept her smile, but the joy in her eyes faded.

"Fortunately, international incidents are more difficult to cause than you'd think. Otherwise, we wouldn't bring Meira *Schmeira* within a hundred miles of the Theocracy."

"But she's our High Priestess."

"She doesn't like the archbishop. I'm not sure why; he's not a bad guy. But she's always at odds with the church. Bit of a revolutionary, that one." Etolié's smile softened into something sincere. "I'm one to talk, but still. Staelash's brand of Sol Kareena worship is much more in line with what Meira wants. And in her defense, it's why our kingdom *isn't* chomping at the bit to fight Nox'Kartha, despite a number of our citizens being pledged to the Goddess."

"What's the difference?"

"Sol Kareena isn't keen on necromancy, something the Theocracy actively preaches against. Meira focuses more on ritual behaviors and worship. That said, Nox'Kartha has a religious freedom policy that puts any Sol Kareena worshipper on edge. They have temples to every god in their city—*demon* gods even. If you're a cultist for The Lurker, you'll find friends. Sacrificing for Onias? As long as you aren't hurting other citizens, do what you will." Etolié stopped, thoughtful. "I ought to go there. I've heard there's a temple to Eionei that puts any party to shame."

Though shy at the idea, Flowridia said, "I'd love to go with you, if you do."

"We'll make it a diplomatic mission, then. I'll go party with the acolytes, and you can play chess for eight hours."

Flowridia blushed. "Oh, Etolié–"

"Sorry, sorry," Etolié said, laughing, "you can go to church, too. Ayla looks like she knows a few things about idolatry; I'm sure she could get you to cry out to a few gods–"

"Etolié!"

Etolié's laughter only increased, and Flowridia wished for nothing more than to sink into her seat. The open road mocked her as it echoed Etolié's amusement.

The carriage continued moving, but one of the doors opened slightly. Marielle's voice rang out. "And what are you two talking about?"

Etolié continued cackling. "How to get Flowridia to touch her goddess. *Get in touch* with her goddess, sorry."

Etolié was not sorry.

The carriage slowed to a stop, and Marielle herself appeared from around the corner, hands on her hips. Her expression said annoyance, but her whispered words implied something else. "Your conversation sounds much more interesting than theirs." She tilted her head toward the carriage. "Can I sit with you?"

"We'll make room," Flowridia said, and she scooted her bottom over as far as the bench would allow. Marielle was hardly small, but between Flowridia's dainty frame and Etolié's near emaciation—starlight did not provide more than a bare minimum of nutrition—they managed to squeeze the buxom queen between them. The carriage continued rolling forward.

"Sora and Meira were discussing temple rituals for Sol Kareena," Marielle said, pursing her lips. "All very important in the grand scheme, I'm sure, but I'll be holy-ed out by the end of our visit." She then glanced up toward the sky and spoke loudly. "Not that holiness isn't important."

Etolié nudged Marielle with her elbow. "Sol Kareena doesn't care. She has better things to do than take offense to a bit of harmless blasphemy."

"Well, that's good," Marielle said. "I was a bit worried, given I agreed to a trade agreement with her chosen kingdom's sworn enemies."

"So you do have a sense of self-preservation." The ice in Etolié's words could have frozen Onias' Hell.

"They'll hate me anyway if I marry Zorlaeus," Marielle continued, perhaps purposefully ignoring Etolié's slight. "I might as well be allied to Nox'Kartha before that."

"A girl and her demon—a love story for the ages," Etolié said, her bright words marred by bitterness. "Can't think of anything cuter."

Marielle, staring out into the field surrounding them, apparently missed the obvious wink Etolié gave Flowridia.

"We're stopping. If I don't walk around, I'll die."

Etolié proclaimed them done for the night, and Flowridia was inclined to agree. They would reach the Theocracy within the week, but in the meantime, they would camp.

Flowridia relished the chance to stretch her legs and followed Demitri as he hopped through the tall grass, the little wolf frolicking as he chased down whatever vermin he found scavenging. Flowridia kept a close watch, following him when he ran too far.

Sora stepped up beside her. "Do you have experience tracking wild animals?" the half-elf asked. Flowridia was small, but she was hardly short—average perhaps—yet Sora stood nearly a head taller, surpassing even Etolié in height.

"I spent hours in the woods as a child following animals." Demitri pounced at what she realized was a cricket, and she giggled as it jumped away, narrowly missing the snap of her wolf's jaws. "I'd like to think I know how their minds work."

"Catching predators and catching prey are two very different things," Sora said. "Prey animals leave little marks, footprints, trails. They might even help their killer out, leave accidental invitations and such if they don't know they're being hunted. To catch a predator though . . ." Sora watched Demitri as he pounced again, this time successfully ravaging the cricket with his teeth. "Sometimes, the best way to catch a predator is to follow the prey."

"I've never been hunting," Flowridia admitted. "I only ever followed for fun."

"I haven't done it for survival in years. I'll only do it for fun, or to stay in practice." Sora smiled, sincere as far as Flowridia could tell. "But you know about surviving in the woods, right? That's where you lived before Etolié picked you up."

Flowridia forced a smile, unwilling to elaborate. "For a time, yes."

Sora studied her, visibly intrigued. "But you're a child."

Flowridia shook her head. "I'm older than I look. And I wasn't alone. When I *was* a child, my familiar, at the time, taught me how to survive in the wild. She was larger than anything else in the woods, so that kept me safe."

"Was she also a wolf?" Sora asked.

She realized she hadn't spoken of Aura to anyone since her passing. It felt odd, the memories dusty on her tongue. "She was. Her name was Aura." Demitri came bounding up to her then, and Flowridia knelt to greet him. "Those crickets don't stand a chance against you, dearest Demitri."

49

Someday, I'll be able to fit a whole horse in my mouth.

"I believe in you."

"Whatever my talents," Sora said as she watched the exchange, "I can't actually talk to animals."

"I can only talk to one," Flowridia said, squeezing the wolf tight to her chest.

"Flowers!" Etolié called from beside the carriage. "Help me with the tents! You'll want to learn this."

Flowridia expected poles and tarps. But Etolié held only a small box in her hand. Curious, she followed the Celestial to the far end of their chosen clearing. From within she withdrew what Flowridia could only describe as a miniature tent. Etolié set it on the ground and took several steps back. Fingers placed together, she stared at the tiny object, and when her fingers pulled apart, the tent grew.

From the size of her palm to larger than the carriage in seconds, the tent was extravagant. Etolié ran toward it and opened the flap, revealing a small bedroom, bookshelves, and other finery. Flowridia stared, struggling to articulate a response to the bit of sorcery she had just witnessed. "So," she finally mused, "you set it up at home, and then you shrunk it. You put it in a box, and now we're here?"

"Close, but I didn't set it up. That's what servants are for. Now, come on. There's one for you too."

A bit of a mad genius, that Etolié.

A tent for each of them surrounded the perimeter of camp. Darkness had descended, but in such warm company, there was no fear. Etolié regaled them with tales of revolution.

"Oh, it took practice, sure," Etolié said, taking a sip of her flask. "I'm Celestial, not infallible. But, and I hate to say it, once you've liberated one slave camp, you know how to liberate them all. It isn't complicated."

. . . Said the near demi-goddess.

Demitri sat in Flowridia's lap as she chewed on her dinner of dried fruit and nuts. All sat by the fire and watched as Etolié stood, her eyes reflecting the firelight as she continued her tale.

"I remember once," she said, holding out her flask, "after using my feminine wiles to stab the leader of the camp forty-seven times with a paring knife, it took some convincing to get the slaves to actually leave. I was new—I didn't speak many languages of your realm yet—so it took a bit of shock and awe for them to understand I was their savior–"

On cue, Etolié's ethereal, tendril wings suddenly flashed, spreading wide from her back. They reminded Flowridia of some undersea creature, the way they floated, how she could just barely see the outline of the forest through the shimmering of silver light. The Celestial often kept them hidden through illusion; she had more than once decried them as a nuisance. "But all was well. No casualties. I shipped them off to Solvira and went on my way." She took a long sip from her flask, grimacing when she put it down. "Until, of course, I'd freed approximately a kingdom's worth and Solvira came after me. Do you know that story, Flowers?"

"You tell it at least once a week," Flowridia said demurely.

"Well, time to fill my quota," Etolié replied. She took another sip, then tossed the flask away. A faint sparkle in the air, and the flask vanished. "Cue me, Etolié, Daughter of Stars, Chosen of Eionei, Savior of Slaves, and bane of the emperor's sensibilities– blamed for the influx of uneducated, 'lesser' races to the hoity-toity Solviran Empire."

Flowridia had heard her tell the tale, verbatim, countless times. It seemed the others had as well, as demonstrated by Marielle busily wrapping her hair around strands of cloth—her head would be a mass of curls by morning—and Sora carving a stick with her knife. Meira's white eyes made it impossible to say if she were paying attention, but her head was turned toward the night sky.

So Flowridia, pitying Etolié's drunk, one-woman show, kept her attention sharp, occasionally mouthing the words with her.

". . . *years* tracking me down. But Emperor Malakh Solviraes placed a pen and a contract in my hand and bound me to co-rule the plot of land—a client kingdom, one could say. With me–" Etolié gestured to Marielle. "—Clarence Vors, brother-in-law to the emperor, and the most insufferably dull man I ever had the pleasure of calling my friend. They wanted me as queen, I said no, Clarence was crowned king, etc, etc . . ."

Etolié waved off the words, dramatic in her stance, her wings actors of their own with how they shone and posed with her body. "With the impossible, experimental task of turning an eclectic group of former slaves into productive members of society came the necessity of keeping the co-rulers safe. Cue, my absent friend, Khastra—legendary war-hero, general, and friend to the Solviraes. They pay her a substantial amount of gold to be here. Way more than they ever offered me."

"How much?" Flowridia asked, and in tandem with Etolié said, "Half our taxes!"

"Thank you, Flowers. You pass with flying colors."

Flowridia applauded, smiling as Etolié bowed.

"You still leave to liberate slave camps, though." Sora's voice surprised them both; she had been listening, apparently.

"I . . ." Disappointment swallowed up Etolié's previous enthusiasm. "I occasionally scout them out, but then I point Khastra and the provided Solviran soldiers in their direction. Though, with the emperor's recent death, perhaps I'll have a bit more freedom under Lara's reign."Etolié's smile radiated conspiracy, but the half-elf kept peppering her with questions.

"Have you ever had any major casualties?"

Etolié's wings faded from view. With the disappearance of her wings came a downtrodden expression. "Yes," Etolié replied, and the flask appeared back in her hands. "Many times." She shot back another gulp of ale, then turned her sights on Flowridia. "Tell us a story, Flowers. Cheer me up."

"What sort of story?" she whispered, shy as her companions' attentions were turned to her. Her fingers dug into Demitri's fur, his steady breathing a comfort to her agitated soul.

"Hero stories. Join our party."

"I'm not much of a hero."

"They don't have to be real," Etolié continued, nudging against her. She handed Flowridia the flask. "What sort of tales did your mother tell you as you drifted off to sleep?"

"Trouble sleeping, Flower Child? Let me tell you the tale of your father . . ."

"A paladin," Flowridia began, shutting her eyes as she reminisced, "heard tales of a kidnapped maiden during his travels. He hailed from the Theocracy of Sol Kareena, a champion of her holy name, and he was a decorated warrior, skilled in combat, but his prowess in battle paled for his penchant in healing magics. They say Sol Kareena herself laid claim and infused him with power."

"He sounds like a bore," Etolié said, chuckling to herself.

"This is how my mother told it."

"Carry on."

"The paladin rode through a village on the edge of a swamp where a demon told him the harrowing tale of a brutal kidnapping—a beautiful maiden, stolen in the night by the hag who resided there. The hag had terrorized the village for decades, stealing children and coercing men to her home where she slew them and ate their entrails." Flowridia paused, unsettled at her own words. "But the paladin had fought worse in the name of righteousness. He rode into the swamp, resolving to save the maiden and slay the beast.

"They said the hag had drawn wards to keep visitors away, but with Sol Kareena's aid, he was able to burst through the enchantments and find the cottage in the center of the swamp. When in sight, his horse was suddenly struck dead by a spell—a spell meant for him. Standing at the door, the most hideous and wicked of creatures met him—the Swamp Witch, Odessa.

"She cackled, and his blood turned to ice. But his sword shone with holy light. He swung; she dodged, but her laughter only increased. Over and over, he swung and missed, and Odessa swiped at him with her claws. Her hair took sentience and grabbed him, tossing aside his sword as a child might toss a stick.

"His blood soon gushed like summer rain. The battle seemed lost as she drew him close, but with a prayer to Sol Kareena on his lips, he blasted her with a spell of light. Overcome by his power, the hag fell, twitching, trembling, until the paladin removed her head with his sword.

"Injured but standing, the paladin entered the cottage and saw the fair maiden. She praised his bravery, her tears falling in gratitude, and kissed him chastely, for she was virtuous and good above all else. The paladin, struck by her

53

beauty and innocence, allowed her to remove his armor and dress his wounds. But with every touch, the paladin felt his heart succumb to the maiden and . . ."

At Flowridia's hesitation, Etolié nudged her yet again. "They lived happily ever after, right?"

"*. . . she, sweet and shy, let him claim her for his own. Lost in their lovemaking, he never did see the dagger coming . . .*" Mother's smirk twisted her beautiful visage. "*One swipe, and he was dead, but his purpose was fulfilled. She ate him raw, content at the fullness in her belly . . . and in her womb.*"

A pause, and then Flowridia whispered, "Until the end of his days, yes."

Etolié immediately broke out into applause. "Ten points to our shy little flower."

"Wasn't Odessa an actual legend?" Marielle asked. "I swear I've heard stories before."

Flowridia managed a nod.

"I don't think I've ever heard that one. Is that really how she died?"

This time, Flowridia managed a shy shrug, staring down at the sleeping wolf in her arms. "It's one my mother told me," she echoed, acutely aware of the warm flame against her face. "I think it would have been trivial for someone like Odessa to have faked her death, so perhaps not." Definitely not. "But it's nothing to worry about. Who can say what's real and what's legend?"

"Well, being a witch, you must know lots of stories," Marielle pushed, and Flowridia sensed sincerity behind her earnest expression. Perhaps she thought she was helping by coaxing Flowridia to speak.

"I haven't really met any others."

An awkward silence settled, one Flowridia refused to fill. "Sora!" Etolié suddenly explained. She stole the flask back from Flowridia and tossed it over the fire toward the half-elf. "Tell us a story."

Grateful for the shift in attention, Flowridia heard little of Sora's tale—some story about an elf trapped in a library. Instead, her eyes squeezed shut, the burning of her tears against her eyelids enough for her to flinch.

She willed them away, focusing on the soft fur against her fingertips.

Chapter 4

An enormous statue of the Goddess gazed down to greet them, forever guarding the gates of the city. She towered over their carriage, her great wings spread wide and her face covered in a cowl. Still, the artist had done well in conveying her benevolence; she smiled with her eyes, and Flowridia felt compelled to smile back.

Sol Kareena accepted all, and those who accepted Sol Kareena were held to a high standard of righteousness. But her rewards were great, or so they said, and Flowridia wondered if Meira truly had been enlightened for her devotion.

As they passed the gates, they stated their purpose, and Queen Marielle presented a royal seal to prove herself. They were allowed inside, past the stone walls, over the moat, and beyond the statue of the Goddess.

A certain richness pervaded the city, shown in the paved stone roads and impressive statues. Ancient stone made up the buildings, and Flowridia couldn't begin to guess their age. She thought each citizen must be truly blessed, with their elaborate clothing and smiling countenances.

Seated within the carriage, she turned to Etolié. "Are there peasants? Everyone I've seen looks wealthy."

"This is only the capitol city, Flowers. Peasants wouldn't be rich enough to afford living here. Undesirables are booted out to maintain appearances."

Flowridia recalled seeing miles of farmland, but she still frowned. "I'm not sure if I believe that."

"Everyone in this city," Meira said, staring blankly through the window, "is a hypocritical sheep."

Flowridia peered out the window, watching to see if what they said was true. She, in her simple shirt and skirt, would be severely out of place among the populace.

The carriage rolled to a stop in front of a spiraling cathedral, pure white and gleaming in the sunlight. Meira and Sora moved to exit, but Marielle, it seemed, noticed Flowridia's admiration. "Do you want to go inside? We have some time before we're meeting with the archbishop."

Flowridia whipped around to face Marielle. "Are you sure? I don't want to inconvenience you."

"We came all this way," Marielle said, practically pushing her out the door. "We might as well sight-see." Once she had stepped out, she turned to Etolié, still sitting in the carriage. "Are you coming?"

Etolié bit her lip, staring at the enormous, wooden doors resting at the top of the stone steps, carved in Sun Elven characters. "I suppose I am." She stepped out, her dress swooshing around her legs in a sea of glitter. Flowridia swore she hadn't been wearing glitter a moment ago. "Eionei's temples aren't quite so pretentious."

"There are no drinking gods in this city, Etolié," Marielle said, nudging her in the ribs. "Come on—Flowridia wants to see." Marielle's boots clicked along the stone steps. She placed a hand at Flowridia's back and pushed her forward.

Flowridia realized she was still barefooted. At least her skirt would cover that.

Two guards stopped them at the door. "No pets inside the cathedral," one stated, and Flowridia pulled the small wolf tight to her chest.

"He's not a pet," Marielle said. "I am Queen Marielle Vors of Staelash. This is my diplomat, Lady Flowridia, and her familiar."

The guard hesitated, glancing between the wolf and the foreign monarch. "Forgive me," he said tentatively. He settled his gaze on Flowridia herself. "I've never seen a priestess of Sol Kareena with a wolf for a familiar."

"I'm not a priestess to Sol Kareena," Flowridia replied, shy in her words, "but I hold an enormous amount of respect for the Goddess and her followers."

The guard looked torn, and he turned to his companion who seemed equally perplexed. The young man spoke again. "Allowing animals into the cathedral is against policy, except for those who serve the Goddess."

Flowridia nodded, unwilling to risk trouble, but Marielle had no reservation. "Her wolf is as intelligent as the birds who sit on your acolyte's shoulders. Flowridia has as much a right to be here as anyone."

"She does," the guard muttered, facing the floor, "but the wolf will have to wait outside."

Marielle nodded, and for a moment Flowridia thought she might accept the explanation. "We'll be moving on then. I have a meeting with Archbishop Xoran, and I'll be sure to commend you and your attention to the letter of the law. All are welcome to worship Sol Kareena, except for witches, because they have to leave a piece of their soul behind to enter the cathedral."

The orb in her bosom glowed as she spoke, betraying Marielle's anger. When Etolié suddenly popped up behind Flowridia, the guards visibly paled.

"Hello, Magister Etolié, Chosen of Eionei, here. Will you please let the diplomat in before my queen throws a tantrum?"

The guards stepped aside, heads down as they held the doors open.

Flowridia kept Demitri in her arms, protective as she stepped through the illustrious doors. Inside, she nearly gasped at the grand display. Sweeping ceilings held pockets of stained glass, illuminating the floors in bright colors. Candles sat by the windows, unlit for now, and pews lined the floor leading up to the altar.

She saw Meira bowing and praying before a statue of Sol Kareena. Unlike the hooded depiction welcoming all at the gate, this one's hair flowed long and free, her eyes sparkling in splendid stone. Hundreds of candles flickered behind her, each one a prayer from a devoted servant.

The polished floor made little sound as Flowridia stepped forward, basking in the grandeur. "A bit of trivia for you," Etolié began. "This city is ancient. Magic has kept it looking young, but it was founded by Sun Elves some two thousand years ago."

Flowridia glanced at her a moment before returning her sights to the altar. "I wouldn't have guessed."

"However," Etolié continued, "this cathedral is considerably younger. A few hundred years after it was built, it burned to the ground. To this day, no one knows why. The only thing left standing among the ashes–" Etolié gestured to the statue of the Goddess and the altar before her. "Only Sol Kareena herself knows the mystery. Who knows what that statue has seen."

"That statue is two thousand years old?" Flowridia said, jaw gaping.

"Likely more."

Marielle muttered as she approached from behind. ". . . bigotry at the steps of the Goddess' cathedral. I'll have their necks wrung for–"

"Marielle," Flowridia said softly, Demitri's weight in her arms a reminder of the exchange, "don't be angry on my behalf. They only did their job."

Marielle's lip twitched as she gave a curt nod. They continued forward, Marielle's hand gently pushing on Flowridia's back.

The word 'witch' came with a legacy of fear, and there was no other explanation for Flowridia's powers, and for such an odd choice in familiar. Serving angels and Celestials, and being granted a familiar by their power, bestowed the title of 'priest.'

Those who served demons and their ilk were deemed 'witches.' Flowridia had vowed to forget the wickedness she'd learned in her mother's home, instead resolving to be the rare witch with good intentions.

They reached the altar—she, Etolié, and Marielle. A simple stone table served as the altar, covered in the front and hollow within, large enough for a small child to hide inside. Inscriptions along the side—some ancient form of Sun Elven, Flowridia was certain—were the only decoration.

Meira knelt at the side, muttering as she hid her face. Flowridia looked up, shying away from the Goddess' stone gaze. She hid Demitri in a protective stance as she whispered, "Hello."

"Polite, but I don't think she cares." For the second time, Flowridia jumped at Etolié's words.

"Why wouldn't she care?" Sora appeared from beside the statue, eyebrow raised. "She can see everything that goes on in here. Maybe a simple 'hello' would break up the monotony of prayers and begging."

Etolié looked up at the statue, the preamble to her eye-roll. "Hello, Sol Kareena. Hope the baby's well. Give my best to mother."

"Isn't it customary to leave a gift?" Flowridia asked, hesitant under the watchful gaze of Sora and Sol Kareena.

When Sora nodded, Flowridia removed one of the flowers tangled in her hair and knelt to place it at the Goddess' feet. "It's all I have with me," she whispered, and then she stood and turned to Marielle. "We don't need to stay long. I don't wish to keep the archbishop waiting."

Marielle looped her arm around Flowridia's and began to escort her out. "Etolié, are you coming?"

Etolié's stare remained on the Goddess. "No, I'll stay. I'll find you when you're done."

In the carriage, Flowridia sat Demitri down on the seat beside her. "Am I allowed to bring Demitri with us?"

With a permissive glance to Flowridia, Marielle gently ran her hand through Demitri's soft fur. "He isn't your pet. I would hope the archbishop would be held to a higher standard than ignorant cathedral guards."

Self-conscious fear threatened to choke Flowridia's throat. Sol Kareena accepted all, or so they said. Witches who accepted wolves from demons in the woods could be considered outliers. "I can leave him in the carriage."

Reassurance manifested in a beaming smile across Marielle's face. "Bring him. He's a part of you. If you smile wide enough, no one will notice him."

Flowridia nodded, distracting herself by staring out the window as the street rolled by. All along the road, people moved in droves, and Flowridia questioned why she had ever bothered to leave the woods.

When the carriage pulled to a stop, Flowridia wondered if there had been a mistake. A gated, brick home stood before them, but the size and grandeur were nothing of note. Still, Marielle swung open the carriage door, and Flowridia followed. She set Demitri at her feet, listening intently as Marielle presented herself to the guard at the gate.

The gate, metal and spiked, rolled to the side, and the stone path leading to the home itself wound and weaved through a lush garden. Greenery, shaded by the trees and surrounding homes, kept the area cool and moist, and Flowridia dared to step off the path and toward a patch of berries.

She sensed a sickness in the plant and ran her fingers across a leaf. A rot gnawed at the roots, and instinctively Flowridia let a healing spell cross through her skin and into the bush, her strength depleting in tandem with the plant's growth. But the root rot remained. She felt a curse dance across her tongue, but her mouth remained shut. To act so impulsively would undoubtedly harm the plant further. And what use was there in attempting to curse a fungus?

"You would use your spells on plants?" came a masculine voice, and Flowridia, having done what she could, removed her hand and faced the aging gentleman. The man approaching her wore simple robes of gold and white, the only bit of grandeur a gold crown braided into the thick, black locks of his hair.

She felt her chest cave from embarrassment. "I would. It's what I often do at home, for my own garden," she explained, but she caught herself before she began to babble.

Behind her, she felt Marielle's presence. "Pardon us, sir, but we seek Archbishop Xoran. Do you know if he's home?"

The man nodded and smiled as he approached. "You must be Queen Marielle Vors." As the man came closer, Flowridia noticed the richness of his simple robes and pristine shoes, despite the mud clotting the hem. In his hand, he carried a staff—a staff topped with a white, gleaming orb—and on his shoulder sat a small bluebird. "Forgive me. I often lose time in my garden. I am Archbishop Xoran of the Theocracy of Sol Kareena." He gave a respectful nod in response to Marielle's sudden, deep bow, then turned his attention to Flowridia. "And who are you, child?"

"Flowridia," she said, and she bowed before realizing she had given no context or title. She quickly straightened herself, panicked as she said, "*Lady* Flowridia, Grand Diplomat of Staelash."

"In training," Marielle added.

Relief coursed through Flowridia. "In training."

"We must all begin somewhere," the archbishop said kindly. He offered a hand, and Flowridia shook it, his umber skin rough from age and work. "Please, let us go inside." He escorted them toward the brick cottage and even held the door.

Charmed by the gesture, Flowridia took two full steps inside before bothering to realize the magical presence tingling against her senses. A modest home, comfortable, but the wards surrounding the house itself and emanating from within churned her stomach—the sheer magnitude of it nauseating to anyone with a shred of magical sensitivity. She glanced down at Demitri, only to see him stumble and nearly fall. She scooped him into her arms. "Are you all right?"

There's powerful magic here.

It invigorated her as much as it was overwhelming. Pure light surrounded this home. Protective wards established by something powerful and ancient, yet she and Marielle had crossed the threshold with no trouble. What this protected against, Flowridia could not say.

Marielle seemed unhindered in the slightest, though the orb at her chest had begun to glow.

"The wards here are impressive," Flowridia dared to say, intrigue overshadowing her fear. "Did you set them?"

The archbishop smiled at her question. "I maintain them, but the high priestess of the cathedral—my sister—set them using the orb. I'm surprised you can feel them."

"I have enough experience with wards to recognize them."

Archbishop Xoran gestured to a green couch, embroidered in gold. "Please, sit," he said, and Marielle and Flowridia did, with Demitri in her lap. "And who is your pet?"

"This is Demitri." The wolf in question perked up, and he stared at the archbishop with his enormous golden eyes. "He's my familiar," she finished, searching for the inevitable ire on his face.

The archbishop nodded as he sat on a chair to the side and leaned forward, noticeably intrigued. "I have never met a priestess granted a wolf for a familiar. May I ask whom you serve?"

"I don't actually know," Flowridia said, feeling no need to correct the title. "Only that my first familiar appeared to me in the woods when I was very young."

"Interesting," he said, and she sensed no ire in his tone, only fascination. "It tells me you were chosen. Perhaps your god has plans for you."

Her fears exactly. Flowridia simply offered a pleasant smile.

"Archbishop Xoran," Marielle began, every bit of her regal, from her posture to her tone, "as I stated in my letter, I've come to pay my respects for your fallen comrades. The diplomats were guests in my kingdom and in my lands during the attack."

"There is nothing you could have done," he said. "You treated my guests with utmost respect when they were in your care, and while what happened was a tragedy, I know Staelash is not to blame."

Flowridia knew relief must have struck Marielle, but the young queen hid it well and continued to smile.

"Lord Ashwood told us you were busy planning celebrations in honor of Sol Kareena's child."

"Yes, in a few weeks' time we will be unveiling a new statue dedicated to her and the child and hope, on that night, to be granted the knowledge of his or her name."

Flowridia listened with keen interest as Marielle and the archbishop spoke of more civil things—the expansion of her territory, the death of her father—and wondered why Marielle would even wish for a diplomat. She spun words as easily as she wrote songs and music, and Flowridia wondered if the two skills were related.

But when the matter of foreign polities rose to the surface, Flowridia realized the caution in Marielle's demeanor. "I was informed by the Tholheimer ambassador of attacks on the roads to the north. Has anything of the like happened in your borders?"

"No, but I've been told similar rumors. We've offered numerous prayers to the Goddess for the safe return of their prince."

Of Nox'Kartha, when the subject inevitably came up, Marielle said, "Oh, negotiations are always under way."

Flowridia knew what she truly meant. Did the archbishop know of Zorlaeus and Nox'Kartha?

"I've heard rumors of a Nox'Karthan Embassy being built in your city," he said, verifying Flowridia's suspicion. He spoke with pleasant nonchalance, but the statement was open-ended.

"You've heard correctly," Marielle replied. "Staelash has always maintained open borders, however, and not only to Nox'Karthans. We would be open to discussing the same arrangements with you."

"I think arrangements could be made," the archbishop said, "though I have nothing to offer at this time."

The conversation began to dry, and they said their goodbyes.

"I appreciate your visit," Archbishop Xoran said. "The deaths of those in my service weighs heavily upon me, and your condolences do make a difference. It's not often a ruler comes personally to offer such a thing, and it speaks of your compassion."

Once outside, Marielle remained silent until they stood beyond the gates. "I think it went well," she said, and Flowridia could only agree.

A crowd of people blocked the entrance to the cathedral. Concerned, Marielle ran out of the carriage first, followed closely by Flowridia. Caught outside the sea of people, Flowridia's desire to not squish her familiar heavily outweighed any curiosity she had, but Marielle's beckoning finally pulled her through.

"I need to be sure Meira didn't tie herself to the altar," Marielle said.

The danger of leaving a revolutionary inside the cathedral, Flowridia realized.

Marielle dragged her between the rows of pews, forcing them both past onlookers as only a queen could. Flowridia struggled to shield Demitri from the bodies surrounding them.

The statue of Sol Kareena oversaw the scene. Flowridia could finally see what madness lay at the Goddess' feet. She saw her offering—orange and vibrant, though perhaps a bit small—and realized the flower had taken root. It had broken through the cracked stone—stone that had to be several feet deep before touching dirt.

How, though?

Meira stood beside it, unimpressed. "Sol Kareena has spoken, yes," she said to an aghast priest. "She often speaks."

"But it is a miracle!"

Flowridia stiffened when a voice whispered into her ear. "Looks like Sol Kareena noticed," Sora said.

"What does it mean?" Flowridia whispered, staring at the flower.

"The Goddess has claimed you. If you pledge to her, you'll do great things in her name."

Despite the answer, it left Flowridia unsettled. Not for the first time, the memory of a demon in the woods with a tiny wolf passed through her mind. She held Demitri to her chest, now gazing up at the statue.

Sol Kareena accepted all. Even those who had already been claimed.

They spent the night at an inn, and Flowridia wondered at what point they should be worried for Etolié.

But the Celestial appeared the next morning, a pile of books in her hands. "I spent all night in the library. Gotta catch up on my scripture study!"

She proceeded to fall asleep on Flowridia's shoulder as the carriage rolled home. The Celestial rarely gave in to exhaustion, but consequentially she was wide awake when night fell.

A sudden rustling at Flowridia's tent caused her and Demitri to wake. "Flowers!" the whispered voice spat. "I need you awake!"

Tangled in her blankets, Flowridia stumbled out, immediately seeing Marielle seated beside the dwindling fire and Etolié shaking the tent where Meira and Sora slept. "Rise and–"

The half-elf burst out, knife readied. She nearly tripped when she saw Etolié, blushing fiercely as she dropped the weapon. "I'm so sorry."

"I'll know better next time. You can help by rousing Meira."

Flowridia moved to join Marielle. The monarch wore her nightclothes, and in her hands, she held the orb normally situated in her bosom. Flowridia realized that Marielle's chest was red and raw. "Marielle, what happened?"

"It burned me," Marielle whispered. "I was sleeping, and all of sudden, it flared. It's still warm."

Etolié had begun shrinking tents and plucking them from the ground. "Sora, get the horses ready," she said. One by one, she placed the tents into the pouch on her belt.

Sora asked no questions and went straight to the carriage. Flowridia looked to Etolié, then followed her gaze and saw something bright on the horizon. "Etolié, what's happening?"

In the distance, Flowridia saw the sky flash. "According to my headache," the Celestial said, as alert as Flowridia had ever seen, "we're going to have company."

Above them, Flowridia saw clouds gather. The horizon shone like the sunrise, yet daylight was hours away.

The sky rumbled, thunder sounding, but the circle of clouds stirred only above them. Atop the distant hill, illuminated by a flash of sudden lightning, Flowridia saw an armored silhouette.

Etolié rushed to Marielle and stole the orb from her hands—and all at once, Etolié's form was engulfed in brilliant red flame. Her wings, once invisible, spread wide, fire consuming the gentle tendrils.

Gasping, Flowridia ran to Etolié, desperate to free her of whatever enchantment surrounded her.

Lighting shot down from the sky to their camp. Flowridia fell, deafened. But death did not take them—a geyser of flame absorbed the bolt. Etolié held up her arm, the fire bursting from her hand and arcing in a perfect circle back down, surrounding their entire camp.

Etolié, Flowridia realized, did not truly burn, though her face was etched with fury.

The wall of fire parted for a masculine figure. Blue lightning danced along his armor, which bore the colors gold and white. He held no insignia, no seal to show allegiance, and from his helm shone a resplendent halo, one threatening to surpass even the outpouring of flame.

He wielded an enormous sword, held in two hands, taller than Flowridia herself.

The heat grew stifling. Flowridia coughed, finding it difficult to breathe. The armored man towered above them all, even Etolié, who spoke fearlessly as she kept her spell strong. "I'd heard rumors of a mad-man murdering monarchs for orbs," she said coolly.

A masculine voice spoke slowly through the helmet, stifled by his metal helm. "Give me your orb, and there will be no need for murder."

The fire surrounding their camp suddenly dissipated. Flowridia's lungs welcomed the influx of fresh air. The man radiated light, and from within the slits of his helmet, she saw human eyes, the color of tilled earth, flecked with greenery.

Etolié stood with her wings still aflame. Heat visibly radiated from her skin. "Let my comrades walk away; then we can strike an agreement."

Flowridia stood, realizing Marielle had collapsed, perhaps from suffocation. Sora frantically fanned her face.

"I have no time for tricks, Daughter of Staella. Give me your orb. Then, you and your friends can walk away."

Meira joined Sora in trying to rouse Marielle, but when Flowridia went to join them, Etolié's arm stopped her. The Celestial spared a glance for the collapsed monarch. "A pity we can't be reasonable," Etolié said.

The heat Flowridia felt from Etolié's form suddenly radiated across her own skin. Etolié had placed the orb into her hands, and Flowridia clutched it tight, dizzy at the incursion of energy. The orb swirled a furious shade of red, clouded with vibrant orange. Flowridia felt no depth, no limit. Were magic a tapestry, she felt no edge, yet every strand threatened to ignite.

Marielle held little talent for magic, and so the orb was merely a trinket. But in Etolié's hand, it had become a weapon. Likewise, Flowridia felt the potential for destruction, infinite power clutched in her hand. She saw the strings, the raw power free for her to pluck and weave.

She let them be.

The Celestial shot forward, wings still aflame, armor coating her form as she soared toward the man. A sword appeared in her hand.

The armored man braced for impact, swinging his enormous weapon with both hands as Etolié swooped to avoid his blow. The light from his sword glowed not from fire or lightning, but from pure holy light.

Etolié danced across the sky with a nimbleness Flowridia had never seen the Celestial possess. When his sword met her form, she phased from sight, and it swung through clean. Etolié reappeared behind him, slowly leading him away.

"Flowers, get moving."

Flowridia nearly gasped when a translucent Etolié stood by her side, tapping her shoulder. She glanced frantically between the titanic clash and the nigh invisible Celestial and realized Etolié's trick.

"Yes, yes—I'm right here," Etolié said nodding at the armored figment of magic. "But I'm quite acrobatic when I imagine I can be."

Etolié hadn't earned a reputation for illusion over mere conjuring tricks.

"Keep the orb safe," Etolié continued. "I can't mask its aura. That should keep him distracted, but he can still feel it." Etolié then withdrew a small, silver mirror from her pocket, one etched with a pattern of leaves. It glowed at her touch. "Lara, sweetheart, we have a problem."

Sora held Marielle in her arms. "Etolié, we should go."

Etolié held up a hand. "Find us. Get us out of here," she said to the mirror. Then to Sora, she said, "Now, we run—Flowers!"

Flowridia followed Etolié's frantic gaze and saw the armored man charge toward her, weapon readied. The illusionary Etolié flew in his vision, but he stared straight past her.

The illusion vanished. Real Etolié grabbed at the air, and in her hands appeared a quarterstaff, stars carved into the solid wood. She slammed it into the ground, splitting the earth. The cracks ran deep. A chasm lay etched into the ground.

Not ten feet away, the man faltered, stumbling to avoid the crevice. Then, he stepped forward with caution, his feet walking across the gulf with ease. "Your illusions hold no sway to those who know you, Daughter of Staella."

The cracks vanished. The earth remained pristine. Cold fury shone on the Celestial's face. "No more tricks, then," she said, and then her body began to shine.

A vibrant mass appeared in the sky and descended upon her. Their forms collided, the light blinding as a new figure emerged.

Mother had spoken once or twice of possession, of how angelic and demonic entities could only exist in this world with a host. Formless and powerless otherwise, if invited to inhabit a mortal form, they possessed all the power they held in their own plane and more.

Such power often killed the host when the summoned being was god.

Light poured from Etolié's form as she grew and morphed into something lithe and androgynous. Then she—he?—laughed, and the voice that spoke was both Etolié and not. Something else intertwined with the sound, something masculine—something inhuman. "Give me a moment," he said, and when their attacker rushed forward, he held out a hand to stop him. "No need to rush in bull-headed."

To Flowridia's surprise, the man slowed, perhaps confused at the command.

From the air, the glowing figure pulled a flask, not unlike Etolié's. He offered the flask forward but laughed when the man stared silently. "I never enter a fight sober."

The figure brought the flask to his lips, but just as he might have taken a sip, he threw it forward.

An explosion at the armored man's feet caused him to cry out in rage.

The glowing figure laughed uproariously. "Not a fan of my tricks, either? You're such a bore." It took the quarterstaff in hand, prepared to strike. From the sky, stars began to fall, each one striking the man's armor with perfect precision. The man stumbled back with each glancing blow, some of which dented his worn armor.

Etolié—and whomever possessed her body—swung the staff, striking a blow to the distracted, pained man. Another swing, and this time, it met with an enormous sword. "Your kind are a plague on this world, Eionei."

"Oh, so you know me? Can't say I wish to know you."

The man whirled around, just as a bolt of lightning shot from his hand. Eionei, the Drinking God of freedom and laughter and every sort of riotous thing, waved it aside with his staff, the discordant magic striking a tree instead. The staff morphed into a sword—a rapier—and the god darted forward.

Nimble feet dodged heavy blows with ease. The rapier swung quickly, landing precise blows in the cracks of the mysterious figure's armor.

High above, clouds continued to gather. The moonlight disappeared. Flowridia heard thunder.

The rapier's tip waited at the man's neck. "Just a peek," Eionei teased. "Let's see the face behind the–"

From the sky, lightning split the air in a deafening bolt. It struck Eionei, his good humor morphing into a cry of pain.

When the light faded, the laughing god had vanished, leaving Etolié on her knees. The armored man's heavy steps thundered in tandem with the roaring sky.

"The false god you pledge to is a coward," he said, and from the ground, Etolié appeared so small beneath the towering figure. His light grew blinding, the sun engulfing the stars. Etolié tried to stand, but a mere kick sent her weakened form sprawling to the ground. "Pledge to me, and you'll be serving the true Gods of this world."

Etolié's breathing came in ragged, pained intervals. She shook her head and spat on the ground. "Better to be pledged to a coward god than to no god at all. You're nothing."

"I assure you, Daughter of Staella, I am everything. The worlds will remember soon." Lightning radiated against his armor, surrounding him in blue, crackling light. He reached into his breastplate and withdrew a blue and yellow orb, one that matched the light dancing across his armor.

Flowridia felt the strings of magic. This time, she pulled, not expecting to feel something pull back.

Fire erupted at the armored man's feet. His cry echoed across the metal chamber of his helmet. Flowridia felt her body begin to burn, both within and without, the struggle to keep from letting heat consume her nearly overwhelming.

His gaze turned to her, and from the slits of his helmet she saw those soft eyes staring back. Flowridia cowered, stumbling back when he took a step toward her.

"A valiant attempt," he said, voice audibly pained. "And in deference to your courage, I'll spare you if you hand me the orb."

On the ground, Etolié struggled to sit up, burns singeing her form. Amidst the outcropping of trees, Sora and the rest hid, but he would find them in moments if he so chose.

Flowridia took a step back, holding the orb close to her chest.

She heard the armored man chuckle, half-hearted as it was. "You're a brave little fool. What is your name?"

Rather than answer, Flowridia yanked the strings again, this time expecting tension.

There was none. Fire exploded. Heat seared her body, but she heard the armored man cry out in pain.

Then, dizziness struck. Nausea welled in Flowridia's stomach as the world turned sideways. Darkness met her eyelids, and for a moment she floated in space, weightless and helpless as something dragged her across the void. All around she saw a chromatic, silver fire, shined and polished and blinding.

Then, she slammed onto the floor of the council chamber. Lying on the ground, polished wood met her back. The orb rolled from her hands.

When Flowridia turned her head, her vision spun with it. For a moment, she swore she saw the empress, those silver eyes unmistakable.

But her vision kept spinning, and when darkness descended, it held relief.

When Flowridia's consciousness returned, she realized that soft, silver eyes watched from above. "Don't try and sit up," said the gentle, feminine voice. "Some people react poorly to having their bodies forcibly dragged across the planes."

Flowridia obeyed, realizing her head lay in the empress' lap. Demitri's nose poked at her side, and she pulled the wolf to her chest. "You can do that?"

"I can do many things. Etolié called for my help, and for good reason." Fingers traced light lines along the side of Flowridia's face, brushing aside unruly strands of hair. "She says you used the orb to save her life. Your bravery is to be commended."

Lara held the aforementioned orb in her other hand. Etolié had once quietly disparaged Marielle's use of it as a fashion accessory, saying only that it was a gift from the late emperor to Marielle's father to be used in protecting their small kingdom. Technically, the responsibility of keeping it had fallen to the recently crowned queen, but Flowridia had never realized the vastness of its power.

Around them, people scuffled about and spoke frantically. She saw Marielle out of her peripheral, her head in her hands as she sat in her throne with Thalmus to guard her.

A sudden groan pulled her attention. Flowridia instinctively tried to sit, catching a glance of a rather sickly Celestial before Lara stopped her. "Etolié channeled a dangerous amount of energy, as did you. How are you feeling?"

"I feel fine," Flowridia said, and this time when she tried to sit, Lara supported her. She watched as the empress stood up and quickly approached Etolié, worry settling onto her features.

The Celestial lay curled on the ground. Etched scars spread across her arm in fractal spirals, the result of being struck by lightning, yet her dress remained oddly pristine.

Kneeling beside her, Khastra's hands lightly scratched her back. "If you are going to be stubborn, I will drag you to bed myself."

"After the meeting," Etolié managed, and with her bloodshot eyes and sallow skin, Flowridia wondered if she would be conscious that long. Lara sat beside her, her small hands brushing the hair from Etolié's face. "Perfect timing, little moonbeam."

Lara's jaw trembled, but Flowridia watched her force a smile. "Etolié," Flowridia said, and when she moved to stand, she found she balanced perfectly well, "will you let me heal you?"

The empress glanced up at her approach, but Khastra's stare remained fixed on her Celestial companion. Flowridia saw Sora and Meira looking disheveled but alive, and then Etolié shook her head.

"Etolié, please–"

"It's bad shit, Flowers. Calling on gods rips some life out of you. Fortunately, I'm technically immortal." Etolié attempted to sit up, but at her pained groan, Khastra gently pushed her back down. "Ya big lug—you don't have to baby me. I'm fine."

"Etolié," Khastra retorted, "you were struck by lightning."

"Yes, and I feel like a thousand bees are stinging me from the inside. But I'm not going to *die*."

"Perhaps I can't restore years of your life, but I can at least heal what's superficial," Flowridia said. "Please, I'm worried."

From the looks of solidarity on both Khastra's and Lara's faces, Flowridia knew she wasn't the only one. Gaunt, pale features met Flowridia's eye, and Etolié finally offered a nod. "Do what you will, Flowers. Stop before you get hurt."

Flowridia let her senses expand and touch upon Etolié's musculature, feeling the burns within and without that had ripped through her form. A deeper weakness lay dormant, one with no bodily harm yet still unquestionably deadly. Flowridia could not touch it and supposed this was the lingering price of godly possession.

Still, she coaxed Etolié's body to mend itself, watching with interest as the fractal scars on her arms faded. Flowridia sat back, and Lara's hand returned to its spot on her back. Demitri came to sit in her lap, surely as exhausted as she.

"You're really quite spectacular," Lara said quietly, and her stare rested on Etolié's faded scars. "To be able to wield the orb with no experience speaks well of your talents. Perhaps you're suited for more than simply being Etolié's gardener." Her adoring smile settled onto Flowridia, a silent 'thank you' in the gesture.

"What happened?" Marielle interrupted, and Flowridia realized the queen was near tears. "Can we start this meeting, please? Why did Etolié know about a mad-man on the road but I didn't?"

Lara helped Flowridia to stand, but Thalmus stole her and escorted her to her chair, still squashed beside Etolié's. He knelt beside her and moved to brush aside her tussled hair, but she knew it was a guise to inspect her for wounds.

Lara stood at the center of the circle of chairs, Etolié by her side. "Etolié, would you please relay the story for everyone not in attendance, including myself?"

Color had returned to Etolié's face, and she began the tale—of being accosted in their camp by the armored man, of calling on Eionei for aid, and of Flowridia's hand in saving Etolié's life.

Flowridia stared at Lara, however, who listened to the story with intrigue. Lara Solviraes and her silver eyes—

A small puzzle clicked into place, though an obvious one in hindsight. It fit that Lara's family name was a bastardization of her most defining trait—*Solviraes . . . Silver eyes . . .*

"It was an impressive maneuver; kudos to Flowers. But the real challenge lies before us. Past experience has shown that this man is willing to kill for the orbs, and we still don't know why."

"What past experience?" Marielle asked.

Glancing around, Flowridia saw understanding on only a few faces—those of Khastra, Etolié, and Lara. The rest appeared as perplexed by Etolié's announcement as Marielle.

Lara spoke with visible resignation. "Three days before Marielle's coronation, this same man appeared in my castle. He murdered my father and stole the orb he kept."Lara braced herself, steeling her jaw as rage and sorrow battle for supremacy. Bitterness seeped into every carefully chosen word from Lara's lips. "We have no motive, no identity—only the knowledge that he seeks to gather all six, and only from his own tongue. My council has enacted their own search, but tonight is the first we've seen or heard from him since my father's death."

Flowridia's fear of appearing the fool paled to her own quiet confusion. It seemed everyone knew a story she didn't. "Forgive me," she asked shyly, "but what is the relevance of these orbs?"

Lara smiled from the center of the room. "Do we all know the story of the Convergence?"

Flowridia did know, a tale she had heard before her life with Mother, but Lara continued her story anyway.

"No one knows the origin of the orbs, but there are six all together, each providing balance, much like the Old Gods who wielded them. In the time before The Convergence of Planes, some ten thousand years ago, the Gods of Order and Chaos gave them to dragons to aid in protecting our world. But we also know that Chaos, out of boredom or spite—no one knows—used the orbs to smash the worlds together and cause the Convergence. The orbs are why we coexist with Celestière and Sha'Demoni, why we cohabitate with races never meant for our world, and the origin of magic within our realm. Her folly, and the Old Gods' subsequent deaths, ushered in the new era of gods—those powered by belief, and thus godlike, but not true Gods." Lara managed to smile despite the grim mood. "Though I suppose it is blasphemous to suggest it.

"The orbs are unique," she continued, "because they do not merely channel magical energy. They can grant power, yes, but the source of that power is infinite, and the power drawn leaves no weakness to the wielder. In the hands of someone like my father, it would offer limitless capacity for absorption, but when wielded against him, it became his downfall."

Lara spared a glance for the orb in her hand and then offered it to Marielle. "We know only the location of three of the orbs. We have one, the mad-man holds the other, and Archbishop Xoran of the Theocracy of Sol Kareena holds the third. The other three have never been found."

"So, what do we do?" Marielle asked, and she held the orb, reverently cupping it in her hands.

"We kill him." Khastra's chuckle interrupted the somber mood. "This man is only that—a man. Whatever magic he may wield, I have yet to meet a man who can fight without his head."

"I'm inclined to agree," Lara said, the softness in her countenance growing suddenly stiff, "though there's the matter of finding him first. After he stole the orb, he wielded it without question and used it to overload my father's reserves. He knew how to combat the silver fire. My father, he–" Steel threatened to break—Lara's demeanor visibly cracked. "He did what any Solviraes would do: he absorbed the magic the man shot at him, but there was no relenting. I walked in to see my father's light grow blinding seconds before he exploded. Then, the man disappeared."

Flowridia had heard tales of the Solviraes bloodline and of their inborn trait to absorb and wield pure magical energy. A talent otherwise unheard of, it offered the potential for a massive reserve of energy—the extent of which Flowridia couldn't fathom.

A moment of hesitation, and in Lara's held breath, Flowridia saw a modicum of insecurity—not the Empress Alauriel, descended from the Moon Goddess, but an orphaned girl in mourning.

The moment passed, and Lara released her breath, resuming the clench in her jaw. "Find them. Hide them. Orbs lead to orbs and exponentially increase the others' power when together. With some study, we can use yours to try and track down the rest. I've been working tirelessly to find a source of maldectine large enough to house and hide their power from the others, but until then, we must find the ones we can."

Marielle's hands blocked the light of the orb, the faint glow of red reflecting off her gown. "So, we hunt for orbs."

"Or we risk handing them to him on a silver platter," Meira said.

"Why don't we ask another kingdom for help? Someone larger?" Marielle twitched, her hand coming up to touch the orb poking out from her dress. "Staelash is small."

"I would rather keep the news quiet for now," Lara said. "Do you really want the orbs in the hands of Imperator Casvir, founder of the world's largest trade empire? Do you think the elves would come from across the sea to fight for a country they want nothing to do with? The kingdom of Moratham opposes Staelash's very founding principles, and to ally with the Theocracy, though our people share a common goddess, would detrimentally shatter the careful balance your kingdom maintains between them and

Nox'Kartha. Staelash is small, but it has much to offer. And you will always have Solviran aid. You were ours first."

Silence filled the room. Marielle finally whispered, "I'll return to the archbishop. I'll propose a trade for the orb."

"Well, about that," Etolié said, pursing her lips. "I already did."

Marielle stiffened. "What?"

"After your and Flowers' meeting, he and I discussed the orb, though in relatively vague terms. The archbishop isn't opposed, but he does need time to think of a proper counteroffer. The orb is vital to the protection of his city, or so he says."

Slack-jawed, Marielle said, "How did you know about all of this?"

"Lara and I talk. I'm the one who told her to keep the news of our orb-stealing friend quiet for now."

Marielle glared between the empress and the magister. "I'm not sure if this is treason or not."

"Not treason," Etolié said. "Khastra knew too. It takes two out of three to make a governing decision. We both agreed getting orbs was a good plan."

Khastra added, "I still believe crushing his head would be the best plan."

"But you didn't think to include me on this?" Marielle said, and Flowridia could hear fury in her tone.

"Marielle," Lara said, firm but soft, "perhaps we should continue this discussion in private. There is something else I wish to discuss with you."

Marielle frowned but offered a nod. "Meeting adjourned, then."

When Flowridia moved to stand with the rest, Etolié placed a hand on her thigh. "I want you to stay, Lady Diplomat. You'll need to hear this too."

The room emptied, leaving only Khastra, Etolié, and Marielle, who continued to glower as Lara stood before her. "Speak your mind, cousin."

Flowridia wondered if the familial pet name were meant to level the two rulers, one of whom unquestionably reigned supreme.

"Marielle, word has reached me that you've agreed to place a Nox'Karthan Embassy in your city. I was not consulted on this."

Swallowing loudly, Marielle's demeanor grew stiff. "I think strengthening ties with foreign dignitaries is the best solution for us both, long term–"

"Rumor says you're courting their ambassador."

"Not officially."

In the ensuing silence, Lara slowly crossed her arms, silver turning to steel. "Marielle, the conflict between the Theocracy and Nox'Kartha escalates with every passing day. I've seen the riots myself, and there are rumors of failed assassination attempts on Imperator Casvir's life. Citizens of the Theocracy call for De'Sindai blood, and I have no doubt Nox'Kartha is giddy in anticipation of the brewing war. The fire's turned up, and your territory will be directly between them when the pot boils over."

Marielle uncrossed her legs, and then crossed them again, her stare fixed on the orb and not the empress. "I've made no agreements, aside from verbal ones."

"Be careful of what addendums are written in your contract. To demand you recant your agreement would be detrimental to your relationship with Nox'Kartha, but you must understand: while my kingdom holds no quarrel with them, most of mine worship Sol Kareena. I'll be hung in the streets if you tie me into a war against the Theocracy. Be careful."

Gentleness held no place here, not for the Solviran Empress. An odd juxtaposition, Flowridia thought, to imagine the soft-spoken woman she'd briefly met to the ruler sitting before them.

Shame colored Marielle's features. "We'll move forward with caution."

"You will. And you'll consult me before you make any more agreements with foreign powers. Your territory is your own, but you still pay taxes to me. Your first alliance is to my empire." Lara released a long, thoughtful sigh, though frustration still showed in the line of her lips. "Many of our treaties remain unwritten. I would hope to continue a relationship of trust, but I think writing out the fine-print on some would be wise."

"I will consult Etolié about the details in the morning," Marielle whispered, and then Lara offered a hand to Marielle.

"I have no wish for conflict between us." She helped Marielle to stand. "Politics spoil so many things, cousin.

Come visit my kingdom; perhaps we can discuss Staelash and Solvira in more hopeful terms."

Marielle took back her hand, nodding as she did, and left the room with no farewell.

Lara said nothing of it, and instead she gave goodbyes to the rest of them—to Khastra and Etolié both, the latter of whom held her in a tight embrace. "Relax, little moonbeam," the Celestial said before tussling—and thus ruining—the empress' braided hair, but the smile she gave was nothing less than maternal.

When Lara reached Flowridia and offered her a hand to stand, she said, "You're a witch with enormous potential." Lara's hand lingered, keeping Flowridia there as her voice lowered. "If you ever tire of the political game, there's a place for you with me, in my castle."

Surprised, Flowridia simply gave her a nod.

Once in bed, Flowridia collapsed into a dreamless sleep.

Chapter 5

"Thalmus, what does it mean to be claimed by multiple gods?"

From his kiln, Thalmus kept his focus on stoking the fire. A black shadow covered much of his face, stubborn hairs having grown between now and last sunset, and the dark braid traveling down his back could have been tucked into his belt. Flowridia wondered if it were common among giants to take such pride in their hair—or perhaps desert dwellers, as Thalmus' dark skin and features suggested his heritage lie. She had never asked.

"I suppose it would mean you're a nuisance to fate," Thalmus finally said, a wry smile at his lip.

Flowridia carefully stepped up behind him, mindful of the heat radiating from the coals within the iron furnace. "If fate wants my compliance, I wish it would be a little clearer."

"Fate is what you make of it. It's not something I believe in," he muttered, and she watched the fire begin to glow from within the small hole at the front. Thalmus set a large dish of multi-colored glass pieces onto the table. "But I do believe in gods. And it's not unheard of for multiple gods to squabble over the attention of a mortal, nor for mortals to pledge to multiple gods."

She took a step back as he moved around her, forever fascinated at his array of tools. "Are you pledged to anyone?"

A wistful, pained frown pulled at Thalmus' scarred lips. Something changed in his countenance, a chink in his heavily armored demeanor. "No," he said. "I have no need for gods."

Dangerous words, and it struck her as odd that Thalmus, as good a man as she had ever met, would be at odds with any of the benevolent gods. But something clamped at Flowridia's tongue when she thought to press him, as always happened when Thalmus spoke a personal anecdote. She longed to ask. She longed to comfort him. But whatever haunted him seemed well beyond what a hug and an offering of pastries could heal.

Perhaps someday. But not this one.

Instead, she pouted, her mind mulling over her trip to the Theocracy. "So, I don't have to make any decisions?"

Thalmus shook his head, his expression kind. "No, Flowra." The use of her nickname spread a shy smile across her lips. "Be whatever it is you want to be, and don't worry about gods or fate."

A difficult task for one prone to worry, but Flowridia felt some comfort at the words. "I should stop being vague."

"Marielle told me about the miracle in the cathedral. Be aware, Meira will start pushing you to pledge to Sol Kareena. But also be aware that I will stand behind you if you choose not to." His lip twitched, a grimace threatening to mar his pleasant demeanor. "As will Etolié. Her life belongs to Eionei."

"I'm glad to know I have allies," Flowridia said, her posture caving as her hands grasped each other behind her back. "But let's say I did claim Sol Kareena. Can I claim multiple gods?"

"As I said, it's not unprecedented. It would depend on who you are already pledged to."

The turn in conversation churned her stomach. Memories of a demon in the woods passed behind her closed eyelids. "I don't know where Demitri came from," she admitted. "And my first familiar appeared to me when I wandered out into the woods one day. I couldn't have been more than three. But if I unknowingly accepted a god then, can I be held to that?"

"Gods work in strange ways," Thalmus muttered, his rough voice barely audible, "but a god who would coerce a child into an agreement would be a wicked one." Quiet animosity descended onto his face. He placed a hand on her waist and led her to a bench beyond the heat of the kiln. When he sat, she joined him, leaning into his protective touch.

With her bare feet dangling above the ground, she said, "Perhaps accepting Sol Kareena would offer me some protection."

"But protection from what? Perhaps your patron is no god at all, but a higher acolyte. Not all demons are gods. And many demons have good intentions, despite being at odds with angelic gods."

"He would still have to be powerful enough to grant me magic."

His eyes narrowed, and Flowridia realized her mistake in granting the demon a gendered description. "You said someone gave Demitri to you?"

Flowridia nodded.

"Did you see that someone?"

Rare was the witch granted power by something benevolent. She had seen her demon, with his glowing red eyes and a voice like the first rumbling of a volcano—soft, pervasive, and filling her with dread.

"It was dark," she said softly. "But I saw him."

Clicking heels against stone alerted them immediately to a presence. Etolié appeared, uneven steps suggesting drunkenness. But she kept her distance, instead beckoning in exaggerated motions. "Flowers, Marielle needs you." She pulled a flask from the air and offered it forward, though Flowridia still sat several feet away. "And you'll need this."

Flowridia left Thalmus' side to accept the offering. "Why?" she asked, purposefully not taking a sip.

"Nox'Kartha's here. You're meeting with them."

Alcohol would do nothing to help Flowridia's lack of social graces. It would probably do little to hinder them either, but she kept the flask on her vanity unopened.

Marielle had gifted her with a selection of dresses after her unexpected promotion, most of them castoffs from the monarch herself. Flowridia shied away from the finery, self-conscious in any color palette other than brown. But, dressed in soft pastels, Flowridia wrestled with her tangled, thick hair, taming it with some violence as she forced tiny white flowers to weave into the waves.

Demitri watched from his spot on the bed. *Why are you angry?*

"I'm not angry," she muttered, pushing a pin in place to hold the mass of hair from her face.

You look angry.

Flowridia dropped her hands, grimacing as several strands fell away with them. "I'm nervous."

Because of Ayla?

The name 'Ayla' hadn't been said by anyone. There was no confirmation that the sultry elf was making an appearance at the meeting. Still, the mere thought brought a blush to Flowridia's cheek.

Instead, she sighed. "Yes, because of Ayla." She resumed work on her hair, determined not to be bested by the mop atop her head. "I want to look nice."

You always look nice.

"Perhaps 'nice' isn't the correct word." Finally, the pin stuck, and half her hair remained secure behind her head. "I want her to like me."

You played chess. That means you're friends.

Watching Ayla's fingers gloss the board, the memory of her calculating mind mercilessly capturing each piece brought fresh heat to Flowridia's cheeks. But with it came Etolié's ruthless assessment. Had she been a pest? What did Ayla Darkleaf think of Staelash's newest diplomat?

It hardly mattered. The meeting was strictly business, to discuss the construction of the Nox'Karthan Embassy. When cloth slippers donned her feet—she could be bothered to wear shoes for this—Flowridia straightened her gown and said, "I should go." She stole the small wolf from the bed sheets. "Come with me?"

In response, Demitri kissed her chin. His thick fur latched to her dress, dark grey strands clinging to the fabric. Recalling Etolié's warning, she set him down and began plucking puppy fur from her sleeves. *I like Ayla. She smells nice.*

"I can't say I've ever sniffed her," Flowridia said, smiling at the childish sentiment. She let Demitri through the door, then followed quickly after, racing him down the stairs but slowing at the end to let her young familiar win.

She met Marielle in the hallway. The queen, more decorated than a wedding cake with her bustled skirts and made-up face, brightened when Flowridia appeared. "They're inside," she mouthed, pointing to the door. "Lady Flowridia," she continued, loud enough for anyone inside to hear. "Right on time. Are you ready to begin this meeting?"

Confused by Marielle's act, she still managed to nod. "Yes?"

Marielle beckoned her forward, eyes wide as she slowly exhaled, then twisted the doorknob.

Inside, Flowridia paused at the sight of Ayla lounging back, a forced, petulant grin plastered on her face as she glared at a jeweled box on the table. Zorlaeus sat to her right, smiling sincerely when he saw Marielle, but Ayla crossed her arms, glancing between Marielle and Flowridia with obvious reticence. Styled curls tickled her shoulders, and a low bun sat asymmetrically by her slight neck, the hair pulled to entirely cover her left ear. Three light blue gems still decorated her right, elegantly pointing through her black hair. One more glance to the box, then Ayla's gaze settled on Flowridia, her smile turning bitter and sweet all at once.

"It's an exciting day for our kingdoms," Zorlaeus began, staring solely at Marielle. "Queen Marielle, Imperator Casvir sends his personal thanks on behalf of accepting his offer. He looks forward to strengthening the ties between our countries."

Zorlaeus continued, even recited a letter from the Imperator of Nox'Kartha himself, but not once did Ayla's captivating gaze leave Flowridia.

". . . Their Viceroy, Murishani, wishes to add a personal note and offers an upfront gift of ten thousand gold pieces . . ."

Ayla's lip lifted just enough to show her teeth. Was Flowridia's blush so obvious? She smiled demurely, brushing against Demitri as she crossed her legs.

"Here it states that I'll be stationed as a representative. The embassy's construction will be fully paid for and enacted by Nox'Kartha . . ."

Did Ayla just lick her lips?

". . . all I need from you, Queen Marielle, is your signature on the dotted line."

The scratching of the quill pen on paper pulled Flowridia's focus to the contract lying before them. Not a day ago, the empress had warned Marielle regarding impulsivity in Nox'Karthan affairs, but delivered with the awkward charm of Zorlaeus, what chance did Marielle have for intelligent maneuvering?

However, Flowridia's tongue stiffened at the thought of daring to object. Cowardice was better than risking insult to their guests, right?

Once signed, Zorlaeus rolled up the scroll. "We will have an envoy sent to begin work immediately after the groundbreaking." He stood and smiled kindly at Marielle. "I will deliver this and tell them to prepare a stage for tonight. The ceremony for the groundbreaking will be at sundown." Then, he looked to Ayla and pulled a jeweled key from his pocket, one that perfectly matched the box on the table. "Casvir has a gift for your kingdom. Ayla?" He handed the key to Marielle, his fingers lingering against her hand before he saw himself out.

The moment the door clicked, Ayla's demeanor changed. She slouched back in her chair, releasing a heavy, prolonged sigh. "Gods, that was too much banter for me."

"Such is the price of ruling," Marielle said, and Flowridia could see the forced smile. Ayla surely could too. "Imperator Casvir has been generous to our city."

At the mention of Casvir's name, Ayla immediately sat straight. "Oh, Casvir . . ." Ayla shut her eyes, letting the name twirl languidly off her tongue.

Something in her tone raised the hair on Flowridia's neck. "What about Imperator Casvir?" she asked, and she feared Ayla's reply would be a pin to her inflated fantasies.

"He's fair and just," Ayla mused, her tone the same, "but as cruel as they come." She leaned forward, smiling wide before she chuckled. "This is terribly embarrassing." She clenched her jaw, and Flowridia realized she meant it sincerely.

"This is a gift from Casvir?" Marielle asked, ever polite.

"An apology." Ayla stood, and her grimace rose in tandem. "Oh, promise me you won't open it until I'm gone."

"Of course."

Pacified, Ayla smiled coolly, staring at Flowridia directly as she asked, "And will I see you at the ceremony?"

Flowridia withered beneath those piercing eyes, grateful when Marielle answered instead. "You will."

Ayla's gaze shifted. "Oh, excellent," she cooed to Marielle, and her poise straightened. "I look forward to it." Her lip twisted, revealing teeth as she grinned.

When Ayla left, Flowridia felt oxygen return to the room. As she caught her breath, Marielle spoke. "Did she mean to wait until she left the room or the city?"

Flowridia shrugged, wondering instead about Ayla's cryptic words. The way she had bemoaned the name 'Casvir' was downright obscene, but still her words were biting.

Marielle shoved the key into the lock and turned it to the side. "What's the worst that can happen?"

The lid opened. Marielle squeaked. Flowridia shot back in her chair, flinching at what waited inside the box. Jeweled and ornate, the box was lined with velvet, and resting in the center was a severed ear. Pale and pointed, three blue stones studded the side, but no blood dried on the edges.

She remembered Ayla's hair, how it curled, styled carefully to cover one side of her head. Flowridia's hand slowly moved to cover her mouth.

"Flowridia," Marielle whispered, "that's Ayla's ear."

Eyes wide, Flowridia nodded, too aghast to formulate a response. But a small envelope, tucked to the side and stamped with the official Nox'Karthan seal, caught her eye. She reached forward, giving the ear a wide berth. Trembling, she opened it as Marielle watched and handed it over to the queen to be read aloud:

> To Queen Marielle Vors and the noble court of Staelash,
>
> My sincerest condolences on the deaths of the diplomats of the Theocracy of Sol Kareena. Such a tragedy should not have been committed within your borders, and it leaves the rest of us shaken.
>
> I offer such formalities not as an admission of guilt, but of frustration. My own people were in your kingdom at the time and sent with the express purpose of keeping a watchful eye on the happenings therein. Had my people done their duty, this tragedy would have been averted. As a gesture of my goodwill for this slight, I offer this: three wishes, granted by my most accomplished servant. Whisper your intent, and she will be at your command.
>
> I am pleased to hear how the embassy moves forward.
>
> -Imperator Casvir, First and Last of His Name, Tyrant of Nox'Kartha, and Marshall of the Deathless Army

"It really is Ayla's ear," Flowridia said, horrified at the implications. A clean cut severed the pale skin—not a single jagged edge. Her hands shook as she reached forward, resisting the impulse to flinch as she touched cold skin. A chain had been looped through the earhole, creating an eerie accessory. Flowridia lifted it and ran her fingers along the pointed tip, glossing over the studded stones.

What sort of monster was Imperator Casvir?

Marielle leaned away when Flowridia offered her the ear, visibly nauseated. "Ayla will grant us three wishes? What sort of wishes?"

"We could ask her?"

"That would mean admitting we opened her gift."

Flowridia studied the chained ear, letting her senses brush gently across the uncanny gift. It radiated something dark; something she couldn't decipher. "It's her ear. If there's magic involved, she might be listening, even now."

"That sounds horrendously annoying," Marielle said, frowning. "Not only does she get her ear severed, she might be forced to listen to us argue about it. Imperator Casvir is thorough in his punishments."

As she spoke, Flowridia placed it back into the box.

"I'll ask Zorlaeus," Marielle continued. "He knew about the gift, so he must have known what it was. Perhaps he'll know what it's capable of."

Flowridia stood, open box in hand. "Where should we keep this?"

"Etolié might have some suggestions," Marielle said, rising to her feet. Key in hand, she walked over to the door and let it swing open. "She would–"

Ayla stood in the doorway, arms crossed, a single eyebrow raised. Her sanguine smile grew as she plucked the box from Flowridia and handed it to Marielle. Standing so close, Flowridia realized the imposing woman barely reached her chin.

"Do not worry for me," Ayla said, an airy quality to her voice. She took the ear in her hands, then let it fall, catching it so it dangled at the end of the chain. "An ear is not so brutal a thing to lose as you might think." She turned her predatory grin directly onto Flowridia and lifted the chain up over her head and placed it around Flowridia's neck. She dropped it, letting it settle on the silk buttons over Flowridia's chest. Her fingers slid down the chain and gripped the ear itself, tight but gentle. Ayla tugged downward, ever so lightly.

Ayla's smoldering lips drew close. Flowridia's blush grew hot, and as intimately aware as she was of Ayla's mouth, she remained mindful of Marielle standing beside them. Her attention darted away, words tumbling out regarding the first thing catching her eye. "The earrings are lovely."

Horrified, Flowridia internally berated herself. Ayla's mouth only inches from her own, but all she could comment on was her earrings?

"Aren't they?" Ayla mused, her tone caustic. "Casvir said they looked *fetching.*"

Casvir said . . ?

With a laugh, Ayla released the ear, and Flowridia stood up straight. "Take good care of it for me," she said, but the words felt muted, lost in the jealous morass filling Flowridia's chest. Ayla's fingers caressed the chain as she slid away, small hips swaying as she stepped silently down the hallway.

"So, Flowridia," Marielle began, eyes darting between Flowridia's face and the ear resting on her chest, "it seems Ayla–"

". . . is sleeping with Casvir." Flowridia's fists clenched at the thought. Why did that anger her so? Ayla could be centuries old for all she knew. Her and Casvir's history might run longer than Flowridia had been alive. Still, the idea hurt. Oh, why did she even care?

"I was going to say that Ayla entrusted the ear to you." Marielle stepped forward, forcing herself into Flowridia's line of sight. "Which means I'm going to trust you too."

Flowridia nodded, though her heart and mind were far away. With no farewell, she left, Demitri at her heels and the morbid accessory still dangling from her neck.

Demitri's voice broke through her agitated thoughts. *Why are you so unhappy?*

"Because Ayla's sleeping with Imperator Casvir. I'm such a fool, Demitri." She didn't steer toward her room, but to her garden. The sun warmed her skin, cold from Ayla's touch and presence. Frustrated, she slipped off the cotton shoes and let grass tickle her rough, bare feet.

I don't understand.

"You're young," she said with a weary sigh, "and so am I." The stone path brought her to the colorful bushes at the entrance of her garden. Trees shaded her steps, and she slowed her pace. "It was stupid of me to even think–"

Think what, exactly?

She veered off the path and knelt in the grass before setting her focus on a patch of daisies, tiny buds amidst a brilliant floral sea. She pursed her lips; the buds were too small for this late in the season. She placed her hands on the dirt, beside the thick stems of the bush, and poured energy into the ground. Not a spell—pure energy.

"Why not feed the plants directly, Mother?"

"If you do, that's all they'll consume," Mother replied, *weaving the roots into the dead flesh buried in the earth. "But enrich their soil, and watch them flourish."*

Weakness struck her. She pulled her dirt-covered fingers away and rolled onto her bottom, letting her heartbeat steady. When Demitri's nose poked her knee, she did not even turn.

You're distracted. You'll hurt yourself if you keep working like this.

"I know," she whispered.

Demitri's sharp nails dug into her thigh as he crawled into her lap. *Are you sad about Ayla?*

"What's there to be sad about?" Flowridia fell backwards, lying flat in the shaded grass. "It seems Ayla doesn't entirely hate me," she muttered, and she grabbed the ear resting on the chain. Holding it up, she let it dangle inches above her face. "But that doesn't mean she wants anything to do with me."

She gave you a gift.

"Imperator Casvir gave us a gift." Distain pulled at her upper lip. "A pretty horrendous gift, and not exactly the kindest thing to do to someone you're sleeping with." Flowridia shut her eyes and released a steady sigh. The ear dropped into the grass, and the gentle singing of birds lulled her into sleep.

After her nap, disastrous grass stains covered the silk of her dress. The sun hung low in the sky; she would have to run to make it to the groundbreaking on time. Flowridia plucked a few fresh flowers, hiked up her skirts, and ran back to the manor, praying Etolié wouldn't catch her.

A few horrified gasps met her as she ran past a pair of servant girls. She remembered, then, her eerie fashion accessory. Still running, she dropped the ear down the collar of her dress where it settled perfectly between her breasts.

Demitri narrowly avoided being squished by the doorframe. Flowridia inspected herself in the mirror and frowned. "Perhaps Etolié knows spells for cleaning fabric." As quick as her fingers could fly, she removed her dress and stuffed it into the base of the wardrobe. She stole the first dress her hand met—something white and blue, with a neckline to cover the ear—then remembered she'd left her shoes outside in the garden.

The long skirt would hide that.

Flowridia removed the crushed petals from her hair and instead wove fresh ones through the thick locks. Soon, subtle pastels graced her head.

She glanced at the window. The sun had nearly set. She shoved the ear into her bodice and scooped Demitri into her arms, prepared to run.

A knock startled her. With the small wolf securely in her arms, she opened the door to find Thalmus looking down at her. "Marielle and I were concerned when you weren't on time for the groundbreaking," the half-giant said, studying her for any signs of distress.

"I fell asleep outside," Flowridia admitted, holding Demitri up. She wished she could hide behind the small pup and cover her embarrassment. "Lost track of time. I'm sorry."

"Think nothing of it. I only want you safe." Thalmus took a step back, and Flowridia let him escort her down the hallway. "The ceremony will have already begun. Apparently Etolié worried about the repercussions of you being hidden away."

"I'm hardly of note."

Thalmus' hand nearly covered her entire back. "People would notice if you disappeared."

His statement gave her pause. They descended the stairs, and Flowridia dared to ask, "Did anyone ask for me?"

"Etolié did, to question you about your meeting."

Disappointment brewed inside her. Flowridia said nothing further and allowed Thalmus to lead her outside in silence.

Beyond the grounds of the manor, the city flourished, and even far away she could hear a faint, yet booming voice, one magically enhanced for volume.

A crowd met them, but Thalmus escorted her behind the makeshift stage, where Zorlaeus spoke to the enormous assembly of citizens from Staelash. Behind him, a series of seats had been set up. Marielle sat directly to his right, only a few steps behind, with Etolié sitting in a chair by her side. Khastra, armor glittering in the fading sunlight, sat in a large throne beside her, along with an empty seat.

On Zorlaeus' opposite side, a decorated chair sat empty.

Behind the platform, Thalmus whispered, "I'm to help keep peace among the crowd." He motioned toward the steps leading up to the platform. "Will you be fine if I leave?"

"Of course. Thank you for the escort."

"Stay safe, Flowra." Thalmus disappeared around the platform.

She took one step towards the stairs, when a whisper nearly stopped her heart. "'Flowra?' That's adorable."

Flowridia whirled around. Ayla stood directly behind her, smiling from Flowridia's shadow. "I-It's my nickname," she managed to say.

Ayla's eyes were ice, despite her smile. "Flowra," she cooed softly, and Flowridia felt heat blossom across her cheeks. Ayla chuckled. "Sweet Flowra, may I ask your plans following the ceremony?"

That's when Flowridia's heart stopped all at once. "You may ask."

Laughter added charm to Ayla's words. "Oh, clever, aren't you? Allow me to state my intentions more plainly." Ayla stepped forward, and despite being several inches shorter, Flowridia felt she were being stared down. "I find you devastatingly beautiful. I'll meet you in your bedroom. We'll . . . have a bite?" Ayla lifted a single eyebrow.

Flowridia managed a nod, something inside of her melting.

Ayla's grin grew wide, predatory. "I'll see you after the ceremony," she whispered. She brushed past Flowridia, stepping silently up the steps to the platform.

Flowridia stood a full five seconds in pure shock before a child's voice broke through her clouded thoughts. *She smells awfully nice.*

"Does she?" Flowridia released a breath, the first one in minutes. "I hadn't noticed."

Better than you do. The small wolf stood on his back legs and stared up at her. *It's eerie, to be honest. I feel like I'm supposed to like her.*

"Oh, she's quite likable," she said, swaying slightly. A smile spread across her face, and she heard herself giggle. "And I think she might like me too."

She said you were beautiful.

Blushing fiercely, Flowridia brought her hands up to her cheeks. "We, uh, we need to go to the ceremony." She paused, looking at Demitri, and giggled some more as she climbed up the steps onto the platform.

A crowd of people met her view, and Flowridia quickly shuffled to the empty seat beside General Khastra. The enormous woman stared down at her oddly, perhaps noticing her blush and smile, but said nothing, and instead looked back at Zorlaeus, who continued his speech. Something about trade and trust, but Flowridia beamed, her mind singing.

Sitting opposite of Khastra, Etolié peered around the glittering, armored woman. "Flowers," she whispered irreverently, "you're shining brighter than my favorite tattooed beefcake."

Flowridia composed herself, biting her lip as she glanced at Etolié. "I have a date tonight."

Were there not thousands of people staring up at them, Etolié's hand looked like it might fly to her face. Instead, she simply leaned slightly to the side. "Oh, do you?"

Flowridia nodded, acutely aware that Khastra could hear every word whispered between them.

But Etolié pushed. "Is that why Ayla was late too?"

"She waited for me?" Flowridia's heart soared at the thought.

"Apparently."

Flowridia's cheeks grew sore from smiling. "We'll be having dinner."

This time, Etolié glanced over to Ayla, who occupied the once empty seat. The woman looked back at her, a knowing smirk crossing her face as she glanced from Etolié to Flowridia and then back to the crowd.

"Dinner doesn't seem like her style."

"Well, it's what we're doing," Flowridia shot back, defensive at Etolié's tone.

Etolié pulled a flask from the air. After a long sip, she said, "And then chess, right?"

"Sure, Etolié."

She heard Etolié chuckle.

The crowd applauded. Flowridia looked over and realized Ayla had disappeared.

She stood, but before she could move, Khastra blocked her path. With her glowing, pupil-less eyes, Flowridia always struggled to decipher the tattooed woman's expression. Even with the faint smile on her lips, when she stood nearly three feet above Flowridia's head, it painted her aura with menace, deserved or not. "You are meeting with Lady Ayla tonight?"

Flowridia nodded, a blush blooming onto her cheeks.

"Tiny one, I have some suspicions to her character you should know first–"

Etolié's hand appeared, and by some miracle it managed to land directly over Khastra's mouth when she reached up. Not that something so trivial would stop a force of nature from speaking, but Khastra did stop, perhaps from surprise. "And who are we to stop our sweet tiny one from meeting with the Nox'Karthan diplomat for a diplomatic engagement?"

"Etolié–"

"Flowers is a fully blossomed adult. We shouldn't stand in her way."

Flowridia couldn't decide how she felt about this particular use of the word 'blossomed' and wished to melt into the floorboards and vanish.

The blue woman's stark confusion diminished her intimidating aura. "Then, may I discuss it with you, instead?"

"Yes, yes," Etolié said. "But first, I'd like to walk Flowers home." Etolié placed a hand on Flowridia's waist and began leading her away.

"I think I want to know Khastra's suspicions–"

Etolié patted Flowridia's back, then swiftly escorted her down the steps of the platform. "I'll take care of it. Khastra is many things—highly intelligent is one of them.

Tactless is often another. I'll let you know if it's anything important. May I escort you?"

Flowridia glanced out toward the crowd. She spotted Sora surveying the mass of people, but the half-elf didn't feel her gaze, and to the far end was Thalmus.

Telling Thalmus about her plans with Ayla seemed a daunting task. She returned her attention to Etolié. "Yes, please."

They stepped away from the ground and toward the road. At the front of the stage, Marielle stood with her hands on her knees, chattering excitedly with a group of children who giggled at every other word.

"Whatever Marielle's setbacks as a monarch," Etolié said softly, watching Flowridia's gaze, "the people adore her. There's something to be said for that."

Zorlaeus stood behind Marielle, his shy countenance perfectly juxtaposed with the vibrant queen.

Ayla was nowhere to be seen.

They proceeded down the road in silence, haste in Etolié's footsteps. Past the gates of the manor, Etolié finally spoke Flowridia's own quiet fears. "She's using you."

Flowridia's pride reeled at the thought, her desperation to latch onto Ayla's pretty words as truth causing her jaw to stiffly set.

"Everything is a game, Flowers—politics, sex, and convenient dinner invitations. Small, dark, and sneaky looks like the type to do whatever it takes for political gain," Etolié continued, but her face conveyed no judgement; merely rumination, "including buttering-up tiny, flower-laden diplomats. My question is whether or not you're ready to play this game."

Flowridia's feet ceased their scuffling across the dirt path, the implications of Etolié's words wounding her palpitating heart. "Etolié–"

"Don't 'Etolié' me. This is a precarious political situation. Secrets might be the only thing you keep from Lady Ayla tonight."

"That's not the plan."

"Isn't it, though?" Etolié withdrew her flask and maintained perfect eye contact as she took a long sip. When she offered it forward, Flowridia shook her head. "If Lady Darkleaf is soft on you, Staelash might finally have a fighting chance when negotiating with Nox'Kartha."

Instead of replying, Flowridia stooped down to lift Demitri into her arms. They stepped within the gates of the manor and finally went inside. Etolié's words—a warning, really—refused to settle in her mind, instead churning over and over as she contemplated every individual facet.

It was foolish, she knew, but Etolié had implied that Ayla might be soft on her, and it was that notion only that spurned her feet to keep moving forward.

Can I come to dinner too?

Demitri's words jarred Flowridia from her swirling thoughts. As they climbed the staircase, she said, "Of course, Demitri."

Etolié grinned at the wolf pup. "What's Demitri saying?"

"He wants to come to dinner."

Nodding, Etolié's smile grew wide and wicked. "Don't be shy if you need me to watch him."

They reached Flowridia's door. "I don't think that will be necessary–"

When the door swung open, a thousand candles met her view. On every surface they shone, on her windowsill, her vanity, the table to the side of her bed, and on her desk where a basket of fruit waited. Only the bed remained untouched by flame.

Instead, Ayla lounged on her sheets, coy and grinning like a snake.

Mesmerized by Ayla's stare, Flowridia handed Demitri to Etolié. Etolié, in an uncharacteristic display of tact, said absolutely nothing and simply carried Demitri away.

The door clicked shut. The gown draped across Ayla's sensual form at first appeared to be a dark grey, but Flowridia realized it was black, albeit entirely sheer. Ayla's skin, nearly white, created a vision of slight curves and tempting shadows. "Is the fruit acceptable?" Ayla tilted her head, the flickering light casting deep lines upon her face. "I overheard a little bird say you had an odd diet."

Flowridia, struck by the ambience, the unquestionable sensuality of Ayla lying serene in her bed, managed a brief nod. "I only eat what I can grow."

Ayla cracked a predatory grin. "I hope I don't offend you, then." Her eyes managed to sharpen. "I'm a meat-eater."

Flowridia's breath hitched, heat filling her abdomen. "I've been known to make a few exceptions."

Ayla chuckled as she beckoned with a lithe finger.

Drawn by her magnetism, Flowridia obeyed, her entranced steps silent on the rug beneath her. She accepted Ayla's hand when offered and allowed the pale, elven woman to pull her in for a deep, slow kiss. Curiosity and desire overshadowed her inexperience, and Flowridia simply let her lips respond in turn, allowing Ayla's tongue to slip into her mouth. She fell gently into bed beside her. Bony hands, cold even through the fabric of her gown, traced across Flowridia's form. She savored every flush motion of those thin, perfect lips, the innocence of it something to cherish.

It wasn't until one hand reached to cup the gentle contour of Flowridia's jaw that Ayla pulled away. Her fierce gaze kept close contact as she slowly, deliberately, stroked at Flowridia's long hair and removed one of the many tiny flowers she kept braided within. Ayla placed it carefully on the nightstand before repeating the motion. Again and again, so simple a gesture, yet with each movement, anticipation grew. Each touch, so slight, seemed perfectly placed to tease.

Flowridia lacked the words to express what she desired, but whatever storm Ayla brewed, she longed to dance in the eye of it.

Perhaps Flowridia showed her impatience. Ayla's coy laughter filled the room. "I have a weakness for simple, pretty things."

Entranced, Flowridia could only nod in response, and Ayla continued her task, the pile of dainty, colorful buds steadily growing. Flowridia's mind began to wander as her eyes took in the rare, detailed view of the alluring woman—the way her cascading hair, curled and styled to perfection, managed to hide her ear, how the rich shades of black stood in stark contrast to her pallid skin; the candlelight as it highlighted the shadows of her ribs faintly visible above her collar, how the deep, plunging collar of her gown drew Flowridia's eyes. Sudden heat colored her cheeks at the sight of Ayla's breasts, barely covered by the sheer fabric. She looked away, up to Ayla's face, only to be caught staring.

Was that amusement pulling at Ayla's smile? "Sweet Flowra, don't be so demure," she teased. Ayla drew her hands back. She pushed aside one sleeve and then the other, letting the top of her dress fall away, revealing her bare, beautiful chest. Ayla's small breasts bounced when she chuckled, and Flowridia couldn't help but stare at both her slight curves and at the taut muscles visible through the thin skin of her abdomen. Pained heat brewed between her legs as Ayla leaned forward, the magnetic pull between them unlike anything Flowridia had ever felt.

A soft line drew along her jaw as Ayla leaned forward, her fingernail lightly touching Flowridia's skin. Their gaze met again. "I'm yours to admire." Hunger bled into her wicked grin. "And you're mine to claim."

A cold hand pushed against Flowridia's sternum. Plush blankets met her back. Ayla straddled her, and in an instant their lips smashed together. Pure lust radiated from the elven woman, and Flowridia gasped when a bite stung her bottom lip.

When Ayla pulled away, her stare reminded Flowridia eerily of her own wolf before he devoured his meal, but the thought only caused further heat to rise within her. She surged up to meet Ayla's lips but was met with a vicious touch forcing her back down. Ayla shook her head, pupils engulfing the ice in her eyes. With skilled fingers, she traced the collar of Flowridia's gown and began to undo each button down the line.

Before she could finish, her eyes narrowed in amusement as she removed the uncanny trinket—her own ear—from the bodice. She chuckled, and with a wink said, "Perhaps I should have given you an eye as well, if I'd known where you'd keep it."

Flowridia's face grew flush. "Please, don't."

A genuine laugh escaped Ayla's lips as she set the necklace aside. "You are a delight. No, no, Flowra, I plan on making good use of my eyes tonight." With a dramatic flair, she ripped open the fabric covering Flowridia's chest, the chill causing bumps to rise along her sensitive skin. Flowridia instinctively shied, her hands coming to cover her exposed breasts and body, but Ayla's wicked chuckle came with a light grasp on her wrists. "Let me see you," she cooed, more a command than a request, and when Ayla pulled Flowridia's arms away, she didn't fight the touch.

Instead, she released a breath and basked in Ayla's gaze, enamored as she watched that striking blue become a ring around a void of black. The grip on her wrists grew loose, then fell away.

Flowridia felt, for the first time in her life, *devastatingly beautiful.*

And, oh, suddenly Ayla's mouth was on her breast, and Flowridia released a moan as the woman's tongue pleasured her sensitive form. She tried to rise, to arch herself instinctively, but Ayla pushed her down, and Flowridia gasped as she felt another bite on her lip. Ayla's eyes met hers, dangerous yet pleased, and Flowridia smiled, sighing as fingernails traced down her chest.

Ayla squeezed her roughly, something erotic in the sight of her own breasts spilling from Ayla's hands. Flowridia's sigh became a whine when Ayla's fingers took over the work of her tongue and twisted the sensitive buds. Teeth scrapped against Flowridia's collarbone before a sting along the curve of her neck betrayed Ayla's newest act.

Flowridia knew something of foreplay, had read of it in the books kept in Mother's home. She knew of biting, of touching and teasing, of kissing lips and intimate parts, but nothing could have prepared her body for the storm brewing within her.

She reached up, stroking past Ayla's pointed ear, and cupped her head as she pushed the elf against her, the thought of being claimed so visibly causing her breath to grow heavy. She felt Ayla grin.

A hand tangled in Flowridia's hair, pulling tight, forcing her to reveal more of her neck. Compelled to stare at the ceiling, Flowridia realized she had nearly lost feeling in her limbs. Her hands traced Ayla's back, memorizing the lithe musculature, and she dared to skim the barest outline of Ayla's breasts. Despite the growing heat between her legs, her demure heart dared not go further, not until Ayla released her, grabbed her hand—

Ayla pressed Flowridia's hand against her own breast, and Flowridia swore the soft weight—the only bit of softness on Ayla's taut body—was a miracle.

She hardly noticed when Ayla released her hair and traced down across her stomach, until the length of her arm forced her to pull her face away from ravaging Flowridia's neck. Ayla sat up, hunger in her relentless gaze. Still caught in her grasp, she squeezed both of Ayla's breasts in tandem, the tight muscles of her stomach reflecting the flickering candle light. To watch Ayla so visibly revel in her attention stole Flowridia's breath.

Then, Ayla released her hands. Flowridia let hers fall away, no time to be disappointed before Ayla pushed the rest of the dress away. Ayla planted herself between Flowridia's legs, spreading them apart as her fingers traced unknown words across the sensitive skin of her thighs. Flowridia sighed, not expecting such a tender, teasing gesture from her companion, and instinctively thrust against the air. Her body screamed for something her vestal form couldn't name, but it seemed Ayla would force her to, all the same.

"Beg," Ayla said, all pretense of rectitude gone in that simple, boorish command. When Flowridia didn't immediately respond, Ayla took both of her breasts into an iron grip. Ayla's nails dug into the tender skin. "You do want me, right?"

Flowridia managed to nod, her mind hazy from desire.

Ayla squeezed painfully. "Say it."

"I want you." Flowridia's voice was little more than a squeak, but how else was one meant to sound when cornered by a lion?

Pacified for the moment, Ayla's expression grew less severe as she released Flowridia's marked breasts. "You want me to fuck you. Now, say it."

Flowridia tensed in anticipation when she felt a cold finger trace against her wet folds. There was no true choice; Ayla knew what she wanted, and she would take it. Ayla had marked her uncharted body. Now, she would claim it for herself.

Flowridia's body burned for friction, for Ayla to reach inside and quench the very flame she'd kindled. "Fuck me," she said, staring into the icy ring surrounding Ayla's consuming pupils. Desperation bled into her tone. "Fuck me, Ayla, please—"

Ayla's fingers slipped inside her, and Flowridia swore the touch imprinted new writing onto her soul. Gasping, Flowridia's hands dug into the sheet, searching for stability amidst the indomitable storm that was her lover, lest she be swept away. Ayla's thrusts became bliss, each precise motion pulling inarticulate cries from her throat. Relentless, each stroke of Ayla's fingers, and any semblance of control Flowridia may have imagined filtered away.

Ayla's thrusts became deeper, harder. Flowridia felt her body tense unbidden, and she reveled in the fullness inside her, her pleasure surmounting to some grandiose height. When she thought she might burst and scream, Ayla bared her teeth and smiled.

Flowridia came undone at that wicked grin. With Ayla's name on her tongue, her body arched in ecstasy, stars passing through her gaze as pleasure radiated through every inch of her body.

Then, an absence as Ayla pulled out, and a teasing touch on her aching bud.

A weight settled beside Flowridia. Ayla lounged with her head propped up by her fist as she lazily sucked on her fingers. Flowridia felt the beginnings of fresh arousal begin to simmer.

Ayla leaned over and planted a kiss on her mouth, a bitter taste staining Flowridia's lips. "My name on your tongue is such a joy," Ayla said. "Perhaps I'll make you scream it again before the night is through."

A breathless smile crossed Flowridia's face. "I think I'd like that," she said, blushing fiercely. Uneasiness seeped into her tone. "But is there anything I can do for you?"

Intrigue crossed Ayla's features, and she cracked an amused grin. "Convince me."

Fear rose like a tidal wave and slammed against her chest. Flowridia's voice shrank. "I-I did say I—" She stopped herself, allowing the shaking in her voice, along with her breathing, to mellow. "I said I could be meat-eater. I'm dying to know what you taste like."

Flowridia kept her hands clenched together at her chest, but desire flooded Ayla's eyes like a blackhole. "Do go on."

Though she trembled, Flowridia's hands swept aside what hair had fallen into Ayla's face, as tender a gesture as she could summon the courage for, nervous to accidentally brush against where the severed ear had been sliced. Instead, one hand moved to cup Ayla's jaw, her thumb stroking the jagged lines of her cheekbones, and the pale woman turned her head to kiss her palm.

Something electric coursed through Flowridia's blood. Wide-eyed, she stared at Ayla's lips as they brushed past her hand. Flowridia leaned in, both sides of Ayla's face held between her palms, and placed a kiss on her thin lips. Slow, tender, but full of curiosity, Flowridia reveled in the contact, memorizing each movement. Her tongue slipped into Ayla's mouth, and she moaned at the sensation, realizing she could contentedly kiss those thin lips for hours and never bore. Humming, her hand slid back to cradle Ayla's head, bringing their faces closer.

She resisted when she felt Ayla pull away. Instead, she planted kisses on the sides of Ayla's mouth, her cheeks, her jaw, peppering sweet affection along that pale skin. "Flowra," she heard Ayla chide, "are you stalling?"

Flowridia's false confidence withered. She tried to hide her face, but Ayla grabbed her jaw, forcing eye contact.

"Oh, my Sweet Summer Blossom . . ." Ayla fluttered her lashes as she pouted her doll lips. "Is this your first time?" Perhaps she was not purposefully patronizing, but Flowridia felt shame begin to rise inside her.

She chose not to speak, embarrassed to admit her inexperience. When her face fell, eyes to the bed, Ayla moved her hand from Flowridia's jaw to her hair, gripping with menace. Immediately, Flowridia stared forward, locked into Ayla's stare.

Ayla leaned forward, grinning like a starved predator presented with raw meat. "Sweet, innocent Flowra . . ." A dark chuckle met Flowridia's ears. "Not so innocent anymore," she said, and her pupils widened, a black hole ringed with pale blue. "I'll give you a demonstration."

And she did. Over and over . . .

Flowridia didn't taste Ayla that night, but it seemed by the woman's own design; Ayla's true pleasure came from Flowridia's domination, her capacity to own her completely. Names had power, and with each breathless cry of, "Oh, Ayla . . ." she grew both fiercer and more pacified.

Finally, when the burning between Flowridia's legs did not subside, she managed to voice her thoughts. "Ayla . . ." Her words shook from fatigue and light-headed pleasure. Pulled by the change of tone, Ayla looked up from between her thighs. "I might break if we try for one more," Flowridia said, letting a smile settle on her lips.

Ayla wiped her mouth on her wrist, an obscene glint in her gaze. On hands and knees, Ayla crawled up beside her and wrapped her thinly muscled arms around Flowridia's exhausted body. Tenderness filled her, Ayla's naked, bony form providing a strange sort of comfort as she pulled Flowridia close and caressed her hair. A blush bloomed across Flowridia's cheeks when she felt lips lightly trace the side of her head. The predator was still here, but Flowridia felt no more danger in the lion's den—only peace.

"Forgive me for asking," Flowridia said, each breath more serene than the last, "but why all of this?"

Amusement tugged at Ayla's lips. "Flowra, I have lusted after you from the moment I first saw you," she said, a dangerous hunger bleeding into her words. "Captivatingly beautiful, dressed up for Marielle's ball, and with those precious flowers woven into your hair . . ." Ayla leaned close and sniffed her hair, an erotic moan escaping as she released the air. Even in Flowridia's exhausted state, a shot of pleasure coursed through her blood. "I have a habit of taking things I want."

Somehow, the implied threat only caused her cheeks to flush. "If you wanted," Flowridia said, unable to quite meet Ayla's eye, "I'm sure they wouldn't miss me too much."

"Steal Staelash's Grand Diplomat? Oh, Casvir would have my head. And losing a head seems far less pleasant than losing an ear." Teeth scraped against Flowridia's ear, evoking a gasp. Ayla laughed, yet a threat still tugged at her smile. "I do hope you'll care for my ear, for me."

Flowridia nodded, enthralled by her gaze.

The clouds shifted outside the window, letting the full moon shine into the candle-lit room. Ayla began to pull away.

Despite the clenching in her chest, Flowridia said, "Will I see you again?"

Ayla's grin had never left. "You will." She planted a quick peck on Flowridia's mouth, but before she could remove her touch, Flowridia cupped Ayla's cheek, praying her lips would stay. Those small lips parted to return the tender gesture. Slow, passionate, Flowridia hoped the memory would linger and serve as a parting gift.

Ayla stayed at her lips until Flowridia pulled away. "You do have a bed to sleep in, right?"

"Oh, you adorable thing." Amusement flickered across Ayla's face as she stood and stole a single white flower from the pile on her nightstand. "Tomorrow night, Zorlaeus and I will be meeting with Marielle for dinner. I hope you'll be there. Perhaps afterward, you and I can grab another bite." She grabbed the bundle of her dress.

Ayla seemed to vanish, then appeared at the windowsill. Flowridia swore she could feel the kiss blown from Ayla's lips.

THE STING OF VICTORY

With a wave, Ayla fell backwards from the window and into the dark night.

Chapter 6

Flowridia was one to rise with the sun. To awaken still exhausted, with daylight already shining bright through her window, caused her to bolt into sitting.

Sharp knocking at the door had awoken her, she realized. Lightheaded, she let her face fall into her hands.

She was naked. Why was she—?

Flowridia gazed across her nude form and saw a bite-shaped bruise turning purple on her inner thigh. Amorous memories replayed in her head, spreading a smile across her face.

Again, came the knock. "Flowers, I swear on Alystra's Supple Ass, I will blow down this door if you don't answer."

"Give me a moment," Flowridia said, and she stood, careful to avoid stepping on any extinguished candles.

In the mirror, she saw a mess of bruises dotting her neck, forming a necklace along the sensitive skin. Red and blue marked her torso, her breasts, where Ayla's nails had threatened to pierce the soft skin. Littered all over her body, just like her thigh, were bite marks. None drew blood, but Flowridia felt thoroughly ravaged and claimed by Ayla's lovemaking. The thought brought heat to her abdomen.

Flowridia slipped into a long-sleeved night gown, realizing the fruit on the desk remained untouched.

She positioned herself carefully behind the door, letting only her head peek out as she gently turned the knob. Demitri immediately ran inside and began to sniff at her long gown, but Etolié smiled pleasantly, expectantly, as she raised an eyebrow at the obvious bruising on Flowridia's neck.

"I'm sorry I slept so late," Flowridia said, stepping aside so the Celestial could enter.

THE STING OF VICTORY

Flowridia blushed when Etolié began inspecting the aftermath of the night's activities. "So, Flowers . . ." The door shut, and Etolié quirked an eyebrow when she noticed the pile of dried blossoms on the nightstand. "It seems you've been deflowered."

Grimacing, Flowridia asked, "Can I borrow a scarf?"

From the air itself, Etolié pulled a glittering scarf. "Well, Demitri and I had a lovely night. I told him mother needed, uh, alone time."

Having adjusted the cloth to cover her bruises, Flowridia knelt beside Demitri. "I'm sorry about dinner. I know I promised."

Etolié says you decided to eat out instead.

She clenched her teeth and glared at Etolié, horrified at the remark. Etolié laughed.

"I didn't eat a single thing last night," Flowridia said, approaching the tray of fruit.

"Judging by the state of your neck, I'd say Ayla was the one taking a few bites."

Glaring, Flowridia gave Etolié a curt sigh. She stepped into the hallway, petulant at hearing Etolié chuckle.

"Bring your food to the library," Etolié said, coming up beside her. "We'll have a post-mortem."

Flowridia stopped, cringing at the choice in words. "A 'post-mortem?'"

Etolié nodded vigorously, stealing the tray and continuing ahead. "For your childhood."

An odd sentiment, and Flowridia frowned before hurrying to catch up to the Celestial. Of all the stepping stones into adulthood, Flowridia felt losing one's virginity and losing one's innocence were hardly the same.

Certainly an exercise in trust, but Flowridia had felt nothing taken; only given. Her body ached, but the memory of Ayla's smile rising from between her legs would be one to warm her for many nights to come.

Innocence could only be stolen, and nothing could quite patch the wounds those experiences left.

"Slit his throat, Flower Child. He'll patrol the swamp, and once he's collapsed the garden will appreciate the sustenance."

"But, really, did you have a pleasant night?"

Flowridia's expression softened at the thought, pulled from her spiraling memories. "Yes," she whispered, and a fluttering sensation filled her stomach as she smiled.

"Do you think she'll be back?" Interest laced Etolié's words, and when Flowridia turned to face her, she saw cold calculation.

"She'll be at dinner tonight with Marielle and Zorlaeus. She suggested that afterward . . ." Flowridia blushed at the thought. "Well, we'll see."

Etolié raised an eyebrow at her gentle smile, but Flowridia realized she couldn't be embarrassed, not when the memory had yet to cool. She followed the Celestial to the library in silence.

"She disappeared out the window?"

Flowridia, wrapped in Etolié's scarves in the center of the library, held a teacup and saucer in her hands. Demitri paced behind Etolié as the three-quarters angel stood beside one of the many shelves circling the room.

A plate of stale cookies sat on the ground beyond her reach, delivered a day or two ago—Etolié claimed to not remember—by Khastra, who chronically disparaged Etolié's eating habits. They were palatable when dipped in the tea, but otherwise too old to be appetizing.

"She vanished," Flowridia said with an offered nod. The tea had gone cold, but she had nowhere to place it. Etolié had insisted on bundling her up for her 'post mortem.'

To Flowridia's relief, Etolié hadn't pushed for details regarding the sex itself. She seemed much more annoyed at the apparent mistreatment. "Un-classy," Etolié spat. "She should have at least waited until you'd fallen asleep."

"I'm not bothered."

Etolié scoffed dramatically. "That's because you're young. First lust."

A shy smile spread across Flowridia's face. "I wouldn't say I'm in love–"

"Did I say love? Look at you, blushing warmer than the Sun Goddess. You wanted her the moment she danced at Marielle's party."

Flowridia brought the cold tea to her lips and feigned a sip. "Maybe not consciously, but–"

"Well, you have her," Etolié finished, and she stooped down to pick Demitri up and cradle him in her thin arms. "Now what?"

That, Flowridia hadn't considered.

"Are you a single notch on her coffin, or are you planning to see her again?"

Flowridia frowned as Etolié placed successive kisses on Demitri's face. "What are you implying?"

"Do you want to keep her?"

With care to balance the liquid, Flowridia moved to untangle herself from the engulfing pile of scarves and blankets. "Of course I want to keep her. I'm seeing her tonight." Etolié, seeing her struggle, stole the saucer and cup, keeping Demitri secure in one arm. Flowridia managed to free herself. "What do you mean by 'coffin?'"

She set the teacup on a bookshelf. Flowridia stopped in front of the flighty Celestial, forcing her to stop pacing. "Imperator Casvir is known for employing the undead," Etolié finally said.

Flowridia crossed her arms, prepared to offer an objection. An insane idea, to think of Ayla as some sort of ghoul or undead monstrosity. Last night, Ayla had shown such life, such passion, with her cold touch and eerie smile, her unnatural strength . . . her tendency to bite . . .

Had she still been holding the teacup, it would have shattered as her arms went slack. "Ayla's a vampire?"

"Khastra certainly thinks so. It's my best guess too."

Flowridia stepped back, using the bookshelf for support, barely cognitive of Etolié's words. "What do you think, Demitri?" the Celestial. "Wolves love vampires."

The back of Flowridia's nightgown snagged against the bookshelf as she slid down. Ignoring it, Flowridia turned a pointed stare toward the small pup as her bottom touched the floor. "Demitri did say she smelled good." She held her arms out, and Etolié carefully placed the wolf into her embrace. "Does Ayla smell like a vampire?"

The wolf met her stare, intelligent eyes blinking innocently. *How am I supposed to know what a vampire smells like?*

Etolié continued her pacing. "It could be some sort of innate compulsion magic," she said, and suddenly she paused before darting around the corner of a bookshelf and disappearing.

Flowridia placed Demitri on the floor. "What does she smell like, exactly?"

Thoughtful, Demitri's tail began to thump on the floor. *Warm and soothing, like blood.*

"I don't know if blood is soothing, dearest Demitri."

That's because you don't eat meat.

Etolié reappeared, a small stack of books in her hands, and plopped down beside her. The book she shoved into Flowridia's arms gave her pause—*The (Nec)Romance of Undeath.* "Etolié, what is this?"

"There are countless books on undead leeches, Flowers." In her own hands, *Stakes and Holy Stones: Things to Break a Vampire's Bones* was already being perused. "I only wish I owned more. Lurker Spawn are interesting creatures, and I'd love to study one up close—especially one who's diplomatically inclined to not drain me of life fluids."

Lurker Spawn was a colloquial name—given because it was said that the demon god, Izthuni, the Lurker, was incapable of siring his own children and created vampires to serve as his envoys in the mortal realm. Staring aimlessly at the table of contents, Flowridia frowned, a thought poking at her mind. Izthuni was the God of Shadows, sworn enemy of Sol Kareena, the Sun Goddess. "Sunlight burns vampires. Everyone knows that."

Etolié nodded.

"Ayla was outside during the groundbreaking ceremony. It was sunset, but the light touched her."

"Perhaps she's special."

Thoroughly unconvinced, Flowridia continued reading, letting Demitri settle into her lap. "What are you asking me to do with this knowledge, Etolié? None of it proves anything."

"We play the game, Flowers. If we do this right, we can trick Ayla into revealing that she's an undead leech–"

"Etolié, I–" Flowridia stopped herself, nerves silencing her tongue. She swallowed her words, gripping the book tight in her hands as her insides tied themselves into an endless knot.

But Etolié suddenly knelt in front of her. "Yes?"

The knot settled, threatening to make her ill. "I-If it's important to you, I'll be as helpful as I can," she finally muttered. "I could ask her–"

But Etolié leaned forward, eyes narrow. "What's wrong?"

"Nothing is wrong, Etolié–"

Flowridia stopped when Etolié leaned closer still. She couldn't say if she would ever be used to such blatant violations of her personal space. "You don't want to do this."

"I-I never said–"

"Flowers," Etolié said, finally sliding backwards onto her posterior, "when will you accept that you won't be burned at the stake for having an opinion?"

Etolié watched her expectantly. Flowridia mustered her courage, staring at her lap as she said, "After what happened last night, it feels like a horrible violation of her trust. I know I'm a fool to say it, but what transpired between us was . . ." She struggled to find the word she wanted. Her hands fidgeted, grasping the other to quell her nerves. ". . . special. To me, at least. I'd never felt anything like it; I'd never had anyone look at me the way she did–" She stopped, breath hitching, finally daring to meet Etolié's gaze.

Etolié watched in silence a moment. "You need to be careful," she finally said. "I told you—she's playing with you. Pleasure is one thing, but feelings are dangerous. Politics are–"

"A game, I know," Flowridia said, swallowing the sudden rise of emotion in her throat. "I won't let this cloud my judgement in Nox'Karthan negotiations."

Etolié looked skeptical, with her raised eyebrow. Flowridia couldn't blame her.

Thankfully, Etolié had never been one to push once her prying was done. She stole the book from Flowridia's lap and began prattling on about adding a few new shelves to her library and where on earth they would find the space.

Flowridia listened, even though her heart sank.

Dinner transpired with little excitement, though Ayla's use of innuendo was nothing less than inspiring.

"For a moment, I assumed you were the next course, with how prettily you waited–"

"The appetizer is acceptable, but I can think of something far more delicious–"

"Oh, won't you share a bite with me, Flowra? Perhaps afterward–"

But all throughout, she watched as Ayla ate and laughed, inspected her plate for signs of garlic, realized the utensils were all pure silver, yet still wondered if what Khastra and Etolié speculated was true.

And so, when the offer was extended—*"Won't you join me for dessert, Sweet Flowra?"* –Flowridia accepted with a shy smile and followed Ayla up the stairs, all while summoning the courage to simply, well, *ask.*

Furthermore, as they walked, she suppressed the gnawing bit of anxiety whispering that this was merely a game. Ayla would only be in town for one more night, and so Flowridia longed to hold the illusion for a while longer yet.

Once in her bedroom, Flowridia felt her breath leave her when Ayla began to sensuously strip from her clothing. In languid, teasing motions, she let it fall, and Flowridia hardly spared a thought toward the oddity that apparently was Nox'Karthan fashion—for Ayla wore nothing underneath her dress at all. Instead, she shyly took in the sight of Ayla's slight figure, blushing when Ayla turned around and caught her staring.

Ayla smiled, wide and leering. "Shall we?"

Curiosity sparked Flowridia's dangerous question. "May I ask something?"

Ayla stepped forward lightly, her hands sliding around Flowridia's waist. "Go on," the seductive voice cooed, and suddenly Flowridia felt teeth scrape against her ear.

Flowridia sighed, shivering in anticipation. "Are you–" Her breath caught when Ayla's hand cupped her neck, planting kisses along her jaw. A cool hand travelled smoothly up Flowridia's gown. "Are you a vampire?"

"Oo . . . Not quite." The hand at her neck slid down her collar before stopping at her breast. "Something like it. How did you guess?" Ayla laughed, squeezing roughly at Flowridia's form.

Flowridia sighed at the contact, her body craving more. "Imperator Casvir employs the undead," she echoed.

"Yet, you still came." Ayla returned to kissing Flowridia's neck, teeth scraping ominously against the soft skin. Flowridia heard Ayla breathe in her scent, causing a shiver to travel down her spine. "Foolish of you."

Flowridia's hand came up to stroke Ayla's fine black hair, careful to avoid where her ear would be. Pained arousal only continued to grow, and Flowridia sighed, surprised at the tenderness filling her at feeling Ayla's touch. "I trust you," she whispered, and she whined softly when Ayla pulled away.

The naked woman quirked an eyebrow. "Terribly foolish." A sardonic grin pulled at her lips. Her hands shot back to Flowridia. Nothing sweet in the touch; Ayla pushed her into bed.

Claws ripped at her dress. Flowridia gasped, fear and arousal growing at the animalistic display. Ayla leered over her, staring hungrily down at her slight form, muscles tense as she straddled her. "Now you know," Ayla growled, and her lips engulfed Flowridia's.

Bodies touched and rubbed together. Ayla's cold hands grabbed her, held her enthralled, and Flowridia rejoiced at every sensation.

Teeth scraped against Flowridia's neck, and each time she wondered if it would be her end. Hands gripped her hair, crushing the pretty blossoms woven within. Her body screamed, prey cornered by predator, but her mind and senses craved more. To be eaten alive by this woman would be a perfect end.

When Ayla bit her inner thigh, Flowridia nearly screamed. Her hand flew down to touch Ayla's hair, directing those lips to the wanting wetness between her legs. Oh, those skills in diplomacy and charm; the way Ayla's tongue twisted words were but a candle in the dark compared to what her tongue spoke alone. Whatever words Ayla spelled inside her cast a powerful spell, and Flowridia gasped for breath.

Words held power. "Oh, Ayla . . . Ayla . . ."

Flowridia felt those lips grin.

Her orgasm tore from her body, and she screamed at the pained pleasure. Vision faded; limbs numbed. When Flowridia fell back down to earth, she felt gentle lips against her mouth and a bitter taste at her tongue.

Ayla kissed her, and Flowridia's arms flew to trap her there. "Stay?" she whispered.

"For a little while. I have much to prepare before my departure."

Flowridia sat up as Ayla did, reaching out to touch her face, craving contact. Her hand moved to stroke the meticulously styled hair, marveling at how it had stayed so perfectly in place despite the night's antics. She hesitated, however, realizing from one side poked a pretty, pointed ear, while the other . . . nothing.

Ayla offered a scornful grin. "It's terribly embarrassing. But I won't stop you from looking."

With shaking fingers, Flowridia brushed aside the curled strands of hair. There, meeting Flowridia's view, was the scarred hole of where her ear had once been.

Instead of flinching, Flowridia stared, curious at how clean and yet how open the gash remained. She suspected dark magic kept the layers of flesh fully visible and the severed veins from bleeding.

Did vampires bleed?

Ayla watched, perhaps anticipating a horrified reaction she simply wouldn't get. Flowridia had seen far worse—helped in inflicting far worse—and wondered if it still brought pain.

She asked, "Does it hurt?"

"Only my pride. Ghastly, I know. But penance is penance. Once you've made your wishes, Casvir will restore it." A frown marred Ayla's features, and Flowridia wondered if it were the first genuine expression she had seen from her vampiric companion. "I hope."

A thought, impossible yet intriguing, compelled Flowridia to act. From her bedside table, she grabbed the severed ear, realizing it held a lower temperature than its chilled mistress. With intricate care, she removed the chain, staring at the detached pointed ear and the three earrings that decorated the sides.

She placed it against Ayla's face, matching the ear to the hole. Ayla chuckled darkly. "What is this mischief, Flowra?"

Flowridia let her senses expand. She felt the severed ligaments align in perfect sync, prepared to stitch themselves back together.

She released her spell; a bit of healing magic.

Flesh burned, and Ayla screamed. Where magic glowed, the skin seared away in a blinding flash of light.

A hand grabbed Flowridia and threw her like a ragdoll. She hit the wardrobe with a painful clatter, wood cracking under the force.

Ayla's pained gasp forced Flowridia's eyes to open, despite the shock. From the bed, Ayla clutched the scorched flesh, hand covering the raw burn. Her fangs elongated as she turned to face Flowridia. No mere woman met Flowridia's terrified gaze, but a monstrous visage, black pupils consuming her once vibrant eyes, her fangs much too large for her mouth.

"I thought you were naïve, not *stupid!*" Ayla spat. She leapt from the bed but gripped the bedpost, nearly falling into it as she clutched her ruined face. When she released it, Flowridia saw that nearly half her face was charred, sinew and bone visible by the ear itself. The line of sizzling, dead flesh barely stopped short of her inhuman eye.

Tears fell down Flowridia's cheeks as she hid her face from Ayla's wrath. "I'm sorry! I wanted to help you."

The bedpost cracked as Ayla's fingers dug into the dark wood. Then, Ayla stood tall, her slow release of breath more a growl than air. The color in her eyes slowly reappeared, slim rings of blue around pits of black.

Ayla stepped forward, and Flowridia bit back a scream as she flinched, pain tearing through her spine. "I'm going to need some time," Flowridia heard through her own crying.

Silence. Flowridia stayed in fetal position, shaking, sobbing. Ayla had gone. Still, Flowridia remained, fear and guilt battling for dominance. The image replayed over and over of Ayla's burned flesh and exposed bone.

She clung to her hair, struggling to breathe. Oh, she was stupid. She was so *stupid.*

Scratching at the door evoked a gasp. Flowridia stared, eyes swollen, as a small paw reached under the door.

Demitri could sense her feelings. Of course he knew she was in distress. Sharp pain ripped through her core as she tried to move, a cry escaping unbidden from her lips. Throbbing pain emanated from her arm where Ayla had gripped and thrown her. It hung limp; she feared it had broken.

A frantic knock overshadowed the scratching. "Flowers? What's going on?"

"Etolié–" She kept her breaths shallow.

"Everyone cover up. I'm coming in!"

A locked door would do nothing to detour the Celestial. The knob turned with no resistance, and Etolié peeked inside. Her eyes met Flowridia's, and she gasped. "Demitri, get a healer," she said, rushing toward Flowridia's crumpled, naked form. "Flowers, what happened? Are you hurt?"

Flowridia trembled, from shame as much as pain. "Not as much as Ayla." Holding her head up proved a difficult task, so with a pained wince she rested her forehead on the carpet.

"I'm going to turn on a lamp, all right Flowers? I'm still with you."

Light flickered through the shade of her hair. She felt Etolié kneel beside her. Gentle fingers moved to touch her head, but Flowridia flinched, pained at the contact. Ayla's grip would surely bruise. "Can you tell me what happened?" the Celestial asked frantically.

Demitri ran to her side, his cold nose sniffing her form. *What happened? Why are you scared? You're hurt!*

Flowridia managed to look up, but gasped when she saw who lingered in the doorway. Thalmus surveyed the scene, his eyes wide with anger, with sorrow, with shock— Flowridia couldn't tell. She instinctively curled, ashamed at her nude form, but another sharp pain twisted her back when she tried. A cry tore from her throat.

Etolié broke the tension. "She needs a healer."

"Cover her up," Thalmus said, voice shaking. "I'll set her bones; then, she can heal herself."

A sheet gently caressed her broken body, soft enough to cause no further pain. Then came Thalmus' hand on her back, lighter than a leaf on the water, and the deep rumble of his voice. "Your back isn't broken. But I think your arm may be. Etolié and I are going to turn you over."

Flowridia braced herself, unable to hold back the gasp of pain when she felt herself jostled. She shut her eyes, though they still leaked tears.

A pillow met her head before she could set it down. Flowridia released a pained sigh, trying to relax underneath the light sheet. She noticed, then, how Thalmus trembled as he studied her, how his jaw quivered as his hand delicately touched her shattered upper arm.

Pain spiked. Flowridia screeched at the contact. Thalmus stiffened. "I'll need to set this, Flowra. It will hurt, but only for a moment."

She managed a nod, accepting Etolié's hand when offered.

Pain ripped through her arm, sharper than the injury itself. She cried out, squeezing the Celestial's hand until the pain settled.

"I brought healing salves. It should numb the pain enough for you to focus. Will you be able to heal yourself?"

Flowridia managed a nod, letting Etolié support her as she tentatively moved, willing away the shooting pain in her core.

Cream touched her arm, and with it Thalmus' gentle hands. Like a bandage, where the salve touched it hugged the skin, cooling it, numbing it. Underneath, Flowridia felt the lacerated bone. With a bracing sigh, she let her own tendrils of magic caress the ruined portion, knitting it together and leaving it warm and throbbing.

She should have been as shattered as the wardrobe door, but as Flowridia focused her energy, safe in the company of her friends, she felt the residual protections from the flowers braided into her hair.

The pain in her head quickly subsided. Her core began to numb.

"Who did this?" Thalmus whispered, his eyes wide and watery.

Etolié responded. "Ayla Darkleaf."

"It isn't what it looks like," Flowridia said frantically. She knew what it looked like, with her bruised neck and battered, nude form. "I burned her. I tried to heal her."

Through her blurred, tear-stained vision, Flowridia watched Thalmus' eyes roam her form. "Before or after she had her way with you?"

"After. Thalmus–"

"This confirms my suspicions," Thalmus interrupted, his enormous form blocking the light. "Did you know Ayla was undead?"

Flowridia nodded.

"Ayla Darkleaf is held together by necromancy. What heals the living will wound the dead."

Flowridia shut her eyes, releasing a relaxed sigh. Her core had numbed, and she felt the bruising begin to wane. Her arm had become a muted throbbing. "But something must heal her."

"Ayla is a monster spawned from necromancy—one of the great evils of the world," Thalmus replied, his dark eyes narrowing. "When all is right in the natural world, the dead remain dead."

A warm tongue licked her hand. Flowridia opened her eyes, weakened and sore, and caressed Demitri's fur with her fingers.

"Whatever lies she's told you," Thalmus continued, "you didn't deserve this. Stay away from her."

With a wince, Flowridia slowly sat up, clutching the sheet to preserve her modesty. "I really hurt her."

"And from the looks of it, she threw you across the room."

Flowridia shut her eyes, unsure of what she could say. "I'll beg for her forgiveness–"

"You will not!"

Flowridia shrunk at the rage in Thalmus' voice.

"She's a monster. You're a child. She shouldn't be toying with you, much less having her way with you. And not this; definitely not this–" Thalmus quickly shut his mouth, visibly combating his emotions. "My little flower girl," he said, subdued. "I love you. Please, be careful."

What could she say or do, other than simply nod and try to not shed her own tears?

He stood, too quickly, and said, "If you need anything more from me, I'll be in my room." Thalmus stepped out, a tumultuous storm threatening to break.

The door shut. In the corner, barely visible in the shadow, stood Ayla. She watched, hair styled to cover what Flowridia knew was a gruesome sight.

Etolié, oblivious to the ominous presence in the corner, whispered, "He isn't wrong–"

"I need sleep," Flowridia said, staring directly at the shadowed figure. "We can talk tomorrow."

"Are you sure? You don't have to be alone. I can set up some pillows in the library." Concern bled into every word, but the threat of exacerbating Ayla's wrath caused Flowridia to shake her head. "Flowers, please–"

"I'll send Demitri if I need you."

Etolié helped her to stand. No pain in the movements—her body had healed anew; not even bruises lined her wrists. "I'll be awake," the Celestial said.

Once Etolié had disappeared behind the shut door, Ayla stepped out from her dark corner. She glared viciously, expectantly, eyebrow raised as she watched Flowridia sink slowly to her knees before her.

Flowridia let the sheet drop, her form naked and pitiful as she clutched her hands together against her chest, keeping her stare to the floor. "I'm sorry," she mouthed. "I didn't know–"

"Look at me!"

Flowridia's gaze shot up, breath hitching at the enmity etched into Ayla's features, the ice in her blue eyes. She flinched when Ayla brushed aside her hair, revealing charred, ruined skin. "I didn't know," Flowridia said, this time managing to vocalize her words. "I'm sorry."

Ayla's pointed glare sliced through her already shattered resolve. Flowridia withered, crumbling to the ground and clinging to Ayla's skirt. Fresh sobs shook her form.

"I think, in time, I will be able to forgive you," Ayla said, her voice as smooth and cutting as a knife. "All things heal, Flowra. Wounds. Grudges. Trust." When Flowridia dared to look up, she swore she saw fangs behind that cruel and much-too-wide grin. "But you'll have to prove your sincerity."

Flowridia gave a tentative nod. "What can I do?"

Ayla opened her mouth to speak, but stopped, lips pursing. Coyly, she said, "You're the one bargaining. Once you've thought of an offer, do let me know."

She extended a hand, and Flowridia accepted, allowing Ayla to help her to stand. Flowridia stepped forward to offer an embrace, but were Ayla a cat capable of hissing, Flowridia had no doubt she would have—with how she flinched, how she bared her fangs.

Flowridia stumbled back, shaking as she clung to the frame of her four-poster bed.

But Ayla's countenance softened, a forced smile spreading across her face. "Flowra, I don't often give second chances," she cooed, sanguine sweetness chilling Flowridia's blood. "Take this gift, that of your continued life, and know it means I care."

Flowridia flinched when Ayla's face suddenly appeared only inches from her own.

"You are grateful, right?"

Flowridia didn't presume to imagine the threat behind the innocuous question. "Yes."

"Say it."

Flowridia recalled a lesson taught from Aura long ago—that when faced with a predator to show no fear, to poise your body tall and broad, to match their stare and bare your teeth and scream . . . and pray they walked away.

But Ayla was no hungry lion, satiated by flesh. Flowridia cowered, finding neither woman nor beast in those vibrant blue eyes, but something far more sinister. "I'm grateful you've given me this second chance," she said softly, bracing herself for Ayla to strike.

Ayla did attack, but in slow and gentle blows. A hand caressed Flowridia's face, cold and soothing, and Ayla planted a tender kiss on her cheek. Her whisper was soft, a breeze through a shadowed night: *"Good girl."*

The touch vanished. When Flowridia opened her eyes again, she realized she was alone, save for Demitri watching from the corner.

The little wolf ran to her side, standing on his hind legs as he pawed at her thigh. She lifted him into her arms and hid her face, thick droplets of tears soaking his soft fur.

Are you still hurt?

Truly, she was not. Healing magic had purged her body of even the most superficial of wounds. There were no marks on her neck, nor her thighs or her breasts.

Her hair snagged the bedpost. From the thick, dark locks, she withdrew a shriveled flower, the magic once within expended in protecting her.

Flowridia shook her head. "No, dearest Demitri. But I'm afraid."

He curled into her side as she tried to sleep, soothed at the contact of his fur.

She bore no wounds, but, oh, she ached. Ayla had consumed something far more vulnerable than her body, leaving a gaping, bleeding hole in her chest.

"Salvage what you can, Flower Child."

Flowridia peeked around the doorframe, maintaining careful eye contact with the nude woman straddling the dead man beside a pool of blood and entrails.

Mother stood, a bit of dizziness in her step, but Flowridia clung to the damp wood, careful to avoid brushing against splatters of fungal life.

"I need to clean up."

Worry filled Flowridia as she watched her mother's stumbling steps, but the woman disappeared behind the bedroom door. Flowridia held her breath as she knelt before the dead figure on the floor. The knife in her hand reflected the phosphorescent light, glinting in shades of blue and green as it split a thin line at the victim's torso. The half-nude man—they were always men, or young girls; ones Mother deemed unfit for her lineage—lay crumpled on the floor, freshly dead from a head wound. Mother's carving knife still rested on the ground, sticky with brain-matter.

Most organs were useless for spellwork, instead destined for Mother's kitchen, but hearts and lungs were valuable, as were eyes and tongues.

The man's green eyes were marred, glassy, blood from his head having stained the white. When Flowridia plucked it out, she panicked at the blood dyeing the gelatinous substance. Mother would be livid, her doing or not. Imperfect ingredients meant imperfect spells.

An idea, something creative and dangerous, stopped Flowridia's work. Instead, she held the eye in the palm of her hand, releasing a healing spell and letting it trace across her fingertips. Her palm glowed, but nothing changed. Frowning, Flowridia poured more energy into—

"What are you—?"

Startled, Flowridia's fist clenched, and she gasped when viscous slime oozed from between her fingers. She turned, only to cry out when her hair nearly tore from her head. With Mother's grip tight in her hair, Flowridia whimpered as she pled. "I didn't mean to. I'm sorry–"

"Look at me when I speak to you!"

Flowridia clutched the hand at her hair, daring to make eye contact with the furious woman, now dressed in a loose robe.

"You can't heal what's already dead!" Mother threw her down. Flowridia's hands landed in gore. Blood from the floor seeped into her hair and clothing.

Beside her, Mother knelt, inspecting the corpse. She wiped a speck of the ruined eyes from the floor, emulsified under Flowridia's startled grasp. "What was salvageable is ruined. To your room!" Flowridia stood, stumbling as Mother cried, "I'll fetch you when I can stand to look at you!"

Flowridia wept nearly all night, blood and tears staining her pillow.

Chapter 7

Restless sleep meant an early morning. Flowridia awoke before dawn. Her eyes fluttered open, gentler than butterfly wings, and landed on a deep, red rose lying at the center of the table.

Flowridia sat up, head growing light, but not from wakefulness. She trembled as she reached to grab the thorny, delicate flower, mindful to not jostle Demitri. Suspicious of an enchantment or some sort of trick, she inspected the gift, hoping something might explain this offering. Her eyes narrowed, senses expanding as she searched for any trace of magic.

Nothing. Only a plain rose.

Velvet, fresh, and utterly flawless, when Flowridia brought it to her nose, she sniffed, savoring the sweet sensation. With the release of breath came relief.

Paws against her legs drew her attention. *Did Ayla come back?*

"It looks like it." But what it meant, she could not say. *Why didn't she say hello?*

Flowridia said, "She might still be angry," and left it at that. Love, or whatever addictive counterfeit Ayla offered, held a high price. But Demitri was young, and Flowridia hoped he would keep his innocent view of the world.

But she said she could forgive you.

"And this is her way of showing she still cares."

Flowridia placed the rose back onto the table and stood from her bed. She realized all of the candles had vanished. Thoughtful of Ayla, to clean up.

Before donning her clothing, she draped the ear around her neck and let it settle at her sternum.

I didn't even smell her. Flowridia turned around, focusing on the small form wagging his tail at her feet.

118

Ayla had appeared in the shadow of the door and held the talent to vanish at will in darkness. For her to have left a gift and no other trace seemed well within her capabilities. What sort of creature was Ayla? The books had said nothing about vampires travelling through shadow.

Ayla herself had said she was something different.

"Come walk with me," Flowridia said. "I'd like to clear my head before the world awakens."

Demitri followed closely at her heels. She twirled the rose in her hand, wondering how wise it was to let relief overshadow the fear and guilt lurking behind her stolen heart.

In her early morning wandering, she found herself outside, the crisp air startling to her skin. Damp grass kissed her bare feet. Sunlight burst in brilliant beams over the horizon. Flowridia shut her eyes, breathing in the warm sun as it touched her face and hair.

The garden came into view, but the entrance to Thalmus' kiln stood a few hundred feet across. She saw Thalmus himself standing by the wall, leaning quietly against it.

Every morning, he watched the sunrise.

But from the bags beneath his eyes, she wondered if he had slept. Thalmus turned at her approach, relief in his smile as he moved to close the distance. Before Flowridia could even speak, Thalmus scooped her up and engulfed her in a hug.

Though nearly three feet off the ground, Flowridia felt safety in the embrace of the hulking half-giant.

"Did you sleep?" he asked, soothing and soft.

"A little."

Thalmus set her back onto the ground. "You should be resting."

"I'm fine, Thalmus. There's nothing to worry ..." Her voice faded in tandem with his smile. He stared not at her, but at the rose in her hand.

"She came back," he said, something ominous in the deep rumble, like a volcano threatening to blow.

"It was on my bedside table when I awoke."

"Flowra, we're calling a meeting." Flowridia felt tension in his grip on her arm, his curtailed strength as he pulled her along. "We're banning her from Staelash, diplomat or not. Casvir can send another."

"Thalmus, stop!" Flowridia yanked her arm back; Thalmus released her, anger in his narrowed eyes. "I don't care that she came back. She isn't going to hurt me, and I don't want to cause any international incidents."

"She committed a crime against a member of our ruling council. That more than warrants–"

"What crime?!" Flowridia yelled, anger quickly bubbling over. "It wasn't the first time we'd had sex, Thalmus. I liked it. I *wanted* it."

"You wanted her to leave you bruised and battered?"

"She reacted because I *burned her face!* Would you have done any different?"

Thalmus' voice suddenly bellowed. "A mistake doesn't warrant her beating you to a pulp! If she's done it once, she'll do it again. Flowra–" He stopped himself, gritting his teeth as he continued, more subdued. "I searched the castle. If I'd found her, I would have killed her."

Wide-eyed, Flowridia clutched the rose to her chest. "Thalmus, you don't mean that–"

"She raped and beat my little flower girl." A pause; his jaw quivered. "Would you have done any different?"

"That's not what happened," Flowridia pled. "She broke my arm when she threw me across the room, yes, but all the bruises were–" She hesitated, uncomfortable giving details of her affair, but swallowed her embarrassment. "The bruising was consensual. Like I said, it wasn't the first time we'd slept together."

Unwilling to meet his eyes, Flowridia's gaze wandered Thalmus' form, acutely aware of the mass of scars covering his skin. His hands moved to clasp each other, knuckles nearly white despite the dark hue, and when Flowridia dared to look back up, she saw that tears welled in his eyes.

"If I could fall on my knees and beg you not to see her, I would." Instead, when Thalmus fell to his knees, he pulled her into a hug. He shook, his soft crying drawing tears from her own eyes as well. "I know the shame–" His voice stopped abruptly, as though hitting a wall. Perhaps the same wall, so carefully constructed, that protected him against the history of violence written across his skin. She felt him stiffen and shake, felt him tear a rip into those guarded layers. "I know the shame of abuse and the agony it brings," he whispered, each word forcibly torn from his unwilling, broken voice. "It's a burden I carry years later, and if I can spare you any pain, if I can fight for you, please, let me."

Flowridia let her arms snake from her chest to try and properly embrace her enormous companion. She had no words. She had no response, other than to not further harm the gentle man before her, delicate and raw despite his inherent strength.

"If you insist on carrying on . . ." Thalmus' hold grew tighter, protective. "If she returns, will you tell me?"

The question lingered, and Flowridia couldn't help the pit that welled in her stomach. She simply nodded, unsure of her own honesty.

"If Ayla can appear uninvited in your room, the entire castle is under threat. This is about more than last night, Flowra." Thalmus kept his embrace but pulled away enough to face her. "I hope she brings you joy. I hope she cherishes your heart and treats you like a queen because it's nothing less than you deserve." One hand left her back and gently stroked against her hair. Flowridia reached up and grabbed the back of his hand, leaning into the tender gesture. "I also hope you'll come to me, or Etolié, Marielle—*someone*—if anything like this happens again. Please."

Flowridia nodded yet again, more confident in her honesty.

"You're gentle. You're kind. Don't let her change that." He released a deep, pained breath. "I wish you wouldn't see her at all."

When Thalmus' grip grew slack, she pulled away, eyes wide and watery, and said, "May I stay by you today? I could find a book and keep you company."

Thalmus smiled and nodded.

The grass bent under Flowridia's light steps as she returned to the manor, the rose steadily twirling in her hand as she contemplated Thalmus' words. All of these promises she couldn't keep, yet the prospect of disappointing Thalmus lacerated her bruised heart.

She and Demitri made their way down the stairs and through the hall, when an irreverent voice shattered the peaceful morning.

"I'm not going to suck Sol Kareena's dick to appease you!"

No one blasphemed as freely as Etolié. The words echoed off the ceiling and through the hallway. Flowridia lifted Demitri into her arms and increased her pace, curious to know the cause of the altercation. Whatever reply she heard was merely a mumble next to the irreverent Celestial.

"Don't you talk to her! She's a child. Benevolent goddess or not, Sol Kareena won't be coercing any—!"

Flowridia crept inside and peered around the shelves to see the source of Etolié's rage. Meira stood tall and firm, only a raised eyebrow in response to Etolié's shouting. Sora stood behind her, glancing at Flowridia despite her silent entrance.

Flowridia struggled to hear Meira's quiet retort. "To pledge to a god of debauchery would hardly do her any–"

"She's not joining Eionei, either!" Etolié's sunken, bloodshot eyes turned to Flowridia herself. "Flowers, hi! How are you? Get any sleep after last night?"

Flowridia glanced between the two arguing figures, as Meira herself turned and approached her. "Flowridia, I wished to speak to you–"

"No, she doesn't," Etolié said, rushing to Flowridia's side. "Sorry, cult practice has been cancelled for today."

Meira's sightless eyes made her glare all the more ominous. "Sol Kareena would accept us all, but we must choose her. Flowridia, consider how your talents could be used to glorify the Goddess' name." The eerie woman walked away, Sora following behind, and once the door shut, Etolié finally released her hold on Flowridia's shoulder.

"Fun fact, Flowers: The Theocracy of Sol Kareena was founded by a branch-off of elves who thought their own people's antiquated views on the Old Gods were corrupt. Years later, we have Meira *Schmeira* trying to convert Staelash into another branch of worship because she thinks the Theocracy is corrupt." With an aggravated sigh, Etolié stepped away. "Eionei's theology doesn't change. 'Get drunk. Live free.' That's not so complicated, right?"

Flowridia finally set Demitri down. "Does Meira bother you often?"

"Less than she used to. I think Sol Kareena picking you as a champion rekindled her anarchist flame." Etolié's hands shook as she set them on her hips. "Pledge to Sol Kareena if you want, but don't do it because her puppet asked you to."

Concerned at those dark-rimmed eyes, Flowridia asked, "When was the last time you slept?"

"A few days ago," Etolié admitted, and Flowridia didn't question her honesty. "Don't make this about me. How are you?"

"I'm fine. I slept. When did you last eat?"

Etolié scoffed at the question, brushing past her and moving to stand beneath the skylight. "I don't need to eat. I subsist off starlight, remember?"

Etolié's near-emaciated form had always drawn questions from Flowridia. "Be that as it may, I think it's been too long since you last had something other than alcohol in your stomach."

"I haven't had a drink since last night." With her back to Flowridia, Etolié stared up at the hints of light, arms crossed. "Too worried for you. I needed to think clearly." A pause, and Etolié gave a humorless chuckle. "Thinking clearly hurts sometimes."

Guilt clenched Flowridia's stomach, especially when she looked down at the rose in her hand. She said nothing, instead disappearing behind the nearest shelf both to hide and to inspect the books.

"Listen, Flowers," Etolié's voice said, emanating from the center. "I'm sorry. I pushed you to pursue her." Flowridia pulled out a copy of *Eleven Elven Elegies* and peered through a hole in the line of books at the aggrieved Celestial. "This is my fault. I put you in danger."

"She would have pursued me, either way."

"Still, I'm sorry."

When Flowridia reappeared from the bookshelves, Etolié stared at the ground. "You don't need to be," Flowridia said, holding the rose behind her back. "I'm still processing last night."

"And that's fine," Etolié replied. "Processing is good. But don't justify it." Etolié's bloodshot eyes turned to her, sallow skin highlighted in the light. "What Ayla did was wrong."

"Etolié, it truly was an accident–"

"Yes, you burned her. I understand that. But if I were to swat a mosquito on my arm, it'd be no effort on my part to leave nothing but a puddle of blood."

Flowridia said nothing, unwilling to puncture the morass steadily filling her chest. A confession tingled at her tongue, burning to be spoken, of Ayla's return that night and her words, but . . .

Whatever fear Flowridia felt, she dared not cast it onto Etolié, whose bloodshot eyes bespoke guilt. Instead, she offered a smile and nothing else, weaving her way back through the shelves and to the door.

She turned the doorknob, startled to see a familiar half-elf waiting behind it. Flowridia nearly dropped her book, but Sora's hand caught the heavy tome before it could crush her small familiar. "Careful." Sora glanced down and raised an eyebrow. "Elven literature?"

Flowridia shrank slightly at the question. "I don't know much about elves, so–"

"Is that for Ayla?" she asked, gesturing to the rose.

"Yes," she lied, and then recalled that Sora didn't know the extent of their flirtation. "How did you guess?"

"Etolié said the name. And I think we all had our suspicions, after the chess incident." With a smirk, she handed the book back. "Poetry. Smart. Elves love pretentious stuff."

Sora's words brought up an excellent point. Ayla might be undead, but she was unquestionably an elf. And Sora, being half-elven, might know a few more things about elves than Flowridia. "What else do elves tend to like?"

"Well, they don't eat meat, so you'll be among friends. But poetry, art, engineering, invention . . . their culture values creative endeavors and science. It's how they survive without magic in a magical world." Sora shrugged. "I grew up with an education of both worlds; I was raised by my Sun Elven mother, but my father visited as often as he could."

An intriguing thought—Flowridia had never considered that Sora's parents might not have raised her together. "Your parents aren't married, then?"

"Elves are racist bastards. My relatives weren't too keen on my father, and my mother told me later that he was some high-ranking official in his homeland—apparently, news of an illegitimate, half-elven daughter would have hurt his political standing. But it doesn't matter. They've both since passed away."

"I'm sorry to hear that."

"Everything that happened has led me here," Sora said. "Speaking of which, I wanted to talk to you. I know Meira can be off-putting at times."

Flowridia held the rose and book to her chest, as defensive a gesture as she dared to show.

"She really is the wisest woman I know, though," Sora continued. "You don't have to pledge to Sol Kareena, but promise me you'll consider it. Think if what's holding you back is worth it."

Though her tongue grew dry, Flowridia said, "I will," and knew it was a lie. She hoped Sora didn't.

Sora's smile grew as she gestured to the flower held to her chest. "How are you going to get it to her?"

"I was thinking of drying it," she said slowly, hoping if she spoke articulately enough she wouldn't be caught in her lie. "Then mailing it to her through the embassy. When it's complete," she added, realizing the event was weeks away. "I'm planning ahead."

"Have you heard from her since the embassy unveiling?"

"Nothing more than dinner," Flowridia said, her nervous laugh surely betraying her lie.

"Whatever your goals, good luck."

Sora left her alone, and Flowridia took her book outside.

That night, Flowridia lay in bed, a sweet, sleeping puppy at her side and a small pile of withering flowers—those worn in her hair—by her bedside table.

The open window invited the night air to caress her face, along with the gentle singing of wind rustling the trees. Silver wisps of moonlight illuminated the covers of her bed, and when she stared out, Flowridia could see faint speckles of starlight.

Etolié had said the Moon and Stars were wed and had spoken the sacred name—*Neoma*. Legends said a thousand years ago, Neoma, the Moon Goddess, had fallen at the hands of her own child, the first of the Solviraes. But there were many stories of gods and goddesses, most untrue or embellished. The Solviraes bloodline was moon-touched, never diluting despite the passing generations. The empress was Flowridia's only face for Neoma's progeny, and despite her power, Flowridia couldn't imagine her murdering a goddess.

Besides, the stars were Etolié's mother's domain, and though Neoma and Staella were wed, no child could be born between them. The story held a few holes.

Still, Neoma's legacy touched the world, if only by the silver light caressing Flowridia's face.

Never in her life had Flowridia thought to pray sincerely to any god. Instead, she had spent years searching for something far more precious.

The light never breached through the misty cover of trees. For two years, Flowridia had not felt the sun.

All night, Flowridia cowered in her bed, the occasional echo of a knife thumping bluntly against wood and the memory of emulsified gore jarring her from vain attempts at sleep. Someday, she knew Mother would disown her and feed her to the garden, bury her barely alive and let the fungi consume her breathing body. That, or chop her into pieces and use her entrails for spellwork. Mother threatened it often enough.

For now, Flowridia survived.

When the outside world grew silent, Flowridia dropped from her bed to the floor and set her hands against the wooden walls. There were no windows in her bedroom, but if Flowridia shut her eyes and focused, she could feel where the dead wood mingled against the earth and touch her senses against the plants caressing the outside walls. Though sickly from no sun, the plants lived and breathed. She felt the trees, ones that managed to breach above the shadows and feel the sun.

But walls prevented her from searching too far. Mother's wards stopped her from looking out, just as they prevented anyone from looking in.

Did Aura search for her? Every night, Flowridia asked the trees if they had felt a wolf in their midst.

The static of magical wards muted the answer. Perhaps, someday, she could breach it.

"Flower Child?"

The voice at the door came so softly, yet Flowridia's heart immediately seized.

"Come out, my sweet girl. I have a surprise."

Fearful, Flowridia trembled as she turned the doorknob.

Mother stood with a gentle smile, one Flowridia waited to twist and sneer. But the words were sweet, and behind her, Flowridia saw no evidence of corpses or blood. "Come and sit. I've made you some dessert."

When she offered a hand, Flowridia's blood-stained one accepted, and she let Mother lead her through the mushroom garden and to the kitchen.

It was the only room untouched by fungi, with a wooden table and two chairs in the center. A small pile of muffins sat arranged on a plate beside a kettle of tea.

Behind the quaint scene, in the sink lay evidence of blood and entrails, separated from the carved pieces of raw meat on the cutting board. Strips of flesh lined the walls, drying and awaiting enchantment. Over the fire, a cauldron boiled, filled to the top with a stew Flowridia knew better than to ask the ingredients of.

Everything Mother created was perfect, infused with magic and horror.

Mother, with her lace-lined dress, beckoned for her to sit. Flowridia obeyed, skin crawling as she awaited reprimand.

But Mother smiled, her teeth pure white, and both her hands rested gently on her stomach. "Flower Child, my sweet, something wonderful has come from all of this."

In the morning, the flowers had gone, replaced by a single, red rose.

Flowridia rolled over and grabbed it, a frown pulling at her lips. Why had Ayla returned?

Demitri yawned as he opened his large, golden eyes. His clawed feet padded against her nightgown and covers as he came to sniff the gifted rose. *It smells like Ayla. But why didn't she say hello?*

"I don't know, Demitri," Flowridia said, truthful as she mulled over what strange and intricate flirtation Ayla seemed to be concocting.

If she can be bothered to leave gifts, she can bother to say hello.

His petulant little voice drew a smile to her face. "Perhaps if we catch her," she teased, kissing his cheek, "she'll tell us."

But Demitri, it seemed, was utterly serious. *If we catch her, don't you have to tell Thalmus?*

"Demitri, Thalmus doesn't like Ayla."

But he made you promise.

"I know," she said. "But telling him would only worry him."

Because Ayla threw you across the room?

"Yes, and other reasons," she said, flinching as the memory of hateful words—*'Look at me!'*—brimmed to the surface. "But Thalmus wasn't there. He doesn't understand."

You should probably stay away from him. You're a terrible liar.

Flowridia could only nod. "I'm aware." She stood up, her feet chilled when they touched the thin rug protecting her from the floor, and placed the gift into the vase at her windowsill—one housing the rose from the previous night.

The construction of the embassy was underway. Zorlaeus, having been named the official ambassador between the two kingdoms, often visited Marielle, who personally dealt with the day-to-day affairs of Staelash. And though Flowridia was, at Etolié's insistence, the official liaison to Nox'Kartha, why send Flowridia to negotiate with Zorlaeus when it would mean less time for Marielle?

Instead, Flowridia spent her morning alone in her garden, gently touching marred petals and wilting flowers, infusing them with healing magic. She wore only her nightclothes and a robe to ward against the morning chill, and underneath a willow tree, surrounded by patchy grass, an idea prickled in her mind. "Should I leave something for Ayla?"

Demitri ceased rolling his scent into the dirt long enough to reply. Covered in dust, the young wolf looked like the wild animal he truly was. *It might slow her down enough to catch her.*

Flowridia bit her lip, nervous at the thought. "But what would Ayla even want?" She released a heavy sigh, slumping over. "I don't know anything about flirtation." Grimacing, she turned to face the little wolf. "What would you do, Demitri?"

Again, Demitri stopped rolling around, this time turning over onto his feet. He shook his fur, and Flowridia ignored the specks of dirt flung onto her dress. *Wolf mating rituals aren't too different from yours. Keep touching her and kissing her to show you're interested.*

Taken aback, Flowridia said, "Is that all it takes?"

There's more, but I don't know if Lady Ayla wants you to lick her bum, even if it would show you whether or not she's ready to mate.

Flowridia wasn't sure what worried her more—tiny Demitri using words like 'mate' or the fact that acquainting herself with Ayla's posterior actually sounded appealing. Flowridia cringed, however, ignoring the heat that rose to her cheeks. "She's already leaving me flowers."

Mother had always said that roses symbolized love, and that different colors conveyed a different tone. The darker the red, the more beautiful the recipient, and the deep maroon of the rose in her hand was as romantic a gesture as Flowridia had ever received. But there were other meanings in floral spellcraft: a sprinkle of white roses petals for purity, lavender for love at first sight, pink for innocent friendship, and so on. The language of flowers held important meanings in both romance and magic.

"You use your own blood to feed the roses?"

"Yes, Flower Child. The deeper the stain of red, the deeper the affection, as well as the depth of power it holds."

Flowridia shoved the eerie thought from her head.

The moon lilies gave her pause. So vibrant and icy a blue, but they were much too large to be useful in her hair. Lilies were a funeral flower, and this particular breed only grew naturally across the sea in Zauleen—elven lands. The first of her seeds had been a gift from Etolié, a welcome present to help her feel at ease in Staelash. In only a few months, the sprouts had blossomed into an expansive garden, fueled by devoted care and a substantial amount of magic.

Etolié had succeeded. Having a space of her own had helped Flowridia feel at home.

She knelt and plucked a single stem, roots and all, and twirled it between her fingers, wondering if this might be what she left for Ayla that night. But a bit of engineering and magic mulled through her head, and when she passed the gardenias, she stopped and plucked a single bud from the bush.

Breeding inter-species plants was something she had learned from Mother, though she had taken to it much more quickly than her progenitor. Weaving roots together was a matter of detail and, if she were entirely honest, a labor of love her mother held no patience for.

In a small patch of empty earth, Flowridia placed the chosen flowers—the gardenia and the moon lily—and let her magic blend and seal the roots. Now to wait and let nature and time do the work she could not.

"What's the most romantic thing anyone has ever done for you?"

Etolié, from her corner, snacked on a fresh muffin as Flowridia posed the question. No one knew of Ayla's nightly visits, for now. Flowridia would keep that a secret.

Demitri sat by Etolié's side, picking out pieces of fruit from the muffin balanced between his paws.

"No offense, Flowers, but I have yet to meet anyone from the mortal realm who makes my heart flutter."

From the opposite corner, Flowridia had her nose buried in *Thespian Vampires: A Powerplay of Art and Horror.* The odd retort gave her pause. She set the book down into her lap. "Have you ever been in love?"

Etolié shook her head. "Not among my interests. Mom always said I'd find someone if I spent more time partying with the angels, but I think she's projecting."

Gaze narrowing, Flowridia set the book aside and stood. "Have you ever . . ?" To say the word felt daunting. To mime an obscene gesture seemed more appropriate.

"Of course I've done the dirty," Etolié replied. "How else do you break into slave camps, isolate the leader, and stab them in their sleep? I'm gorgeous, Flowers, and men are weak."

Mother had shared similar sentiments. *Let him in, won't you, Flower Child? Seems we'll be having a guest for dinner tonight–" The laughter at her own morbid jest filled the cottage. Mother stared out the window, her coy smile turning lurid. "But an appetizer first. I'm starved."*

"You'd sleep with them, and then you'd kill them?"

"Sometimes during. Sometimes before. They're slavers, Flowers. Getting their rocks off wasn't exactly priority one. But I was a young revolutionary, then. I have more class to my methods now."

Flowridia smiled, as though what Etolié had said wasn't deeply concerning. "But you haven't pursued a relationship?"

Etolié shook her head. "Could I? Sure. But who, Flowers? Who is more interesting than knowledge?"

"Is this a trick question?"

"Absolutely, because the answer is no one. Mortals don't lubricate my gears." Etolié stole another muffin from the plate and took a small bite. "Circling back to your original question, though, I think the most romantic thing that ever happened was when a man offered to sell his wife at the next slave auction if I'd agree to take her place."

"I feel like I can recreate none of that with Ayla, so I'll pretend you didn't say it."

"So, this is about Ayla," Etolié said, and Flowridia saw a hint of ire in the knowing smirk twisting her lip. "Have you heard from her at all?"

Grateful that Thalmus and Etolié never spoke, Flowridia shook her head. Much easier to lie non-verbally.

"But you've been thinking about her?"

"I've wondered how she's been," Flowridia said truthfully. Careful to divert the attention from herself, Flowridia added, "Sora said elves love art and science. It makes me wonder if undead elves would appreciate the same."

Etolié laughed as she withdrew her flask. "Sora loves to talk about elves like she isn't one. Elves are notoriously racist and generally stick to their own. For all you might see here, or in the Theocracy, there are virtually no non-elves across the sea."

Etolié began to drink. Flowridia forgot, at times, that their ruling council was uncommonly diverse, with its inclusion of a half-giant, a Celestial, and who Flowridia was fairly confident was a particularly large De'Sindai. Marielle's father had deemed it necessary; if they were to care for freed slaves, they ought to employ what were historically slave races. A definite risk: Humans and their Celestial counterparts got along well, thus their continued ties to the Solviran Empire.

Other races tended to fight.

"So, you're going to pursue this relationship with Ayla?"

The more Etolié drank, the easier it was to see the forced humor on her face. Flowridia simply shrugged.

"Ambitious of you," Etolié said, and again she took a drink. "You ever had a relationship before?"

"I've never had the opportunity."

Etolié offered the flask forward. Flowridia gently shook her head. But Etolié pushed, eyebrow raised as she held her arm out. "Take it."

Flowridia accepted.

"You're compliant, Flowers," Etolié said, and she suddenly snatched it back, "and that concerns me. If you don't want alcohol, tell me no."

"I don't care for the taste, or the effects," Flowridia admitted, words as shy as she felt.

"Listen, what I mean is, don't go along with things if you don't want them." Flowridia's posture turned inward as she waited for Etolié to say her piece. "Or do, but if you want something, take it. You have my permission to make a few waves."

It left a lingering question, one Etolié had hinted at more than once. Flowridia had never spoken of the life she'd lived before this one. She clasped her hands behind her back, careful to filter the truth as she chose her words. "Coming here, to Staelash," Flowridia began slowly, "has been a dream, and one I don't deserve." Etolié frowned, but Flowridia continued before she could object. "There's no danger here, but compliance is a survival technique. It's a habit that'll take time to break."

Etolié took a tentative step forward, her own posture matching Flowridia's. "Your power isn't something to be afraid of."

"I've seen it do terrible things," Flowridia whispered, and her hands began to fidget.

"If you ever need to talk–"

"I don't."

Etolié's hands came forward, as if to clasp her own, but instead she gripped Flowridia's forearm. Her drunken serenity faded into something fierce. "Ask me to get rid of Ayla Darkleaf, and she'll never speak to you again."

"I haven't made a decision," Flowridia whispered, but the threat of a smile tugged at her lip when she realized Etolié cared, even if she showed her devotion differently than most. Whatever the Celestial's eccentricities, Etolié would never make an idle threat.

Yet, the offer highlighted a truth that unsettled her– that there was a choice to be made.

The Celestial withdrew her hands and disappeared behind the shelf. "Keep yourself busy," she heard Etolié say. "Dust off my shelves if you need a distraction."

Flowridia did so, channeling her anxiety into meticulously dusting off the trinkets and books.

With the ear secure around her neck, Flowridia dressed in her night clothes. "Come to bed, Demitri."

If I get in bed, I'll fall asleep.

"That's the point of bedtime."

Were we going to wait for Ayla?

Oh, that had been jested. Flowridia offered an uneasy smile. "I don't think she'd like that. I-I don't want to ruin her game."

But how can it be a game if you don't know how to play?

Curiosity piqued, Flowridia nodded, despite the pit in her stomach. "I'll wait with you."

Demitri said nothing else, content to avoid bedtime, it seemed. Flowridia blew out the candle lighting her room and crawled into bed. "Goodnight, dearest Demitri."

Goodnight, mom.

The moonlight through the window barely flickered; if Ayla were to appear, Flowridia feared she'd miss her. But she lay in silence, staring at the window through drooping eyelids.

Silence. Shuffling from beneath the bed meant Demitri still stirred. Faint whistling wind from outside stole her focus. Sleeping with the window shut might be the smarter move, but what if that were Ayla's only entrance?

The possibility of Ayla not showing up at all wasn't lost on her. An odd chance she took, to stay up all night, and . . . and do what, exactly? Not confront her. Not even seduce her. What did she want? Contact? Conversation?

The image of charred skin and a hateful gaze still seared her memory, welling guilt in her stomach. At her sternum, she gently touched the severed ear, growing accustomed to the eerie feeling of dead flesh against her fingers.

The entire bed jostled when she turned over. The moon's placement in the sky suggested she had a long wait ahead of her.

Darkness descended; the moon grew dim.

The flickering fire cast a shadow upon the walls that did not quite match Mother's form.

Something monstrous moved with her gestures, something feathered and large. It resembled nothing of Mother's body, even with her barely swollen womb.

The slight tug on Flowridia's head pulled her back into the moment. "Almost done, Flower Child," Mother soothed, the brush detangling her hair by bits and pieces. With pregnancy had come the return of motherly instinct, or so it seemed; Flowridia remained constantly on edge for a cruelty she hadn't seen in nearly two months.

Mother released her, then placed a large mirror in her hands. Flowridia saw Mother's face beside her own, doppelgangers to the other, though Mother's skin held a paler shade than her own amber hues. Flowridia's hair had been pulled into a twist, a large flower—one Flowridia had grown—tucked behind her ear, and she couldn't deny that it looked lovely.

"You're a beautiful girl," Mother said as she stepped away, and with her, the shadow shifted, revealing the oddity of its movements. "Be careful with that. Treasures are often sought to be claimed, and you, my darling, are a gem."

Flowridia felt a rise of something dreadful and unknown in her stomach. Resisting the urge to tear the flower from her hair, she asked, "I don't understand what you mean?"

Mother's chuckle held malice. "I suppose you came here young enough to have avoided the advances of men. Some men are beautiful and good, Flower Child, and I truly hope you meet one who sweeps you off your feet."

Flowridia fought to suppress her rising panic.

"But the wicked ones will seek to cage you, whether you like it or not," Mother continued, any good humor fading into something wistful. "Have I ever told you of Rulan?"

Flowridia shook her head, grateful for the change in subject. "Was he someone you loved?"

Mother cracked a smile. "Yes, but not in the way you mean. He was my familiar—a great, magnificent owl, and the wisest friend I ever had. Rulan came to me when I was but a medicine woman in the village yonder, long ago." Unspoken sadness tugged at Mother's smile, and when she spoke again, sorrow laced the words. "This was in the era when the Solviraes weren't the benevolent monarchs they are now, but tyrants of their empire. Their crimes were many, but most infamous were the witch hunts."

Flowridia had heard of such, when religious purity reigned supreme and all those pledged to demon gods were burned at the stake.

"I was found. Luckily for me, the crown prince personally accompanied the hunting party and deemed me worthy of saving, but for a cost. A marriage proposal . . . and letting Rulan be slain.

"Of course, when I refused, he slit Rulan's throat anyway. All of my power funneled away. I was helpless when he claimed me nonetheless."

Never had Flowridia pitied the woman who birthed her; not until this day.

"I was granted the kindness of keeping Rulan's body," Mother sneered. "As I was taken to the capitol city, I prayed to the demon who had granted me Rulan. I did not know his face or name, but I pled for aid. A voice in my head told me that for the cost of a child, I would be granted all that was lost and more. I agreed."

The glee in Mother's eyes as she spoke of the ensuring chaos and slaughter of her captors prickled at the hair on Flowridia's neck, chills sweeping across her skin. Rulan's power, she said, descended upon her, and they became one.

Though the idea of consuming her familiar revolted Flowridia down to her very soul, her heart understood. She watched the shifting shadow her mother cast, and she felt immutable sadness for the loss.

Flowridia bolted into a sitting position, the faint light of morning threatening to peak over the horizon. Frustrated, she let her head fall into her hands.

Beside her, Demitri slept. When had he joined her?

Her eyes travelled to her bedside table. A single, red rose lay upon it.

Careful to not crush Demitri, Flowridia leaned over and grabbed it. A shy smile spread across her face, the worry of last night evaporating like the morning dew.

Her hands moved to lightly scratch at Demitri's fur. He rolled into her touch, turning onto his back as one eye opened. *I did my part. Let me sleep.*

"Did you see her?" Her long hair moved to frame his little body as she peered down from above. "Tell me that, and I'll leave you alone."

I saw her. Demitri began to roll back over.

"Wait, wait!" Flowridia curled up beside him, staring at his sleepy face. "Tell me what happened. Did she say anything?"

Demitri opened his eyes again, blinking heavily as more words appeared in Flowridia's head. *She saw me watching.* He yawned, his over-sized jaw stretching wide to reveal sharp incisors. *She asked me to tell you something.*

Flowridia hung onto his small, childish voice.

She said when there are twelve roses in the vase, she'll appear. Demitri stood on his hind legs, and his tongue gave a quick lick to Flowridia's cheek. *She also asked me to deliver that. Then, she was gone.*

"Did she kiss your cheek or actually lick it?"

She licked it.

Somehow, that was more arousing.

Flowridia turned her gaze to the vase by the window. Two roses stood tall, soon to be joined by the third in her hand. Her heart fluttered at the thought.

"Thank you, Demitri," she whispered, and she kissed his nose. Careful to not jostle the sleepy pup, she stood and left the room, still in her nightclothes.

Outside, the early morning air chilled her through her thin nightgown, and she wrapped her arms around herself. Dew soaked her feet, but the feeling of sunshine on her face was more than worth the cold. She smiled, letting the sunrise further warm her heart.

Ayla had returned. Ayla would return again. And for a moment, her fear and guilt were assuaged.

In her garden, the ambiance of nature and life filled her senses with joy. Flowridia breathed in the sweet air, the fruits of all her hard work, and let the singing of birds lead her steps.

Alone, she continued to her destination, that of her newest project. Flowridia knelt beside the patch of dirt near the gardenias, where fragile, precious spots of green had already begun to sprout. A shy smile tugged at her lip. Flowridia placed her hands on the dirt, letting pure energy wash into the ground, her own reserve giving life and growth to this new creation. Nothing visibly changed, but Flowridia, upon brushing against a miniscule stem, could feel them sing in joy at the offering.

She went on her way. At the rose bushes, their deep, blushing red gave her pause, and she let her hand stroke against the soft petals. A near perfect match to her own gifted roses, but did she dare tease her shadowed suitor? Ayla had said she would reappear once twelve roses appeared in the vase.

Flowridia, with care to match the length of the stems and the color, went about cutting nine matching roses.

"Flowers!"

Flowridia nearly jumped at Etolié's voice.

The Celestial approached, her light feet barely indenting the dewed grass. "You're a predictable duckling. If you're not in the kitchen, you're always here."

"It's a good place to clear my head," she said honestly. Flowridia nonchalantly kept her arms behind her back, hiding her bouquet. "But I can make you breakfast–"

"While I appreciate the gesture, I'm capable of making my own food." To Flowridia's surprise, Etolié sat down, apparently giving no care to what the grass might do to her silk gown. "That came out poorly. Make me food because you want to, not because you feel like you have to."

Self-conscious, Flowridia gave a slow nod.

Etolié collapsed on the ground, her back to the cool grass. Gentle speckles of sunlight illuminated her fair skin, and her silver hair glittered like the stars she had descended from. "Your garden makes me want to nap. That's not an insult. I think I could sleep sober in here."

Birds sang a comforting song, and the flowers radiated a tune of their own, one of familiar magic and protection.

"This world wasn't meant for magic," Etolié said softly. "It damages the fabric of the dimension. When angels started partying with humans, it brought much more than half-breed children."

Flowridia wasn't sure why Etolié waxed poetic on history, but the serenity on her face spoke volumes. By her own admission, Etolié felt magic, felt it prickling at her skin and tangling into her hair. Drinking, she said, dulled the perpetual annoyance.

"But your magic, the way you weave it into the earth, is the most natural I've ever felt." She released a sigh, pursed lips spreading into a smile. "I don't know how you do it, Flowers."

"Attention to detail?" Flowridia offered, and Etolié chuckled in response.

"I did come here for a reason. Marielle called a meeting. Apparently we've received an interesting letter."

"It's early for a meeting. Will anyone else be there?"

To Flowridia's surprise, Etolié's dress remained pristine, despite the threat of grass stains. "To say Marielle's sense of prioritizing is broken would be an understatement," Etolié replied, offering Flowridia a hand. "I told her unless she served breakfast, it'd be her and me. And you, I suppose, but I'm not convinced you ever sleep either." Etolié clutched the air and pulled a robe from what appeared to be a tear in the sky. She offered it to Flowridia. "Wear this over your nightgown."

Flowridia accepted the night robe, marveled at the weight, and said, "Is it actually real?"

"As real as my dress."

With an amused smile, Flowridia slipped her arms through the illusionary sleeves and followed Etolié out.

In the council room, Flowridia found she wasn't the only one wearing nightclothes—Meira seemed only half awake, her head resting on her fist as she snoozed in her throne. Sora stood at her side, alert for the early morning.

Khastra didn't sit. Instead, the crystal hammer sat in her throne, and Khastra leisurely polished the shaft.

Thalmus sat quietly but nodded at Flowridia's entrance. Marielle, sitting on her throne, smiled brightly. "Oh, good. Flowridia, this involves you."

Panic caused her to stop in her tracks. "What?"

"This is a matter of diplomacy. And you're the diplomat."

"Doesn't mean she's required to fix any bad news," Etolié interjected, settling into her seat. In her hand, she dangled a flask. "But she might be the messenger."

The words did little to soothe Flowridia's concerns.

Once everyone was seated, Marielle withdrew a letter from her robe. "As I think we all remember, we had a meeting with the ambassador from Tholheim after my coronation. We've received news. The missing prince and his comrades have been found." Marielle's hesitation grew palpable, and she glanced nervously between Etolié and Thalmus. "According to the sole survivor's account, there's been a slave camp discovered due north—"

Etolié immediately shot to her feet. Thalmus' grip on his throne grew tense, and Flowridia wondered when the wood would crack. "Oh?" Etolié said.

"The letter *insists* this be approached diplomatically," Marielle said, flinching when Etolié snatched the letter from her hands. Flowridia saw, torn but unmistakable, the seal of the Tholheimer Royal family.

"What I do not understand," Khastra said, inspecting her own reflection in the shined weapon, "is why we need to interfere in Tholheimer politics. If they wish to conduct slavery in their own territory, it is their prerogative."

"Because it's on our border," Etolié all but spat. "And they're specifically asking for our presence to discuss solutions."

Marielle spoke up. "The letter requests I come personally to the border city of Molt."

Etolié frowned as she continued studying the letter. "Why you?"

Marielle frowned, eyes narrowing. "Perhaps in deference to the times my father personally mediated political situations for foreign parties? I should be there. You're too personally invested to–"

"This isn't political," Etolié interrupted. "These are slavers. We're not discussing trade agreements; we're debating how to best smear them across the walls of their own encampment."

"The last time you were on the road, you were attacked by a mad-man," Thalmus said to Marielle, shaking his head. "Their request is out of bounds."

The orb at Marielle's chest began to shine. "And risk starting a war with Tholheim? Let's at least consult Lara–"

"A compromise," Etolié said, still staring daggers at the document. "We go to King Thovir. We tell him our intention to decimate the camp and ask if he'll help. And if he objects, then we involve Solvira. Khastra?"

The general glanced up, the shine of the metallic handle enough to easily reflect her countenance. "If you think it is wise, I will agree. But I would rather not waste time talking when murdering is more effective."

"This is why I keep you, Khastra," Etolié said, her good humor returning, and with a wink, she added, "in the back, far away from foreign monarchs."

Khastra merely chuckled.

"Tholheim will be insulted!" Marielle said, voice rising. "They asked for Queen Marielle."

"I'll play Marielle." Etolié's form melted away, revealing a perfect doppelganger of Marielle Vors. "If anyone can negotiate with a bunch of angry drunkards, it's me."

Seething, Marielle turned to Thalmus. "Well? Will you send Etolié to take the axe for me?"

"She volunteered," Thalmus replied. "And I will accompany her for protection. Khastra will stay with you."

Marielle's knuckles had turned white as she gripped the chair. "Fine," she spat. The orb in her bosom glowed at the word.

"Flowers will come with me, in case I need to make any decisions. We'll pretend she's me," Etolié said with a wink.

Flowridia's fingers delicately stroked against her sternum, the chain around her neck barely exposed. Eyes wide, she said, "Are you–" She bit her tongue, gently amending with, "You aren't joking."

"I'm quite serious, Lady Diplomat."

"How far do we have to travel?"

"It's over a week's ride to Molt," Etolié said. "We'll need everyone ready to leave by tomorrow morning."

In a week's time, a dozen roses would be blossoming on the windowsill, and Ayla would be waiting. "Etolié, I–" *I can't do my duty because of a date? Ayla Darkleaf, distrusted diplomat of Nox'Kartha, requests my time?* Nothing she could say would change this. Still, her heart felt it might seize. ". . . I'll be ready," she finished, voice quiet.

"Khastra, send your best to accompany them," Marielle said.

Khastra's grandiose smile revealed white teeth. "Marielle, I am the best."

"Yes, but they insist you stay here in case it's a trap and Etolié ends up dead. Send your other best."

Marielle huffed, and when she stood, Flowridia noticed that the edges of her hair seemed to flicker with flame. "Are we done, then? We're done. Meeting adjourned. For those of you going, meet here tomorrow at sunrise with everything you'll need."

Marielle left with no further comment. As the rest cleared out, Sora hesitated at the door. "I-I know I work for Meira, but with her permission, I could accompany your party. I'm good with a sword, and I can hide if I need to."

"We may have to disguise those ears of yours," Etolié said, a defensive hand raised at the statement. "Don't take it personally; you know how dwarves are."

Etolié said more, but Flowridia was slowly losing the fight to remain composed. Rather than burst into tears in public, she quietly stood and slipped away, then ran to her bedroom.

Once the door shut, tears began to flow. Oh, Ayla would be so angry. Flowridia slid down the wooden door, letting herself crumple. The nine roses fell to the ground in a heap.

Her entrance had awoken Demitri—the little wolf crawled in between her knees. *What's wrong?*

Flowridia sniffed, still forcing back the rush threatening to overwhelm her. Only a few tears leaked out. With forced composure, she relayed the tale.

It isn't your fault you have to leave.

"I know, I know, but I don't want to disappoint her."

Ayla had duties. Ayla was a diplomat. Ayla would understand.

But, oh, how Flowridia wanted to stay.

She wandered to her desk and sat, grabbing a paper and pen before scribbling:

> *Ayla,*
>
> *I've been called away to assist my kingdom in diplomatic negotiations at our northern borders. It pains me to say I will be gone for the twelfth night and those leading up to it. Upon my return, I will do all I can to fall back in your favor.*
>
> *I'm so sorry.*
>
> *Yours,*
> *Flowra*

Why did this have to cut so deep?

That night, the bouquet upon the nightstand held a passionate display of red. A dozen roses bloomed, and with the accompanied letter, Flowridia hoped it served well as an apology, and perhaps as a bit of humor.

Demitri lay by her side. *Do you really think it will work?*

"No," Flowridia said. "But it may make her laugh before I disappoint her."

A clever solution. Creative, even, yet something icy stirred in her gut. As Flowridia settled in to sleep, she tossed and turned. What sort of reaction would it invoke?

She remembered her last bit of 'creativity' regarding Ayla—creativity that had gotten Ayla disfigured and Flowridia thrown across the room.

With care to not jostle Demitri, Flowridia sat up. A walk to clear her head, a drink of water, or something. Living with Mother had taught her all sorts of coping mechanisms.

"Still awake, Flower Child? Well, make yourself useful. Grab a mop before the blood dries–"

In the dark, her reflection cast an eerie doppelganger, of herself and of the meticulously clean room. The hazed shadow, barely lit by the celestial lights outside, followed her movements in perfect sync.

Beside her wardrobe, her treasured chess set stood ready to play. A beautiful work of art should not be hidden, she had long ago reasoned. The sight brought comfort, memories of afternoons spent with Thalmus learning the intricate rules of warfare.

But as her fingers skimmed the pieces, one lay missing. Frowning, Flowridia realized an empty square rested where the white queen should be. Had she never returned it after her game with Ayla?

The display on the nightstand no longer filled her with joy, but dread. She approached the moon-lit bouquet, the silver wisps gently caressing the fragile flowers. Her hands shook as she moved to rearrange them. A better presentation would endear to Ayla more, perhaps.

In the dark, she flinched, a sharp pain piercing her finger. She shot her hand back, the skin tearing against the thorn. Blood, dark and rich, seeped from the puncture and dripped onto the windowsill.

Tears welled. Flowridia withdrew the nine roses with infinite care and held them a moment to her nose, the alluring fragrance distracting from the pain they had caused.

With a gasp to mask her sob, she stepped toward the window, prepared to throw them out—

But a touch on her waist froze her to the core.

"Clever girl," came a smooth voice from behind. Flowridia's breath hitched as chilled hands slid around her waist.

The flowers fell to the floor. Flowridia trembled as she reached down, her hands settling over Ayla's as they continued to caress her form. They trailed along her stomach, her sides, settling on her breasts where they lingered, taunting at the unfulfilled promise. At Flowridia's sigh of want came a chuckle. "Real life so often interferes with games. Twelve flowers in a vase is all I ask. Once it is accomplished, I'm yours for the night."

Such tantalizing implications in that single promise. Flowridia's body craved contact. Desperate, she squeezed, Ayla's hands under her own moving in tandem.

One hand broke away, sliding down her stomach as the other continued its pleasured massage. It teased over her skirt, lightly touching the heat between her legs.

Then, both hands pulled away. "I don't break my promises, Flowra," Ayla cooed, then teeth tugged at Flowridia's ear. Gasping, she turned, finally able to look down and see the fierce, coy figure standing before her.

Her breath caught at the sight of Ayla's face, the charred skin still fierce and exposed. No hints of her skull but blacked, ruined skin, shriveled and raw around her ear, spread out to her hairline and to her eye.

Flowridia's hand flew to cover her mouth. "Your face," she managed to say, guilt drowning her lust.

"It will take time to get used to," Ayla cooed, and Flowridia swore she heard sardonic teasing in her tone. Her lip twisted into a cruel smile, the lines of her mouth marred from disfigurement.

Speechless, Flowridia slowly let her hand fall.

Ayla's predatory smile looked capable of tearing out Flowridia's throat. "You precious thing." She licked her lips, leering as she withdrew a single red rose from behind her back. She pressed it between Flowridia's breasts, perfectly centered.

Flowridia wrapped her hand around Ayla's and the rose stem, gripping tight when Ayla moved to pull away. "Ayla, I am so sorry."

Ayla's eyebrow flickered up dangerously as she slid out of Flowridia's touch. "Best keep my flowers safe."

Ayla stepped backwards into the dark shadow of the dresser, waving as she did, and vanished, her form fading into blackness.

Breathing heavily, Flowridia waited a moment for her head to stop spinning before investigating the shadow.

Ayla truly had disappeared.

"There's an intruder in our swamp, Flower Child. I've let him in as far as I can, but I'll need you to coerce him inside. Use whatever means necessary."

'Whatever means necessary' meant very different things to the two of them. But with Mother's womb beginning to protrude, Flowridia would do what she could to help.

Outside the cottage, the evening light barely filtered through the trees, heavily shadowed through the thick foliage. Noxious odors met her nose, and by the door, the usual array of ghosts watched as she left. Harmless, but not illusions—most were men, brutalized in their final moments, some missing heads. A few were little girls, younger than she. A warning, with their bloodied clothes and dismembered limbs, to what fate might await Flowridia should she step out of line.

But she braced herself, already hearing footsteps through the bog that weren't her own. The young man appeared from the trees, eyes darting all about but never settling on the shrouded cottage. He would never see it, not if Mother's wards willed it, but Flowridia stepped forward, and the startled man gasped and drew a sword.

"Wait," she said, holding out a hand. "Please, don't hurt me. Will you hear me out?"

The man—though he appeared barely older than she—kept his sword aloft as he took a step forward. He said nothing, but what did one say to a mysterious young woman in a swamp?

She smiled kindly and offered a hand, practiced charm in every word. "You're very brave to find your way here."

Like threading a needle, all it took was a bit of finesse. She recalled Mother's words—that to kill with only a touch was beyond even she, but that eternal sleep was nigh indistinguishable and trivial to cast—a matter of simply knowing which strings to twist and pull.

The moment their hands touched, the boy collapsed, asleep before he hit the water.

Flowridia shuddered, scrubbing her arms with her hands, unsure of what she even wiped away. She bent over to lift him before he drowned and pulled him through the murky water and up the stairs, the damp wood snagging his shirt and trousers, ripping into the worn cloth.

When she finally dragged him through the doorway, she heard mother's voice. "Flower Child?"

Flowridia gasped, turning to see Mother in a loose-fitting gown waiting in the doorway of her bedroom.

"He's a handsome man. I was going to say to enjoy yourself before you killed him." She raised an eyebrow, a slight frown at her lip. "Though you've made a mess of swamp water on my floor."

So much of Mother's words touched her soul as invariably *wrong*, but Flowridia managed to smile and shake her head. "He's not dead. Only sleeping."

In the doorway, Mother chuckled darkly, placing her hand on her swollen stomach. "You darling thing. Have your fun, then clean up and take care of him, will you? The child is starved, and so am I." She disappeared behind the door and shut it behind her.

Flowridia looked down at the prone boy. She wondered his name, and she knew she could wake him and ask him, then ask of his family, his life, what foolhardy quest had brought him to the swamp with a sword. His clothing didn't speak of riches. Perhaps someone he loved sat on the doorstep, ethereal and cursed to haunt their place of death.

It mattered not. He would join them. Flowridia grabbed the carving knife from the wall, her tears splattering the shined blade.

Chapter 8

They left in the morning. Flowridia sat in the carriage with Thalmus, and Etolié rode at the back, as usual. Sora rode outside with the guards, each among Khastra's elite, who surrounded them on horseback.

In her hair were fresh flowers. Her hands fidgeted, even though she and Thalmus spoke of pleasant things, the urge to distract herself by picking apart those protective buds a constant temptation. Flowridia's heart lie elsewhere—worry for their safety as they travelled this worn road, and worry for herself, Ayla's talk of games confounding her mind.

Out the window, she stared, the blinding sun bringing reminders of armored monsters in the night.

"Flowra?"

Startled, Flowridia turned at Thalmus' voice.

"Perhaps there is reason to worry, but there's still so much we don't know."

With her hand resting on her fist, Flowridia asked, "Do you think we'll run into him again?"

"I don't know," Thalmus replied, understanding in his distant gaze. "Leaving the orb behind means he has no reason to trail us, but I won't pretend to understand it."

Flowridia gave a curt nod but said nothing else, content to slip into companionable silence and stroke soothing lines against the wolf pup in her lap.

At night, they camped.

All was silent around the fire as Flowridia chewed on her dinner. Sora sat by her side, silent as she sharpened her dagger, the flickering fire reflecting against the polished blade. Guards scattered around them, some relaxing by the fire and others put to work. Thalmus stood among them, directing and helping to assemble tents.

"Etolié," Flowridia said, observing the quiet scene around them, "won't you tell us a story?" Memories of her travels with Etolié, Marielle, and the rest floated through her head. "I always love hearing about your adventures."

Etolié shook her head, staring down at an unraveled scroll. "There's a time and place for tales of revolution, Flowers."

Surprised at the rejection, Flowridia studied the Celestial's jittery demeanor. "Are you sober?" she asked curiously.

Glancing up from her book, Etolié quirked an eyebrow. "That's offensive to presume," she replied with a wink, and then she returned to her reading.

"I apologize," Flowridia whispered, and she returned to eating her dinner.

Alone with only Demitri, she later lay wide awake in her bundle of blankets. She had been offered a tent, yes, but the promise of a thousand glittering stars to soothe her to sleep had been too perfect an offer to dismiss this time. High above, galaxies swirled, stars providing light the new moon could not, while the Daughter of Stars sat only a few feet away, taking first watch by the fire.

Sleep evaded her, thoughts of angelic goddesses drifting, instead, to her own ever-present goddess. A few more nights under the stars, but then what? Another night of pleasure? Ayla's game prickled at her nerves, and Flowridia had never actually chosen to play. She found herself smitten, but for what?

To think of Ayla, of her grace and power; Ayla's allure came from intoxicating words and a proud, dominating presence, one that dared you to approach, to plead for the honor of her company. Too fierce to be beautiful, yet Flowridia thought her the most perfect creature she'd ever seen.

But while Ayla had claimed her, Flowridia knew she herself held no sway. To think of Ayla tamed and docile . . . bent over for Imperator Casvir—

Flowridia flinched at the horrid thought.

An odd comfort, but Flowridia let her hand slip into her nightgown and grip the ear resting between her breasts. Three wishes, and if the worst came of their quest, a wish for the safety of her companions seemed a worthy endeavor.

Exhausted from travel, but more exhausted from her thoughts, Flowridia dared to brave the chill of night. She stood, leaving Demitri bundled among the bedspread. Etolié smiled as she approached, patting the space beside her. "Come to join the thrills of first watch?"

"I'm having trouble sleeping," Flowridia admitted, hoping Etolié wouldn't press for details.

Fortunately, it seemed Etolié had her own inner turmoil. "I'm sorry for depriving you of the epic tales of my slaver-crushing adventures," Etolié said, subdued. "I do love telling stories, but . . ." Etolié shut her eyes, the firelight luminous against her delicate features. "For all my victories, there are so many more failures."

Confused, Flowridia said, "But, Etolié, you've done so much good–"

"I've done good, yes, but now what? I'm caught up playing a political game, caring for the people I've freed, but what of the rest? For all the progress I've made, there's still slavery. There will always be slavery." Etolié stared up, past the fire, into the dark night. "People are free because of me, but people are also dead. Some of my failures hit closer to home. I try not to gloat when he's around."

Flowridia followed her gaze, realizing there was only one 'he' Etolié could be referring to.

"Half-giants make up a significant portion of our population, and Clarence thought it would do them well to see one of their own on the council. Which isn't to say he didn't earn it. There's a certain wisdom you can gain only through suffering."

Half-giants only existed because of slavery, bred as the result of atrocity and violence between giants and humans. Their lineage continued only because of the profitability of selling the offspring as slaves. In some countries, they were mere cattle, auctioned for their strength, sold as gladiators or cheap labor and bred amongst themselves to create the perfect workers, the perfect fighters, the perfect monsters . . .

Flowridia thought of Thalmus—gentle Thalmus, with his quiet demeanor and the thousands of scars littering his body.

Etolié released a soft sigh, her jaw quivering slightly. "'Etolié, Savior of Slaves,' they call me. My legacy continues. They sing songs of my deeds, light candles for my worship, and those in captivity pray to me for liberation. But you can't save everyone, Flowers. Sometimes, despite a lifetime of prayers, the Savior of Slaves never comes." Now, she shut her eyes, and a few silent tears spilled down her cheeks.

In the tentative peace of night, Flowridia's hand ran soothing lines along Etolié's thin figure.

Mother slept serenely in her bed, though one eye opened when Flowridia entered.

A lazy smile spread across the witch's face. "What mischief are you up to, Flower Child?"

Flowridia shut the door behind her, the plate of muffins balanced carefully in her hands. "I know you haven't been feeling well, so if you can't eat them, it's all right."

Mother chuckled and beckoned her forward. "Help me stack the pillows. I'll sit up and take a few bites."

Flowridia set the plate down on the bedside table and helped Mother sit comfortably in her bed. Her womb protruded quite obviously now. A month more, and Flowridia's sister would join them in the world.

Mother's sudden pained groan evoked panic from Flowridia. "Are you all right?"

Mother nodded, visibly forcing a smile. "Nothing your baking can't fix."

"Forgive me," Flowridia dared to say. "This seems like so much pain, but for what?"

Mother laughed, though her pale face betrayed her illness. "This is nothing compared to the pain of childbirth. But I've done this before. I'm perfectly capable."

"Aren't there any spells to help you? I could try and make you something."

"If you, my clever girl, wanted to try, I wouldn't stop you. But life requires sacrifice. We come into this world through blood and pain. Most of us leave the same way."

Flowridia paled at the thought, shying when Mother began to chuckle.

"I will be fine, Flower Child. I have a plan, I have sacrifices prepared, and all will be well. Little Demeter will be brought into this world, and you'll have a sister to love."

A hand on her wrist caused Flowridia to stiffen, but with care Mother placed it gently on her swollen stomach. "If you wait a moment, she might kick again."

Flowridia kept her hand still, sitting on the bed as she waited. There it was, a slightly nudging against her hand. She nearly laughed, so wide was her sudden smile.

"Magical, isn't it?" Mother said, and she released Flowridia's hand and placed her own atop her stomach. "I wasn't much older than you when I gave birth to my first daughter. A fierce little thing, and the only one I raised from infancy. But she died centuries ago, felled by soldiers from the Theocracy."

"I'm sorry," Flowridia whispered, but Mother shook her head.

"It was long ago, and I took my revenge. Those soldiers were the first to feed my garden."

An eerie thought, but Flowridia sincerely contemplated a moment if she'd do the same for her own child. She offered the plate of muffins forward. With a smile, Mother accepted and took a small bite of one. "You've always shied away from the men who've come here."

Her hands turned white as they gripped the plate. Chilled by the statement, Flowridia set the plate down for fear of dropping it.

"There's no shame if you don't feel ready for children–"

"I've never really considered it," Flowridia interrupted, hands fidgeting as she debated how to change the subject.

"No? Never spent your days as a little girl dreaming about a prince to sweep you off your feet?"

"Did you?"

"Many times. I grew up terribly poor, so I spent many nights dreaming of rich men carrying me off to their castles." She cracked a wry grin. "Funny how fate works."

Flowridia jumped at the opportunity for a subject change. "A castle would be lovely."

"But you wouldn't fill it with my granddaughters?"

Her slight shrug caused Mother to chuckle. "Like I said, I've never considered it. I don't think I could ever love a man enough to have his children."

"You don't have to love a man to have his children." Then, a wicked glint in Mother's eyes caused Flowridia's limbs to grow cold. "You don't even need a man at all, with the right spells . . . and the right woman."

Blushing fiercely, Flowridia's hands began to sweat as they gripped at the other. Stammering, she managed to say, "T-That's not what I meant."

"But it's what you want."

Flowridia could summon no response. When Mother laughed, she shut her eyes, willing away embarrassed tears.

"My little Flower Child," Mother said, wrapping her arms around Flowridia's stiff form, "who spends her nights dreaming of princesses to sweep her off her feet." Mother's chin rested on her shoulder, and she planted a kiss into her hair. "It's uncommon, but far from unheard of. The elves and the angels have done it since the dawn of time, penning great epics of beautiful women loving beautiful women. No need for shame, little angel. You are full of surprises."

Tears did leak from Flowridia's eyes, but of relief. No more fear.

For seven days, they travelled. Seven roses lay secured in her bag, and with each addition came a growing sense of dismay.

Tonight, the elusive twelfth rose would be delivered. Flowridia hoped Ayla held enough tact to not deliver the promise of her body with it, acutely aware of Thalmus and Etolié's proximity.

A slight headache weighed on her, minimal sleep having taken a toll, she figured. Peering from the window, the landscape held odd protrusions. Grasslands, yes, and cleared forests, but in the distance, enormous dirt towers stood erect.

Flowridia frowned, realizing holes littered the surface, reminding her of termite towers she had observed in her youth. With Aura by her side, Flowridia had once spent hours watching them skitter within a fallen tree. Their strength came from numbers, thousands of them steadily tearing it apart.

"Thalmus," she asked, "what are those towers?"

With some difficulty, Thalmus managed to strain his neck enough to see out the window. "Skalmite structures."

"What's a Skalmite?"

"When the planes converged, creatures other than demons and angels touched our world. Giants, gnolls, merfolk—creatures not meant for our atmosphere. Most acclimated. Skalmites never did. They weaken in the sunlight, and it's rumored the presence of magic drives them mad."

Etolié's voice and a fist against the back wall interrupted their conversation. "We need to stop. Flowers, grab your suitcase."

The carriage rolled to a stop. Flowridia swung open the door, allowing Demitri to jump out before letting her bare feet join him on the dirt road.

The surrounding guards all attempted not to gawk, but Etolié simply frowned, her wings serenely floating behind her back, apparently unperturbed by fact that she was entirely naked. Flowridia stopped, averting her eyes. "Etolié, what happened?"

"Can't you feel it?" Etolié asked, staring out into space. Her translucent wings did little to shield her modesty. "The magic here is twisted, like the strings got tangled. Don't try casting any spells, Flowers. You might get murderous results."

Thalmus appeared behind her, but the moment Etolié came into view, he immediately spun on his heels. He braced himself against the side of the carriage, growing stiff, avoiding Flowridia's eye when she came around. "Can you get me my suitcase?" she asked, and she wondered at the panic in his eyes as he processed her words.

Then, he released a steadying sigh. "What happened to Etolié's clothing?"

"I'm assuming she'll tell me once I get her a dress," Flowridia said carefully, sensing something raw and festering beneath Thalmus' stone exterior.

She watched as the stark shock on his face faded into something more void and resigned, annoyed even. Slowly, he reached up above the carriage and pulled her bag from the pile. Once he'd placed it on the ground, he hurried himself back into the carriage, slamming the door with more force than Flowridia deemed particularly necessary.

Flowridia carried her bag to where Etolié waited. "None of this explains why you're naked."

153

"Illusion spell. Fabric irritates me."

Frowning, Flowridia stopped. "You mean to tell me you never wear clothing?"

"Not a single day you've known me, Flowers."

Perhaps she tossed the dress with more force than necessary, but at least Etolié had something to wear. She quickly reshuffled the contents, unwilling to answer any questions about the roses cushioned by her underclothes.

"I'm going to have to ruin this. Wings and all."

"It's not mine, anyway. It's one of Marielle's."

Etolié ripped the back of the dress, creating enough of a hole for her wings to slip through. "Thanks."

Flowridia stood on the bench and managed to shove her suitcase back onto the roof. She sat beside Etolié, holding Demitri secure in her lap once the carriage began to move. "You never wear clothes?"

Etolié shook her head.

"Don't you get cold?"

Again, she shook her head.

Realization struck, and with it, horror. Flowridia struggled to find her voice. "So, when you loaned me a dress at Marielle's ball . . ?"

"It was as real as you believed it was."

Now that she thought about it, it had disappeared come morning. She'd assumed Etolié had taken it back. "What about your flasks? Where do you keep things?"

This time, Etolié grinned. When Flowridia cringed, she burst into laughter. "Flowers, it's all magic. I keep them all in my room, or in an extra-dimensional space, or even in the carriage, until I need them."

Flowridia frowned at the Celestial's crass implications. "You say all this like everyone has this knowledge."

"We're all born with different gifts, Flowers. I can manipulate planes and cast illusions. You're all about healing, and damn good at it too. Nothing wrong with that."

Flowridia shrugged. "All the talent in the world will mean nothing if I can't cast." Frowning, she added, "Etolié, what did you mean earlier, about murderous results and such?"

Etolié opened her mouth, and then shut it again, suddenly thoughtful as she looked from Demitri to Flowridia. "I don't know quite what it's like for you, having a familiar," she said slowly, "but as a Celestial, magic is an innate part of my being. I feel it. I breathe it. But here I feel . .

." She trailed off, biting her lip. "I feel muted. If magic is a tapestry, all the strings are crossed. I fear if I try to pluck at it, I'll touch the wrong one, or pull a few extras with it. I think if I focus, I might be able to conjure up something, but the risks of unintended results are astronomically high."

Flowridia considered this and the headache clouding her senses. "Demitri, what do you think?"

To her horror, Demitri simply stared. Understanding met her gaze, but no words filtered into her head.

Pure magic connected the two. Staring, she spoke again. "Demitri, if you're speaking, I can't hear it. Nod your head if you can understand me."

Demitri nodded, giving a slight bark as he did.

Flowridia pulled him close, realizing now what part of her senses were muted. "Etolié, I can't talk to him."

"It's a risk," Etolié said, reaching out to scratch the little wolf, "but if you focus, you might be able to hear him."

Flowridia shut her eyes, focusing, reaching out her senses to try and touch upon the natural world. She felt it clearly, as Etolié had said—it was as if a fog covered the tangled mass of magic surrounding them. She searched desperately for the single string connecting she and Demitri.

She knew the feeling of total isolation. After Aura's passing, her connection to her talents had vanished. This was something else.

Focused, she searched, hoping to navigate the minefield of energy. Several minutes of silence, and then a perfect, young voice. *I feel you!*

Flowridia's eyes shot open, and she smiled as she kissed him. "I don't know if I should do it again. But if you need me, we can talk."

"That said, Flowers," Etolié interrupted, "be careful. We don't know what's causing this."

"Have you ever felt anything like this before?"

"There are substances that can mute magical energy. When the Convergence happened, all sorts of nasty things fell into our world . . . stones, crystals, and other cursed things. I once met a slaver who utilized collars imbued with maldectine—a crystal that creates a void of space no magic can penetrate. Which, yes, if you snapped something like that on me, I'd be useless. Can you imagine the nasty weapons you could make out of that?"

Flowridia's breathing became steadily hurried. "And we're walking right into this?"

"If we can't use magic, neither can anyone else."

Then, a cry from afar. "Oi! We have guests!"

Flowridia immediately perked up. The carriage stopped. But the return cry was more vicious. The guards surrounding the carriage rushed forward, the hooves of their horses swift upon the ground. Sora, from her own horse, came from the front, stopping before Etolié and Flowridia, dagger drawn.

Thalmus burst out from the side of the carriage, nearly ripping the door from its handles. Set on the outside of the carriage, he took his treasured axe, one fashioned from the glass he lovingly tended.

An arrow embedded into the throat of one guard, blood spurting as he fell to the ground. Flowridia grabbed Demitri, instinctively cowering as a group of men appeared from behind an outcropping of trees. Small in stature, but stocky; they were unquestionably dwarves.

One met her gaze, and Flowridia saw animalistic fury. Scars ravished his skin, barely visible behind the tangle of hair grown into a beard. Brutal red sunburns blasted his form—all their forms—skin peeling in droves. Flowridia knew dwarves to be sophisticated and rational, if at times stand-offish; these men had lost their minds, it seemed.

Six of them rushed, all wielding large battle axes. Etolié grabbed Flowridia and cried, "Disappear, Sora!" before she shot into the air. Ethereal wings burst from her back. Translucent and floating, pure light radiated, but a shriek filled the air as arrows pierced the stunning display. Etolié spiraled downward, clutching Flowridia to her body as arrows began to rain into the air.

Etolié fell. Flowridia braced herself as her stomach threatened to fly out of her throat.

Stone arms stopped their impact. Thalmus held the three of them—Etolié, Flowridia, and Demitri—in one hand while wielding an axe in the other.

Guards cried out from the other end of the carriage. Thalmus swung, and four of the dwarves were swiped away with the ease one might brush aside saplings in a forest. Not dead, but flung aside, leaving only two.

Flowridia wrenched herself out of Etolié and Thalmus' grip, falling to the ground but managing to roll onto her knees. Just in time—a dwarf swung an axe at her shoulder.

Thalmus brought his weapon down. Through the skull, down the spine, splitting her would-be attacker in two. The halves fell aside, gore spilling onto the road, and Flowridia covered Demitri's eyes, but failed to protect him from the spray of blood.

Thalmus' axe swung again and missed, stunted by Flowridia's proximity. A dwarf leapt toward his knee, but a sudden kick to his stomach from Thalmus' gargantuan leg sent him flying.

But more dwarves appeared from the road, all as bloodthirsty as the rest. They came from the hills, the road, the trees, and Flowridia heard the horses cry out in terror. For all their talents, she knew they would be overwhelmed in moments.

"Tell them who we are, Thalmus!" she cried, and she leapt onto the bench of the carriage. "Tell them we were called from Staelash!"

With that, the dwarves suddenly stopped. Thalmus trembled from adrenaline, axe high in the air as the swarm of men slowed.

One spoke. "You're royalty?"

Flowridia felt her courage falter but managed to nod.

The dwarf turned to his companion, one with a bloodied face, and the two swapped words in a language Flowridia didn't understand. He turned back, victory etched into the cracked lines of his face. "We'll escort what's left of you to our leader," he said simply.

Looking out, Flowridia counted thirty armed dwarves staring back at them. Even if all the guards had survived, they were outnumbered twice over and more. To fight meant death. Flowridia stepped down from the bench and stood beside Thalmus.

Etolié groaned when Thalmus moved her into a cradled position, and Flowridia thought she might cry from relief—proof the Celestial still lived, pained as it was. Thalmus, however, stared at the crowd of dwarves, his dark eyes visibly calculating. "I need a moment to stabilize this woman," he said, but when he knelt down, an arrow flew past his head and into the carriage wheel.

"You'll be coming with us first," a dwarf said, bow readied.

Thalmus surveyed Etolié's limp form before standing, murder in his gaze. But he followed when told, and Flowridia grabbed his hand, fearful of separation.

In one arm, he cradled Etolié, and with the other he held Flowridia to his side. As they passed the other side of the carriage, she saw that her worst fears had come to pass. All the guards—all eight—lay dead and mutilated on the ground.

No sign of Sora, however. Flowridia prayed the half-elf found help quickly.

They walked, surrounded by a sea of dwarves, but Flowridia dared to speak. "Will she live?" she asked Thalmus, and the half-giant nodded.

"If I could remove the arrows from her back, she would be more comfortable. But Celestials are sturdier than they look."

Flowridia realized Etolié watched her. The Celestial smiled. "Don't worry, Flowers. Worst that can happen is I party with the acolytes for the rest of eternity."

The dark humor caused Flowridia's head to grow light. Tears prickled at her eyes, and she clutched Thalmus' shirt in her hand.

Skalmite mounds lay scattered across the scenery, growing dense in frequency as their group walked. Each mound was dotted with holes large enough for a dwarf to pass through with ease. Dwarves historically were underground dwellers, making homes of elaborate stone fortresses and simple burrows in the ground. Flowridia had never seen them, but it was well-known, and she wondered what interest they would have in grand, dirt towers.

Ahead, one structure jutted out far higher than the rest. Rising hundreds of feet into the air, the main entrance looked capable of accommodating even Thalmus with ease; two of him, even, one stacked upon the other. Full rings circled the odd structure. She wondered if it extended as far down as it did up.

At the base of the structure, a large encampment awaited them. Fires burned, even in the midday heat, and dwarves rushed between tents. All of them carried similar, painful sunburns. As underground dwellers, the sun didn't treat their pale skin with any kindness. But the brutality of it was unlike anything she had ever seen—raw blisters and peeling, angry burns coated every inch of exposed skin.

It was said Sol Kareena's light would burn those who lost her favor. Flowridia wondered what they had done.

Centered in the camp, there stood a cage filled with odd creatures, ones Flowridia had never seen. Standing as tall as she, they resembled vibrantly green insects, with skittering claws and enormous, bulging diamond eyes. They languished in the bright sunlight, most of them collapsed onto the ground.

Skalmites, Flowridia reasoned. Creatures not meant for this realm, or for the sun. With their insect-like physiques, she was reminded that there were bugs who chewed and spat. Perhaps this was how they had assembled the enormous towers.

They were stopped before a particularly large tent. A squat, muscular dwarf met them at the front, a parasol in hand. Perhaps stolen from an unfortunate traveler, it held a floral pattern, an odd juxtaposition to his leather armor and scarred skin. Flowridia, however, wouldn't have dared to comment on the dainty accessory, for fear of him ripping her lips from her face.

He surveyed their group, his large eyes settling on Flowridia. "They tell me you're the envoy from Staelash."

"Yes," Flowridia replied, holding tight to Thalmus. "We were on our way to Tholheim but your people–"

"Did exactly what I asked them to." The man stepped closer, his head not quite reaching her chest. "Which of you is Queen Marielle?"

Etolié looked out weakly, but Flowridia realized she was in no position to negotiate. Desperation fostered her courage, and she said, "I am Queen Marielle." Standing tall, she trembled as she stared. "Why did you attack my companions?"

"I sent for you. Don't you think I can forge my father's signature? I am Prince Falrir of Tholheim."

Whatever trap Flowridia had anticipated, this hadn't been it.

"We'll make this simple," Prince Falrir continued, studying her form. Flowridia's grip on Thalmus' shirt grew tighter, uncomfortable under the scrutinizing view. "Where's your orb?"

"My orb?"

"Queen Marielle always carries an orb in her breasts. You have no room to hide anything in those peaches of yours. Where is it?"

His crass choice of words unsettled her. When Thalmus pressed her closer to his side, she knew she wasn't the only one. "I don't often travel with it."

The Prince of Tholheim stared at her a full three seconds, his eyebrow furrowing, before barking out an order. "Tie them up!"

"Wait!" Flowridia cried, but her words meant nothing. Rough hands began to pull at her, ripping her away from Thalmus. "Do what you will, but let us heal my companion, please!"

"Who is she?"

"Magister Etolié, Chosen of Eionei–"

Scarcely had the words left her mouth before the prince cried, "Stop!" The dwarves immediately stepped away, unhanding Flowridia and the rest. "Eionei?"

Flowridia gave a quick nod.

"Chosen of the Drinking God?"

This time, Etolié managed to give a quick wave. Thalmus helped her sit up and face Prince Falrir. "And granddaughter, technically," Etolié said weakly. "Not for much longer if I keep bleeding out, though."

"Set her down! Give this woman some help!"

Thalmus watched them closely as he set Etolié on the ground. For the first time, Flowridia saw the wounds ravaging her body –her shoulder had become a bloodied mess, the fabric of her borrowed gown drenched in gore. Arrows embedded in her back added to the ravaged mess, and her wings, fully visible, hung limp and lacked their lustrous glow. The delicate skin, entirely translucent, had torn, puncture wounds leaving them ruined.

Had she been a mere mortal, Flowridia held no doubt she would have bled out.

When the dwarves tried to approach, Thalmus raised a hand to bat them away. "Leave her to me," he warned and plucked the offered rolls of bandages from their hands and proceeded to stop the wounds himself, ignoring the Celestial blood staining his arms.

As he worked, Flowridia turned to Prince Falrir. "What do you want from us?"

"A trade," he replied. "I'll forge a letter for you to sign. Your kingdom sends the orb, and we return their queen. Your kingdom sends the orb and a generous sampling of Etolié's personal brew, and we return their queen unspoiled."

"And what use have you for an orb?" Flowridia asked, not daring to contemplate what 'unspoiled' might mean.

"A gift for our God," Falrir said, and he gestured to the enormous dirt mound. "And we're promised a great reward."

Flowridia stared up at the colossal cave entrance, where no light seemed capable of breaching. "What's in there?"

"There's an artifact that would fetch a high price, but these bug bastards are protecting the damn thing. Our God has sworn to give us this and more in exchange for the orb."

Demitri shuffled fitfully in her arms. Flowridia adjusted her protective hold. "Who is your god?"

"You're a poor negotiator to be asking so many questions."

Bruised at the slight, she dared to follow when he returned to the entrance of his tent. "One more question, then, from the poor negotiator. What use has a god for an orb? Gods have no physical forms to wield them."

"The true Gods of this world have every use for them." The prince turned, and Flowridia followed his gaze to the Celestial lying on the ground. Blood-soaked bandages staunched the wounds littering her body. "These are our honored guests," his voice boomed. "And with the promise of ale, we'll be treating them kindly, you hear?" He turned to Flowridia, any good humor draining from his face. "If any of you try to run, we won't hesitate to roast the rest of you on a spit."

Flowridia barely managed a nod before the prince disappeared into his tent.

She nearly collapsed at Thalmus' side. He kept his focus on Etolié, but he leaned into her touch. "I overheard," he whispered.

"Something's going on. Something bigger than merely us."

Blood stained Thalmus' arms and hands as he pulled them away from Etolié's form. The Celestial stared up at them weakly and smiled. "Don't worry, Flowers," Etolié managed, though she cringed when she inhaled a pained breath. "Staelash will pay through the nose to keep us." Etolié sat up, though not without a whimper and Thalmus' hand on her back. "And if any of us can get more information from them," Etolié struggled to say, "I have the best chance. Dwarves love their alcohol."

"They already demanded a 'generous sampling' of your wares in exchange for a safe return."

"Help me stand," Etolié said, and she held out a hand. "I'll strike a deal with them."

Before Flowridia could object, Thalmus held out a hand, helping to leverage the wounded Celestial into standing.

Flowridia would never understand how Etolié could enthrall drunken men with such ease, but within the hour a roaring party had kindled by the largest bonfire. Even with her egregious wounds, Etolié managed to stand—with support—and captivate them with tales of her slavery-ending exploits. The ale in their barrels never seemed to end, and as the party continued, even the prince himself joined in the celebration.

Evening fell, and Thalmus and Flowridia watched the ruckus from afar. None dared approached them, not with Thalmus' palpable anger.

The ale kept flowing, and Flowridia attributed that to Etolié: if Eionei willed it, why would their alcohol run out? They said if one fell out of favor with Eionei, your brew would go sour or simply disappear. Their change in demeanor toward Etolié was a shot of luck she hoped would flow as endless as the stream of alcohol.

This meant gods could channel magic through the void, she realized.

Thalmus never went farther than an arm's reach from Flowridia, watching the growing shadows and unruly crowd with concern. The dwarves seemed at no risk of blacking out from drunkenness.

Flowridia whispered, her gaze kept to Etolié. "It was clever of them, to claim there was a slave camp. How could Staelash resist?" When Thalmus said nothing, she looked up to follow his gaze, far beyond the camp. "Are you thinking of running?"

"If I thought I could succeed, I would have already grabbed you and run."

Music met their ears. Etolié led them, despite her teetering form, in a riotous song, singing praises to the Drinking God who bestowed their ale upon them.

"And if I thought you could run," he continued, voice barely rumbling, "I would do what I could to cause a distraction. If your magic wasn't muted, we could succeed."

"You'd die, though."

"My life is mine to forfeit, if I so choose," he said gently, sincerity in the words. "I'd do it for you."

"Why though?" she pled softly. "You could run. If you left me, you'd survive. You could even take Demitri with you."

"It's my sworn duty to protect you, Queen Marielle," he replied, his fond smile revealing his jest. His arm settled against her back, holding her close. "There's nothing I wouldn't do to save my little flower girl."

Her fingers dug into his shirt.

She saw a flicker of movement—a frantic gesture from a lithe, dark-hued hand. Flowridia withheld a gasp when she saw Sora waving to get her attention from behind a tent.

With her hood pulled up over her head, it seemed the fire didn't dare to cast a shadow upon Sora's form. She moved quickly, darting silently between tents toward them. Flowridia nudged Thalmus, drawing his attention to the half-elven interloper as she crept into the open, but vanished after only a moment behind Thalmus' bulk. They stood back to back, and she offered a quick wink to Flowridia.

Thalmus sat on the ground, and Sora matched pace, keeping in the dark shadow cast by his back. Flowridia watched, aware of the dwarves who wandered the tents. Not all were drinking. Surely they'd notice a half-elf.

But Thalmus' body blocked her from view of the fire, at least. "I thought you would have gone to get help," Thalmus whispered.

"I couldn't send help if I didn't know where the camp was," Sora replied, and Flowridia swore anyone listening would only hear the wind. "But I overheard what the prince said, that they wanted an artifact in the Skalmite mound. I went inside to find it."

"None of them saw you, right?" Flowridia dared to ask.

Sora shook her head. "None of the dwarves know I'm here, trust me. They have camps set up inside, but the cave is enormous. I swear it goes deeper underground than it does above. And it's all a maze. They've barely tapped the surface. But I thought if I could fetch the artifact for them, they'd let you go, orb or not." She hushed her words, exhaling when a trio of dwarves came within feet of their small group.

But they continued on, seeing nothing amiss. "I found the Skalmites," Sora continued. "They're holed up at the bottom, thousands of them, all surrounding an enormous green crystal."

Flowridia remembered Etolié's comment about crystals capable of diluting magical energy. This must have been the dwarves' prize.

"They saw me, but they didn't attack. They let me come forward. Their leader spoke to me." Sora's gloved hands stroked lines against the dagger at her hip, prepared at a moment's notice to grab it and strike. "They don't speak like we do, but he touched my hand, and I swore it felt like he was riffling through my brain. Like, an initiation or something. Then, I heard a voice in my head. He asked for my help. The Skalmites are highly sensitive to magic. It drives them mad, and so they worship these crystals. The underground area used to be full of them, and for thousands of years they've protected them and lived in peace. They assembled them together into a single rock, sealing it with their own spit, but as it's grown larger, it's grown more powerful. It's attracting attention.

"The dwarves have been camping here for months now," Sora continued, "but they don't know how to navigate the tower. They come in raids and take prisoners, but now the Skalmites huddle in the center for safety."

"They won't stop," Flowridia said, forcing her trembling voice to stay quiet. "They say their god will come to steal it for them."

"We have to protect the crystal," Sora said. "God's will or not, these people will die without it."

But what hope did they have? Marielle would surely cave to Prince Falrir's demands. Within days, the orb would be delivered. In the meantime, there were only four of them, all with talents but stunted in their magic. Sora seemed unhindered, and Thalmus maintained his strength and will, but Etolié could only distract their capturers for so long. Even with magic, Flowridia knew she hadn't a wish to try and save them.

. . . a wish?

"Sora," she said, shifting to hand Demitri to Thalmus, "how important is this?"

"You're asking me the importance of preventing genocide?"

"Yes, but if you had three wishes in the whole world, would you use one on this?"

Sora frowned. "That's oddly specific."

Flowridia stood up as her hand plunged into the collar of her dress. She withdrew the ear and immediately felt both sets of eyes on the ghastly accessory. Flowridia looked up at the mouth of the cave, imagining the poor Skalmites huddled at the center, recalling those who languished within the camp, and trembled as she contemplated what to say.

"What is that?" Thalmus asked, his tone severe.

"A gift from Nox'Kartha," she said, purposefully cryptic. "Marielle entrusted it to me."

Sora remained in the shadow. The bonfire sat only twenty feet away at most, and dwarves still walked freely back and forth. "What does it do?" the half-elf asked.

"Grants wishes. We have three." Flowridia stared at the eerie artifact, the smooth lines, the pointed tip. It felt cool in her palm, and the earrings, as blue as the eyes of she who owned the other set, glittered in the firelight. "I don't quite know how it works," she admitted, and braced herself. She took a deep breath and spoke. "Ayla, I–"

"Ayla?" She only vaguely heard Thalmus' voice.

"I don't know if you can hear me, but . . . Protect the crystal, and let us go home. Please." Then, to punctuate the words, she kissed the ear, right on the lobe, just as cold lips nibbled at her own.

Flowridia gasped, turning to see Ayla's disfigured face peering from behind her shoulder. "Hello there, Flowra," she cooed, and she placed the twelfth rose into Flowridia's hand.

Ayla vanished. Flowridia heard nothing but her own breathing.

Screams erupted from the bonfire. Flowridia turned in time to see Ayla's entire arm burst through the chest of one of the dwarves. She withdrew; his spine came with it. Whirling around, the force shattered the skull of another, the spine embedding itself within. She dove at Etolié, but missed her body, vanishing instead into the Celestial's shadow.

Ayla emerged not a second later from a larger dwarven shadow, twirling as she ripped his back from base to neck with a single swipe of her dagger. She threw it at another's neck and pulled a second from her belt.

Each light step held such grace as she danced through the battlefield. Any partner who dared to match her met a swift, choreographed end. Creative cruelty became her signature; she sliced one's stomach with careful precision, then plunged her hand into the slit and withdrew a ribbon of entrails. She pulled the viscera apart and wrapped it around another's neck, a noose she dragged behind as she continued her onslaught.

Blood sprayed. Screams muted. Ayla danced, and each smooth motion brought death. The stage cleared in mere seconds, decorated with severed heads and blood-stained dirt. Ayla turned to Flowridia, delight in her wide grin, her eyes void of color. Fangs jutted from her gore-splattered face.

She dove into Etolié's shadow, the Celestial the sole survivor among the display of mutilated bodies.

Flowridia's frantic heart nearly stopped when Ayla stepped out beside her. Claws gripped her arms. "Care to spark the main attraction?" When Flowridia didn't immediately respond, Ayla released a gleeful laugh.

The claws on her arms suddenly gripped tight, and Flowridia gasped when nails pierced her skin. Blood welled, but Ayla kept her hold strong, pressing into her arms. Flowridia whimpered, fear outweighing the pain, and still Ayla laughed, withdrawing her hands and running for the mouth of the cave.

Shaking, Flowridia's arms wrapped around her body, and she shrieked when strong hands grabbed her. But it was merely Thalmus, who pulled her into a protective hold, his face etched with shock and fury.

The two watched as Ayla leapt up and gripped the top of the cave. Who could say how she balanced, but with Flowridia's blood on her fingers, she began to paint a symbol at the top of the entrance.

It spoke of a legend, one her mother once told, of the ancient monster who chilled the blood of every creature— The Endless Night. Living in the deep recesses of the underground shadows, stories said it could be summoned and turned upon one's enemies by writing the symbol upon their door.

And there, in Flowridia's blood, Ayla drew that ancient rune, large enough for all to see. Once completed, she landed on the ground with nimble feet and inspected her work, casually licking her fingers clean as she did. Flowridia watched as she stopped and grinned, tongue twirling languidly against her forefinger.

Ayla turned. "Stay to watch the show, darling. You'll see me at the next sunset," she said, and with a coy wink she blew a kiss towards Flowridia.

Ayla disappeared inside the cave.

In the ensuing silence, Flowridia's head grew light. Hands trembling, she let the ear drop to her chest. The rose shook her in hand.

"What is that?" Thalmus' voice rumbled.

"'The Endless Night,'" Flowridia said. "My mother said it was an ancient being who dwelled in the deepest parts of caves."

"It isn't only an underground legend," Sora whispered. "The elves called it 'The Scourge.' It was the story every child was told to keep them in their beds, but it hasn't been heard from in centuries."

"Flowers!"

With Thalmus supporting her, Flowridia jumped at the sudden exclamation. Etolié stumbled toward them, her borrowed dress splattered with dwarven blood. She looked near collapsing; Sora ran to steady her. "What the *fuck* was all that?! Why is Ayla here?"

Flowridia held the ear up from where it dangled freely at her neck. "This is a gift from Imperator Casvir," she whispered, "after the death of the Theocracy's diplomats." She stared entranced at the mouth of the cave, at the symbol written in her blood. "Marielle entrusted it to me."

"Oh, did she? Funny that the rest of us hadn't heard of this–" Etolié's sudden coughing fit interrupted her rage, droplets of blood falling to the earth. Sora's grip tightened as she pulled the Celestial against her body for support. After a few painful heaves, Etolié managed to say, "Whatever it all means, Flowers, we're not sticking around to find out."

"Ayla said I should stay–"

"Ayla wrote an ancient demon symbol on the wall with your blood, so her opinion is invalid–" Again, Etolié's words were stolen by violent coughs.

Sora helped guide her to the floor. "With due respect, Magister Etolié, you're in no position to travel. If you're able to last, I can run and send word–"

"It took us a week on horseback to get here," Etolié interrupted, holding her head in her trembling hands. "But you can make it to the carriage. My mirror is there, in my bag. Dig it out, then go beyond the bounds of this non-magic void. You can contact Lara; she'll send help."

"Of course." Sora stood immediately, and with an affirming nod to Etolié, ran off into the night.

From within the insect mound, faint cries of terror were heard.

Thalmus knelt down beside Flowridia, inspecting the wounds on her arm. "Not too deep, but let me at least stop the bleeding." He tore off the ruined sleeves and, with what remained of the bandages for Etolié, tentatively wrapped her upper arms.

Flowridia said nothing, silent as she stared at the mouth of the cave. A gaping maw, screaming faintly—soon, blood would spill forth in droves.

Once done, Thalmus stood. "I'm going to check the camp for survivors," he said gravely, stepping out to inspect the mutilated bodies.

Flowridia's lip trembled, and she managed a nod, unable to say anything more. In slow movements, she turned and moved to follow Thalmus, who inspected each bloodied figure scattered about the bonfire.

With her bare feet, Flowridia stepped carefully. To think of treading on spilled organs or mutilated flesh made her queasy. She lifted her skirts, knowing full-well that bloodstains never quite faded.

The images of corpses, torn apart and ruined, were hardly an oddity, not to her. Shredded flesh and crushed organs littered the area. Bits of bone threatened to sliver into her feet; Each gouged eye stared up to the night sky. Flowridia let her gaze linger at each one.

"Clean up this mess, Flower Child." Mother pointed at the floor, then returned to the cutting board, the 'slunk' of her knife against the wood and flesh sickening to Flowridia's stomach. "Use the mop to push what's left into the swamp."

Suddenly queasy, Flowridia stumbled out of the circle of carnage and shut her eyes. Deep breaths filled her lungs, yet the scene of fresh blood seemed inescapable.

Thalmus' gentle voice cut through her sickness. "Flowra, Prince Falrir is dead."

Her mind thought, 'good riddance,' but still her heart ached.

Thalmus stepped toward the captive Skalmites, all of whom stared in abject horror at the scene. They cowered in

Thalmus' presence, gathering together at the center of their cage.

Metal sheared and cracked. Thalmus ripped the door aside, then let them be.

Flowridia stepped out of the ruined camp. Rose in hand, she stared at the mouth of the cave, letting every faint scream caress and sing at her senses. A penance. Flowridia shut her eyes.

She knew not how long she waited before the cries in the cave grew suddenly louder. A group of dwarves burst from the shadowed entrance, all of them bleeding, limping, and with eyes wider than saucers. One by one, they ran, each more desperate than the last.

From the cave, a white claw swiped out and grabbed the straggler. A quick cry, a sickening squish, then silence. Blood seeped from the darkness.

Not Ayla's claw. Too large to be Ayla's.

The dwarves—there were only five—stopped once they reached what remained of their camp. Ignoring Flowridia and Etolié, they set to work patching their wounds.

Thus began the pattern of the night. Every few hours, dwarves ran from the cave, all of them damaged, bleeding, some mutilated beyond what even magic could repair. Most of them escaped the cave and ran into the wilds, but others, those with injured companions, remained behind, tending to their wounded and keeping their distance.

Sunlight flickered above the horizon. Thalmus, at Flowridia's admonition, slept, and Etolié lay with her head on Flowridia's thigh, not asleep but resting. She coughed, and blood stained Flowridia's skirts.

Demitri sniffed the ground within arm's reach of Flowridia. Though exhaustion pulled at Flowridia's eyelids, to shut her eyes meant to see white fangs glinting in the darkness.

Instead, she watched each group as it fled the cave, flinching if claws grabbed the last few.

Around midday, a group of Skalmites appeared.

Seeing the insect-like creatures caused Flowridia to freeze, but then she realized that they, too, were damaged and bleeding. Green liquid seeped from deep wounds, and Flowridia felt Etolié shuffle and sit up.

"I assume attacking our bug friends wasn't part of the agreement?" A hint of sardonic ire seeped into her voice, exhausted as she was.

"I didn't ask for that," Flowridia whispered. "I asked for her to protect the crystal." Realization clenched her gut. "I *only* wished for her to protect the crystal."

Guilt brought tears to her eyes, but Flowridia forced them back, tentative as she approached the wounded Skalmites. They had joined with those formerly caged, the ones Thalmus had freed, and though they visibly languished in the sun, Flowridia saw joy at their reunion.

With careful steps and open palms—the universal sign for peace—she approached the group. They eyed her with suspicion, pincers snapping as a threat. Flowridia nearly forgot her crippled magic, daring to summon a bit of light—

Only to have it fizzle with a spark.

Apparently her good intentions were conveyed, because while the Skalmites remained visibly wary, their aggression lowered to a mere simmer, then finally ceased.

Keeping careful watch on the healthy ones, Flowridia knelt beside one whose limbs seeped viscous, green liquid. She tore a strip of cloth from her skirt and offered it forward. When it showed no aggression, Flowridia hesitantly moved to wrap the cloth around the exoskeletal-wound, wondering if it would do any good at all.

Skalmites had an entirely foreign anatomy, but pressure did stop the seeping liquid. When the Skalmite offered another injured extremity, Flowridia reasoned she had done something right. She smiled gently, not showing her teeth in case it indicated aggression, and tore another strip from her long skirt.

To her surprise, another Skalmite removed the fraying, make-shift bandage from its companion, then, from its odd, proboscis-like mouth, spat on the wound. A murky, gelatinous substance covered the injury.

It used the cloth to wipe away green liquid from another cut on the Skalmite and spat again. Flowridia followed its lead, helping to clean Skalmite wounds before another came to seal them shut.

And so, she spent her afternoon aiding the wounded Skalmites and steadily drowning in the guilt of knowing it was she who had caused them this pain.

The day progressed. More survivors left the dark cave. The screams never stopped; not entirely.

Night fell, and perhaps a hundred total Skalmites camped around them. The bonfire still burned, casting insect-like shadows across the dark landscape and illuminating the few dwarves who remained.

Loud cries echoed through the cave, a sign that more survivors might soon emerge. A group of dwarves ran from the cave entrance. One, two, three—

Something grabbed the last and pulled it back. A slight 'thud' echoed across the silent night. The decapitated body rolled from the cave entrance.

A slight clink of claws on rock, and a monster slowly emerged, nearly as tall as the mouth of the cave. Flowridia shrank as it turned its glowing eyes upon her. Vivid blue, the same shade as Ayla's, but the creature facing them was elongated, twisted, limbs too long as it skittered forward on all fours. Its skeletal face held a nightmarish mouth of endless depth, fanged and stained with blood. A burn covered half its face, raw and meaty, with exposed bone and muscle quivering as the jaw hung slack.

Flowridia slowly stood, gripping her gifted rose in her hand as she stared up at the beast. "Ayla?"

The creature stepped forward, and the grin spreading across its face was one and the same.

It leapt. Flowridia gasped, falling to the ground as the monstrosity flew toward her. She shut her eyes, only to hear bone crunch. Thalmus stood above her, his axe meeting the monster's chest and batting it away.

The creature rose, twice taller than Thalmus. A grotesque roar, wet and guttural, ripped from its throat. Again, Thalmus swung, smashing its ribs to bits. Flowridia watched in horror as the creature toppled but immediately leapt to its feet. Bone visibly shifted inside its form, knitting back together.

Flowridia stood up as Thalmus moved to swing again. The creature dodged and bolted forward, tackling Thalmus to the ground and screeching in his face, guttural and shrill all at once, before looking up at the trembling Skalmites and grinning with palpable glee.

"Ayla, stop!" Flowridia screamed, vocal chords tearing at the force.

To her surprise and horror, it listened. It stepped off Thalmus and stared at her with glowing, pupil-less eyes. Petrified, Flowridia quivered as she came forward. "Ayla, please," she begged, and she offered a hand. "The wish is fulfilled. The crystal is safe. Please, let everyone go."

A curious gaze matched her own. Unmistakable, that grin. It reached out a clawed hand, one that matched her own body in size. They touched—

Light suddenly blinded them. Etolié approached, wings aloft, her entire form lit from within.

The monster shrieked at the approaching combatant. Claws gripped Flowridia's body. Nails shredded the skin of her stomach and chest as the monster threw her aside, her form ripped from base to neck. Flowridia landed sprawled, searing pain radiating across her skin. Blood seeped from beneath her ruined dress.

Though darkness threatened to steal her consciousness, Flowridia watched as Etolié's form twisted and grew. In her hand, a summoned quarterstaff appeared, and Etolié—but not Etolié, morphed together with her god—dodged what might have been a killing blow to the neck.

The monster leapt. Light burst from the staff. Bombarded by an otherworldly source, the monster screamed, thrown aside like a ragdoll. Etolié's eyes held the same vibrant glow as the monster's, pupil-less and ominous. No playful banter this time. Bathed in ethereal, holy light, she raised a hand. Stars fell from the sky, pelting the creature, tearing through those thin, elongated limbs.

A shriek filled the night. The monster reared onto its hind legs, mouth wide as it screamed. It leapt.

In a single sweep, Etolié's quarterstaff ripped through the monster's neck. The light burned through. A headless monstrosity fell to the ground.

The body turned to blackened dust, raining upon the ground and sweeping away in the wind. Flowridia's eyes closed, finally succumbing to darkness.

Chapter 9

Flowridia awoke to daylight and a relieved cry. "Thalmus, she's awake!"

Sunlight burned her sensitive eyes, but as Flowridia blinked into consciousness, she saw the outline of Sora's face staring down at her. Pain shot through her as she tried to sit up. Lithe hands pushed down on her shoulders. "You need to stay down."

Flowridia managed to nod as Thalmus' shadow blocked the sun completely. His finger moved to stroke her hair. "How are you feeling?" he asked gently.

A wet tongue on Flowridia's cheek made her smile. Demitri nudged her hair. "What's going on?"

Clicking from above stole her attention. She turned and saw a Skalmite casually stare, then dare to approach. "I had nothing to stitch you up with," she heard Thalmus say. "But they stepped in to save you."

The Skalmite in question leaned in close to her chest, and Flowridia followed its gaze, realizing that the same murky, gooey substance they had used to bind their own wounds now formed a trail from her sternum to her hips. The blood-stained gown hardly held together, the dress having torn along the same line as the searing wound.

Before she could sit up, Thalmus held her shoulders, just as Sora had. "You're fine. You're safe," he soothed. "You gave us a scare, but the wound is shallow."

The Skalmite continued clicking over her, reminding Flowridia of a mother hen to its chicks. Still, the news of her continued survival did little to soothe her, not with the memory of leering teeth behind her eyelids. But with it came the image of the headless monstrosity.

"I'm fine, if a little bruised. I'm not sure about Etolié."

173

Panic coursed through Flowridia. "What's wrong with Etolié?"

"She called upon Eionei. However . . ." He looked over, frowning at some sight in the distance.

Flowridia turned her head and saw Etolié bent over by the cave. Retching could be heard, but instead of vomit, blood spilled from her mouth. Sora stood at arm's length, stiffly patting her back.

"Something tore inside of her, channeling that much power through her body. She won't let me look at her, says she's fine." Thalmus grit his teeth. "She also hasn't had a drink since the dwarves were slaughtered. Withdrawal hasn't been kind to her."

"We need to get her to Staelash," Flowridia said, trying again to sit up.

But Thalmus kept her down and shook his head. "The empress' people are on their way. Sora returned before sunrise. She says they've sent a carriage with medical supplies. Etolié refuses to leave without securing the crystal and looking for more Skalmite survivors." Thalmus surveyed the horizon, and Flowridia realized it would be evening soon. "The dwarves left, those that survived, at least."

Those that survived . . . Flowridia turned again toward the cave, her mind in a fog, and watched as Etolié struggled to walk, using the wall as a support.

Above the cave entrance loomed the symbol of The Endless Night.

Demitri appeared in her view, his inquisitive nose sniffing her face. His tongue licked her forehead, conveying what comfort he could.

When he stepped away, he returned with a blood-stained rose between his teeth.

In the aftermath of so much blood, a little more did nothing to disturb her.

As Flowridia tried to soothe the shrieking infant, it threatened to slip from her arms, still covered in fluids. She thought it looked more like a demon than a child. Yet, it pulled a tenderness from her she never expected.

As Mother rested, she cleaned the baby of blood and other fluids and found pink, soft skin, each stroke of the wet cloth revealing something more and more human.

She loved him, this odd little crying creature in her arms. Flowridia held her brother to her chest and soothed his scared soul.

She wondered if Mother would keep him, or if he would be sent away like the rest of her children. Flowridia hoped he stayed.

"Flower Child," came the exhausted plea, "bring her over. She needs fed."

Flowridia obeyed and brought the infant over to the blood-soaked bed. "He," Flowridia corrected. "He needs fed."

Mother's pale face quirked an eyebrow. "You're either being funny or idiotic."

With care, Flowridia held the cleaned infant forward, placing him gently into his mother's arms. "Neither," she said, offended at the remark. "This child is a boy."

"And so it is," Mother replied as she held the baby in her arms. "I've never birthed a boy before."

Flowridia kept her gaze on the squirming infant, watching as he reached for his mother with tiny, pudgy fingers. "I still like the name 'Demeter.' I know it's a girl's name, but we could change it. Perhaps—"

With an exasperated sigh, Mother stood, bracing herself against the wall as she steadied herself. "Useless," she spat, and she tore from the room.

Flowridia followed, confused and panicked. "What do you mean?"

"Boys can't inherit my potential. Have you ever heard of a male witch, Flower Child?"

Flowridia had not, and she gasped when Mother nearly dropped the baby into her arms.

"Take care of it," Mother said, and in her other hand she offered a knife.

The roses rested at her chest, one splattered with blood. Flowridia flinched when she attempted to sit up. The scars remained tender, and against her wishes a pained sigh left her throat. The Skalmite's spit had wiped away without a trace, leaving only patched skin for her to heal with her own magic.

A carriage had been sent, a rip between the planes created by the empress allowing it to appear outside the bounds of the crystal's power.

Thalmus watched from the opposite bench. The carriage rolled smoothly, lulling Flowridia's tired body. His voice did little to soothe her troubled mind. "You talk in your sleep."

Flowridia shut her eyes. "I know," she whispered.

Thalmus said nothing else, for which Flowridia was grateful. Though her wounds had healed, the thought of speaking brought pain.

In the early evening, Marielle and Zorlaeus waited at the gates. Flowridia had scarcely stepped out when she felt herself pulled into a careful hug. "Oh, Flowridia, I was so worried," Marielle said, letting her fingers trace lines against her back.

The embrace was enough to pull tears from Flowridia's eyes. "So was I," she replied, but she couldn't summon the laugh meant to accompany it.

"Are you injured?"

Flowridia shook her head. "But I would like a bath. And sleep. I healed myself."

"Once Etolié has returned, we'll have a meeting," Marielle said, and she pulled away enough to study her face. "Are you sure you're all right?"

Flowridia knew Marielle didn't refer to her physical well-being. "I need sleep," she repeated.

Marielle nodded, but Flowridia could see her skepticism. "If you need anything at all, please find me. Or Thalmus. Someone." She engulfed Flowridia again in a hug. "Don't be afraid to talk."

Flowridia nodded in her arms, eyes still glistening. She wondered what Marielle knew.

It didn't matter. She would know everything after their meeting.

Demitri kept close by her heels, and she carried her bag by her side. *You've barely said anything.*

"I don't know what there is to say, Demitri," Flowridia replied, voice soft. The young wolf brushed against her knee as they walked. "I need to be alone."

Without me?

Up the stairs, and then Flowridia managed a smile. "No, dearest Demitri. I always want you."

She swung the door open. The flickering of a thousand candles met her gaze, and Flowridia immediately knew.

Stepping fully inside, she braced herself as she turned to see Ayla by the window. Her black dress, painted on by appearances, left little to the imagination, though Flowridia was intimately familiar with what lay underneath. A coy grin graced Ayla's face, still burned and charred. "Good evening."

Flowridia kept her gaze down and turned when she realized Demitri had already begun trotting down the hall. "Demitri–"

The small wolf turned. *You need alone time.*

Flowridia shut the door, knowing he was right. "You look like you're feeling better."

Ayla chuckled darkly and said, "Oh, your little group was adorable." Her grin turned wicked. "The crystal is yours now. Who better to protect it?"

Gaze to the floor, Flowridia nodded.

"You and yours are home safe."

Again, she nodded. Flowridia shut her eyes, angry at her welling tears.

"You could map out the catacombs and set up an impressive stronghold, your treasure vaults are full of dwarven spoils, and–" Her tone grew dark, intense. "... you and your friends will never be forgotten. Stories will be told for generations about the return of The Endless Night and those who heroically fought it. A bit of collateral damage, sure, but heroes never escape unscathed."

Flowridia sniffed, her form trembling as she fought to push away her tears. "But at what cost?"

"Now, now," Ayla cooed, "you got exactly what you wanted." Flowridia heard the faint rustling of fabric; Ayla approached. "Exactly what *you* asked for." With a gentleness that caused Flowridia to tense, Ayla put her hands on either side of Flowridia's face and placed a kiss on her forehead.

"I–" Flowridia took a step back. "I-I still have scars from–" A tear trailed down her face. Instinctively, she turned away, dabbing at her eyes with her long sleeves. "You don't want to see them."

"Scars have never bothered me." Ayla's hands gently pulled her back. Flowridia stiffened as Ayla began planting small kisses along her jaw and down her neck, trailing down to the top of the brutal gash at the collar of her dress.

Flowridia stood still, unsure of how to react. Ayla leaned up and said, "You did bring my flowers, right?"

When Flowridia stepped away, Ayla let her, and she dropped to her knees and rummaged through her suitcase. She withdrew the roses, though they had wilted in the passing days, and offered them forward.

Ayla took them and smoothly tossed them to the ground. Her grin spelled triumph, and she offered a pale hand. "Come."

Flowridia stared down at her lithe fingers, trying to reconcile the view of those gentle hands with the claws that had torn through her like paper. Not days before, blood had seeped through those fingers, raining down and snuffing out the lives of thousands.

Flowridia reached out to accept the offering and realized the blood soaking Ayla's hands had stained hers too. When she looked up, it wasn't Ayla's smile she saw, but the fanged grin of the monster before it ripped her to ribbons.

"Flowra?"

A torrential sob ripped through Flowridia's body. Her hands flew to cover her face, though tears leaked through her fingers. The memory of pain and turmoil, of screams and horror and blood-stained earth, roared through her mind, yet paled to the all-consuming shame threatening to drown her.

She managed one word: *"Why?"*

The answer came in sensuous tones, along with a light touch upon her waist, one that would surely lead her to hell. "You faced an enemy you had no hope to defeat."

"The Endless Night was–" Flowridia gasped when the soft hands at her waist turned to claws, threatening to pierce her skin.

"Was it The Endless Night who threatened to force itself upon you and kill your friends? Funny, I seem to recall it saving your life." Ice steadily rose in Ayla's voice, freezing Flowridia to her core as she whispered, "When faced with monstrosity, become the greater monster. The sting of victory will fade with time."

When Flowridia said nothing, Ayla's grip softened again. Her voice cooed, "There is no monster here, my sweet Flowra. I'll show you there's no need to be afraid."

When cool hands slid across her dress and groped her, when kisses were peppered along her neck, Flowridia shook her head, gasping sobs stealing her voice. "Ayla, I—I can't–"

Ayla released her, and Flowridia crumpled to the floor, weeping into her hands. Amidst her cries, something soft brushed against her; instinctively, Flowridia reached out and clutched the fabric of Ayla's dress, desperately clinging within the storm of her tears.

Flowridia looked up, and through her misted, tear-stained vision, she met an indifferent gaze, one bearing nightmarish features—a burn hardly healed. Ayla raised a single eyebrow. "Pathetic doesn't suit you."

Mother's sneer crippled her already waning resolve. "Pathetic doesn't suit you," she said, grabbing Flowridia's trembling hand. Together, they stabbed the knife down, plunging it into the stomach of the screaming infant.

Flowridia felt the same blow, stomach pained at the sharp remark.

"I'll return in the morning, once you've cried yourself to sleep. Perhaps you'll remember to be grateful for all I've done for you."

"If I'm such a burden," Flowridia whispered, lip trembling despite her words, "don't come back."

Ayla stood straight, stare suddenly sharp. "I beg your pardon?"

The urge to hide from that pointed glare nearly overwhelmed her, but Flowridia matched it as she trembled from tears. "I'm sorry I burned you," she managed, words shaking, "but now the debt is repaid." Her hand touched the top of the scar that peaked at her sternum, shined and tender. "Please, go."

When Ayla stepped forward, Flowridia shrunk back, prepared to accept death as penance for her crimes. Such pride in Ayla's face, but something else, something severe beyond even the disfiguration spreading out from her ear. Ayla turned aside, her body vanishing behind the cracked door of the wardrobe.

Alone, Flowridia crawled onto her bed and curled into a ball, grabbing the blankets and wrapping them around her shaking form. Crippling sobs tore through her, tears falling fast. No relief; only pain. She buried herself underneath the thick blankets, disappearing as the sun set outside her window.

Then, a familiar voice drifted through her head. *Mom?*

Flowridia sat up. At the foot of her bed stood Ayla, and in her arms, gently stroked by her thin fingers, was Demitri. Trembling, Flowridia reached out. Ayla placed the pup in her arms.

Flowridia held Demitri tight, breathing ragged as she pulled comfort from his soft fur and the lick on her jaw. She kept her stare for Ayla, who watched the scene with an odd vulnerability. Ayla's gaze shot to the ground, and in meticulous, stiff movements, she climbed on the bed and slid herself toward the pair.

Arms snaked around Flowridia's form, but Ayla said nothing as she pulled Flowridia down into her lap. She brought the blanket up to cover Flowridia's shoulders. "Try and sleep," Ayla whispered, her fingers soothing against Flowridia's bare arm. "I cannot promise I'll be here when you awaken."

With Demitri cradled in her arms, Flowridia settled herself against Ayla's body. Despite her dirty clothes and shoes, the blood that clung to her hair, she breathed in deep and shut her eyes. Tears still fell.

Soft, barely a whisper in her ear, Ayla began to hum. Far from unpleasant, her voice held an airy quality, but the tune she sang, heartfelt and melancholy, resonated through Flowridia's head.

She clung to the sound, letting it soothe her to sleep.

The next morning, twelve roses sat in a bouquet on her bedside table. Flowridia steadily blinked into wakefulness, smiling fondly in the dim morning light.

The scratching of a pen on paper alerted her to the presence beside her. She turned over, only to see Ayla sitting in her bed, legs under the covers. The lithe woman, still fully dressed and hair well-kempt, glanced down from the nondescript book in her hand. The other held a pen. "Good morning," Ayla said, and she turned the book toward her.

Flowridia saw a detailed ink drawing of her own sleeping image, her breath leaving her as she studied the near-perfect likeness. Each individual strand of hair seemed ready to burst from the page, her lips glossy, and even the gentle blemishes of her face—her faint freckles and hints of scars—held a delicate beauty about them. A stunning image, and Flowridia felt heat color her cheeks.

This was how Ayla saw her. "It's beautiful."

"You can have it. I have others like it," Ayla said, and she ripped the page from the book and leaned over to place it on Flowridia's table. She set the book aside and slid down next to Flowridia and the still-snoozing Demitri.

"I didn't expect you to be here," Flowridia said softly, and when Ayla pressed their lips together, she smiled wide.

A vicious grin tugged at Ayla's mouth as she pulled away. "What's the worst Casvir can do? Kill me?" She chuckled and snaked her arms around Flowridia's waist, keeping their bodies flush together. "Besides, I got carried away with drawing. After you fell asleep, I realized how peaceful you are to watch."

An odd statement, and Flowridia raised an eyebrow. "I would have thought you already knew that, with how often you'd snuck into my bedroom."

"Clever girl," Ayla said, and she planted a kiss on Flowridia's cheek.

Feeling brave, Flowridia dared to add, "And you have other drawings like it, you said?"

A wide and dangerous grin spread across Ayla's face. "Most are from memory. But it's been a long time since I've had as pretty a subject as you."

Somewhere in the depths of Flowridia's sense of self-preservation, she suspected she ought to object to this, yet this sudden change in Ayla's decorum, while jarring, wasn't unappreciated. Instead, she said, "How did you learn to draw so well?"

Ayla chuckled. "When you've lived as many centuries as I have, you pick up a few hobbies." Her hand moved up to stroke Flowridia's hair, her neck, and as she traced down, Ayla flinched at the scar. She glanced down and leaned in to place a kiss at the top, above the collar of Flowridia's dress. "Give it time. It will fade."

Demitri stirred, perhaps awakened by their conversing. In clumsy motions, he approached Ayla, even as she leaned away, visibly wary.

"It's all right if you touch him," Flowridia said, smiling softly. "You don't need my permission; only his."

In tentative motions, Ayla offered a hand forward, but Demitri ignored it. Instead he settled into Ayla's lap, curling into a ball while Ayla kept her hands up, oddly stiff.

But before Flowridia could comment, Ayla lowered her hands, letting one settle onto Demitri's back with a quiet smile.

Flowridia watched them fondly, the peaceful scene warming her tender heart. "Ayla, last night . . ." Her breath hitched when Ayla glanced up. "I shouldn't have told you to leave. I'm sorry."

Ayla held her gaze, her smile fading as she shook her head. "We both said terrible things." When she returned her attention to Demitri, Flowridia knew Ayla would say nothing more.

"You mentioned something else," Flowridia dared to push. When she hesitated, Ayla reached over to cup her cheek, softness returning to the undead woman's expression. "Are you The Endless Night?"

"Oh, Flowra," Ayla said, amusement in her words. "I promise, I am no demon." She scattered kisses across Flowridia's forehead, and with each one Flowridia felt her body relax. A firm kiss pressed against her lips. "No need to worry yourself."

Ayla said nothing more, instead continuing those sweet gestures. Each kiss brought a deeper blush to her cheeks until, giggling, Flowridia dove in to return the favor. Their mouths met, and when her tongue parted Ayla's lips, she reveled in the soft moan her cold companion released.

With an apology, she sent Demitri away. Alone with Ayla, Flowridia savored every unmapped curve of her body, before finally settling at the valley between her legs. Bitterness, she discovered, was the sweetest taste of all. Ayla's pleasure rose with the sun.

A knock at the door interrupted their play. Flowridia froze, Ayla's breast in her mouth. "One moment," she said, the words muffled by Ayla's slight chest, but when she looked back at Ayla's face, the woman held a dangerous glare. "Please, Ayla, it'll only take a minute," she whispered. She took Ayla's face in her hands and kissed her roughly, smiling when she felt Ayla's tense pose relax.

Flowridia stood and quickly threw a nightgown over her nude form. She opened the door no more than a crack and stared out at Marielle. "Good morning."

"You missed breakfast," Marielle said kindly. "I wanted to know if you were all right."

Flowridia gave a slow nod. "Exhausted, but well."

"Etolié has returned and wants to meet as soon as possible. She brought home an interesting souvenir."

"A council meeting, then?"

"Once you're dressed, we'll begin."

Flowridia's heart sank. "I should bathe first. Give me a few minutes. Please?" she added, and when Marielle nodded, she smiled. "Thank you."

Still, the queen watched with concern. "I'll tell them half an hour."

Marielle left, and Flowridia shut the door. She whipped around, relieved to see Ayla still lying nude in her bed. "You'll be leaving me, then?" Ayla said, if a bit dramatically.

"I have duties," Flowridia replied, remorse in her words. "But you don't have to go."

Ayla sat up, the blankets pooling around her waist. She leaned back, her tight stomach flexed, ribs severe but her breasts enticing. "I do, unfortunately. I should have left last night." Her head fell backwards, and bitter annoyance escaped with her groan. "Casvir will have missed me."

Heat filled Flowridia's cheeks, but not from arousal. Of course Casvir would care. Did Ayla care that Casvir cared? Flowridia stepped forward, hands fidgeting as she sat at the edge beside Ayla. "Casvir will have missed you . . . in his bed?"

The silence grew tense, though perhaps only in Flowridia's head. Ayla burst into laughter. "Flowra, my sweet, I beg your pardon?"

Relief vastly overshadowed her embarrassment. Flowridia sighed, releasing tension she hadn't realized she carried. "You aren't sleeping with Casvir?"

"Gods, no," Ayla replied, hilarity lacing her words. "Even if I were inclined to, he wouldn't have me. Haven't you heard the jests? That he's more monster than man, immune to the temptation of flesh? I don't think he's ever so much as wet his cock on a woman's mouth, much less her cunt."

The mocking in Ayla's tone meant this must have been a common jest, and Flowridia felt her face grow hot. Ayla surely felt her red cheeks when she moved to cup her face. "I'm sorry for accusing you," Flowridia replied softly. "When I first met you, I thought you and he–"

"Were sleeping together? Oh, Flowra . . ." Ayla drew her in for a soft kiss. "How you amuse me." Her gaze lingered, and then her words continued. "I work for him. Nothing more. I am indebted to him, but not happily so."

"Why though? Why must you work for him, or for anyone? Did–" Flowridia bit her lip, recalling Ayla's past words. For five years, she had worked for Casvir, and if Etolié was to be believed, he only employed the dead. She continued, slower now. "Did he turn you into . . . this?"

Ayla shook her head. "Had Casvir twisted my mortal form into an undead monstrosity, I would be more compliant to his will. Such is the nature of necromancy: ruthless domination; your will against your slaves. No, Flowra, I have been around a long time. Longer than Casvir, and I expect to survive well after his death, at which point I'll be free again for my own pursuits. Had Casvir wished it, he could have attempted to break my mind and will and control me like a puppet, but he wanted my intelligence as well as my skill set. Instead, the viceroy bound me into a contract, until Casvir's death or mine."

"Forgive me," Flowridia said, posture caving in, "but I'm surprised you haven't tried to kill him."

Ayla spoke through uproarious laughter. "Oh, Flowra, you are too sweet and innocent for this world." She placed a kiss on Flowridia's lips. "I have tried. Many times. Someday, I'll succeed." Her hands moved to touch Flowridia's clothed waist, pulling her close as she placed a kiss against her cheek. "I should go. If you show up at the meeting still dirty from travel, your precious Marielle will be suspicious."

Something of ire spoke in Ayla's tone. "I don't care," Flowridia replied, shyly matching Ayla's stare. "Do you not want them to know you're alive?"

"They'll find out sooner or later. I don't care, but I believe they'll be rightfully wary of me after that bit of fun with Etolié." Ayla's wink caused Flowridia to blush. "If my time with Casvir has taught me anything, it's that consequences are unavoidable. I've made my bed, and now I must lie in it."

No regret; simply acceptance. "They'll distrust me too, if I'm caught lying in bed with you," Flowridia said, and then a wry grin tugged at her lips. "But you've made my stay pleasurable."

Ayla chuckled. "Clever." Her fingers traced lines through Flowridia's hair, softly caressing the thick locks. "I would like to propose an official visit, then; a diplomatic gesture from Nox'Kartha. The embassy nears completion, and what better timing? Perhaps it will make your stay in my bed less complicated, if I make peace with those running your kingdom."

"I don't know if they'll accept it, Ayla," Flowridia said, concern bleeding into her words. "Thalmus was already out for your blood, and surely Etolié doesn't feel much better. I want you safe."

But Ayla smiled as she waved her words away. "If Nox'Kartha deems it my duty to oversee the embassy's completion, Marielle will concede to it like the sheep she is." Before Flowridia could balk at the insult, Ayla leaned forward, expression light. "It would be a wonderful excuse to spend a few days with you. I'll spoil you, Flowra. I might even cook for you. While it has been centuries since I followed a mortal diet, as an elf I know a few recipes you might appreciate."

The mere idea drew a wide smile to Flowridia's face. A romantic notion, beyond what she could have dared to hope for, yet . . . "I would love that, but Ayla–" Flowridia stopped her words, shrinking at the caress of Ayla's finger against her chin. "Why all of this?"

Whatever answer she hoped for or expected, she did not receive. Instead, Ayla whispered, "I ask myself the same." Then, after a quick peck on Flowridia's lips, Ayla continued. "Expect to hear from Nox'Kartha soon." Her voice lowered, eyes bright with conspiracy. "And myself. For now, though, I must go, and you must bathe." Ayla pressed their lips together once more, lingering at the touch. When Flowridia pulled away, Ayla followed, letting their kiss deepen instead of part.

Flowridia bathed and ran to the council room, feeling naked without the usual sweet scent of flowers woven into her hair. After the meeting, she would tend to her garden.

In the council chamber, all eyes followed her as she plopped into her seat. Demitri jumped from Etolié's lap to the ground, and Flowridia saw the Celestial smile faintly as she watched his movements. Never had Flowridia seen Etolié look so disheveled, so sullen. Pale and emaciated, Etolié had also never appeared so alert. She twitched, and did Flowridia imagine the slight shaking of the Celestial's hands?

She soothed her nerves by clinging to Demitri, who settled in her lap. Marielle stood, drawing their attention, eyes wide with morose. "Whatever we had intended to happen . . ." Marielle's jaw trembled as she glanced at the faces staring back. "Obviously it went terribly wrong. I want to know everything."

When Marielle's gaze fell to her, Flowridia knew she was expected to speak. "Tholheim needs to be informed that their people are dead," Flowridia said softly, staring out. Khastra came without her weapon, nothing to distract her wandering attention. In a reversal of norms, Meira stood, and Sora sat with sunken, dark rings around her eyes, staring at the floor.

But Thalmus' gaze was kind, as was Marielle's, and Flowridia braced herself to continue. "We were attacked on the road. They wanted your orb."

"Flowridia spoke personally to Prince Falrir," Thalmus added. "They were promised the crystal in the cavern in exchange for delivering the orb to their so-called 'God.'"

"A crystal now in our possession," came Etolié's exhausted voice. "But that's a story for later."

Marielle stood silent as she contemplated Thalmus and Etolié's words. "Lara needs to hear of this development." Hesitant, she clutched the side of her throne, bracing for the next question. "Tell me how we managed to commit genocide on an entire species."

Genocide? Surely there were more Skalmites than simply . . .

Or perhaps not. They couldn't adapt to a world of magic. Perhaps the crystal had provided a haven for those few remaining.

Thalmus looked to Flowridia, and she realized she would have to give her account. "Marielle, do you remember a certain 'gift' Nox'Kartha gave our kingdom? One you placed in my possession?"

Marielle's face snapped forward. "You made a wish."

Flowridia nodded.

"Tiny one," Khastra said, looking intrigued as she lounged in her enormous throne, "you will have to explain."

"Do you have it with you?" Marielle asked, looking to Flowridia.

Shamefaced, Flowridia lifted the ear from her bodice. She realized one of the earrings had cracked and dulled. "It's Ayla's ear, a gift from Casvir," she said softly, inspecting the ruined stone. The bottom two still held their vivid blue. "It grants wishes."

"You never told us we have a vampire on a leash." Khastra looked not at her, but at Marielle.

"Ayla entrusted it to Flowridia, so I thought I would too."

Khastra chuckled, deep but feminine, and she rested her chin on her fist. "Marielle, you are queen, but that is not how decisions are made here."

"It's Lady Ayla's ear," Marielle snapped, "and if she wants Flowridia to have it—"

"Look," Etolié said, and Flowridia heard fatigue, "we'll discuss this later. Let Flowers give her speech."

With a huff, Marielle returned her attention to Flowridia. "Flowridia, will you please tell us what you wished for?"

"I wished to protect the crystal," Flowridia whispered. In her hands, she stroked the fine lines of the ear, immune to its ghastly nature. The gems threatened to cut her thumb.

She thought of Ayla, hardly disheveled after dancing through the camp with her knife and her nails, the screams from the cavern, the monster emerging to rip her open—

She realized, as her mind wandered, that Etolié had begun giving the same account. Hearing it spoken so plainly cut deeper than the monster's claws. To reconcile that night with the woman who had loved her so tenderly only hours before . . .

Etolié regaled her victory against the monster with little aplomb.

"What you are describing," Khastra said, curiosity in her words, "is demonic possession."

Etolié frowned. "It's not demonic if it's done by Eionei."

"I mean Ayla. She invoked the name of The Endless Night, used the tiny one's blood to summon it, and then Ayla's form twisted to match the demon inside her."

Etolié's frown deepened, visibly thoughtful at the idea.

"But she's dead?" Marielle asked. "Ayla Darkleaf is dead?" She stared directly at Flowridia, waiting for confirmation.

"She's not dead." Sora's words cut the tense thread of silence. "If she's dead, who was singing in your bedroom last night?"

Flowridia felt her face pale as every eye turned to her. Tension brewed with each passing second. Truth or lie, she had to speak.

All she could manage was a weak, "She's alive."

Marielle pursed her lips. "At least we won't have to navigate that political nightmare. Etolié, won't you tell us what happened in the cave?"

Flowridia kept her stare at Demitri as shame drove away her relief. It had seemed so simple that morning; Ayla had stayed. Ayla had comforted her. Ayla promised to return and set things right with the ruling council of her kingdom.

But the wicked question of 'why?' threatened to shatter the image, the answer given that morning only a paltry supplication, and she knew it.

". . . wasn't about to leave it unguarded, not after the Skalmites were willing to die to keep it," Etolié said, and Flowridia realized how flush the Celestial's cheeks were. "What I saw in the cave–" Etolié steeled her jaw, emotionless as she continued. "Absolute slaughter. Everywhere I turned, bodies—dwarves and Skalmites alike. Not simply killed. Mutilated; torn to shreds. There must have been thousands."

Flowridia's heart sank with every word, nausea filling her stomach, but nothing was as vile as the dread in her soul. She shut her eyes as Etolié continued, images of the bonfire massacre filling her head. Torn limbs, bloodied earth, crushed spines—

"But I did find the center. I found the crystal." Etolié's lower lip trembled, a single tear escaping her eye. "The Skalmites had clustered around to protect it, and their dead bodies formed a wall. They must've known they'd die if it were broken. But now there's no one left in there to protect, so with some help from the party sent to retrieve us, I took it."

No one left to protect . . . Flowridia felt her throat begin to choke. An entire species nearly gone. What few remained faced an uncertain future.

"It's unique in that its aura can be dampened, I've discovered. It has a temporary home in the library, until we figure out what to do with our new refugee friends. Useful, that thing. I'll be playing with it."

Khastra asked, "Refugee friends?"

"I'm currently in the middle of a heated debate with Lara about which kingdom has the resources to take the surviving Skalmites in."

"I think for now," Marielle said. "I want you to take time to rest. I'd like to adjourn this meeting." She looked to Flowridia. "I need Flowridia to stay a minute, though."

Dismayed, Flowridia remained seated, even as the rest of the council cleared out. Sora hesitated by her chair. "I didn't mean to cause trouble."

Flowridia simply stared.

"I figured it wasn't you singing, though, unless you know elven tunes."

Flowridia didn't, but she couldn't find the words to articulate that. Sora left her alone, and Flowridia was grateful.

But Thalmus lingered, and Flowridia saw the scowl on his dark features. Flowridia clutched Demitri, wishing he were larger so she could disappear into his fur. Marielle spared him a glance and said, "Ayla is alive?"

Flowridia nodded.

"Does she often visit you at night?"

Flowridia stared at Thalmus, watching fury settle onto his features as she said, "Not all the time. But she has before."

"You said you'd tell me if she ever came back," Thalmus said, muted anger seeping into his words.

"I-I was going to–"

"Is this the first time she's come back?"

Flowridia couldn't summon a response.

"Is it?" Thalmus pushed, and Flowridia shrunk into her chair.

"No." Tears began to well in her eyes. "She's come every night and left a rose on my table. I only saw her one of those nights, but–"

Marielle's eyes narrowed. "How?"

"I've never asked."

"Does the imperator know this?"

This time, Flowridia bit her lip. "I don't think he does."

Marielle turned to Thalmus. "If Ayla can sneak in to see Flowridia, she can go anywhere she wants."

"Which is precisely why I asked Flowra to tell me if Ayla ever came back," Thalmus said, disappointment in his dark features.

Oh, that stung. It stung worse than the scar on her chest.

"She doesn't mean any harm," Flowridia dared to say. "She isn't our enemy."

Marielle released a slow sigh. "I will talk to Zorlaeus and see what he says on the matter."

"This can't continue," Thalmus said. "Ayla will be forbidden from–"

"You can't forbid anything!" The tears threatening to fall from Flowridia's face finally did so, angry and hot. "You aren't the queen, and you aren't my father–"

"Then you'd best keep her far away from me–"

"No arguing!" Marielle snapped, and from her bosom the orb flashed bright red. "Flowridia, Ayla is dangerous. Zorlaeus doesn't trust her, and now we know what she's capable of."

"It was because I wished it," Flowridia said, shrinking into her chair.

Marielle opened her mouth to speak, but Thalmus' words came faster. "Don't. Don't you *dare* blame yourself for this again, Flowra. She'll say anything she can to get herself back into your bed, only to rip you open all over again–"

"That's not what happened!' Flowridia yelled, and Demitri nearly fell when she suddenly stood. She managed to catch him, placing him back into the seat. "Ayla came to see me, yes, but she stayed. She comforted me. She brought Demitri and held me all night, and in the morning we talked–"

"And you think she gives a damn about you?!" Thalmus stood now, standing several feet taller.

Flowridia had no fear to mask her fury. "You don't know what she's like when we're alone–"

"I know she leaves you bruised and battered!"

"I burned her!"

"Both of you, stop!" This time, the orb flashed, and flame sizzled from Marielle's feet and hair. Her footsteps left scorch marks. "Meeting adjourned. Flowridia, Ayla is a breach in security. I won't forbid you from seeing her, but you will *tell us* when she visits. Thalmus, you can't control the diplomat. Now, both of you will exit in different directions and not speak until you can both be civil. Am I clear?"

Flowridia glared between Marielle and Thalmus, the latter of whom matched her simmering rage. "You're clear," she said, and she turned on her heels and left the room.

In the library, an enormous crystal floated in the center, perhaps ten feet above the pile of scarves and blankets. Larger than Flowridia, it bobbed gently, shining a florescent green and glowing vividly. To her surprise, the edges were jagged, as though ripped from the earth, any smooth edges ending quickly in rough cuts.

Etolié sat beneath it, Khastra kneeling beside her. Flowridia caught the end of the general's fervent chide: ". . . you have not eaten in days, Etolié."

"It's difficult to keep shit down when I'm vomiting blood every hour, you bastard spawn of a–"

They both turned simultaneously at Flowridia's entrance. Upon seeing Flowridia, Etolié gave her an exhausted smile. "Hi, Flowers."

Khastra kept her frown as she looked back to Etolié. "I will bring you something liquid."

Khastra hardly acknowledged Flowridia as she left the library.

Etolié attempted to stand, and when Flowridia ran forward to help, the Celestial all but fell into her arms. Flowridia held her slight form with care, allowing Etolié to pull her into a tight hug. Her skin, where they touched, was clammy and cold. "You're not bleeding anymore."

Etolié nodded as she stepped back. "Lara's people got to me." She knelt and hugged Demitri, planting kisses all over his face.

Flowridia looked over her shoulder, toward the exit. "Khastra seemed–"

"She's like that when she's worried. Nothing to do with you."

Studying the dark rings around Etolié's eyes, her sullen features, Flowridia understood Khastra's fears. "Can I get you anything? I know teas for soothing fevers and chills."

"If you really want to help, sneak me in a pint. Khastra won't let me have a drink until I can go half a day without puking blood." She smiled with no amusement. "Everything hurts, and I'm dying."

Flowridia sat down beside her. "Perhaps you should go lie down. Working won't help you heal any faster."

"It won't slow me down, either. Knowledge over health."

"Etolié, if everything hurts and you're dying–"

"I'm not really," Etolié said, holding up a hand. She pulled Demitri into her lap and gently scratched at his neck. "We Celestials are tougher than we look. I won't be partying with Eionei anytime soon."

Flowridia gave a slight nod and stood up, not wanting Etolié to see her worry. Instead, she walked toward the crystal and stared up at the faintly glowing stone. "What is it?"

"It resembles maldectine, but I can turn it on and off, though it's not something I want to play with quite yet. I'll get better at controlling it with practice. I could teach you."

"I think I'd like that," Flowridia said, still looking up. Even from here, she could feel the radiating power, not unlike the cold that emanated from her lover.

"So, Ayla's alive."

Etolié's voice drew her back to earth. Flowridia whirled around to face her. "She is."

"I'll have to apologize for popping off her head." Etolié mused, still staring at the crystal.

"She has no grudge. It was part of her game: our kingdom will go down in history as the ones who killed The Endless Night . . ." She trailed off, shrinking when Etolié slowly turned and glared.

"Forgive me," Etolié said pointedly. "Game?"

Flowridia nodded warily. "Politics are a game–"

"Genocide of an entire civilization isn't a game, Flowers. It's not funny. It's not clever." Etolié tore her gaze away, but Flowridia still felt its sting. "The symbol she wrote was The Endless Night, but I've seen demons. That was–" Etolié stopped, shaking her head. "Forget it. I don't want to give that bitch more credit than she deserves."

"I know it sounds insane," Flowridia said tentatively, "but she's been nothing but kind–"

"Bullshit, Flowers!" Etolié's gaze bounced back to her. Flowridia flinched. "Kissing you better doesn't mean she didn't rip you open in the first place. Don't forget that."

Anger welled in Flowridia's chest, but with it brewed the harsh knowledge that Etolié was right.

"I'll accept that it's Ayla's nature to cause destruction," Etolié continued, more subdued. "You can't fault a cat for killing birds and mice." A pause, and then Etolié lowered her voice. "Cats play with their food before they strike. Be careful, Flowers."

Her words burned, and Flowridia stepped back, turning quickly before Etolié could see the hot tears welling in her eyes.

"Flowers–"

Flowridia whirled around.

Etolié stood tall, stubborn in her pale, sickened state. "Tea would be nice."

Blinking heavily, Flowridia nodded, managing to run from the library before the first of her tears fell.

A letter arrived later that day stating that Lady Ayla Darkleaf of Nox'Kartha would personally be overseeing the completion of the embassy. In two weeks' time, she would come.

That morning, the news would have brought butterflies to Flowridia's stomach. Now, she felt only dread, especially when Marielle responded with an affirmative.

She knew the council's true feelings. She feared they were right.

When she entered her room that night, Ayla sat at the foot of her bed, the beautiful half of her visage turned toward the door. Flowridia paused, stunned, but when Demitri began to back away, Ayla shook her head, revealing the burn marring her features. "He can stay. I won't be here long." She stood, though it did little to increase her height. "Casvir was quite unhappy with my disappearance."

Flowridia shut the door, never moving her stare away from Ayla's face. "I'm sorry," she began to say, but Ayla shook her head.

"It was my doing, staying the night. But you should know he is now aware of the two of us," she said, a grimace in her tone. Her expression steadily fell, until only a sneer tugged at her lip. "I'm good at lying. He's better at discerning."

Panic coursed through Flowridia's veins. "What will this mean for us?"

"Presumably nothing," Ayla replied, though chagrin seemed permanently etched into her mouth. "He seemed concerned for your well-being, amusingly enough."

Flowridia would be a rich woman if she had a gold piece for every person who expressed concern about her and Ayla.

"I came to tell you that," Ayla continued, "and to inform you that you won't be seeing me again until my official visit. No more gifts. No more stolen kisses."

Was it disappointment that flashed across Ayla's face? Flowridia reached forward to take her hand. "Has Casvir forbidden it?"

"No." Ayla brought Flowridia's hand up. "But I am more than simply his diplomat. I have a bit of espionage to embark on, and it will take all my focus." Thin lips kissed the back of her hand, and Ayla let it linger by her face, breathing in the scent.

The gesture unnerved her. Flowridia drew her hand back. "Ayla, be careful."

Ayla grinned, vicious and predatory. "I'm the best at many things, my Sweet Flowra." She laughed, but Flowridia shook her head.

"Ayla, they know you've been visiting me."

Ayla's expression immediately turned dark. "Oh?"

"Someone heard singing last night."

"Odd, that they would assume it was me."

Flowridia stepped forward, settling her arms around Ayla's waist, nervous at the accusatory tone. "I didn't tell them anything, Ayla. Sora heard you singing and knew it was an elven tune."

"Oh, did she?" Ayla mused, and though Flowridia wondered at the suspicious tone, she reached up to cup Ayla's cheek.

"My point is, please be careful." Flowridia looked down at her beautiful face, one marred by a hateful sneer. "Is this a dangerous mission? What sort of–"

Ayla interrupted. "Who is Sora, anyway?"

"Sora is our stablemaster. Ayla, what I'm trying to say is–"

"You have an elven stablemaster?"

"She's a half-elf. Ayla–"

"What sort of half-breed knows ancient elven music?"

"Ayla Darkleaf, listen!"

Ayla finally focused, a glare souring her features. "Yes, Lady Flowridia . . ." Her eyes narrowed, though not from anger. "What's your surname?"

Incredulous, Flowridia nearly balked at how distractible her elven companion proved to be. "I don't have one."

"Makes it difficult to petulantly call you by your full name if you don't have one."

"Ayla, please," Flowridia said, exasperation leaking into her tone. "Listen for a moment."

Ayla stared, raising an expectant eyebrow when Flowridia didn't immediately continue.

"Swear to me you'll be careful," Flowridia said softly. "Don't let your pride get you killed."

"There's very little danger of me getting killed, Flowra."

Flowridia's hold on Ayla grew tight, her fingers gripping the thin, soft fabric of her dress. "I'll still worry while you're gone."

Ayla watched her with no tension, despite the silence. She stood on her toes to plant a light kiss onto Flowridia's mouth. "In two weeks, I'll be sleeping by your side, I swear it. Casvir and the world be damned." She rocked back onto her heels, smiling faintly.

A knock interrupted Ayla's speech. When Flowridia tried to turn, Ayla's grip tightened possessively.

"Flowridia?"

Sora's voice. Flowridia whispered, "I'll get rid of her. Give me a moment."

Murderous intent stared back, but Ayla loosened her hold. She stepped to the side of the door, invisible in the shadow.

Flowridia opened the door and saw Sora waiting, hands on her hips. "Can I help you, Sora?"

"I wanted to apologize," Sora said, leaning against the doorframe. "I didn't mean to call you out during the meeting."

"I can't fault you for telling the truth."

"You seemed–" Sora suddenly stopped, eyes growing wide as she stared past Flowridia's shoulder.

Flowridia turned and gasped when Ayla's leering grin waited only inches behind her. "I've heard you've been creeping around my Flowra's room. Tell me, what kind of bastard elf knows elven music?"

The terror in Sora's visage surprised Flowridia. She placed a hand on Ayla's shoulder, feeling tension beneath the thin skin. "Ayla, I don't think she meant any harm."

"I'm sure not," Ayla replied, haughty as she straightened her pose. "What's your name, Stablemaster Sora? Perhaps I killed some of your pure-blooded ancestors."

Sora stepped back, still maintaining eye contact.

"There aren't many blunt-eared bastards in the world, Sora *Fireborn*." Ayla let the word trace obscenely off her tongue. At the use of her full name, or perhaps the slur, Sora flinched, and Ayla laughed. "You are a Fireborn, right?"

Sora quickly shook her head. "You have me mistaken–"

"A bit of human swine in your blood does nothing to mask the taint of your scent. You're a Fireborn." Ayla's grin grew wide and toothy. Flowridia didn't presume to imagine the lengthening of her fangs. "Finding a census was trivial. I made certain to check the whereabouts of as many of you gnoll-benders as I could."

Sora simply stared, either stunned by the insult or incapacitated by fear.

"I have no wish to murder in front of my sweet lady, but give me a reason, and you'll be a smear on the walls." Ayla pushed past Flowridia and placed a hand on the door. "Give my regards to Mereen." The door slammed. Ayla turned around. "Watch that blunt-eared tart."

Flowridia stared, jaw agape. "Ayla, what was all that?"

"Why did I threaten Sora Fireborn? Amusement, pitiful as it is." Any humor in Ayla's grin seeped away, leaving nothing but menace. "Fireborns have a habit of locking me in coffins."

Flowridia stared down, unsure of what to say. "I forget I know nothing about you," she finally whispered.

"Next time you see me, I'll answer of a few of your questions."

Ayla turned as if to leave, but Flowridia reached out to grab her hand. "Answer me one now? Please?"

Ayla turned as she raised an eyebrow. "Yes?"

"If I find out there's any sort of danger to you, what do I do?"

Ayla stepped forward, her lithe hands suddenly at Flowridia's waist and then skimming up her bodice. Her fingers lightly cupped Flowridia's breasts, barely touching. Flowridia's breath hitched as one of Ayla's hands dipped into her cleavage and withdrew the ear. "Whisper with intent, and I'll hear everything you say." Ayla let it drop. It fell against the fabric outside her gown.

Ayla's mouth pressed against hers. "I'll give you a sign, Flowra. No need for panic."

Flowridia shut her eyes, basking in those lips brushing against her own. "Safe travels, Ayla."

This time, the kiss held more urgency. Ayla held the back of her neck, crushing their lips together. Flowridia savored the contact, letting her hand stroke Ayla's hair, until the small woman pulled back quite suddenly.

Something unreadable settled onto Ayla's tense expression, the furrowing of her brow, the twitch at her lip. But then she smiled and planted a kiss at the back of Flowridia's hand. "Farewell, Flowra."

She disappeared out the window.

"Demitri, stay here," Flowridia said, stuffing the ear back into her bodice. She immediately went to the door. Ayla was gone, and that meant she was free to pursue answers on her own.

No sign of Sora. Flowridia ran down the stairs, avoiding eye contact with all she passed. The half-elf was a near zealot to the Goddess, and Flowridia had only one guess to where she might try and hide.

Outside, a warm breeze swept Flowridia's hair across her face. Her bare feet tapped along the stones, toward the enormous iron gate outlining the perimeter of the manor. Flowridia ran to the entrance, seeing the gate slightly ajar—

A knife appeared at Flowridia's throat.

She gasped, prepared to scream, but just as quickly the knife withdrew. Sora stood at the other side of the gate, eyes wide, breath hitched. She tucked the knife into the sheath at her belt. "I'm sorry. I thought you were her," Sora said, releasing a long breath. "I suppose if she wants me dead, I won't hear it coming."

Flowridia still hadn't breathed, but she managed to speak a few nervous words. "I want to know what you know."

"Not out here," Sora replied, her stance still prepared to fight. She glanced about, twitching at every shadow. "I'm going to the Temple of Sol Kareena. If you join me, she won't be able to listen. Vampires can't enter holy places."

Flowridia nodded, keeping her skepticism to herself.

Lamps burned bright outside shop doors, the sun having long set. The sparse streets made little noise, and Flowridia followed Sora through the winding, dusty roads toward the temple. Not nearly as ostentatious as the cathedral in the Theocracy, it still harbored its own subtle beauty. Flowridia had only ever seen the outside, built from rough stone and smaller than the enormous manor housing the royal council, but beautiful stained glass windows depicted images of angels, of Sol Kareena and her pantheon.

Inside, it appeared as a smaller version of the cathedral, with pews and an altar at the front. Sora shut the door behind them and quickly approached the statue before the altar. It stood smaller than Flowridia, but placed upon a pedestal, it managed to tower above them all the same. The half-elf knelt and gestured with her hands, silently mouthing a prayer to the statue staring down.

When Sora opened her eyes, she asked, "Have you pledged your heart to Sol Kareena, yet?"

Flowridia shook her head.

"She's claimed you. Choose her, and you'll be protected from evil."

Flowridia would be a fool to not hear the condemnation in Sora's words, the implications rampant in the word 'evil.' "That wasn't my plan for the night," Flowridia said as she stood beside Sora. "I wanted to apologize for what Ayla said. She doesn't mean you harm. She asked me to give you her best and admitted that she may have been harsh."

Sora stood, her full height several inches taller than Flowridia, and stared up, studying the hooded image of Sol Kareena. "I'm somewhat of a pariah among my extended family. But I grew up on stories of the monster my grandfather managed to lock into a shadow-less coffin underground. I don't know if Ayla is impossible to kill, but despite a thousand years of war, no one could. He only managed to lock her away."

Flowridia's hand moved up to cover her mouth. "Why though?"

Quiet a moment, Sora looked down to the plaque at the Goddess' feet, one bearing the phrase: *The light will burn away all your fears.* "Elves cling to old ways of life. Most still pledge to the Old Gods, Chaos in particular. But we Sun Elves swore allegiance to Sol Kareena, and The Endless Night became the monster my people came to fear above all else. What happened to the Skalmites and the dwarves was a tragedy, but their deaths are drops in a tidal wave. Forgive me—for you to say she doesn't mean me harm is a blatant lie, whether you realize it or not. I'll be keeping my distance."

It stirred a thought, one that sat unwell in Flowridia's stomach. "You've known this all along," she said, stifling her slow-brewing anger. "You've known who Ayla was, but you encouraged me to pursue her. Why?"

Sora's fists clenched. "You're a cute kid. I thought you would be good for her–"

"You don't lie well when you're cornered."

Sora turned, one hand drifting toward her belt, and Flowridia watched her grip the hilt of her dagger, prepared to run if the half-elf turned on her. "I didn't know what she was, not until she manifested as The Endless Night. But I had suspicions, and if she was sweet on you, I could keep an eye on her."

Sora said nothing more, but Flowridia felt her own fury begin to simmer. The gentle caress of leather against

199

metal sang across the walls of the cathedral. Sora's dagger glinted silver. True silver—a bane to most undead creatures.

"You've meant to kill her," Flowridia said, and she glanced from Sora's dagger to her face, watching for any shift in demeanor. Sora glared, the hunter cornered by her own prey. "If you, the pariah of the Fireborn family, brought the head of Ayla Darkleaf, why wouldn't you be welcome with open arms?"

"My motives aren't so petty," Sora said, her knuckles white against the hilt. "You could help me. You'd be doing the world a service."

Flowridia spat on the ground at Sora's feet. "Never."

Sora could do many things, but slay Flowridia on Sol Kareena's altar was not one of them, so what had she to fear? The half-elf slipped the dagger back into her belt. "Watch yourself, diplomat. She'll ruin you, and you'll never see it coming."

Flowridia made no move to stop Sora when the half-elf stepped past her. She froze, watching until the door slammed shut, the sound echoing across the vacant cathedral. She turned back, studying the altar, and stepped forward, each bare footstep a quiet mar on the silence of night.

Sol Kareena gazed down, her pupil-less eyes an eerie sight. A whisper in Flowridia's soul beckoned her forward, and Flowridia wondered if this was what Meira experienced when the Goddess tried to speak. Underneath her sightless shadow, Flowridia knelt and shut her eyes.

A whisper said, "Do you want me to kill her?"

Shocked, Flowridia opened her eyes. Peering upward, she gasped when she saw Ayla's face beside the Goddess'.

She grinned viciously, showing her teeth, and slid down with ease. Her feet touched the floor without a sound. "I ask again—do you want me to kill her? All you need do is wish it, and I'll receive no reprimand from Nox'Kartha."

Flowridia shook her head. "I don't want anyone to die."

A wicked chuckle echoed in her ears. "Flowra, you are too good and innocent for this world." A pale hand extended; Ayla helped her to rise. "Let me escort you home. It wouldn't do well for a lady to be caught alone on a dark night."

When Flowridia nodded, Ayla's fingers interlaced with her own. With Sol Kareena at her back, Flowridia walked forward with Ayla and felt her worried heart begin to speed, though not from fear. It fluttered; it burned.

Flowridia didn't know what it meant, for Ayla to hold the door open and escort her, hand in hand, but she followed, her steps unhurried.

Chill night air stung her face, the breeze whipping her hair. "I thought you'd gone," Flowridia said softly.

"And leave you alone with that Fireborn tart? I wished to see what you would do." Ayla chuckled, something wicked in the sound, but brought Flowridia's hand to her lips and placed a kiss on her knuckle.

Ayla didn't take them toward the road but to the dark shadow cast by the temple. "Hold tight to me, Flowra," Ayla warned, and she slipped her arm around Flowridia's waist, keeping their bodies flush together. "Whatever you see, nothing can take you unless I let it. Let me lead you."

They stepped into the shadow, and the entire world shifted. Flowridia saw jerking, muted shades of grey; manifestations of the cathedral, the road, and all of Staelash. Like an underwater scene, but in a colorless blur, and Flowridia saw beauty in the dark, ethereal ambience. She only had a second to glance, a moment to memorize the glowing eyes staring from the dark—formless creatures, ones that whispered and beckoned for her to follow. Ayla took a single step, and the scene changed. Suddenly, the gates of the manor stood before them.

The white skin and black hair of Flowridia's companion blended with perfection into the shifting environment. Only her eyes, still a brilliant blue, revealed her as an interloper. Another step, and the scene whizzed past, that of the halls and the stairs. Ayla navigated with ease, leading her past the twisting hallways. No door stopped them, but living creatures moved as colored blurs when they passed, their features hazy, words muddled.

Ayla and Flowridia stepped from the shadow of a bed, and the world grew sharp. No more whispers; no haze of shadow or dark creatures. Only Flowridia's bedroom, the gentle breeze from outside, and a small wolf pup fast asleep on her pillow.

"Sha'Demoni is a broken world, forced to share a space with the inhabitants here but stretched impossibly thin," Ayla said, leading her to sit at the edge of her bed. "Time flows differently; a day in Sha'Demoni might be an hour here, or less. Most demons were destroyed in The Convergence, like the angels, but unlike Celestière, Sha'Demoni remains a perilous world. Only the ruthless survive the eternal battle between the gods residing there. But it did adopt me when I had nowhere else to go. As a child, I saw the thin lines separating the planes and begged to join the inhabitants within. I hid in the shadows, and the shadows comforted me, helped to raise me when I had no one."

"It sounds like a beautiful tale," Flowridia said, but her voice faded away when Ayla slowly shook her head.

"No, but to trade the knowledge it gave me for a happier childhood is a sacrifice I would not make. Instead, I travel between planes with the ease you walk through a doorway."

"Is it magic?" Flowridia asked, but even as she spoke, Ayla shook her head again.

"I've no talent or patience for magic. To dance in shadow is a matter of learning to see the cracks between worlds."

"And those creatures watching us, those were demons?"

Ayla nodded. "That is the colloquial term, yes. Most are as benign as you or I."

Neither of them were particularly benign. Flowridia knew beings like Etolié could ask for passage to the angelic realm of Celestière, but she was a near demi-goddess. For Ayla to consort freely with demons meant to stand tall among gods. "Have you met many demons?"

"I have. Like I said, most are benign, indifferent to my presence. And the few I've met who aren't let me pass after some convincing."

"Like the one you let possess you? The Endless Night?"

Ayla chuckled, her brilliant smile revealing slight, pointed fangs. "And how did you figure that one out?"

"Khastra said that's what is was, when Etolié described it," Flowridia replied, hoping she had said nothing damning.

"Dangerous knowledge, to recognize demonic possession." Ayla brought her hand forward to stroke the hair from Flowridia's face, letting it linger as she said, "The Endless Night is a title; not a demon. It is also a question for another time. I've tarried here too long."

Flowridia turned into the touch, her cheek rubbing Ayla's hand. "Will you stay until I fall asleep?"

Tension settled. Flowridia feared she had overstepped her boundaries, until Ayla's expression softened. "Until you fall asleep."

Flowridia stood and quickly stripped from her day clothes, self-conscious when she felt Ayla's gaze on her bare back. A silly insecurity—Ayla had seen much more of her than this; Ayla gave no care to her scars—yet the gesture was so familiar, so comfortable. She slipped on her nightgown, silent as she climbed into bed.

Flowridia took care to not jostle Demitri. Ayla settled behind her and pulled her against her chest. Flowridia breathed alone, no heartbeat or other sign of life to soothe her. Until, suddenly, Ayla began to hum.

Airy and somber, the familiar tune lilted into Flowridia's ears, the very same that had damned Sora. She whispered, "Ayla, what song is this?"

The humming stopped, replaced by Ayla's soothing voice. "It's an old tune, written by one of my first lovers as a birthday gift. She was a minstrel–" Ayla stopped, and Flowridia felt the arms across her body grow slack. "I never did get to hear it in life. Instead, it echoed through my mind as I crawled from my grave."

"She sang it at your funeral?"

"She did." A kiss brushed the back of Flowridia's head. Then, Ayla slowed her tongue, thoughtful with each word. "Much of my life before death is a distant, shattered thing. I don't recall the words. But I remember her voice. Even in heartbreak, it was as pure and beautiful as the sunrise."

Flowridia wondered at Ayla's reminiscing, her dreamy tone as she spoke of the past.

Ayla said nothing more. Instead, her humming once again softly stroked Flowridia's senses. Lulled by the sweet sound, Flowridia fell asleep.

Chapter 11

Flowridia awoke to gentle breathing against her side. Demitri had spread out along the length of her torso; he grew with every passing day.

Her baby Demitri, aging right before her eyes. Flowridia placed a kiss at his nose, giggling when her companion squirmed. "Good morning, Demitri."

Demitri opened one eye. *Did Ayla leave?*

So he had heard them enter, or perhaps smelled her in the night. "She did. But she'll be back, remember? Two weeks."

Two weeks, and hopefully the hot temperaments of her council would die down. Etolié had made her feelings quite clear, Sora plotted her death, and Thalmus . . .

The sun already shone above the trees. Flowridia rushed to put on day clothes and ran outside, Demitri at her heels. If she hurried, Thalmus would still be watching the sunrise.

No such luck. But smoke from the chimney of his workshop became her guide, and Flowridia ran inside with no hesitation. Thalmus stoked the fire, his black hair braided down to his belt. Flowridia's voice came out in a flurry. "Thalmus, I still love you. Can we talk?"

The half-giant turned, an amused smile tugging at his lips. "I love you too. Would you help me with something first?"

Flowridia stepped up to Thalmus' side, confused to see an enormous spear resting in one hand—one with no head.

"Hold this," Thalmus said, and Flowridia frowned. A gorgeous piece, carved with vines across the wooden handle and rose petals embedded into the sturdy wood, lovingly polished to perfection, but it stood taller than Thalmus himself.

"I don't think I can lift that."

"The wood is nearly weightless—there's a tree found across the sea called a *tsipouren* that grows hollow branches as strong as steel." He offered it forward, and Flowridia hefted it high above her head with ease. "I'm still working to finish the blade."

She giggled. "Where did you get something like this?"

"Khastra has connections across the sea."

With care, Flowridia set the wood back onto the table. "Never thought I'd have potential with weapons," she teased.

"It's for you."

Flowridia frowned, taken aback, and said, "Thalmus, I can't ask that of you."

His hand appeared at her back and pulled her into his side. She breathed in his warm, smoky scent, relief coursing through her as she reached her arms as wide as they could go. "I sincerely want you to have it."

Flowridia's embrace grew tight. "Thalmus, I'm sorry I yelled at you. I know you're worried. I don't . . ." She hid her face in his shirt, refusing to shed the threatened tears. "I don't want to lose you over this."

"You will never lose me, Flowra." Coals crackled in the kiln, the only sound aside from the faint singing of birds from outside. "Though I will struggle to remain composed if I'm forced to see Ayla Darkleaf again."

"I'll keep her away from you, if it'll help," Flowridia whispered, and she stepped back when she felt him shift.

He looked down, the first hints of fury simmering beneath his composure. "My comfort isn't what I want you to worry about."

"Thalmus, I swear to you, she's not what you think," she pled. Flowridia squeezed her eyes shut, bracing for backlash. "Ayla came to see me again last night."

Thalmus' stare was suddenly stone, and Flowridia's words flooded the rocky shore. "Nothing untoward; merely to say she *wouldn't* be back to see me, not until the completion of the embassy. Casvir has sent her on some sort of mission." She released a sigh, praying her next words were no betrayal to Ayla's trust. "She can cross into Sha'Demoni. It's how she can sneak into the manor without anyone seeing."

"Is she a demon?"

"No. She didn't say much, only that she slips through the cracks between worlds."

"Interesting," Thalmus replied, his deep voice reverberating between them. "It raises as many concerns as it soothes, but I thank you for telling me."

"I don't understand." Flowridia tugged at his hand as he stood up.

Thalmus turned toward his work. Flowridia saw an array of half-finished projects: pottery, a tea set, a spear-head, and many more. "Our library holds next to nothing on elven history," he said, studying the wall. "I've often wondered what merit Ayla has to Imperator Casvir. If she can slip between worlds, that's a valuable slave to keep. And with her penchant for knives and stealth, it makes me wonder if 'Grand Diplomat' is her only title."

A fact Ayla had all but confirmed the night before, with her amusement at her own 'espionage,' but Flowridia said, "I feel like you're hinting at something—"

"Clarence Vors was found with a single stab wound, slipped perfectly at the back of his ribcage. No struggle; an instant death, and no sign of anyone breaking in or out."

Flowridia recognized the implications and said, "Thalmus, that's not—"

"What I'm telling you will have me arrested if anyone finds out," Thalmus said. Flowridia's face grew pale. "His murder was shortly after it came to light that Marielle, Clarence's daughter and heir, fancied the Nox'Karthan recruiter, Zorlaeus. Clarence had rejected numerous offers from Nox'Kartha for an alliance; convenient, then, that within months of his death, Marielle was made queen, and Zorlaeus was promoted to ambassador."

There were leaps in the story, but nothing Thalmus said was wrong. Flowridia whispered, "So you believe Imperator Casvir told Ayla to assassinate Clarence Vors?"

"I don't know what I believe, only that the timeline calls for suspicion."

"Who else knows about this?"

"Etolié and Empress Alauriel first made the connections. Khastra agreed and keeps a guard stationed at Marielle's room every night. Marielle knows of the assassination, but none of our suspicions."

Each day, it occurred to Flowridia more that Marielle was merely a figurehead.

Still, an implication had been made that raised Flowridia's hackles. "Why blame Ayla? If she's Casvir's knife, he still wields it."

"Even if Ayla is a slave to Casvir, she's done enough on her own accord for me to hate her. The envoy from the Theocracy, the ones found torn apart, held evidence of bite marks. We have no true proof, but we know they insulted her before they left for the night. Strange that Imperator Casvir would apologize when his kingdom wasn't to blame."

The word 'slave' would have meant nothing, but Thalmus had used it twice, and Flowridia was acutely aware of the scars on his arms, his face, the violent history haunting his weary countenance.

Flowridia swallowed and dared to ask, "But weren't you forced to do awful things when you were a slave?"

Nothing in Thalmus' demeanor changed, but he grew stiff, and Flowridia realized she'd cornered him.

"I'm sorry," she continued, shame causing her cheeks to grow hot. "I shouldn't have assumed–"

"Did Etolié tell you?" She'd never heard Thalmus speak with such ice.

Flowridia shook her head. "Etolié didn't have to. It's not surprising. Many citizens of Staelash are freed slaves Etolié sent–"

"Etolié didn't free me." Thalmus moved to step out of the workshop, his hand gripping the opposite forearm, thick muscles flexed as he fought for composure. Flowridia dared to follow. She stepped in front of him, gazing up with wide eyes, and placed a soft hand over his own, his dark skin pale from tension.

But under her touch, she felt him relax, and then he whispered, "As a child, I sent prayers to Etolié every night. I heard whispers of her, the so-called 'Savior of Slaves,' and asked her to save my mother and I before I could be taken from her and sold." Thalmus' jaw grit, and he gently shook his head. "I was never taken and sold. Instead, my mother died from a miscarriage, and I was kept, deemed valuable because of my obvious giant lineage. In the end, I saved myself. I don't need the indulgent benevolence of drunk Celestials.

"Yes, I did terrible things as a slave," Thalmus continued. "And terrible things were done to me." He shut his eyes, and Flowridia felt her face pale when she realized her error. "I would prefer my history not be compared to Ayla Darkleaf's."

Flowridia stared at her own small hand covering his, the deep hue proof of his desert-dwelling heritage. Thalmus' words stung, but not for malice. Flowridia had overheard Etolié once, in a state far more drunken than Flowridia had ever seen, cry to Khastra about a liberated camp of broken men and women, most with giants' blood in their veins—*"forced to fuck and make the perfect monsters, otherwise they'd be beaten. The price for running was severed limbs, Khastra. The women didn't need those—"*

One camp liberated meant a hundred others still flourished.

Thalmus remained kind and good despite his rage, and gentle despite abuse Flowridia couldn't begin to comprehend. With care, Flowridia slipped her fingers between the rough skin of his forearm and hand to try and hold it. "I'm sorry."

"I know. I forgive you."

She squeezed his fingers, realizing he trembled. "I've hurt you. I'm so sorry."

A smile, sad as it was, replaced Thalmus' frown. "You haven't hurt me, Flowra. It's a joy to share your company. But let me keep my secrets, and I'll let you keep yours."

She wondered what he knew, what he'd heard when she muttered in her sleep. Flowridia simply nodded. Her hold on his hand became her only support as she rested her head against his thick forearm.

"Slow, Flowers. Slow!"

In the library, Flowridia kept her focus on the small crystal in her hand.

"You've got a fist-sized shield of useless-ness," Etolié said, her bloodshot eyes staring at the crystal. "See if you can't make it bigger."

Before shipping the enormous crystal off to the Solviran Empire, Etolié had surreptitiously carved small pieces off and distributed them as she saw fit. She'd gifted one to Flowridia, and with practice, Flowridia had managed to expand a field of anti-magic large enough to engulf her hand.

"Push it, Flowers."

"I like drunk Etolié better," Flowridia muttered.

"So do I, Flowers. So do I. Now, expand the damn thing."

Flowridia pushed, feeling sweat drip down her forehead. She felt herself meld with the odd trinket, felt her own influence begin to expand.

The faintest hue of green created a sphere as wide as her elbow. Flowridia grinned and let it shrink back.

"Flowers, you had it. You had it, and you let it go."

"I thought it was good progress," Flowridia said, wounded at the reprimand. With a pout, she expanded the crystal's radius yet again to the length of her elbow. She let it expand and decrease, expand and decrease—

Etolié groaned, looking nauseated. "You're giving me a headache."

"Etolié, the world gives you a headache."

The sober Celestial could only nod.

A creak at the door signified an intruder. Etolié perked up when Khastra, eight feet tall and grinning wide, appeared from behind the shelves. "I'm assuming the appearance of your lovely self in my domain means my project is done?"

Khastra chuckled. "Admire my work."

Etolié stumbled forward, her hands fluttering excitedly like a little bird. She plucked a small, green object from the blue woman's palm. "Your generosity is outmatched only by the girth of your biceps. Oh, it's gorgeous," Etolié gushed. "Flowers, did you know Khastra has lapidary tendencies?"

Perhaps Flowridia's confusion was obvious, because Khastra clarified with, "My fifth husband was renowned for cutting gemstones and taught me his trade. It is a relaxing pastime."

"Stop being modest. You elves are all the same," Etolié said, holding her hand up toward the light. Speckles of glittering, vibrant green sparkled against the floor. "Beautiful."

The new knowledge that Khastra might hold an elven heritage paled to the realization that she had lived long enough to be married at least five times. But for fear of being rude, Flowridia held her tongue.

"May I see, Etolié?" Flowridia asked, and Etolié held her hand forward. Several metal rings were joined together by green crystal, the sharpened points forming a dangerous weapon should Etolié decide to punch an attacker. A larger chunk of crystal attached at where the palm would grip, giving the weapon support. A practical and dangerous creation, Flowridia held it in her hands, marveling at the design and the weight. "How did you craft this? I wouldn't have thought you could use magic on something like this."

"No magic," Khastra replied. "Only skill."

"Khastra's an artisan; not a magician. But if I ask her nicely, she might make something for you too."

Flowridia handed the crystal weapon back to Etolié. "I wouldn't want to put her out. I'm happy with my shard."

But Khastra extended her hand, motioning for Flowridia to offer hers. Flowridia reached up, and the tattooed woman immediately set her fingers around Flowridia's wrist. "You are tinier than I thought. Ring or bracelet?"

"I beg your pardon?"

"You already wear a creepy necklace. Ring or bracelet?"

"Bracelet?"

Khastra released Flowridia's hand. "I will set to work tonight."

"That's very kind of you," Flowridia said, and she inspected the enormous, muscled woman, curious now that she had a hint to her heritage. Khastra bore elven features, with her pointed ears and prominent, almost delicate cheek bones, but the glowing blue eyes and horns, and certainly her tail and digitigrade, hooved legs, set her apart. The tattoos along her arms and neck bore a language Flowridia had seen in Mother's books but never learned to read, and she wondered if they extended along her entire body.

"Etolié has already been generous in her payment."

"What does she pay you?" Flowridia asked.

Khastra's laugh, bombastic as ever, echoed from the wall to the skylight. "I will be selling my crystal shards to Nox'Kartha for a hefty profit. It is useless to me; I have little patience for magic."

Yet another elven trait. "Forgive me for asking, but I hadn't considered it before. You're an elf?"

"Half," Khastra replied, utterly unoffended.

"The other half can't manifest on this realm without a host," Etolié added, and Flowridia struggled to hide her shock.

Flowridia had met many De'Sindai, but they always bore a human lineage. Elves were hell-bent on purity; demon-descended elves were unheard of. And being half-demon, Khastra's knowledge of demonic possession made an awful lot of sense.

"I never thought to ask," Flowridia said, demure despite the general's good humor. "I hope I haven't offended you."

"I cannot be offended or shamed by the truth."

The statement struck a chord with Flowridia, but she found herself too shy to press.

"Khastra's lived on this planet longer than most mortals—and immortals," Etolié said. She pointed to the far corner of shelves, filled with precariously stacked tomes. "I got some of my best elven novels from her, since she's older than most of the dirt covering them. You'll have to check it out, Flowers. Some might even be older than your favorite bloodsucker."

Curious, Flowridia followed Etolié's directive, her steps quiet as she went to the shelves. She heard Khastra say, "Etolié, try something."

Flowridia spared them a glance and realized Etolié had expanded the shield in her own hand. "Make it bigger," the half-demon said, and from her back, she unstrapped her enormous, crystal hammer. It fell to the ground with an earth-shaking 'thud'—Flowridia realized it had cracked the wooden floor.

"Khastra, why now? My head might split and seep Celestial brain slush all over the floor."

"I will get a mop if it does."

Flowridia saw the shield expand to cover the hammer and realized Khastra's experiment; when the circle of magic touched the hammer, the faint glow of the purple crystal faded. It reflected only sunlight.

Flowridia grabbed the first ancient novel her hand touched—*Old Gods of the Elven Providences*—and slid to the ground as Khastra held out a hand toward the hammer. Nothing happened. "Good to know," she mused, and she stooped down, muscles heaving, expanding, to lift the gargantuan weapon with both hands.

"Still good for smashing though," Etolié said, her eyes unfocused. Flowridia realized she held the crystal far from her body, but that anywhere the shield touched, her clothing disappeared. The sleeve of her dress had gone, as did small bits of where it draped on the floor.

Khastra either didn't notice, or simply didn't care. "Exactly. Always make sure you have a bigger stick than your enemy."

Flowridia wiped dust from the pressed collection of paper, marveling at the hand-written words when she peeled open the front cover. It bore an old style of elven syntax, only a handful of words recognizable as she thumbed through the pages, pausing here and there when she came across an illustration.

One such illustration gave her pause. Intrigued by the faded ink and the figures represented, Flowridia studied a mosaic of the two Old Gods. The woman had no details to her picture—only a lithe, black silhouette and fire at her feet. She looked away from her counterpart, yet their hands touched at the center, her small one held in his large, gloved one.

He stared wistfully at her image—even depicted on ancient paper, Flowridia saw longing—yet her breath caught at the image of the picturesque man. Brilliant and armored, a halo gleamed around his head, and even in a monochrome depiction, Flowridia could practically see the golden light.

"Etolié," she said, and something in her visage must have spoken of panic. Etolié placed her toy on her shelf of gifted trinkets, the gemmed weapon fitting in well with the rest, and approached, Khastra following behind. Flowridia tapped the image of the gleaming man, one who bore a sword and no sigil, the same man who had called her a fool and asked for a name.

Etolié sat beside her while Khastra leaned against the shelf, looking confused as she stared down at the offered picture. But Etolié said, "Well, Flowers, Prince Falrir did say the true Gods of this world have every use for orbs." The Celestial stole the book, immediately squinting at the text. "Khastra, I need your knowledge of ancient elven literature."

Khastra set her hammer down and sat beside Etolié, her armor brushing against what Flowridia knew was an illusionary dress.

"What does this mean, Etolié?" Flowridia asked, watching as Khastra's eyes scanned the ancient text.

"It means we either have a committed imposter," Etolié replied, and already she pulled out the small mirror she kept, "or a very big problem." She tapped the reflection, and Flowridia watched as it began to glow, and then Empress Alauriel's face appeared.

Lara smiled, her silver eyes kind when she saw Etolié. "Hello, Etolié."

Etolié wasted no time on pleasantries, instead turning the mirror over to face the book. "This is our man."

"I beg your pardon?"

"Flowers found this. This is the dead God of Order, and he looks exactly like the man who murdered your father."

While Etolié and Lara hashed out the impossibility of the claim, Flowridia watched Khastra frown over the text and turn the page, revealing yet another depiction of the dead Gods. An artistic rendition of an elven woman in childbirth, yet from her womb burst a cacophony of angels and demons. A grotesque image, truly—she lay as though dead, her eyes rolled back—and held above her head, spilling from her hands, were six orbs.

"Khastra, what is this?"

"The Convergence and Chaos," Khastra replied, still skimming the text. "A metaphor for creation—when the worlds converged, it killed the Old Gods to bring in the new."

She was dead, then. Flowridia frowned at one small detail, though. "She was an elf?"

"That is wildly disputed. Elves like to claim it, but elves do not typically worship non-elves."

Flowridia sat back, frowning as she recalled Prince Falrir's claim, that their God had promised rewards for their loyalty, that historically they had worshipped Order, that Gods gained power through belief . . .

But why would a dead God wish for orbs?

Thoughtful, Flowridia turned the page back to the depiction of Order and Chaos as two opposite entities and saw the longing in Order's stylized view, wondering if perhaps. . .

Two halves of a whole. A beautiful thought, two deities ruling their own world, until one used the orbs to converge the worlds together.

"Order and Chaos were opposites in all things," Flowridia said aloud, and saw Etolié and Khastra—and Lara in the mirror—all look to her. Shy, she continued with,

"Chaos used the orbs to combine the worlds. What if Order wants to tear them back apart?"

"It would destroy Sha'Demoni, and probably Celestière with it," Etolié said, looking over Flowridia's shoulder at the book.

Lara, in the mirror, said, "I will discuss this with my council and give them this new information."

Flowridia looked to Etolié. "You think it holds weight?"

"I don't know. But even if he's only a delusional mad-man playing God, with the power of six orbs, it'll nearly make him one."

Etolié handed down books. They spent the day reading.

Chapter 12

Ayla had promised two weeks.

On the appointed day, they received a letter from Archbishop Xoran—an invitation to their official unveiling of the statue of Sol Kareena and her child, along with a request for a meeting between his council and theirs. An offer could be made for the orb, he wrote, but he would only discuss the details in person.

Dirtied from a morning spent gardening, Flowridia kept her dirt-encrusted fingers hidden in her skirts as Thalmus berated the willful queen.

"You won't be going," Thalmus said, in response to Marielle's palpable excitement.

The queen pouted, the letter falling to her lap. "I can't stay cooped inside this city forever, so Flowridia and I–"

"Will leave us alone with Ayla Darkleaf?"

In the council chamber, Thalmus, Marielle, Khastra, and Flowridia were present. Etolié had been summoned, but the sober Celestial hadn't left her library since Flowridia's discovery.

Flowridia tentatively raised a hand, but quickly drew it back, recalling her soiled fingers. "The embassy is only three days from now. Can we make both events?"

Marielle squinted at the letter, visibly making calculations in her head. "If we leave the morning after, we can make it–"

"Twice now," Thalmus interrupted, "there have been attempts on your life, even if Flowra had to bear the brunt of the second."

"There will be no danger this time," Khastra said, but she barely paid attention, instead focusing on the cloth she used to polish the crevices of her gargantuan weapon.

"Because this time, I will be accompanying Etolié. Who would dare?"

With palpable ire, Marielle slunk back into her throne. "Fine, send Etolié and Khastra and leave me and my orb here unprotected–"

"Etolié already thought this through," Khastra continued, easily speaking over Marielle. "She has commissioned a box made of her crystal, big enough to hide an orb inside. Even if he comes here, he will never find it."

Flowridia had to admit it was a clever plan.

"Queen Etolié has spoken, I suppose," Marielle said, and Flowridia saw her distorted reflection glowering in the crystal weapon. "Meeting adjourned. I've promised to see Zorlaeus, so if Lady Ayla shows up early, warn me."

Flowridia left the council room, Marielle's request dredging up her heart's insecurity. Two weeks of longing, wondering, worrying . . .

Realizing the tangle of her hair and the mess of her dress and hands, Flowridia went to her bedroom for a fresh dress, then to the washroom to bathe.

Flowridia shared the washroom with all members of the ruling council—aside from Thalmus and Khastra, who had their own respective wash areas to accommodate their sizes—and was grateful to find the room and large brass tub, unoccupied.

A clever assembly of pipes and well-placed splits in the planes—set up by Empress Alauriel herself, Etolié said, given her talents for bending the structure of reality—allowed water to gush from pipes into the tub. Flowridia removed her nightgown and underclothes, then folded them neatly into a pile on a small table by the door. On top, she placed the ear.

Her hair fell in thick waves as she removed bits of brush, leaves, and forgotten flower petals, ones she let settle across the surface of the water once the tub had filled.

Warmth enveloped her body and soul. Flowridia sank until only the barest hints of her shoulders peeked above the water. Releasing a deep breath, she reached for the soap, sliding it along her thin arms as she forced stress to seep from her pores and into the water. Bubbles gathered along the surface, congregating around her exposed skin.

When would Ayla be here? With no need for sleep, she seemed to live in her own timeline. Perhaps Flowridia would fall asleep alone but awaken in the arms of the enticing woman.

Heat colored her cheeks at the thought of awakening in a soft embrace. Beautiful Ayla with her sharp eyes illuminated by candlelight, her dexterous fingers as they pulled each flower petal from Flowridia's hair, the reveal of her body, sensuous and slight—

Flowridia bit her lip, demure at her own scandalous memory. Two weeks apart had brought worry but also a dissatisfaction she could only label as 'impatience.'

Her shoulders glistened as the soap glided along their sharp contours. Flowridia sat up, washing her neck, her breasts, shifting her thoughts away from how smooth and soft they would feel beneath Ayla's hands. Instead, she thought of the future, of how to entertain Ayla in the upcoming days. There had been the coy offer of dinner, and Flowridia hoped Ayla fulfilled her tantalizing promise, curious at what sort of menu an elven vampire—or something like it, she corrected herself—would concoct.

The soap slid down to her stomach, and then Flowridia heard, "A little lower, Flowra."

Flowridia gasped, the soap slipping from her hands, and curled against the metal wall of the tub to hide her body. Ayla Darkleaf managed to fill the entire doorway, despite her small figure, her hands gripping either side of the wooden frame. Her fingers slid down the wood, and Flowridia felt a blush radiate across her face and chest.

"No, no—do continue," Ayla said, eyebrow quirked. The grin spreading across her face held a dangerous sort of mischief, exacerbated by the burn still brutally marring her face. Would it forever? "Gods know I've done the same thinking about you. Give me a show."

Breathless, Flowridia grabbed the soap, nervous but aching beneath Ayla's gaze. Beneath the water, the soap rubbed against her thighs and up—

The heat between Flowridia's legs rose at the touch. The soap drifted from her hand, and with a permissive glance to Ayla, she touched that small bud oh so gently.

Her breath hitched. Ayla's smile grew wide. She stepped forward, coolly slipping the sleeves of her dress off her shoulders. Mesmerized, Flowridia watched the slow reveal of Ayla's sensuous form. Her finger dipped lower, and despite the water she could feel warm, thick wetness begin to seep.

Ayla asked for a show, but she was the one who gave it, her dress pooling around her feet. Ayla was as alluring as she was in memory, but Flowridia's imagination could never recreate the regal way she held herself, her proud stance, and of course that grin. Utterly nude, Ayla came closer, her thin skin revealing every minute movement of her musculature.

When Ayla knelt, Flowridia felt air brush against her ear and Ayla's eyes on her body beneath the water. "Oh, Sweet Flowra, you're such a sight." When Flowridia's hand paused, she heard Ayla chide, "No, keep going. Let's see how I fuck you in your memory." A wicked chuckle caressed Flowridia's ear. "You are thinking about me, right?"

Biting her lip, Flowridia moved her fingers, letting them stroke against the soft folds before two disappeared inside, her body alight at the touch. A whine escaped unbidden from her throat. She held it in, even as she moved her fingers slowly in and out, the water causing friction.

From behind, Ayla's hands appeared on her shoulders and slid beneath the water, the temperature shift shocking. She stopped at Flowridia's breasts, squeezing as she whispered, "Don't be so demure. Let me hear how much you've missed me."

Immediately, a moan escaped Flowridia's throat, pleasure simmering as Ayla's hands groped her. Her own fingers moved smoothly inside her body. Lips against the back of her throat brought the promise of sweet marks, and as Ayla sucked on her skin, Flowridia said, "I missed you."

"I know."

Flowridia slowed the pace of her fucking, Ayla's hands on her breasts a delight she longed to savor. "Perhaps I shouldn't ask–" Ayla suddenly pinched the peaked buds, forcing a gasp from Flowridia's throat.

"Shouldn't ask what?" Ayla said, voice muffled by Flowridia's neck.

"How was your mission for Casvir–"

Again, Ayla pinched her, the pain lingering until Flowridia yelped. Ayla released her breasts entirely. "Is Casvir what you think of when you fuck yourself, Flowra?"

Flowridia shook her head.

"Then shut *up*." Flowridia felt her stand, but her nail traced a threatening line along Flowridia's shoulder. Ayla appeared at the side of the tub, then stepped inside, the water chilling as she sank her body down. The small woman leaned forward, no amusement in her features. "What were you thinking of?"

Flowridia shrunk back, the words, "I wanted to know that you were safe," tumbling out before she could collect them into something articulate. "I-I'm sorry if–"

"No, Flowra," Ayla said, her tense posture fading as the woman forced a smile. "This only means I need to try harder."

The water parted as Ayla lowered herself down, engulfing her as she disappeared below the surface.

Flowridia watched, concerned until she felt Ayla's lips against her thigh. Pressure welled in her abdomen as she felt Ayla's teeth scrape against her skin, trailing up until Ayla's mouth kissed her vulva.

Flowridia gripped the edges of the tub, head suddenly light. The raging force of her lover dominated every corner of her mind, her pleasure too loud to be shied by any semblance of sanity. Ayla's skilled tongue pulled cries from her body, and Flowridia hoped her ecstasy could be heard beneath the water's surface.

Climax came quickly. Every nerve of Flowridia's body lit in stimulation, bursting first beneath Ayla's tongue and then spreading through her limbs.

Pleasure soon waned. The slight trickling of bathwater and Flowridia's own heaving breaths became the only sounds.

Ayla rose from the depths with a vicious grin. Flowridia was reminded of some great monster from below the sea, but she pulled Ayla into her arms, fearless in the presence of the tamed beast.

Her lips brushed Ayla's before she settled her head between the woman's small breasts. "I'm glad you're back."

Ayla said nothing, simply indulged Flowridia's need for affection, as her own hands settled onto Flowridia's waist and hips.

Flowridia's thumb drew light circles against Ayla's skin. "The embassy won't be opening for a few more days," she whispered. "Does that mean you're staying?"

"Yes, I'll be staying. I suppose I ought to announce my presence for the sake of propriety."

Flowridia leaned up and placed a languid kiss on her companion's lips. "Let me keep you for myself a little longer," she whispered. She batted her eyelashes, nervous as she met Ayla's gaze. "Please? Once they know you're here, I don't know when we'll get a moment alone."

"If I want you alone, I'll get you alone," Ayla replied, venom in her voice. "But I'll indulge. Do with me as you will."

Flowridia felt herself cringe at the harsh words, but spoke nonetheless. "I can't hold my breath as long as you can," she said, a slight smile pulling at her lips. "Come to bed with me?"

Ayla lifted her up and carried her from the tub. "Dry yourself. I'll meet you in your bedroom."

Ayla vanished in the shadow of the doorframe.

"Flowra, where do you keep your knives?"

In the kitchen, Ayla moved like a whirlwind, procuring ingredients Flowridia knew they didn't have from the cupboards. Whatever trick was involved, Flowridia didn't ask, content to watch the graceful woman as she danced between the shelves and assembled supplies.

Perched on the countertop, Flowridia pointed to a drawer nearest the iron stove. Even with the windows open, the kitchen quickly heated to an uncomfortable degree, but Ayla seemed immune. She withdrew an enormous carving knife and inspected it in the light. "Do you *ever* sharpen your knives?"

Flowridia didn't know the answer, but she shrunk at the patronizing tone. "I–"

"Forget it. Dull is still workable," Ayla said, and she immediately began stealing from the pile of precariously stacked vegetables. Pepper, onions, and other assorted edible plants awaited, and Flowridia found herself impressed at Ayla's finesse with a knife.

Demitri paced at her dangling feet, her toes tickled each time his fur brushed against her. When Ayla grabbed a fistful of small mushrooms, Flowridia felt herself pale. "Ayla?"

Ayla continued chopping the fungal growths and said, "Yes?"

"Mushrooms make me ill."

Ayla stopped, tense, but then wordlessly took the wooden board of half-chopped mushrooms and dumped them out the window.

She said nothing else. Flowridia withdrew further into herself, anxious at Ayla's erratic mood.

Within minutes, unique, warm smells began to emanate from the kitchen. Ayla darted tirelessly between chopping, stirring the boiling pot at the stove, and heating whatever decadent array of vegetables awaited them. Flowridia smiled faintly at the sight, content when the mood grew less tense. "Would you like me to help you?" she offered shyly.

Ayla paused, stirring the pot and flipping the roasting vegetables in tandem. "No, Flowra. Tonight, I'm spoiling you. You need only stay sitting like the pretty picture you are."

Flowridia blushed, yet still her nerves wouldn't settle. From another cupboard, Ayla withdrew a small wooden box and set it on the counter. She flipped open the lid and grinned, withdrawing a tiny, black pod. Over the pot, it crumbled to dust, scattering into whatever concoction she brewed.

"What's that?" Flowridia asked, and she obeyed when Ayla beckoned her over.

Ayla withdrew another small pod and popped it into her own mouth. "A delicacy of my homeland." Then, without warning, she planted a kiss on Flowridia's mouth.

Heat sank through her lips, burning her mouth at the contact. Flowridia pulled back, squeaking as Ayla laughed uproariously. "That's hot!"

"Not nearly so hot as what awaits you tonight," Ayla replied with a wink.

"That's not–" Flowridia closed her mouth, realizing she was being toyed with. "I don't think I can kiss you until you wash your mouth out."

"You'll kiss me if I tell you to kiss me."

Ayla wasn't wrong.

Ignoring the heat flaring across her cheeks, Flowridia sat back down on the counter. "Do you cook often?"

"Hardly," Ayla replied, still chuckling to herself. How she managed to jump so smoothly between the oil-filled pan, the boiling pot, and the cupboards, Flowridia couldn't guess. "I only eat for appearances."

"Who only does what for which–" Etolié's entrance pulled no reaction from Ayla, who continued her frenzy in the kitchen. The Celestial, however, raised an eyebrow. "Lady Ayla, nice to see your headache has gone away."

Flowridia flinched at the remark, but Ayla turned with a charming smile. "I'm feeling much better, thank you."

"I mean, it's not all the way . . ." Etolié gestured, palm wide, across her face, mimicking where the burn marred Ayla's otherwise flawless features, but let it drop. She turned to Flowridia with a wide smile and panicked eyes. "Does Queen Marielle know the Nox'Karthan diplomat has arrived?"

Flowridia shook her head, but Ayla said, "My arrival party was small but more than satisfying. Flowra has made pleasurable accommodations for me." The wink she gave Flowridia was nothing less than obscene.

"With that innuendo, I'll be cracking out the alcohol a little ahead of schedule," Etolié said. "I'll tell Marielle you're here."

"Tell her dinner will be ready soon," Ayla chimed, her tone dripping with sincerity. "It's the least I can do for my friends in Staelash."

When Etolié left, Flowridia went to shut the door. "It's kind of you to prepare everyone dinner," she said, coming to stand behind the elven woman.

"As I said, the least I can do," Ayla replied, still smiling, but Flowridia swore she saw it crack.

Small paws patted her leg, and Flowridia stooped down to lift Demitri, his young voice mingling silently in her head. *Lady Ayla is being so friendly.*

"Ayla is very friendly, yes."

Make sure she doesn't poison Etolié. I like her.

Flowridia nearly dropped the pup, shocked at his rudeness. Instead of responding, she said to Ayla, "How long will you be staying in Staelash?"

"Casvir expects me to return after the embassy's official unveiling. I'm early, I know, but I have little to do at home, so I thought I might spend some time with you." Ayla turned from her cooking, the smile on her lips the first bit of true sincerity Flowridia had seen all evening. "You're a puzzle I have yet to solve, Sweet Flowra."

A bit of fluttering joy filled Flowridia's stomach. Unable to help herself, she set Demitri down and carefully placed her hands at Ayla's waist. When the woman didn't stiffen, Flowridia let her hands slide around Ayla's body as she set her head against her bony shoulder.

"I'm happy you're here," Flowridia whispered amidst sounds of sizzling vegetables. She placed a kiss at the top of Ayla's head.

The door creaked open, and Flowridia released Ayla when Thalmus entered the room. He stared oddly at the pair, but Ayla beamed at his entrance. "Thalmus, a pleasure to see you again–"

Thalmus turned around and left.

Something crackled, and Ayla nearly jumped as she removed the pan from the stove. "I swear on Onias' Hell if I've burned this . . ." Ayla's angry muttering switched into elven curses as she resumed her whirlwind, speaking in a dialect Flowridia couldn't hope to understand.

Thalmus reentered, and Flowridia quickly stood up, noticing the iron set of his jaw. Ayla smiled at his entrance. "I may not be the best cook, but there's something blissfully pleasant about cooking for those you appreciate–"

"Lady Ayla, may we speak in private?" Thalmus glowered, making no effort to hide his displeasure.

Ayla quirked a coy eyebrow. "I'm at a pivotal juncture in my cooking. I wouldn't want to burn anything. Can it wait until after dinner?"

Thalmus turned to Flowridia. "Flowra, would you mind if I spoke to Lady Ayla alone in the kitchen so I don't interrupt her cooking?"

Flowridia, nervous at being roped into their standoff, gave a quiet nod. But Ayla's claws on her waist stopped her. "Flowra–" The use of the affectionate title caused Thalmus' frown to deepen. "My sweet summer blossom, there's no need to leave." Ayla looked again at Thalmus. "Whatever you say, she'll find out anyway."

"Then I'll speak as though she isn't here." Thalmus crossed his arms, his imposing height comparable to his scowl. Yet, Ayla stood tall enough to match him in demeanor, her half-smile victorious. "I will be brief: hurt her again, and you'll be ripped in two before you can slink into the shadows like the snake you are."

Ayla's smile only grew. "Are you threatening a foreign dignitary, Sir Thalmus?"

"I am threatening you. If I have to stand before Imperator Casvir and explain why I tore the head off his favorite diplomat, I'll tell him she hurt my little flower girl."

223

A dark chuckle left Ayla's pursed lips, but Flowridia saw that Thalmus' eyes glistened behind his pointed glare. "You're willing to die for this cause?" Ayla's nails suddenly dug into her side. "Noble of you. Is it love?"

"Not a love you could ever understand," Thalmus replied, and Flowridia withheld a gasp when Ayla's fingers threatened to draw blood. But Thalmus stood firm, even as Ayla's stare grew venomous. "She's worth fighting for."

Thalmus stepped back, his gaze falling to Flowridia before he turned aside and left the room.

The food sizzled, but Ayla's focus remained on the door. Flowridia tried to remove the burning food from heat, but when she moved, Ayla's grip grew painfully tight. "Ayla, you're hurting–"

Ayla's hands left her side so suddenly that Flowridia nearly toppled. She might have, had Ayla not immediately steadied her. With gentleness, she held Flowridia up, mouth severe but eyes wide. One hand stayed clutching Flowridia's arm as she removed all the pans from heat, silent as she worked.

When Flowridia moved to step away, the grip grew tight again. Not painful—protective. Ayla held on until Flowridia finally spoke, gently, so as not to startle the mercurial predator. "Can I help you? I'll set the table."

Ayla's arm dropped, staring incredulously. "Do you even have servants?"

"We do, but it's early for dinner." Flowridia moved toward the cupboard where the dishes were held. The small woman held a spiteful glare. "Truly, I don't mind. It'll only take a moment," Flowridia said, and when Ayla didn't immediately pounce on her, she took action.

Separated by only half a wall, the private, casual dining room waited, and Flowridia quickly set eight places. Would Zorlaeus be joining them? She would relinquish her own seat if needed.

Would Ayla be eating?

"Ayla?" Flowridia peeked her head around, shyly watching her companion. "Will you be eating too?"

Ayla tilted her head back, smiling coolly. "I'll at least give the appearance of it, for the comfort of your friends."

"I don't think they'd–" Flowridia stopped herself. They would mind. "I'll remember that," she said instead, and she moved to grab a tray.

Flowridia froze when a hand suddenly grabbed her wrist. Ayla glared, and Flowridia was surprised she didn't growl with how she raised her hackles. "Sit," Ayla commanded, pointing to the dining table.

Flowridia obeyed. Ayla fluttered in and out, setting trays and pots and dishes Flowridia didn't remember her cooking. She watched in silence from her seat at the table, the only correspondence being an occasional wink from Ayla.

Soon, the table was set. Delicious smells wafted from the unique dishes, including the one laden with whatever potent spice Ayla had inflicted upon her.

Ayla sat beside her, at the head of the table, and began to spoon various foods onto Flowridia's plate. "Flowra, eat. You're terribly thin."

Flowridia frowned, though not with any true anger. "Your remarks cut as sharp as your cheekbones."

Ayla merely blinked, visibly confused.

Nervous, Flowridia continued, praying her backtracking didn't land her into trouble. "You're much smaller than me. The irony of you scolding me for being thin . . ." Flowridia shoved a fork-full of food into her mouth, shutting up her embarrassed words.

Whatever touched her tongue held an intricate array of flavors, nothing Flowridia had ever tasted before. She smiled as she chewed, even as Ayla's confusion settled into annoyance. "Forgive me for being so pointed, but need I remind you that I'm *dead*." No question laced the statement.

"This is delicious," Flowridia offered shyly. Blinking prettily, she felt her stiff form relax when Ayla's expression softened.

"You are welcome, Flowra."

Etolié peeked her head around the door, but Khastra pushed past and moved to join Ayla and Flowridia at the table. "Etolié said you made everyone dinner," the half-demon said, and she sat at a chair at the opposite end of the table, one of two that were noticeably larger than the rest.

"It's a delicacy from Falar'Sol, the Sun Elven homeland," Ayla said, and she began to place food onto her own plate, gesturing for Khastra to do the same. "I haven't been there in ages, but I do recall a few recipes."

"I know where Falar'Sol is," Khastra said, accepting the serving utensils. Etolié sat beside her, a slight wall between she and Ayla Darkleaf.

Ayla raised an eyebrow, as though a challenge had been issued. "I spent much of my life in Star Tree, though it's been a few centuries."

"I have been to Star Tree, but not in your lifetime," Khastra said.

Ayla grinned, amusement in the gesture. "Oh, I don't know. I'm quite old."

"I am older."

Again, there was that competitive glint in Ayla's eye. "I was born before the Sun Elven Purge."

Khastra sat up straight, swallowing her bite of food before saying, "When I was born, Sun Elves were still pledged to the Goddess of Chaos."

Ayla leaned back in her chair, looking somewhat impressed. "I concede."

Khastra said nothing else and instead began piling food onto Etolié's empty plate.

"General Khastra," Ayla added, her smile slowly twisting with intrigue. "I do believe I've heard your name. But what business would the Bringer of War have in this charming little kingdom?"

Khastra stole a glance in Ayla's direction before placing the serving utensils back in their respective places. "Perhaps for the same reasons as you, Izthuni Spawn. But I would never be so forward as to ask."

Awkward silence began to brew. Some power play had ensued, and Flowridia might have said something had she not been acutely aware of Ayla's foot tracing lines along her leg.

Etolié nervously glanced between the pair. "I couldn't find Marielle or Zorlaeus anywhere," she finally said, and Flowridia noticed the open flask in her hand. It seemed the Celestial's fast had ended. "Thalmus said he wasn't hungry."

"More for us, then," Ayla said, casting a coy glance to Flowridia.

"Star Tree is nowhere near the sea," Etolié said, and behind her, Khastra watched the exchange with a full mouth. "How did you end up here?"

Ayla smiled, her cheekbones threatening to split her cheeks. "Opportunity. Casvir offered a business arrangement I couldn't refuse."

Flowridia suspected the statement was literal.

"He seems like a strict employer." Etolié said it with every ounce of politeness she possessed, Flowridia was sure, but Ayla's smile twitched nonetheless.

"Employment is stifling."

"Agreed. My days of personally obliterating slave camps are over, but at least I have more time for research." Etolié's wistful tone suggested this may have been a paltry substitute.

"I have a bit of a set-up myself in Nox'Kartha. Respectable employment doesn't have to mean the end of pet projects." Ayla gestured from Etolié's empty plate to the plethora of food. "Eat, please."

Etolié put up a polite hand. "I don't actually need to eat food."

"Neither do I," Ayla said, taking a small bite.

"You make a compelling argument," Etolié replied, and she began sampling the array of food Khastra had placed on her plate. "Everyone knows I founded a kingdom. Has Flowers ever told you the story of how she ended up here?"

Flowridia blushed lightly, setting her fork down onto her mostly empty plate. "Oh, Etolié–"

"It's a great story." Etolié brought her flask to her lips, then with a dramatic flourish, offered it to Ayla. The undead woman accepted it with a conspiring smirk. "Found her in the woods. I had been visiting the late emperor when I received word of Clarence Vors' death, and on my way to Staelash, I found her swaddling what I thought was a baby."

Demitri's head popped up from underneath the table, revealing his spot on Etolié's lap. "Turns out, I wasn't quite wrong," Etolié continued, cradling the wolf pup. "I couldn't leave a baby alone in the woods, or the adorable little witch who owned him. Marielle immediately fell in love and said they could stay."

"And why was a delectable little thing like you alone in the woods?" Ayla cooed, leaning close to Flowridia's ear.

Ayla held no ire in her tone, but the question made Flowridia's head buzz. She brought her hands together, fidgeting underneath the table. "I lived there," she said, and it was not a lie.

"The headache she gave me told me she was something special. She's been my ward ever since." As almost an afterthought, Etolié quickly amended, "And, of course, was promoted to Grand Diplomat. Our little shrinking violet will be a wonderful stand-in for myself when I inevitably light myself on fire to escape the political world–"

The door burst open. Marielle and Zorlaeus entered, both of them beaming. "Everyone, Zorlaeus has proposed! We're getting–" Marielle stopped when her eyes matched with Ayla's. Zorlaeus, too, had all joy suddenly drain from his countenance. "Lady Ayla," Marielle said stiffly, "I didn't realize you had arrived."

"No, no," Ayla said, standing and rushing to them. "No need for apologies. Not with such a spectacle to celebrate. Oh, Lae Lae, I'm so happy for you!" She enveloped Zorlaeus in a crushing hug, and Flowridia didn't miss the flinch of pain from Marielle's intended. "We had all been wondering when the big day would be."

"We hope for a short engagement," the De'Sindai managed to say, and Ayla pulled away, smiling wide.

"Come sit, both of you." Ayla gestured to the table. "This calls for a celebratory drink. Give me a moment–"

She vanished into the shadow of the pantry door.

Silence settled. Marielle and Zorlaeus awkwardly sat.

Khastra, however, side-eyed the door. "She fits in the pantry?"

Unsure if she could reveal to everyone the explanation of Ayla's unusual talent, Flowridia simply shrugged.

Ayla quickly reappeared, and in her hand she flashed a black, metallic flask, one bearing the official Nox'Karthan seal. "From Casvir's personal stores. Strong enough to wake the dead."

Balanced in her other hand, she held six stacked glasses, ones she arranged in a row on the table. Barely a drop of liquid in each, and Ayla handed one to Flowridia with a slight shake to her head. "A toast to the new couple."

At arm's length, Flowridia could smell whatever toxic brew wafted from the glass.

Only Etolié and Ayla partook at first. Ayla flipped the glass back and took it all in one swig.

Etolié tilted back the glass . . . and fell into her chair.

Ayla watched the scene with visible disappointment. "Too much for you, Favored of Eionei?"

Flowridia heard Etolié mumble, "Strong stuff."

From across the table, Khastra took a tentative sip and winced. "Highly effective."

"Well, I have no wish to intrude on personal matters," Ayla said, placing a sincere hand on her chest. From the flask itself, she took another gulp. "I'll leave your council to celebrate in peace."

Ayla turned to leave, and Marielle made desperate eye contact with Flowridia. She nudged toward the door.

Flowridia understood.

Ayla had nearly disappeared down the hall by the time Flowridia left the kitchen. "Ayla, wait!"

Ayla turned slowly, a vicious glint in her eyes. "Sorry," she cooed, serpentine as she smiled. "The mood was nauseating. I'll be in your room if you wish to celebrate Lae Lae's engagement to that bitch."

It rolled so smoothly off Ayla's tongue that Flowridia swore she misheard. "I'm sorry?" Flowridia stopped and placed her hand on Ayla's arm. "Ayla–"

"You can't hate a dog for chasing after swine. I'm happy he's happy." Ayla ripped her arm away and continued walking, her glare pointed straight ahead as she barreled forward.

Pressure crushed Flowridia's ribs, as though an iron hand suffocated her. "I didn't realize you had such strong feelings toward Marielle," she offered tentatively. "Or Zorlaeus."

Ayla stopped, her grip on the flask tightening as she slowly turned around. "I despise him," she seethed. "He's a pathetic little cur, but what does it say if I can't keep even that skulking wretch under my control? My name could once hush a room to silence, Flowra. I was a whisper, because who would dare to speak and summon me? Now, I'm nothing."

"You're not nothing," Flowridia whispered. "You've never been nothing to me."

Ayla took a slow drink from the flask, the ice in her eyes directed at Flowridia as she topped it, tossed it aside, and pulled Flowridia forward into a rough kiss.

Metal clanged against the stone floor. Flowridia craved the contact of Ayla's cool embrace, but the strong stench of alcohol made her flinch. She pulled away as Ayla gripped her arm and dragged her down the hall toward the stairs. "Are you drunk?"

Ayla stopped, staring in disbelief. "How naïve are you? I'm *dead.*"

Flowridia cringed at the harsh words. But the wall suddenly appeared at her back, and a crushing kiss stole her reply. Desperate hands groped her form. Flowridia turned her head and cowered, trying in vain to push Ayla away. "Not here, not here–" A gasp escaped her throat when Ayla suddenly whisked her into her arms and carried her up the stairs.

In her bedroom, Ayla kicked the door shut and nearly threw Flowridia onto the plush mattress. The slight form dominated her before she could breathe, but alone, Flowridia felt no need to fight it. Instead, she melted into the touch, letting Ayla's hands roam her body. Despite the taste of noxious liquor, Flowridia savored the contact. Her own hands settled lightly onto Ayla's waist, fingers grazing the thin fabric of her dress.

Flowridia gasped when teeth nipped at her throat. Fear and arousal spiked in tandem, and Flowridia wondered absently if this would be her end.

Ayla's mouth drew away, her burned visage nightmarish in the setting sunlight. Whispered words tingled at Flowridia's senses. "You're mine," her perfect voice seethed, and a shiver shot down Flowridia's spine.

Steel and ice met Flowridia's gaze, but she dared to reach her hand up and lightly cup the sharp lines of Ayla's face. Flowridia whispered, "I'm yours."

Ayla flinched, eyes wide. Her hand moved to cover Flowridia's, cold to the touch and trembling.

Then, anger twisted those cutting features. She tore Flowridia's hand away.

Flowridia gasped when Ayla grabbed the collar of her dress. Ripping fabric joined the chorus of moans. Exposed now, the cool air touched Flowridia's skin only a moment before Ayla's hand gripped her breast. Nails threatened to tear at the tender skin, and Flowridia moved to stroke Ayla's fine, black hair.

But she was stopped, her wrist grabbed and forced above her head. Ayla's icy glower reflected the fading sun. "Beg," she said, quiet menace simmering beneath the controlled storm. "Beg for me to claim you."

The grip on her wrist grew tight, painful. Flowridia nodded, gasping. "Take me, Ayla, please."

Shivers coursed along Flowridia's skin as Ayla released her and drew careful lines with her nails. Down Flowridia's arms, her torso, and finally to her thighs. Ice became her prison, Ayla's stare unrelenting. When a single, lithe finger stroked a line down her dripping heat, Flowridia said, "Please, Ayla–"

Two fingers moved smoothly inside her. Pleasure came in tumultuous waves, Ayla's hand breaking upon her wanting shore. Oh, such perfection, to be so connected. Flowridia gripped the sheets, unable to contain her inarticulate cries.

Her blood burned with each thrust. Soon came the rush, a new high as her mind met the same pleasure as her body. A burst and a falling as sweeping reality met her too sensitive senses, and Ayla, so perceptive, slowed her pace as Flowridia fell back to earth.

Flowridia's eyelids fluttered shut, a shy smile coming unbidden to her lips. Ayla pulled out, and after a coy stroke to her aching bud, she wiped her hands against the sheet and crawled on her palms to face Flowridia. Their bodies didn't touch—not quite—as Ayla held herself above her.

Breathing heavy, Flowridia reached an exhausted limb up to touch Ayla's face. Emotion threatened to burst from her chest, foreign, warm feelings that grew every moment they were together. Shyly, she said, "Ayla–"

"Satisfied?" Ayla said, the word smooth against her tongue.

Through Flowridia's clouded, emotive thoughts burst despair. Unwilling to articulate, she pulled Ayla's face down to meet hers. Their mouths met with urgency; Flowridia prayed it hid her hurt.

Ayla pulled their lips apart, perhaps sensing something amiss. Flowridia engulfed her in an embrace, holding the smaller woman against her chest as her fingers ran along the bony contours of Ayla's back and ribs.

"Something displeases you." Ayla's voice, though muffled between her breasts, was unmistakably cutting.

Flowridia shrunk. "I would only hope . . ." Her words faded, and she felt Ayla snake her lithely muscled arms around her. "I hope you know this is about more than my satisfaction. I care about you."

A paltry substitute for truth.

Ayla pulled away to face her. She removed one hand from Flowridia's waist and let it trace faint lines along her face. "My Sweet Flowra, I apologize. I have been unbearable."

"No, no!" Flowridia quickly shook her head, panic in her words. "Ayla, you've been perfectly cordial."

"You blush so prettily when you lie. No, I've been intolerable." Ayla's voice caressed her ears with the same slow sensuality as her touch. Resignation settled onto Ayla's features. "Nothing to worry yourself over, Flowra. It's merely been too long since I've had a proper meal."

A soft smile tugged at Flowridia's lips. "Ayla, you made a beautiful dinner–" The smile vanished. The terrible truth slammed her like a brick.

Flowridia had seen Ayla's fangs in the presence of blood, watched her lick it from her fingers. Yet, she'd never considered the truth, that necromancy called for life and that Ayla was a creature born of dark magic.

"Blood is the price of life, Flowra."

"Must you kill, though?" Flowridia's voice was as shy as she felt.

"Gods, no," Ayla said, light laughter in her voice. "I only need a small bite. But I wouldn't dare hunt in your kingdom." Her voice lowered. "Casvir would have my head."

"What if it were offered freely?" Flowridia's voice faltered as her companion turned her questioning gaze onto her. But her courage held, though her blood ran cold. "Take mine."

Ayla shook her head, her eyes magnetized to Flowridia's.

"Ayla, please. If blood is the price of life, then would it help . . ." Her words trailed away as she dared to trace the charred line of Ayla's burn.

"Healing would take more blood than a simple feeding. I could hurt you."

Flowridia's hand reached forward to brush aside the hair from Ayla's severed ear, revealing the exposed bone. "Will it help?"

"Perhaps. But, Flowra–"

"Let me right what I've done." With sincere tenderness, Flowridia managed what she hoped was a reassuring smile. "I offer myself as a gift."

When Ayla pursed her lips, Flowridia saw the barest hints of her fangs. Flowridia sensed animal instinct, barely contained. "I could kill you."

"But you won't. I trust you. Won't you please let me show you?"

Ayla leaned forward, her pupils a black mass consuming all semblance of rectitude. Flowridia placed a finger against her lips. "If you're going to bite me, put it somewhere no one will see."

Oh, there was that grin—the predator bore her teeth, and for the first time Flowridia felt true fear seize her heart at the sight. Her imagination had not betrayed her; Ayla's fangs grew long.

As Ayla drew back, Flowridia stiffened, her fists growing tight. She shut her eyes, bracing herself against whatever pain she had told to strike.

But instead, a hand wrapped around her tense fist. A gentle hand, familiar and cold—one whose touch brought intimacy and pleasure, one that made love with no reserve.

Flowridia opened her eyes and saw Ayla's hesitation. The elven woman's mouth, closed now, seemed too small to encompass her teeth. "We don't have to do this."

Flowridia shook her head and unbound her fist. Dread faded away, and she interlaced their fingers. "I want to."

Ayla kept a careful stare as she lowered her head, her colorless eyes calculating as she drank in the sight of Flowridia's bare torso. "Somewhere no one will see . . ." The animal returned—the very image of hunger and lust—and Ayla sank down and kissed the side of Flowridia's breast. With a confirming glance, Ayla bared her teeth and let her fangs prick the soft skin beside her peaked bud. Hardly a sting, and Flowridia watched the surreal vision of blood beading from two perfect pinpricks at her breast.

Ayla lowered her mouth. Flowridia's fingers tightened around her lover's as a strange coldness descended upon her. Pleasure radiated from the touch, even as limbs began to numb. She watched, mesmerized by the beautiful woman serenely feasting upon her. Ayla looked so content with her eyes shut, the very picture of vulnerability. Flowridia felt a protective, tender instinct grip her heart.

Ayla's eyes opened. Their gazes met, a power binding them, and Flowridia felt something shift in her heart. A well of feeling pooled in her eyes. Never in her life, not even during their lovemaking, had she felt so exposed, yet so protected.

Her hand cradled the back of Ayla's head, and Flowridia felt the grip on her fingers tighten. Flowridia stroked her black hair and wondered if Ayla felt it too—this wave of raw emotion threatening to flay Flowridia's soul into ribbons.

Weakness grew within her. Ayla finally withdrew her mouth and stared, hints of blood staining her lower lip and the fangs innocently protruding from her mouth. Color returned to her wide eyes, a curious frown tugging at her lips.

Suddenly, Ayla sprang forward, crushing their lips together. Blood passed between them, but Flowridia didn't shy at the metallic sting. Ayla pulled Flowridia tight to her chest, yet her touch held no lust. Something different drove her actions, the way she held Flowridia close, how her arms wrapped themselves around Flowridia's weakened form. It was intimate, desperate. Flowridia embraced her, overwhelmed at the sudden rush. She felt words threaten to burst from her lips—

"I love you."

Flowridia's eyes shot open. The words were not her own. She pulled away, head swimming at the motion, and realization of how her limbs tingled, how her eyelids tugged from exhaustion—somewhere it whispered like quiet rain. But Ayla's words were thunder echoing across the gentle night.

The vulnerability in Ayla's stare ripped at Flowridia's open heart. A watery sheen filled those brilliant, blue eyes. "I–" Ayla shut her mouth. Her breath hitched, though she did not breathe. "I love you, Flowridia," she repeated. "Please, never leave me."

"Never," Flowridia replied. "Ayla, I love you." She leaned forward, their lips barely brushing. Ayla's delicate sigh held relief.

When Ayla pulled away, shyness in the smile she fought to suppress, she pressed their foreheads together and whispered, "You're freezing." She grabbed the blanket from the side of the bed and wrapped it around Flowridia's shoulders.

"I'll be all right," Flowridia said, the joy in her heart a quiet, gentle thing.

"Hush now," Ayla said, taking Flowridia into her arms. She laid her down with the care one might give an infant. "I may have taken more than I should have, and you need your rest." Fingers ran through the tangles of Flowridia's hair. Tiny kisses touched her cheeks, along with Ayla's gentle tears. "Sleep, Flowra. Your mortal form needs to recover."

With each stroke of Ayla's fingers, Flowridia felt her eyes grow heavier. Finally, they fluttered shut, her breathing growing steady and deep.

Chapter 13

Flowridia awoke with a pounding in her head and the faint light of morning to lull her into wakefulness. She rolled over, realizing Ayla no longer held her. Pressing the blanket to her bare chest, Flowridia sat up.

On the bedside table sat a pitcher of water and a bowl of pumpkin seeds. No note. No explanation. Flowridia poured herself a glass of water, hoping it could soothe the burning memory of Ayla's words: *"I love you, Flowridia. Please, never leave me."*

Yet, Ayla had left. Sworn to warm her bed but vanished.

Ignoring the bruising at her wrist, Flowridia took a handful of the pumpkin seeds and ate them, realizing last night's adventure had left her starving. Blood loss led to hunger; this much she knew.

A knock interrupted her focus. Flowridia carefully stood from her bed, struck by weakness as she tried to support herself. "One moment, please," she said, holding her head. She leaned against the bed frame, head swimming until her vision focused.

With care, she grabbed a nightgown from her wardrobe. When she finally answered the door, Khastra, fully armored, stood as tall as the doorframe. "Etolié said to deliver this." She extended a tattooed arm, and a florescent, green crystal bracelet sat in her large palm. "Lady Ayla's alcohol bested her, otherwise she would have come."

Flowridia accepted it, intrigued at how Khastra had soldered it to a metal ring, one that slipped around her hand and settled against her small wrist. "It's beautiful. Thank you."

"Where is Lady Ayla?" Khastra asked, peering past Flowridia.

"Out. She'll be back." Hopefully it wasn't a lie. Either way, it appeared Khastra accepted it. The half-demon took a step back, but Flowridia came forward to stop her. "Have you seen–"

"You have severe blood loss."

Taken aback, Flowridia leaned against the doorframe. "I'm perfectly fine . . ."

Khastra's raised eyebrow was enough for Flowridia's words to wither. "Making assumptions has gotten me into trouble over the millennia, but it seems Lady Ayla took a bite. Am I wrong?"

Praise Khastra for being so forward, but damn her as well. At least it spared Flowridia the embarrassment of having to explain herself. She shook her head, realizing the doorframe supported her more than she'd thought.

"Was it with your permission?"

Although shame welled in her stomach, Flowridia nodded.

Khastra glanced past her, at Flowridia's bedside table. "She left you with sustenance. Responsible of her. Drink lots of water."

When Khastra stepped back again, presumably to leave, Flowridia couldn't help but softly say, "You don't care?"

The general stopped, amusement tugging at her lip. "What you and Lady Ayla do in your bedroom is not my business."

"Don't tell Etolié, please."

Khastra chuckled. "Etolié has little understanding or care for sex. I would not wish to scar her."

Khastra really didn't care, it seemed. Surprised at the relief it brought, Flowridia said, "Thank you. I–" She stopped herself, shy to ask what had prickled at her mind for days now. "May I ask you something?" she finally whispered.

"You may." Khastra frowned. "But sit down first. You look faint."

Lightheaded, Flowridia managed to sit at the foot of her bed. Khastra joined her, picking up the bowl of pumpkin seeds and placing it in Flowridia's lap. "Eat. No leaving this bed until you've finished them all."

Tentatively, Flowridia took a small handful and popped it into her mouth. "I never knew you were half demon," she said when she'd swallowed.

236

"It is not a secret," Khastra replied. "Though I did cast away my lineage long ago. My mother is the demon goddess, Ku'Shya."

Flowridia nearly choked on her next bite of pumpkin seeds. Demons weren't nearly so cohesive as their angelic counterparts, most of whom deferred to Sol Kareena. To say Ku'Shya—Goddess of War, The Great Spider, rumored to feast upon the flesh of those slain in her name—ruled Sha'Demoni would be false. But she held a greater following than any other, perpetually at odds with Izthuni, the Lurker.

Coughing, Flowridia took a sip of water, carefully selecting her next phrase. "Are you ever ashamed?"

Khastra shook her head. "I could not have chosen my mother any more than you could have chosen yours."

She knew Khastra couldn't have meant to imply Flowridia's mother was as twisted as a goddess who gained power through brutal, bloody deaths. Still, the memory of dark words lingered forever in her head, spoken by a woman whose image she bore and whose power and knowledge she had inherited: *You're a gem in my lineage, Flower Child."*

"You over-think," Khastra said, and Flowridia whipped her head around, realizing she had been staring at the bowl of half-eaten pumpkin seeds. "There is no heavier burden than a secret, tiny one. Whatever is on your mind, tell it to someone you trust. And then, tell it again. Each time, it will be easier."

Flowridia took another handful of seeds, only half of the bowl gone despite her full stomach. "That's what you did?"

"After a few thousand years, it is as easy as saying, 'good morning.'"

Perhaps, at a later date, Khastra would be a trusted ear, but for now Flowridia's thoughts lingered on Ayla.

With a slow nod, Flowridia moved to stand. A strong hand on her shoulder pushed her back down. "I told you to finish eating."

"I'm full, though," Flowridia said, cringing at her own pitiful words.

Khastra glanced at the bowl and without hesitation took an enormous handful. "You have taken after Etolié's appetite," she said with a chuckle. She stuffed the seeds into her mouth and left the room.

Flowridia popped the last of the seeds into her mouth and swallowed without chewing.

Ayla was nowhere—not the kitchen, nor the garden. Flowridia wondered if she were at the embassy and returned to her bedroom to change into proper attire for trekking across town.

In her room, Flowridia found her quarry. With her back to the door, Ayla sat hunched at the foot of Flowridia's bed, legs folded, a shining rod in her hands. She stared down, dark hair loose and shielding her face, as she turned the odd object over in her fingers.

Flowridia shut the door, cautiously moving to seat herself at the side of the bed.

The burn that once ravaged Ayla's face had vanished.

With a light tap against Ayla's hand, the rod sparked with golden light. Flowridia gasped when the skin of Ayla's palm sizzled and burned away, leaving raw, charred flesh. She flexed her hand, the whites and meaty pinks of her tendons twitching in turn.

By steady degrees, Flowridia watched the wound stitch itself together. Layers of skin grew and reformed. The ghastly wound healed in seconds.

Again, Ayla tapped her hand. Skin burned, but Ayla didn't flinch. The wound sealed shut, not even a scar left in place. "Were I to tap this against you, it would heal the marks I left on your neck. I stole it from a temple in Nox'Kartha," Ayla said, her words void of feeling. She stared blankly at her palm as she repeated the gesture, over and over, until she pressed the rod harder into the skin, and Flowridia clenched her own fists, unable to hide her horror as the flesh burned, the rod penetrating deeper, bones snapping like sticks.

When Ayla finally stopped, the burn remained. She stared a moment at her mutilated hand, then offered it forward. "With focus, I can slow the healing," Ayla whispered, her eyes to the bed, "but I can't stop it entirely."

Ayla took her hand back, the skin slowly knitting together. "It's a delight, what guilt can do, the power I can take from it." Ayla set the rod aside. Her face fell into her hands, fingers tangling into her hair as she revealed the empty hole of her ear and the utterly pristine skin around it.

Flowridia understood. Ayla's fingers gripped her hair, but Flowridia felt them clenching at her chest.

Ayla finally looked up, her vibrant eyes glistening. "Casvir hadn't believed it when I said some mewling cunt had interfered with my mission to spy on your household. I told him your name, and he had the audacity to laugh. I hated you, but I couldn't stop thinking of you, how you insulted my pride with your game of chess. I resolved to break you. So, when you so spectacularly burned my face, you unknowingly gave me a gift."

Each word stripped Flowridia's heart into pieces, layer by layer. Tears welled in her eyes. Flowridia's hand moved to cover her trembling lip, but Ayla continued. "What fun I had. You had taken power from me, so I resolved to steal everything from you—your body, your heart, enthrall you to my whim. I've killed for far pettier things. But I couldn't steal what you freely gave."

On nimble feet, Ayla suddenly stood, hands flying out to grip the bedpost. She turned, eyes crazed as she matched Flowridia's gaze. "I sought to own you, but I'm enslaved by your presence. You dance through my mind, obsessively, *perpetually*, the scent of your flowers driving me mad." The wood cracked under Ayla's grip. "But more than that, more than your beauty or the touch of your skin, you cared."

Flowridia's fists clenched to staunch the threatened tears, and her bleeding heart drowned any words her mind could dare to spell.

When she stood up, Ayla flinched, stepping back against the wall and sliding down as her words continued spilling. "So many have loved me, have worshipped the very air I allowed them to breathe, but you worried for me. You saw me not as a monster, nor a weapon to wield." Ayla pulled her knees to her chest as tears streamed down her cheeks. "With you, I feel loved; I feel . . ." Her eyes shut, her words silent until Ayla whispered with hushed veneration, "I feel *safe*. With you, I can be merely Ayla, and that is enough."

In careful, measured movements, Flowridia stepped away from the bed. Ayla shook from quiet sobs, face buried in her hands. Never had Flowridia seen such raw, shattered guilt so personified.

Ayla seemed to sense her approach. She stared up, tears falling fast. "I have done nothing but hurt you and push you away." Her composure dangled on a thread, Flowridia saw, summoned only by desperation. "Tell me to leave, I beg of you. To fall in love is a weakness I cannot bear to have."

"I did tell you to leave, once," Flowridia whispered. "You came back."

Ayla fell forward, gripping Flowridia's skirts, wetting them with tears as she clung to her legs. On her knees, she sobbed. "I'm sorry, I'm so sorry . . ."

Oh, it stung, like claws raking her tender heart, that confession. The terrible truth, that Thalmus was right, Etolié too: the monster Flowridia had denied had been real all along. She shut her eyes, refusing to let her angry, hot tears fall down her face. But the memories of tears she had shed for Ayla, all the worry and the pain, steadily rose, a swamp in her chest that threatened to drown the sincere love she felt for the weeping woman kneeling before her.

Love, she did. Flowridia loved Ayla. And Ayla, quite unwillingly, loved her too.

"You'll have to prove your sincerity," Flowridia said, and Ayla's eyes shot up, wide as she hung onto every word. "But all things heal with time—even trust and broken hearts. I forgive you."

Glass shattered in slow motion. Ayla crumbled, sobs shaking her form, and Flowridia knelt to collect the pieces. Clinging, cold arms held Flowridia tight.

"I'm yours, Ayla," Flowridia said, the words reverent against her tongue. "If you'll have me, I'm still yours."

"I will live every day of my eternal life proving myself," Ayla said, voice muffled by Flowridia's neck and shoulder. "Flowra, I love you."

Like the wounds on Ayla's palm and face, Flowridia felt her lacerated heart begin to mend.

"Is something wrong, Ayla?"

The chill of night clung to the grass and the air, despite the sun having already risen. Flowridia held Ayla's hand as she led the way toward her prized garden. Birds sang in the trees, compelling the sun to rise higher in the sky, and a sweet floral scent met them at the entrance.

But Ayla stopped, her sharp eyes darting between the countless bushes dotting the sides. "I know little of magic, but there is an odd feeling here."

"Weaving spells into plants is my specialty. Mostly protective wards, spelled into the roots. I wanted a sanctuary, a place to call my own here in this foreign kingdom." Flowridia's grip held tight as she pulled Ayla forward, a tentative smile at her lip.

Ayla stepped through, and Flowridia felt the invisible barriers ripple and sway, parting for Ayla's entrance as smoothly as dew dripping from a leaf.

Relief came with guilt, realizing she still held reserve for Ayla's intentions. Trust would take time to rebuild. "Is this something you've done before?" Flowridia dared to ask. "Toy with hearts to try and break them?"

"Many times, I suppose, in varying ways."

Flowridia broke away from their interlaced fingers, feeling Ayla's eyes as she knelt before a patch of roses. Tiny buds, not yet bloomed, dotted the scene, and Flowridia stripped them of thorns before weaving them into her hair.

"There's power that comes from subduing someone in bed," Ayla continued, watching with interest, "and I've always resented what I couldn't control."

"Did you always kill them afterward?"

Ayla shook her head. "A few I let live, otherwise there would have been no one to remember me."

Flowridia recalled what Sora had said, that The Endless Night was a monster the Sun Elves came to fear above all else. There was much still she didn't understand, but the painting of Ayla's legacy grew more vibrant and bloodstained with every new piece of information.

With practiced fingers, Flowridia wove a second bud into the crown of her hair. "Have you ever fallen in love before?"

"Yes." Ayla watched with curious eyes as Flowridia worked. "But never during my undeath." Cold hands wrapped around Flowridia's waist, but Ayla made no move to stop her from threading a third rosebud into her thick locks. "My life has not always been kind to me. I've had to shutter and seal my heart to keep from aching. So, let me focus on the present, my sweet summer blossom." A faint smile tugged at Ayla's thin lips. When Flowridia dropped her hands, Ayla gently swept her in for a light kiss.

Flowridia let their foreheads touch as she breathed in the fragrant scent of the garden and of Ayla. She heard the whisper, "I would think this was a dream, except I do not sleep."

Again, their lips touched. When Flowridia pulled back, she helped Ayla to stand and led her forward through the grassy path. "Walk with me? I've wanted to show you my garden for some time now."

"It's impressive," Ayla said, as she glanced about. Her eyes never settled on any one thing for long, content to absorb each individual leaf. At a patch of tulips, she knelt, her fingers nearly as white as the petals. "A hobby?"

Flowridia quickly surveyed the array of flowers and plucked the most pristine, white as snow. Held lovingly in her fingers, Flowridia offered it forward. "Plants hold endless potential as spell components. Something my mother taught me—how to use them and what meanings they hold." When Ayla accepted the gift, Flowridia said, "White tulips ask forgiveness."

Ayla studied the flower, twirling it in her hand as she said, "I should be offering it to you." She glanced up, brilliant eyes wide. "Of all the lovers I have had, you may be the most endearing."

"Have there been many?"

"I'm quite old."

"I'm not jealous," Flowridia said, and like a duckling, she followed when Ayla moved, never more than a step or two away from her lover's magnetic presence. "But I am curious. I don't know if it's rude to ask an undead woman how old she is but–"

When Ayla held up a finger, Flowridia stopped. The grin Ayla bore ran a shiver down her back. "Perhaps 'lover' is a crass term, given that love isn't something I've experienced during my time in undeath. But I couldn't count them if I tried, my bedmates, those I've fucked into submission." Ayla glanced briefly at Flowridia's lips before adding, "I'm one thousand, seven-hundred and thirty-six years old." Flowridia's jaw grew slack. "I was trapped in a coffin for four hundred years of it."

"It makes we wonder what you see in me," she said, realizing she couldn't even fathom such a number. Ayla, being an elf, might have naturally lived to be several hundred years old, but to think she'd spent over half a lifespan trapped in a coffin alone . . .

Flowridia would be lucky to see seventy.

"Experience is a greater indicator of maturity than age." Ayla stepped toward the next patch of floral beauty. Flowridia didn't miss how she skipped from shade to shade. The sun might not burn, but it did seem to cause her discomfort. "I suppose it's a foregone conclusion, but I must ask: have you been in love before?"

Ayla stood at the base of a tree, her hand extended. Flowridia accepted it, smiling when Ayla laced their fingers back together. They continued forward, but now Ayla's focus seemed solely set on her, blue eyes studying Flowridia with the same scrutiny she had studied each leaf and petal. "Passing fancies," Flowridia finally said, "but never love. You're my first in every sense."

"I'd wondered, with how sweet and shy you've been." Ayla stood on her toes and placed a light kiss on Flowridia's cheek. She lingered, though, placing her nose in Flowridia's hair and breathing in lightly. "You smell like your garden."

"Do I?" Flowridia asked, laughing.

"A bit of earth, a bit of sun, flowers, and trees, and it all gets tangled in your lovely hair. I noticed on our first night together. It's followed me ever since." Ayla dropped back to her feet and kissed Flowridia's neck, breathing deep as an erotic moan left her throat. "All that masking something sweet and alluring underneath."

Flowridia stiffened, uncomfortable at the gesture, but Ayla simply laughed. "My Sweet Flowra, you'll always be a temptation," Ayla cooed, pulling her close again. "I will take nothing without your express permission. Your blood is a delight, but you are the far sweeter thing."

An eerie compliment, yet it made Flowridia blush a vivid scarlet. But it welled an insecurity Flowridia hesitated to voice. "You think very highly of me and my innocence." Ayla's hand slid down her neck and chest, brushing past the severed ear beneath her clothes. Flowridia gripped it when it settled at her sternum, enthralled against her heart. "If that's all that endears me to you, I think you'll be disappointed."

"I find you endlessly interesting, down to the number of hairs on your head." Intrigue filled her piecing gaze. "But tell me a story, Sweet Flowra."

Flowridia thought of Demitri, his childish voice and innocent worldview, and said, "I don't know what demon grants wolves as familiars. Demitri is unique." She pulled away, stepping towards a bush of pale, yellow roses. She spotted a blemish and stroked it with her slight fingers. "But he's not my first," she whispered, keeping her thumb on the bruised petal. A faint trace of light leapt from her fingers, and when she pulled away the rose shone with glossy, perfect petals.

Flowridia didn't flinch when Ayla's face suddenly appeared inches away from hers. "Demitri is young."

"Not even one year old." Dread filled Flowridia to think of what she'd lost, the friend she'd let die at her mother's hands. "My first companion–" Her throat seized up at the memory of the name. "Aura," she finally choked. "Her name was Aura."

Ayla seemed to sense the reverence in the word and held Flowridia's gaze with intrigue. She spoke slowly, each word carefully enunciated by her sensuous tongue. "And Aura is no longer with us."

"No." With a slight tug, she pulled Ayla away from the rose bush and farther down the grassy path. Nothing but chirping birds met their ears.

At the end of her garden stood an enormous tree, one that shaded a small alcove. A carved stone bench rested at the center, surrounded by a sea of grass, and a wall of smaller trees and bushes blocked the view from within and without. Flowridia beckoned her companion to sit, their fingers drifting apart when she began to pace. "I have told no one of this. Not even Demitri."

Flowridia stared up to the sky, the filtered light cast through the shade of trees caressing her face. With her eyes shut, she breathed in a steadying sigh and released the air and her fear with it.

She hung her head low, her thick hair shielding her from Ayla's view. "I killed her," she whispered, stinging tears welling in her eyes. The statement lingered, the breeze in her hair nothing to the torrential wind of her thoughts. But she let none of that bleed into her voice. "Not personally, though I might as well have. Aura died because–" She squeezed her eyes shut, forcing herself to calm even as tears trailed down her cheeks. ". . . because I was stupid."

A cold hand met the small of her back. Ayla suddenly stood beside her and pulled her into an embrace. Flowridia's breath hitched, and Ayla's gentle hand ran down the thick waves of her hair. "Perhaps you should start at the

244

beginning." Her lips grazed Flowridia's jaw before their eyes met, and she stood on her toes to kiss a tear at the corner of Flowridia's eye. Fingers slid along the contours of her back and waist. Ayla grabbed both of Flowridia's hands and led her away—not to the bench, but to the enormous tree sheltering them.

With one arm, she scooped Flowridia into a tight hold. Conspiracy tugged at her lip as she reached up, and then she pulled them onto the lowest branch.

Flowridia froze, trusting but nervous, and closed her eyes until she finally felt Ayla's other arm wrap around her and place her safely in her lap. When she looked down, she saw the bench and the grass perhaps ten feet down. Ayla sat secure on the bough of the tree, cradled by branches, caressed by leaves.

Flowridia rested her head against Ayla's lifeless chest, reveling in the sound of birds, whispering trees, and all the lively things encompassing them.

She closed her eyes, letting nature's quiet melody fill her with peace. "Nearly four years ago, I ran away from home. Not a traditional home—I grew up in an orphanage, surrounded by other girls, some of whom I helped to raise. But every night I crept into the woods and spoke to Aura. She practically raised me and taught me most of what I know of magic and nature. I kept her a secret, but when we were discovered, we had to run. Witches were feared in my village."

"Any girl pledged to a demon would be feared among ignorant human swine," Ayla said, spite in the words. "You're lucky Etolié found you."

Flowridia shook her head. "My life would be very different, had Etolié found me then. Instead, I felt . . ." She slowed her words, each one meticulous in its choosing. "A tugging in my soul. That was what it felt like. There was something out there waiting, and I couldn't ignore it any longer."

"Did you ever find it?" The intrigue in Ayla's voice caught Flowridia by surprise.

"I did." Flowridia remembered the face in her nightmares, her mother's smile and laugh, but when she opened her eyes, she saw only Ayla's entranced stare. "I did. My mother, Odessa."

Realization flashed through Ayla's features. "That's a famous name. The Swamp Witch was a legend I heard whispers of even living in Nox'Kartha. I heard she birthed children to sate her unusual appetite."

"She ate the ones she deemed unworthy of her legacy," Flowridia managed to say, and the embrace around her body tightened. "But often, she would birth them and leave them on the doorsteps of unwitting families or swap them with their own infant daughters.

"For three years I learned from her," Flowridia continued, but her voice stopped. Her hand instinctively clenched at Ayla's dress, and she gasped as memories flooded her mind—

"You've come so far, Flower Child. Look at you, constructing wards—

"I'll strip you of skin and boil it for my next meal if—

"Someone approaches; let him in, won't you? If you're more his taste, let him have a bite—

"One more for the garden. Flower Child, will you grab my carving knife?"

To speak of hell was to invite its company.

"For three years, I stayed," Flowridia whispered, drops of wetness staining the fabric clutched to her face. The breath she took stung her throat, rough and gasping. "And I wish to say nothing more."

Ayla held her tight, pressing Flowridia's face against her dress. Cool fingers caressed Flowridia's hair. "I can imagine enough, given the whispers I've heard. But what of Aura?"

"My mother offered me the choice, to either consume my familiar or have her be cast out." Flowridia glanced up, her eyes surely swollen, but Ayla's gaze held no judgement. "Should I explain?"

Ayla shook her head. "Witches are known to lose their humanity to the temptation of higher power. Consuming a familiar gives a witch an immediate and substantial boost in power, but they're stunted from then on."

Flowridia clung to every word. "How do you know so much about this?"

"I have lived a terribly long time, Flowra, and it hasn't all been fun. Study before play."

Flowridia settled back into the embrace, hair brushing the exposed skin and fabric of Ayla's chest. "She offered me a choice, and I chose to let Aura live. What I didn't know was that Aura never left. My mother had terrorized the swamp and lands around it for generations but was never found—

not unless she wanted to be found. She constructed wards to protect her home and hide it. All that time, Aura paced the boundaries, trying to break her way inside.

"I learned the secrets of her wards," Flowridia continued. "My mother wove them into the earth as I do, but she had a different sort of garden—mushrooms, fungi; all sorts of glowing beautiful things. Her 'greatest joy,' as she called it. She drew them into runic shapes, infusing the earth and her home with their power, but underneath–" The imagery of half-eaten corpses caused her to flinch. Ayla's nails threatened to draw blood, as though clutching her could protect Flowridia from the horrors in her head. "She buried her victims alive—her lovers and her children—to feed them."

"Genius and madness so often overlap," she heard her elven lover say.

"There's so much more, but her garden was a particularly vile bit of ingenuity. The fungi were the key to her wards, and once I learned to manipulate them myself, I could reach through them. I felt Aura's presence and resolved to leave. I helped her step through–"

Flowridia cut off her words, the gasping pain of speaking too much, too soon. Not once had she cried for this, not since that fateful night. Like an arrow to her body, each word drove it deeper inside, her sobs rising to match her pain. She spoke of Aura, she spoke of Odessa's death, and she spoke of the despair of that awful, bloodstained night.

But though the arrow pierced deep, it worked its way through, and when she finished, she felt that her raw wounds might finally heal. Tears stained Ayla's dress, and Flowridia lightly brushed the bony contours of her sternum, her thin skin grounding.

"I buried her," Flowridia whispered, the peaceful end to her harrowing tale. "I buried my mother too. And her victims. I dug them up from the garden, one by one, and gave them a proper burial. Even if I couldn't carry them beyond the swamp, I could give them a better fate than what they had."

Whispering trees spoke around them, their words unfamiliar to Flowridia's ears. Perhaps they offered comfort, but just as likely they condemned, her complicity in so many crimes a burden to her soul.

Ayla's silence reeked of fury, but finally Flowridia felt her lover shift beneath her. Ayla's voice was colder than her skin. "A pity you killed her. I would have reveled in prolonging that monster's death."

"Not all she did was wicked," Flowridia whispered, "and not all I did was pure. She was still my mother, and she treated me with kindness in her own way. I'm so much like her, and with the knowledge I have, with the spells I helped her to brew, what I am but–"

"*Flowra.*"

The sharpness in Ayla's tone caused Flowridia to flinch, but a gentle hand against her jaw coaxed her to look up and match Ayla's icy stare. "You spent three years groomed to continue Odessa's legacy," Ayla said, severity in the phrase. "You are a much stronger person than you know, to have walked away."

Shame gripped Flowridia's tongue, and her words felt as weak as her will. "I did so many awful things, Ayla–"

"Perhaps, but you survived," Ayla said, and she pulled Flowridia up, their faces now level. "A monster came to claim you, and you survived. Your fate is not her fate."

"So instead my fate is to be claimed by monsters like her–" Flowridia snapped her mouth shut, the implications of her words damning and insulting all at once. "I don't mean that. I don't think you're a monster. You're a woman—an undead woman but a beautiful undead woman—and I only mean–" Flowridia stopped, tongue stiff, knowing she could say nothing to withdraw her terrible words.

Terrible, because deep down Flowridia knew her lie. She braced herself, awaiting reprimand.

The silence grew loud, louder still when the wind picked up. The branches swayed. Leaves rustled. But Ayla's whisper, when it came, cut through nature's stifling song. "Don't speak lies, Flowra. The world proclaimed me a monster, and so that's what I became. I found it much more beneficial to be frightening than to be beautiful."

She remembered Ayla's reprimand from time past, her mocking of Flowridia's innocent trust after an invitation to her bed. "Am I stupid to trust you?"

Ayla's fingers were soft as she stroked Flowridia's hair. She felt Ayla breathe, and with no need for air, Flowridia knew it was for pleasure, to soak in her scent. "We'll find out together."

Flowridia rested her head against Ayla's hollow heart, her dead blood stagnant with no heartbeat. A reminder of

Ayla's undeath, and Flowridia wondered if her life would be forfeit because of their love.

Yet, the burdens in her soul did seem lighter. Speaking of her pain let a weight drop from her chest, and Ayla was here to steady her unbalanced form. Flowridia shut her eyes and wondered how mad she must be to feel peace in the arms of the monster.

Chapter 15

Done with the garden, Ayla helped her scale down the tree, and Flowridia suddenly felt a familiar prickling at her senses. A new figure slipped past her wards with ease. She glanced down the path, unsurprised when Demitri appeared, sheepish in his stance.

Flowridia beckoned the little wolf forward, taking his body into her arms when a shy voice filled her head. *I know you need alone time with Lady Ayla, but Etolié is still sick from alcohol.*

Flowridia held him as she stood up and said, "My dearest Demitri—are you lonely?"

A little.

"Come and help me make some tea for Etolié. I'll make you some too."

Flowridia set him on the ground and went to pluck listrous root.

"It's odd that he speaks to you," Ayla mused. "Does he sound like one of us?"

Flowridia smiled, nodding as she dug into the earth by the patch of listrous flowers, picking a few of the orange blossoms and their roots.

When they reached the kitchen, Flowridia set a kettle on the stove and began to rummage through the cupboards for her teacups. She thought of Etolié, how odd it was to think of the Celestial ill from a hangover, but with that came a realization. She turned, watching out of the corner of her eye as Ayla knelt and stroked Demitri's fur. "You said you couldn't get drunk."

"I will admit to being a bit intoxicated last night. But only Nox'Kartha brews substances strong enough to inebriate the undead."

"It must be difficult to get hung-over, then."

They matched eyes. Flowridia saw a glint of cruel humor flash across Ayla's face. "You didn't want to go on the hunt, either."

Flowridia blushed unbidden and instead turned her attention to assembling Etolié's tea. Amidst the paired sets sat a lonely teacup, one emblazoned with lavender buds, whose paired saucer rested beside it. Flowridia frowned at the missing teacup but stole the single ceramic piece, resolving to search her bedroom. In a second cup, she placed a few extra orange petals. Demitri liked fruity teas.

On the ground, Ayla presented a hand, letting Demitri move first before offering her respects. Flowridia watched Ayla's caution and said, "You're always careful around him."

"Animal affection isn't something I'm used to. Living creatures can smell undeath, and most instinctively run from it. Or bite. But a small few are drawn to it, like wolves or bats, spiders."

Demitri jumped up and tried to lick Ayla's cheek, but she was faster, catching him as she flinched. She set him down, this time allowing him to place a small kiss at her chin.

To think of Ayla as nervous around animals proved too amusing, and Flowridia couldn't help but chuckle. Demitri looked up, his childlike eyes large and shining in pure gold. *Tell Lady Ayla she smells nice.*

Flowridia relayed the message, and a genuine smiled tugged at Ayla's lips. Whistling sang from the kettle, and Flowridia moved to pour the prepared water into the teacups.

"Demitri," Ayla said politely, "I appreciate the sentiment. Given that I don't sweat, I smell good more often than not."

"You don't sweat?" Flowridia asked, realizing in all their love-making, she hadn't seen even a shine of liquid at Ayla's brow. "That makes sense. But you do have some bodily functions."

"There's a bit of dark magic and mystery holding me together." Ayla rose and followed Flowridia from the room, the teacup and saucer held in Flowridia's hands. "I can cry, but I don't bleed. I can have sex, but I can't digest food."

"What do you do when you eat for show?"

"I force it back up. Otherwise, it'll rot inside me."

Flowridia grimaced, embarrassed at the topic, yet oddly endeared that Ayla would share it. "That sounds terrible. What about your hair? Does it grow?"

Ayla shook her head. "But there are magicians in Nox'Kartha who can work wonders. Changing my hair is a spell, not a biological function."

At the library, Flowridia crept on silent feet as she navigated the bookshelves.

Engulfed in scarves and blankets and resting underneath the floating crystal was Etolié. The Celestial stirred and opened one eye. "Flowers, hello," she whispered. "Everything is too bright. Say nothing. Leave the tea and walk away." Her eyes looked to Demitri. "Leave the wolf. He's cute."

Flowridia resisted the urge to laugh at her pitiful mentor. Instead, she set the two teacups down beside Etolié's head and smiled when Demitri began to lap at the one meant for him.

"Tell them I'm dying and won't be at the meeting."

Flowridia nodded and stepped back, taking Ayla's hand to lead her out.

"Nox'Kartha will by paying for everything, of course. They ask for six months. They . . . may have implied providing a rather substantial dowry as well."

Sitting in on the meeting with Marielle and Zorlaeus proved a boring event, even with wedding planning. In the council chambers, only a select few sat in to debate foreign affairs—Thalmus, among them, the most frugal of their counterparts. He kept his face buried in a notebook, scribbling furiously, and only looked up to glare at the undead woman sitting at Flowridia's side. Ayla sat in Etolié's chair, watching the room like a spider might watch a fly.

"What I want to know," Marielle said, grabbing the letter from Zorlaeus, "is how they found out before an official announcement to our own kingdom was issued."

Flowridia watched as Zorlaeus turned his nervous stare toward Ayla, frowning as she placed a hand on her chest. "Are you implying that *I* informed Imperator Casvir of this scandalous proposal? That I looked him in the eye as I stole his personal flask from his belt and that Viceroy Murishani nearly wet himself in excitement?"

Zorlaeus smiled curtly and nodded.

Ayla shrugged innocently and glanced at Flowridia. "I can't imagine why he'd think it was me."

"What's important," Zorlaeus continued, "is that I've been respectfully fired as a conflict of interest. A replacement ambassador will be sent."

Marielle reached over and grabbed Zorlaeus' hand. The ring at her finger flashed nearly as bright as her orb, illuminating the room in red. "I can't be sad about this. More time for us to be together."

"I'm your maid of honor, right Lae Lae?" Ayla said with a wink. Her dress swept dramatically as she brought her legs up into her chair, perched on her knees. Flowridia had never realized how jumpy Ayla could be. "With as good a dowry as it seems you're worth, you're sure to be a blushing bride."

Marielle looked like she might peel the smile from her face and impale Ayla through her exposed sternum.

Zorlaeus began scratching nervously at his forearm. "I don't know if I can argue with that sort of offer–"

"I can," Marielle offered brightly. In her bosom, the orb began to glow. "Lady Ayla, with due respect, we'll be going a more traditional route. If anyone is to be Lae Lae's maid of honor, it'll be Casvir."

Ayla's hand twitched nearly as violently as her smile. Flowridia covered it with her own.

"Moving on," Marielle said, looking to Thalmus, "the embassy. It opens tomorrow. I was thinking of having a small reception afterward."

Flowridia perked up. "You are engaged, Marielle. What about a party?"

"An engagement party," Marielle mused, smiling faintly. "I suppose we do have to announce it to the masses, since Nox'Kartha is bound to let the secret out. A small party, then." A frown stole her enthusiasm. "Put together in less than a day."

"All we would need is food, and perhaps music," Zorlaeus chimed in. "We could hold it at the embassy reception hall."

"I think that sounds lovely," Flowridia said, and she lightly squeezed Ayla's hand.

"I so rarely get to play my instruments," Marielle said. "Perhaps I'll scavenge up a band myself. Would it be inappropriate for a monarch to play music at her own party?"

Thalmus said simply, "It would save money."

Marielle beamed. "And so, it is written. What about food?"

Flowridia didn't hear Thalmus' response. A reception event for all the Nox'Karthans in the embassy and her council, but that hardly mattered. Flowridia felt a plot form in her head, and when she looked at Ayla and those vibrant blue eyes, she realized she had a perfect gift for the occasion.

Ayla caught her stare and quirked an eyebrow. Blushing, Flowridia looked away, back to the meeting.

Ayla's other hand moved to cover Flowridia's. Flowridia beamed brighter than Marielle's ring.

In the pitch black of night, once passionate moans faded to a lull of soft breathing and gentle kisses. Cold hands stroked Flowridia's hair. "You're exhausted, Flowra. Sleep." Ayla's bright eyes pierced the dark like a lighthouse through fog. "I promise to guard your bed and stay until morning."

A blanket separated their naked forms as Ayla tucked Flowridia in. "You don't sleep," Flowridia remarked. "I don't wish to bore—"

"I'll entertain myself by counting the hairs on your head," Ayla replied, amusement in her tone. "Vampires don't sleep as you do, but we do shut our eyes and recharge, as any creature."

"You said you weren't a vampire."

"Not *quite* a vampire, no." Ayla cupped Flowridia's chin, coaxing her to meet her eye. "I don't believe there's a word for what I am. If I drained you of blood and buried you in the ground, you'd rise as a true vampire. But that was not my origin. For me, vampirism is a curse in a literal way, but not one I know how to break."

"You don't know how to die?"

Ayla shook her head. "Despite countless mortal attempts to end me, I have persevered. Fireborns finally locked me in a shadow-less coffin to subdue me, and my body and mind atrophied from starvation. I screamed until my throat grew raw and torn, scratched until my nails and fingers were in shambles. But though I dried to a brittle husk, I never lost awareness. You know something of blood magic, yes?"

Blood was dark magic, the most evil of necromancies. To slay a living being and use their blood to grant undeath was the highest of crimes, and Mother often bemoaned the vagueness of the principles involved in blood magic rituals:

"'An infant's worth of blood?' What sort of measurement is that? Children come in all shapes and sizes." Mother stopped her pacing and scoffed at the cauldron. "Remember, Flower Child, it is often the letter of the law and not the spirit."

Flowridia nodded.

"When Casvir found me, crippled and starved, he offered restoration in exchange for a contract. I'll never forget the euphoric strength flowing through my veins, the blood dripping from my naked form as I stood for the first time in centuries." Ayla's grin twisted into a sneer. "And Casvir, expecting me to bend like a dog to his will. I'm free upon his death, but despite my best efforts, he still walks this plane. Instead, I've done all in my power to be a thorn in his side. Perhaps he'll tire of me. That, or I'll finally succeed in slitting his throat." Ayla cupped Flowridia's cheek and chin in her hand. "Someday," she cooed wistfully.

"Etolié removed your head," Flowridia dared to remind her. "Or was that an illusion?"

"Not an illusion, no," Ayla replied, a knowing grin dominating her pale features. "But I've sustained far worse injuries as an undead, and The Endless Night has nothing to fear from Eionei."

"And—" Flowridia bit back her words, too shy to directly ask what question burned her tongue. "And so why has The Endless Night not slain Casvir?"

Ayla's smile faded, a grimace on her pointed features. "Per the contract, I cannot, lest my soul be forfeit. Casvir did his research."

"What demon is The Endless Night, Ayla?" Flowridia finally dared to ask, and the sheets shifted as Ayla sat up. Flowridia followed, the blankets falling away to reveal her bare chest. "You said it was a question for another time—"

"Yes, and I also told you that The Endless Night is a *title*, my Sweet Flowra. Not a demon." Ayla's tone held reserve, and Flowridia leaned forward to embrace her.

"Will you tell me, please?"

Ayla leaned into her touch, her bare back pressing against Flowridia's breasts. But she turned her neck, their eyes meeting as she said, "It's a bit of damning truth, though not a secret among my own people. I am and have always been Izthuni's mortal form. The Endless Night is our legacy on this world."

It should have been no surprise—that if Ayla were to channel a demon, why not let it be a god—yet still she forgot to breathe. Ayla searched her face, curious eyes awaiting judgement. Flowridia said softly, "You are pledged to The Lurker, then?"

"I am. I told you that as a child Sha'Demoni adopted me. There, I endeared myself to him, and upon my mortal death, years later, I became his first creation. Perhaps it's why I scoff at sunlight and all things holy—all the other vampires trace back to me, and I am Izthuni's first and greatest."

Perhaps it was why Ayla always held her head high— she truly did walk freely among gods, though not the gods Flowridia knew.

"Flowra?"

Flowridia held Ayla's stare, unsure of what she could say.

Ayla walked among gods and bore a blood-stained legacy Flowridia knew only whispers of, but here, alone in Flowridia's bed, her eyes watered, vulnerability marring her pride. "Please, say something."

Flowridia's arms held Ayla tight, and she pressed her cheek against the undead woman's shoulder. She spoke gently, knowing Ayla's hope was as fragile as a flickering candle and that she held the words to blow it out. "I don't care who you're pledged to out there, as long as you're mine in here."

Ayla turned, her nimble form shifting until their bare chests pressed together, and then tucked her face into the crevice of Flowridia's neck. The silence became punctuated only by Flowridia's soft breathing, and she savored the intimacy, the touch of Ayla's skin against her own.

When her eyelids grew heavy, Flowridia heard, "You should sleep, Flowra. You're exhausted."

Ayla moved to pull away, and Flowridia memorized the faded lines of Ayla's body in the darkness. "You don't have to stay all night." Self-conscious, she added, "I don't wish to bother you. I'm told I talk in my sleep."

"You do." So gentle a tone, yet the remark threatened to topple Flowridia's careful defenses. Ayla pressed their bodies together, leading Flowridia down into bed. "I'm quite confident, if I were cursed with the need for sleep, I would be the same."

Never had Flowridia heard so vulnerable a phrase from her companion. She opened her eyes, but her words were silenced with a kiss. "Sleep, Flowra. I'll protect you from your nightmares."

Flowridia settled into Ayla's embrace, whispered words leaving her lips. "You'll let me protect you too, right?"

"Darling, I'm the monster in the dark. There's nothing to protect me from."

Humming met Flowridia's ears. That same song, somber and sad, lilted softly in the night, and within minutes, Flowridia drifted into sleep.

In the morning, the sun shone through the window, and Flowridia awoke to Ayla Darkleaf positioned on top of her, peering at her head. Blue eyes met her own. "I apologize. I lost track around 147,000. You kept moving."

Flowridia turned over, quirking an eyebrow as she stared up at the lazily smiling undead elf. "I beg your pardon?"

"I told you I would number the hairs on your head." Ayla placed a lingering kiss at Flowridia's temple. "If you would lay still, I might be able to give you an exact count."

Flowridia giggled at the thought of sitting in a chair while Ayla riffled past each individual strand of hair. "I appreciate the sentiment, but it's information I can do without." She waited for that grin, for Ayla to join her laugh and reveal her jest.

But Ayla, it seemed, was utterly serious. "I'll try again, the next time I'm able to spend the night."

"You mean tonight?" Flowridia's expression fell when Ayla's didn't change. "What do you mean, 'the next time?' You said you would stay until after the embassy unveiling."

Regret flashed across Ayla's face, any semblance of joy fading. "The reception is tonight, and I am to leave at its conclusion. Casvir expects me back."

Truly, the thought hadn't occurred to her, that Ayla couldn't stay forever. The euphoria of revealed love had enraptured Flowridia, caused her to forget her duties and Ayla's. To return to real life seemed so tragic a thing. "You'll be back someday, right?"

Scarcely had the words left Flowridia's mouth before Ayla burst out with, "Of course!" A protective embrace gripped Flowridia's body. Cold hands stroked her hair. "To have you now, only to have you ripped away, is a tragedy. But I'll be back, Casvir be damned."

Flowridia saw sorrow in Ayla's beautiful face, but with it, conviction. Flowridia leaned up to kiss Ayla's lips. "You know I'll be waiting."

"You deserve so much more," Ayla whispered. Her lithe fingers drew lines across the sides of Flowridia's face. When her thin, doll lips parted, Flowridia saw the barest hints of fangs.

Flowridia hesitated, shy as she reached up to hold Ayla's hands, and asked, "Would you ever take me with you to Nox'Kartha?"

Ayla's humorless chuckle doused the flicker of hope Flowridia had ignited at the statement. "You wouldn't like it there. It's a thriving, beautiful city, but it's full of undeath and all sorts of terrible secrets." Her hands clenched, Flowridia's still covering them, and then she stole one away, bringing Flowridia's hand to her lips to kiss her palm. "You wouldn't like who I am when I'm there."

"I could never hate you," Flowridia said, and again, Ayla laughed.

"I've lived a long time, Flowra. There's much still to learn about me. I pray you never have to."

To pry seemed inappropriate. Flowridia instead said, "Then we run away. Not today, but someday. You and I. And Demitri."

Sorrow threatened to drown the sweetness of Ayla's smile, and Flowridia feared she might tear up. But she remained stoic, released a shuddering sigh as she gripped Flowridia's hand. "It's a beautiful dream, Flowra."

The words held finality, and Flowridia's heart sank. She gave a slow nod, smiling despite the sting of rejection. "I understand," she said softly. "All of this still feels so new, so surreal, and I haven't put much thought into the future. Our future. And I shouldn't. It's presumptuous of me to–"

A finger on her lip silenced her rambling. "Not presumptuous," came Ayla's reply, and in meticulous, slow gestures, Ayla placed a kiss on each of Flowridia's fingers. She lingered on her ring finger, lips curling into a smile.

Flowridia leaned up and stole the smile from Ayla's mouth. Their lips touched, butterfly kisses passing between them. A gentle whisper, reverent as a prayer, met Flowridia's ears. "Darling, darling . . . I love you so."

She took the phrase and spun it to gold, each kiss on Flowridia's form a testament to that statement. Touch wrote a song, one Flowridia sang with Ayla in tandem. A perfect duet, accompanied by soft whispers and sweet moans.

A moment of peace; only for them.

Ayla left to survey the final accommodations for the embassy reception. Flowridia declined to follow, instead running out to her garden to inspect the results of her floral experimentation.

Among the gardenias, her pet project flourished; a perfect blend of tiny blossoms and vibrant color. Moon lilies had provided the palette for her gift, that of a flower to match her undead lover's gorgeous eyes. Gardenias had offered a workable size, Flowridia's own flower of choice for her hair.

The blossoms were small and delicate, none of them larger than a coin. She plucked them, one by one, careful not to crush any petals in her palm.

Once a proper pile had formed, she covered them with her skirt and quickly ran back to her room. No sign of Ayla. Flowridia opened the drawer to her bedside table and tucked the dainty flowers inside.

With Demitri content to sleep beside her, she settled in on her bed with a stolen book—*Crystalline Charisma: A Study in Anti-Magic*—content to wait.

The sunlight through the window had shifted when a touch at her shoulder nearly caused her to squeak. When she turned, Ayla sat by her side, smile wide and toothy. "All goes well at the embassy. The party will be starting soon, and I'm expected to arrive early. A foregone conclusion, I hope, but . . ." Ayla planted a kiss on Flowridia's forehead. "Will you accompany me?"

"Yes," Flowridia said, and she leaned in and captured Ayla's mouth.

She stood when Ayla did, accepting the offered hand. Flowridia stepped toward the mirror, smoothing her hair and adjusting the flowers dotting the waves. "Do you need to borrow a dress, Ayla?"

Ayla surveyed her wardrobe, fingers skimming past Flowridia's gifted gowns. "Pastels aren't particularly my taste," she said, and before Flowridia could comment, Ayla stepped inside and disappeared.

Flowridia watched, fingers still moving in practiced sync, until Ayla finally reappeared, hair woven and half down, dressed to perfection in black—as always—and her plunging neckline reminded Flowridia of the dress she had worn at Marielle's ball. She held two dresses: one dark blue and one a deep maroon, both embroidered and stitched from an unknown, rich material. "Both of these are the height of Nox'Karthan fashion. Which one do you like best?" Ayla asked, coy as she bared her teeth in a grin.

"For what?"

"For you, of course. I'm inclined toward the red—I think it would add richness to your hair—but I'll accept whichever you choose."

Flowridia, her hair woven with tiny, white buds, held out her hands and accepted the dark maroon, noting the deep neckline and long sleeves. Being meant for Ayla, the dress would fit like a glove, if it fit at all. "Ayla, I couldn't accept—"

"I'll have some made for you, more suited to your modest taste. But humor me. Try it on?" Ayla's expression softened, eyes batting cutely, and Flowridia couldn't help but blush and nod.

With her back to Ayla, Flowridia slipped into the borrowed dress, one that clung to every curve of her slim figure and exposed more skin than she would ever be inclined to outside the bedroom. She turned to face the mirror, slouching demurely, and instinctively brought her hands up to cover the exposed cleavage. Ayla stepped to her side and gently pulled her arms away. "Oh, you look delicious. I could eat you up." Flowridia's blush darkened, and Ayla cupped her cheek and met her eyes. "Truly, Flowra, you look beautiful. You'll be perfection tonight; more than even myself." She glanced down, a bit of mischief glinting in her eye. "Though you may need to wear shoes. In the future, I'll be certain all your dresses are long enough to hide your darling feet."

Flowridia still felt like a child masquerading in stolen clothes, but Ayla's reassurance brought confidence, and she managed to stand taller. Once shoes were donned, Flowridia said, "Before we go . . ." She couldn't help the smile pursing her lips. She took Ayla's hands and led her to sit on the bed. "Do you trust me?"

Ayla stared a moment, uncertainty marring the exquisite, sharp lines of her face. For a moment, Flowridia worried she might have over-stepped her bounds.

Ayla finally nodded. "Yes?" she replied, though confusion laced her tone.

"Close your eyes."

Ayla's hand went to rest at her sternum, exposed between the plunging fabric cuts of her dress. But she obeyed, and she shut her eyes, visibly growing stiff.

Flowridia stepped lightly toward the bedside table, withdrawing the flowers, stems and all, and returned, standing before Ayla as she whispered, "Hold out your hands."

Ayla's fist clenched at her sternum, but then she brought it down, uncertain, hesitant. Both hands lay open, and Flowridia placed flowers into her waiting palms. At her touch, Ayla opened her eyes, frowning as she stared at the offering.

"I grew them for you," Flowridia explained, "to match your eyes. Moon lilies are a perfect color, but they're much too big." Flowridia separated a lock of Ayla's fine hair and stole a flower from her hand. Her nimble fingers quickly braided it into the strand of hair. When she began on the second, she said, "Gardenias are small; I thought breeding them might make a perfect match." Ayla simply stared, eyes rapidly shooting between Flowridia's working hands and the flowers resting in her own. Silence welled insecurity. "It's silly, I know, but—"

"No," Ayla said softly. "I love them."

Flowridia smiled unbidden as she finished her work. Ayla stood and pulled her into an embrace. "I mean it. I love them. Thank you."

THE STING OF VICTORY

"Tonight, we celebrate not one union, but two." Ayla's dangerous smile leered at the audience, charm lacing every word. "In uniting two people in matrimony, we see our own future, that of two kingdoms working in tandem to create a better future."

The Nox'Karthan sector spread far and wide, populated by shops and dwellings for the richer migrants. Centered in the district was the embassy itself, shining a brilliant white, its marbled stone exterior spiraling up in a single, rounded tower. Backlit by sunset, it cast a shadow upon the city, a reminder of Nox'Kartha's eternal presence.

The populace watched—citizens of Staelash and the few Nox'Karthans who already populated the sector. Soon, it would thrive. For now, only a few scattered De'Sindai stood among the collection of humans, Celestials, and others.

Ayla continued her speech, Marielle and Zorlaeus standing to her left on the make-shift stage. "Thus, we sign a treaty for trade and prosperity. A brilliant future awaits us all."

Flowridia stood behind the stage, enraptured by every word.

Thalmus approached, simply stating, "She gives pretty speeches," as he placed a hand on Flowridia's shoulder.

"Those are Imperator Casvir's words," Flowridia replied. "But she delivers them well."

Thalmus nodded slowly, expression neutral.

Flowridia dared to continue. "Ayla apologized for her past treatment of me."

"Did she?"

"She did." Flowridia looked up, regretting her words but realizing she had no choice but to continue. "She's been so good to me, Thalmus. She cares for me very much—"

"Did she give you that dress?"

Flowridia gave a self-conscious tug on the long sleeves. Slouching would only amplify her cleavage—as unsubstantial as it was—so she stiffened instead, cursing the blush on her cheeks. "She's letting me borrow it."

The grip on her shoulders grew strong, protective. She braced herself for reprimand, vowing to remain non-combative.

Instead, it grew loose. Then it fell away. "You're growing up," Thalmus said, finality in his tone. "I don't like her at all; you already know that. But I'll stay quiet if she's sincere in her affection."

263

"She is," Flowridia replied. "Thalmus, she truly is. And if there's anything she can do to prove herself to you—"

Thalmus held up a hand, glowering as he looked down. "Flowra . . ." He sighed, resigned. "Ayla could be a shining paladin of Sol Kareena, and I would still have reservations."

Flowridia chuckled. "I don't think I'd know how to get along with a paladin."

"What I mean," he continued, expression softening, "is you're my little flower girl. I'll always be protective of you. But you have to make your own choices."

A smile pulled at Flowridia's lips. Instead of a reply, she nudged him with her hip.

It hit above his knee.

He nudged her back, an affectionate smile on his face, and it landed at her back.

For as lovely as the reception hall was, one particular sight outshone the rest.

The room seemed out of a storybook, decorated with draped fabrics and glittering lights. Candles lined the walls, and at the ceiling shone globes of light—summoned by Etolié, Flowridia guessed. Tables lined with food skirted near the entrance, and a dance floor dominated the room, though not so large as Marielle's ballroom. Outside, a glass door led to a balcony where stars gleamed, scarcely visible in the soft lighting.

But in the center, Ayla awaited, a picturesque island of blue and black in a sea of glowing lights. Her gentle smile juxtaposed oddly with what Flowridia had so often seen, that of predator about to consume its prey, but the effect was the same: Ayla beckoned, and Flowridia followed.

The guests, the food, and even the music seemed to fade when their hands touched. Ayla placed Flowridia's on her shoulder. "Allow me," Ayla said, a bit of amusement in her tone. "Follow my steps. You'll do well."

The smaller woman led with one hand on Flowridia's hip and the other clasping her fingers. She moved effortlessly, smoothly, and Flowridia clumsily followed, half a beat behind.

"If you keep staring at the ground, you'll never improve."

Flowridia looked up, meeting Ayla's expectant eyes. "I'm afraid of stepping on you."

"I promise not to bite if you do," Ayla replied, teething showing as she chuckled. "Be brave, my darling. Eyes on me; your feet will follow."

Flowridia matched her stare, realizing she did, indeed, move easier if she focused on her partner.

A master of her craft, Ayla twirled in time and helped Flowridia to do the same. Fast or slow, the songs would change, and Ayla instructed her steps. It seemed she was a master of all arts, from lively jigs to sensual ballads, or perhaps simply talented enough to make it up as she went. Flowridia listened, following closely with the rhythm, and at times letting Ayla pull her around. Sometimes she stumbled, but Ayla simply laughed and helped her to stand.

Ayla laughed so prettily. When Ayla danced, she looked so carefree, genuine joy in her smile. Never had she appeared so at ease, and Flowridia wondered where she'd learned.

A question for another night. Flowridia was content to bask in Ayla's radiating light.

Marielle socialized when she didn't play, but when she joined the band, Flowridia thought her harp a perfect addition. Thalmus only watched the partygoers, a visible void of guests around him. Etolié and Khastra chatted in the corner, and somewhere in her head, Flowridia wondered what the Celestial thought of the scene.

But her focus remained on Ayla. In the blur of lights and music, Ayla's face shone brighter than them all. When exhaustion pulled at her eyelids, Ayla's laughter kept her moving on.

And for hours, she danced.

The party dwindled. The lights began to fade. Her head rested against Ayla's shoulder, and a voice cut through the music. "Let me take you home, Flowra."

Despite Ayla's diminutive size, she scooped Flowridia up, her unholy strength funneled into the tender gesture. Flowridia rested her head against Ayla's shoulder, cradled as she stepped past the guests and out the door. Once alone, she slipped into a shadow, the familiar, fogged landscape too stimulating for Flowridia's tired eyes. Instead, she looped her arms around Ayla's neck, curling into the protective embrace.

Soon, a plush bed met her back. Flowridia opened her eyes and realized they had returned to her room. Demitri's tongue met her cheek. *Did you have a nice time?*

"I had a wonderful time," she whispered, both to her familiar and to the breathtaking woman standing beside her bed.

A hand caressed her cheek. "Perhaps I'll stay a little longer," Ayla said, and Flowridia felt her light weight press against her in bed. Cold, caring arms tucked the blankets around her and then wrapped around her body.

Flowridia fell asleep.

Flowridia awoke alone.

But there, on the bedside table, a scripted note and a single, red rose:

The dance was sublime. I love you, Flowra

Chapter 16

The festival at the Theocracy of Sol Kareena awaited.

With her head resting against Etolié's thigh, Flowridia slept on the bench for most of their first day of travel. Exhausted from a night that shone in her memory, the afterglow managed to cast out the looming fog of loneliness threatening to descend and drown her. She clutched a hand to her chest, drawing what comfort she could from the accessory resting between her breasts. A piece of Ayla, morbid or not.

There weren't many steeds capable of supporting the robust general, so Khastra rode in the carriage with Meira and Sora, her massive weapon strapped to the roof. Flowridia was awoken by bombastic, familiar laughter, along with an accompaniment of chuckles.

Beside her, at the back of the carriage, content to sit in the sunlight, she heard Etolié scoff. "I think Khastra is the only one capable of making Meira even crack a smile."

"She's quite charming, in her own way," Flowridia said, and she felt Etolié shift as she looked down at her.

"She's hoping we run into trouble. You wouldn't believe how petulant she was after the Skalmite incident. She insists she could have handled it."

Flowridia saw her scan the horizon. With Khastra out of Staelash, it left Marielle vulnerable, even with her intended's doting presence, as Etolié had explained. Instead, Marielle's orb lay sequestered on Etolié's person, hidden within a box crafted from the crystal Etolié lovingly studied.

"I suppose she and her hammer would have been useful."

Etolié chuckled. "She has a few more tricks up her sleeves than just her weapon. If fate has a sense of humor, this will be the safest trip we've ever been on."

The conversation drifted off into idle things. Flowridia questioned the wisdom in tempting fate, but her worry was for not. A few boring days of travel passed, and the towers of the Theocracy appeared on the horizon.

The statue of the Goddess rose to meet them, her arms outstretched and a hood shading her benevolent smile. Flowridia had remembered to change her outfit this time, and with shoes on her feet she watched Theocracy citizens from the carriage. A strange sort of confidence flowed through her veins, helping her to sit tall. In the weeks between now and their last trip, Flowridia felt as though the shifting sands beneath her feet had finally started to settle. So much had changed.

Including the inside of the carriage, which had substantially shrunk. Seated between she and Etolié, Khastra's bulk took up a significant amount of space; with Demitri on her lap, Flowridia pressed herself against the door to avoid invading anyone's personal space. Etolié had no such qualms. Half-asleep, her thin arm settled around Khastra's forearm, her head resting against the general's bicep.

Excitement radiated from the city. Flowridia watched it bustle and move, preparations for the evening's celebration finishing up. The statue would be unveiled in the cathedral itself, and as foreign guests, her council had been promised entrance. But parades and festivities would be conducted outside. Flowridia watched booths be assembled, the beginnings of spectacular costumes donned, and various art celebrating the Goddess displayed.

She heard Meira scoff and mutter, "All ritual. No substance."

They stopped outside the cathedral. "So, you'll be joining us?" Etolié teased as Meira stepped out.

The High Priestess glowered but nodded an affirmative. "I have put off the inevitable long enough."

Demitri walked beside Flowridia, standing at her knee as he absorbed the sights with his curious eyes and nose.

A familiar pair of guards straightened at their approach. The two of them spared a quick glance to Demitri, before darting to Khastra, and then Etolié, who spoke. "We have a meeting with Archbishop Xoran."

"Wait in the chapel," one of them said, his nervous eyes now falling onto the sizeable weapon strapped to Khastra's back. "Someone will inform him of your arrival."

The grandeur of the cathedral's chapel still struck a chord deep in Flowridia's soul. Stained glass shone a rainbow of colors onto the floor, and candles lit the corners and the altar. The familiar statue—the one Etolié claimed survived the same fire that long ago devastated the building—stood before the altar of candles, but behind her, something larger, covered in a sheet. This must have been the new statue, Flowridia reasoned, but that wasn't what stole her attention.

At Sol Kareena's feet was the offered flower from long ago, carefully preserved with a dome of glass. Flowridia stepped past Etolié and the rest, Demitri at her heels, and nearly ran toward it, stopping only to stare at the accepted offering.

Perhaps miracles didn't happen as often as she thought. The flower thrived despite the platform of stone.

When Flowridia looked up, the Goddess' gaze bore into her. She shied away, wondering whether there were boundaries to her unconditional acceptance. Flowridia loved a woman too dark for this world, one who stood at ultimate odds with the Sun Goddess, yet Sol Kareena loved Flowridia still.

"Consider what you could do in her name," said a voice, and Flowridia saw Meira come to stand beside her, staring down at the offered flower. "True greatness is achieved when you give the Goddess your heart."

Greatness, yes, but Flowridia's heart was no longer hers to give.

"You gonna pledge to the Goddess' kiddo, Meira?" Etolié asked, her impish smirk betraying her jest.

Meira, however, looked merely annoyed. "My loyalty is to Sol Kareena. I will celebrate her joy, but her child must prove itself before it earns my respect."

A door opened, creaking wood echoing through the aged cathedral. A small girl, seven at most and wearing the garb of a priestess, approached. She smiled with her eyes. "Archbishop Xoran is ready to see you. Will you please come with me?"

Etolié smiled kindly at the little girl. "Of course," she said, and all followed as the girl escorted them to a door at the back wall.

Flowridia whispered, "I didn't realize you could train to be an acolyte that young."

"She's unquestionably an orphan," Etolié replied, just as softly.

Flowridia's bleeding heart ached, her eyes growing wide as she watched the girl who led them.

"She lives a happy life here, Flowers. There are other children like her who are well-cared for under the Goddess' watchful eye."

They were taken to a meeting room, one with a single rounded table and the archbishop himself seated at the far side. In his hand, he held the staff topped by the white orb. Beside him sat a woman wearing similar garb as Meira, save for the crown woven into the thick, black locks of her hair, not unlike the archbishop. She could have been his near mirror, both in her kind smile and deep-hued skin, and at her shoulder, a small bird sat perched.

Archbishop Xoran stood at their entrance. "Magister Etolié, a pleasure to meet with you again," he said, and he immediately went to shake her hand. Then, to Flowridia, he smiled. "Lady Flowridia, it is wonderful to renew our acquaintance."

She shook his hand, struck by his sincerity.

To Khastra, he said, "I've heard of your legend but never had the pleasure of meeting you. General Khastra, is it?"

Khastra nodded. "I could say the same."

And to Meira, simply, "Priestess Meira, I appreciate you taking the time to come." He made no effort to shake her hand. Then, he turned to Sora. "I'm afraid we haven't met."

"Sora Fireborn," she said, and she offered a hand. "I serve under High Priestess Meira."

The archbishop accepted the gesture, and once he'd shaken her hand, he pointed at the woman seated at the table. "Joining us today is the High Priestess of the Cathedral—my sister, Lunestra." The woman smiled, the lines of her aged face growing deep, and Flowridia found her stunningly lovely.

"Please, sit," the archbishop said, and after a slight push from Etolié's hand, Flowridia obeyed. Demitri circled the chair before settling his small body at her feet.

High Priestess Lunestra spoke up from her seat. "Before we begin," she said, "I would ask your permission to cast a ward of secrecy. What we say at this meeting must not be overheard by foreign parties."

"Who would want to eavesdrop?" Khastra asked.

Etolié looked pained at Khastra's interjection. "Cast what you'd like," she said. "We'd prefer to keep our quest quiet as well."

"I appreciate you accommodating my need for security," the archbishop said as Lunestra stood. From him, she accepted the staff with the orb. It glowed at her touch.

What began as a white light, near blinding, became a circle that expanded to fill the room.

Flowridia reached out to touch the magical light, intrigued at how it tingled against her fingers.

A burning pain suddenly seared her chest. Flowridia gasped, clutching her dress as the pain subsided, the circle forcing past her to surround them all.

"Flowers?" Etolié said, and Flowridia realized they all stared.

"I-I'm fine," she said, patting where the ear lay between her breasts. "Startled, is all."

The archbishop and Lunestra seemed to accept this, but Etolié's smile grew increasingly forced as she followed the movement of Flowridia's hand.

In her head, she heard a young voice. *What happened?*

"Later, Demitri," she mouthed, and she realized Sora, too, had followed Etolié's gaze.

Archbishop Xoran spoke, the staff now back in his hand. "Your kingdom still seeks the orbs."

"We do," Etolié said.

"I will keep our proposition simple and transparent. You received a gift from Nox'Kartha. Bring it to us, and we will give you the orb."

Immediately, Flowridia sat up. Heart seizing, she said, "What? Why?"

Never in all her months residing in Staelash had she seen so vicious a glare on Etolié's pointed face. A warning, directed at her, but before Etolié turned back to the archbishop, her face returned to something more serene and less sober. "I would prefer to not involve other countries in this discussion."

The archbishop shook his head, gripping the staff tight. The orb glowed under his hold. "This is a matter more pressing than diplomatic relations."

"The ear was a gift," came a voice from beside them. Meira spoke, making no attempt to mask her suspicious gaze. "What use have you for an artifact of pure necromancy?"

"We wouldn't use it. We would put a leash on the monster it was severed from."

The word 'monster' drew heat to Flowridia's face. "What's your interest in Ayla Darkleaf?" she dared to ask. Etolié fists clenched under the table, but Flowridia found she didn't care.

"Ayla Darkleaf is a monster only barely caged. Under the thumb of Imperator Casvir," Archbishop Xoran said, slowing his words, "she is at least held accountable for her monstrosities. But the ear is a way for her to funnel her chaotic streak unhinged. What happened to the Skalmites was a terrible tragedy, but it's only a taste of the potential for danger."

"It is," Etolié said, her tone cool. "There is great potential for danger. It's why we're protecting it."

"It doesn't need protection," the archbishop said, frustration growing with each chosen word. "It needs to be destroyed. Do you realize the power you wield? Do you realize the legacy of the monster you claim to control?"

"I know she is no monster," Flowridia said, and the scraping of her wooden chair against the stone floor startled all but her as she stood. Instinctively, her hand flew to her sternum, the weight of the pointed ear soothing to her livid soul. "What would you do with her?"

The archbishop took a breath to speak, but High Priestess Lunestra held up a hand and spoke instead, her words calm and kind. "She is no friend to Sol Kareena, Lady Flowridia, but it seems she is a friend to you."

Flowridia's lip trembled, though from rage or tears, she did not know. Perhaps both.

"Let us explain ourselves," she continued, "because while I respect your wish to not involve foreign parties, Nox'Kartha is already involved. The orb fuels protections set around my brother's home. Were we to give it with no recompense, they would dissolve. Not two weeks ago, another attempt was made on his life."

Archbishop Xoran stared between Etolié and Flowridia, but Flowridia reserved her shock for Lunestra.

"Something scratched at the wards around his home but couldn't break in. Holy magic only detours one sort of creature."

Only a creature held together by necromancy—

Ayla had admitted to embarking on 'espionage' for Casvir—

"Y-You have no proof," Flowridia said, stuttering in her panic.

"The only thing standing between the stability of our kingdom and Casvir's subtle knife is the orb," Lunestra said, finality in her tone. "Unless we have a way to fight back, we cannot consider–"

"So, you would murder a foreign dignitary—!"

"Flowers!"

Etolié's sharp reprimand caused Flowridia to shrink. The glare she gave, once meant for the archbishop, withered as she turned to Etolié. The Celestial turned, her fist settling against the table. "Flowers," she said, stern but subdued, "I need you to leave this meeting."

"Etolié–"

"I won't ask again."

The archbishop and Lunestra kept their gazes to the ground, but all the rest watched her. In the ensuing silence, shame brought heat to Flowridia's cheeks, and she trembled as she turned on her light feet.

She stepped past the barrier of light with no trouble. The door clicked shut behind her. Tears streamed down her face as she brought her ear to the door, desperate to hear something, anything of Ayla's fate.

Nothing.

Flowridia stood, realizing she had left Demitri behind in the meeting. Perhaps he could relay what his young mind held to.

At her chest, the ear had burned when seared by holy light. The barrier, it seemed, allowed one to exit, but not enter—easier that way, to protect a one-way street—and alone, she slipped her hand into her bodice and gasped when she withdrew her prize. Her own sternum was red and raw, but the ear had burned, the once sharp edges shriveled. If she stared, she could see the burns slowly smoothing, the skin sealing and patching.

This was but a glancing, accidental blow. Were the Theocracy to acquire their prize, Ayla's pain would know no bounds.

Flowridia stepped out of the hallway, following the path back to the chapel. Abandoned, closed to the public for the evening's preparations—

But, no. A lone figure stood before Sol Kareena's statue, quiet acrimony on her sharp features. Flowridia knew that stance, Ayla's proud poise. Lithe, pale fingers brushed

273

against the altar, and when Ayla knelt, it was not before the Goddess, no, but by the altar. She peered inside the hollow opening, even her small stature too much to fit underneath.

The elven characters written inside had been too faded for Flowridia to decipher, their cadence bespeaking a time long past. But perhaps Ayla could read it, her age granting wisdom Flowridia could never understand.

When she turned to face Flowridia, a burn radiated from the hole of her missing ear, nearly healed, but not quite. Ayla ran at her approach, her cold hands a comfort as she dug into Flowridia's skirts. "Sweet Flowra, do not fear," Ayla voice soothed, but Flowridia could not help her tears.

"Ayla, your face–"

"Yes, it was terribly uncomfortable."

But Flowridia shook her head. "They'll have you killed, Ayla. They'll kill you in exchange for the archbishop's orb–"

"I know. I heard everything."

Flowridia gasped, daring to match eyes with Ayla's icy stare. "But, how–"

Ayla's finger on her lips caused her breath to hitch. Her finger gently trailed down her chin, her neck, finally pausing at the collar of her dress. Ayla withdrew her own severed ear. "Don't act surprised. Casvir has madness to his methods."

Flowridia felt her face pale. "This whole time–"

"Except in your garden. Your protections are stronger than even the archbishop's." Ayla let the ear fall and land on Flowridia's chest. Then, she stroked the soft contours of Flowridia's face, standing on her toes to place a kiss on her lips. "Gods, I've missed you," she whispered, and for a moment, Flowridia forgot the horrid reveal. She savored those lips against her own, reveled in the soft fabric of Ayla's dress bunching in her hands as she pulled her closer.

The world grew soft, a fog of tentative peace.

Flowridia's body craved contact, but more pressing matters stole her attention. Etolié's reprimand, the archbishop, the meeting . . . All of it simmered in her mind until she finally dared to say, "Ayla, I'm so afraid–"

A door echoed across the cathedral walls, interrupting her words, and when she turned, she felt Ayla disappear from her grip. Into her shadow, it seemed. Ayla vanished as Etolié entered the chapel.

The Celestial came alone, Flowridia realized, the others still in their meeting or perhaps having gone a different way. Did Demitri still listen?

Silent, Etolié stopped beside her, her gaze drifting from the flower at Sol Kareena's feet to the Goddess' smiling face. Flowridia wondered if Ayla watched. "Pretty stupid of you, bringing something like that into the meeting."

The ear, Flowridia realized, dangled outside her bodice. She stuffed it down her dress. "Etolié, it's burned from the high priestess' spell. If we give it to them–"

"Relax, Flowers. I turned them down." Ire laced Etolié's tone, her bitter gaze resting on the Goddess. "And Khastra agrees to everything I do."

Relief threatened to bring fresh tears. Flowridia released a shaky sigh. "Etolié, I'm sorry–"

"Stop," Etolié said, her words sharp. "Flowers, even when we disagree with what our political counterparts say, we at least grant them the respect of *listening*. We might have been able to sway them to a different offer, but because of your tantrum they're soured against us, perhaps for years to come. Rulers hold grudges, like everyone else. The orbs transcend politics, but convincing them this is anything but a political ploy will be all but impossible now."

Flowridia had nothing to say, shame filling her at Etolié's words.

Etolié stood silent a moment, nothing but the faint sounds of radiating excitement from outside filling the tension. "Love so often damns otherwise good people," she finally said. "Marielle's engagement to Zorlaeus has doomed the future of our neutrality in ways she'll never foresee. And your love for Ayla has struck another nail into the coffin."

"What they asked for–"

"Was entirely inappropriate, yes. And on those grounds alone we could have rejected it. But now they know of your affection, Flowers. Why would the Theocracy ever try to consult with Staelash on political matters when its queen is married to a former Nox'Karthan ambassador, or when they know our diplomat will topple an entire discussion off the table because they called her 'friend,' Ayla, a monster?

"For now," Etolié continued, "we set this orb aside and accept that it's safer than any of the others. We turn our focus to finding the ones in the wild. But remember, Flowers, that sometimes we have to set duty before our hearts."

Flowridia forced a stable composure, and when she said nothing, Etolié turned. "Tell no one you have that thing with you," she said, and her clicking heels echoed through the chapel as she stepped down the aisle and disappeared out the door.

Flowridia was unsurprised to feel a soft touch skirt across her waist from behind. "No need for fear, Flowra," came the whisper, and Flowridia turned into the touch, desperate for Ayla's hands. The burn on Ayla's face had all but faded, only a single singed circle around the eerie hole when Flowridia brushed aside her hair. Their lips pressed together, Ayla moaning at the contact.

Flowridia's hips touched the altar when Ayla pushed her, legs splaying as her bottom sat atop it. Ayla's touch grew less innocent, her hands groping Flowridia's thighs, pushing aside her skirts. "Ayla," Flowridia said, already breathless, "we'll be caught–"

She was cut off by Ayla's mouth on her lips, stealing any objections from her tongue. Ayla's hands tugged at her collar and tore the fabric, enough to reveal the chain and slight cleavage hiding her ghastly accessory. She gripped Flowridia's breasts and withdrew one from her dress, the cold air touching Flowridia's sensitive skin only a moment before Ayla's mouth settled to warm it.

Fingers skirted up her thighs, beneath her clothes, and before Flowridia could speak, Ayla's fingers thrust inside her.

Flowridia's hand fell to the altar, the stone a support against Ayla's pleasured touch. The other, she tangled into Ayla's hair, where she cradled her face against her breast. Each thrust tore pleasured cries from her throat, ones she stifled, lest they echo through the abandoned chapel.

Before her, Ayla all but knelt, worship on her tongue. Sol Kareena stared, her stone visage ambivalent to the sacrilege on her holy altar; the prayers Flowridia sang were for Ayla alone.

When her pleasure peaked, Flowridia shuddered and sobbed, the rush of emotion bombarding her frazzled mind. All the relief, all the hurt ripped away, leaving her raw. But Ayla held her, moving from her breast to her mouth where she kissed Flowridia's full lips. Flowridia ached, her seeping warmth swelling against Ayla's fingers. In gentle motions, Ayla withdrew, and Flowridia mourned the loss.

She gasped, her hand wrapping around Ayla's body as the undead woman straddled her on the altar. A comforting embrace held Flowridia tight.

Flowridia opened her eyes, and through her blurred, tear-stained vision she saw a figure standing by the wall. She stiffened, recognizing Sora, her heart seizing at what the half-elf held in her arms—Demitri, caught in his espionage.

Ayla must have sensed the change. She turned, her soft demeanor twisting into something coy and wicked. "Sora Fireborn," she cooed, "nosy little tartlet, aren't you? Curious how your bastard parents conceived you?"

Ayla stepped onto the floor. Flowridia immediately adjusted her clothing, hiding her exposed breast and dripping vulva. Panic filled Flowridia and Sora both, it seemed; the half-elf stepped back at Ayla's approach, keeping Demitri in her arms.

Flowridia matched Demitri's golden eyes. She heard his voice. *Mom, she has a knife.*

"Ayla, stop," Flowridia whispered, staring now at Sora.

But Ayla sauntered forward. "Little blunt-eared bastard, trying to be a hero. What's your plan? Going to tattle to Sol Kareena that I wiped my lady's pleasure on her altar?"

Ayla's smile revealed teeth. When she didn't stop, Sora withdrew a knife and held it to Demitri's throat.

Ayla stopped, her humor vanishing. Flowridia gasped as her hands flew to her face. "Sora, please, don't–"

Mom, she wants the ear!

Sora's hand trembled as she glanced between Flowridia and Ayla.

She told the archbishop she would give it to him in exchange for the orb.

But Flowridia hardly heard it. Her own heartbeat threatened to deafen her. "Sora, don't do this."

Sora glanced between them, hands shaking as she dared to match eyes with Ayla. "Don't you dare take a step."

There was no knife to grab and fling, no weapon to wield, save for her words. Fear stole her breath, and she barely managed to plead, "He's only a child. He knows nothing of any of this; he's innocent."

Flowridia swore she saw the knife press against Demitri's throat. Her little wolf gave a whine, one that ripped into her motherly heart. She screamed, *"Ayla, do something!"*

When Ayla leapt, Sora dropped Demitri, her silver knife glinting off the candlelight before the statue.

The knife plunged. Silver embedded into Ayla's sternum.

Flowridia's gasp ripped from her throat, pained and rough. Demitri's claws skittered across the ground as he bolted toward her. She fell to her knees and gathered him into her arms, felt his racing heart, and saw Ayla glance toward the knife protruding from her chest.

She laughed.

It echoed across the high ceilings, the apparent hilarity at what would have been a killing blow to a mortal too much to bear.

In Flowridia's arms, Demitri squirmed, a pitiful trill leaving his throat as he attempted to bury himself in her embrace. She touched his neck and realized blood seeped from a thin line at his throat.

For as quickly as Sora managed to strike, Ayla leisurely wrapped her fingers around the blade and pulled it downward, skin and fabric ripping to the chorus of snapping bone. "Your ancestors tried and failed a thousand times to slay me. Did you think it would be so easy?" When the blade reached her navel, she withdrew the shined weapon, hardly a hint of red staining the tip. Before Flowridia's eyes, the skin stitched itself together, bone reformed, and Ayla's smile grew wide as her teeth elongated.

Her sweet Demitri's precious blood stained Flowridia's hands, even as a fog of red clouded her vision. A healing spell began to tickle her bloodied fingers, but as she leaned over her dearest companion, from her torn bodice, the ear slipped out and dangled on its chain.

The half-elf held her hands up, slowly backing away from the knife Ayla held. Enmity pulled Ayla's lips into a sneer. "Whatever I do to you, Casvir will surely do to me, tenfold. But keep skulking around my Flowra and her familiar, and I will be *very* tempted to strip the flesh from your bones–"

"Unless I wish you would," Flowridia heard herself say. She clutched the ear in her hand, blood staining the pointed tip. Perhaps she had no knife to throw, but to save her familiar, there was still a weapon to wield. To the ear, she whispered, "Kill Sora."

The earring cracked. Ayla immediately whirled around, startled, it seemed, by Flowridia's words. Her grin revealed fangs. "With glee."

Sora stepped back. "Wait, Flowridia–"

"But no one can know," Flowridia said, louder now as she stared into Sora's wide eyes. She could summon no remorse. "Not of this wish, and not that it was you."

Ayla's predatory smile turned to Sora scarcely a moment before she pounced. The knife fell from her hands, but before it could clatter to the floor, Ayla's hands reached Sora's neck. They thrust into her mouth—

And tore out her tongue.

Blood sprayed. Ayla's arm wrapped around Sora's neck and covered her mouth, a gurgling, horrified cry escaping the half-elf's throat as blood poured from her mouth. Ayla held the dismembered organ in her hand. "Sweet Flowra, do not fear. A slip of the knife, and we celebrate our victory soaked in Sora's blood." Seeping from Sora's lips, blood stained Ayla's fingers. With a sickening crack of bone, Ayla broke Sora's jaw open. "Hold this, please," she cooed, and she forced the tongue back into Sora's mouth, ignoring how she screamed and sobbed.

Flowridia clutched Demitri to her chest, head light as blood drained from her face. "I'll make short work of this one," Ayla continued. "Distract yourself until tonight, Flowra. Bother your Celestial counterpart until the ceremony. Neither you nor I will be implicated in any crime."

Numb hands caressed the wolf pup in Flowridia's arms. Though her head swam, Flowridia said, "Go," and prayed she would live to regret her wicked deed. "I trust you. Go."

Ayla smiled, and despite the tortured half-elf trapped in her arms and the blood staining her body, her face conveyed adoration. "I love you, Flowra. I'll be watching all night."

"I love you, Ayla." She meant it. She prayed it was enough.

Into the shadow of a doorframe, Ayla and Sora vanished.

A healing spell finally met Demitri's throat. The tiny wolf made no attempt to escape her embrace when she stood up. *Mom, are you all right?*

Casvir's subtle knife, as the high priestess had said, and as Flowridia stared at the splattering of blood on the floor, she wondered how many had fallen to Ayla's blade. Contemplating her familiar's question, she pulled a handkerchief from the pocket of her dress and quickly wiped the droplets from the floor. The white cloth spoiled, but the smeared, deep red blended with the stone floor.

There was no remorse, no hesitation in Ayla's action. Clarence Vors, the Theocracy's envoy, now Sora, but surely there were others –an entire country, if Sora was to be believed—and there would be more to come. Ayla stretched her leash longer each day, and Flowridia was certain it would someday be enough to wrap around the imperator's neck.

But, no. Sora's death was not on Ayla's hands. Ayla twisted the knife, but Flowridia had wielded it.

"I fear," she finally said, sparing a glance for the blood-stained handkerchief, "that Sora's death won't be the last."

"Did she say anything else?"

On the steps of the cathedral, Flowridia sat apart from the crowd fighting to enter. Sunset neared, and the unveiling had surely already occurred. Lines of worshippers had gathered, most with candles lit in the child's honor, prepared to be placed at the statue's feet.

No, Etolié left like she said. That was when Sora decided to talk to the archbishop and hurt Lady Ayla.

Guilt had descended, but the time had passed for regret. Sora was surely long dead, and soon the rest would discover whatever morbid mess Ayla left behind. Sora's fate would draw no sympathy from Flowridia; not when Demitri had so nearly met his end.

"Flowers?"

The familiar voice and pet name bespoke only one person. Flowridia looked up and saw the Celestial grab her illusionary skirts and dart up the stairs. "I would have thought you'd go in without me. What happened to your shirt?"

"Tripped. Are we late?" Flowridia asked, and she accepted when Etolié offered her a hand to stand.

"Khastra's already inside. Meira's furious—seems Sora ran off somewhere. No one's seen her."

Flowridia simply nodded and followed Etolié to the entrance of the cathedral. "Do we need a candle?"

"Only if you're pledging. Each candle is a prayer to the new god."

"God?"

"Not every angel is a god," Etolié said. "Not even close. But with as many followers as this kid already has, he or she certainly has a bright future."

At the door, the guards nodded at their entrance, allowing them to bypass the lengthy line of worshippers.

The archbishop stood with the orb and staff in hand, surveying the crowd of onlookers. People clumped together in a mass as they filed through the line, the cathedral bright from candlelight. But standing tall behind the ancient statue, the unveiled Goddess smiled at all in attendance. Cradled in her arms, a small baby, one with alert eyes and a halo outlining a full head of hair. Carved in white stone, the robes fell lifelike across their bodies, their eyes vibrant and kind.

Something in the stone churned Flowridia's stomach, suspicions bubbling in her gut. "Etolié, when was the baby born?"

"Weeks ago. A few days before Marielle's coronation, if I remember right–"

Shattered glass broke her words, and with it a child's scream. A small priestess grabbed the archbishop's robe as she pointed frantically to the window, sobbing. Flowridia heard gasps from the crowd, and when she turned, she saw a body pressed against the broken window, face mutilated and bleeding.

Glass splintered, the windows smashing as bodies fell and crashed against them. Screams erupted from the crowd, and Flowridia felt Etolié yank her between the pews to avoid being trampled by terrified worshippers.

Then, from the ceiling, a final body fell, strung up by the neck, and Flowridia saw what fate had befallen both Sora and the unfortunate ones outside. The ears were cut, the tops sheared and rounded, head shaved, fingers stumped. The blood-stained body was nude, her face a mass of seeping holes. But carved into her stomach was the word 'blunt-ear,' and embedded in her torso, straight through her sternum, was Sora's own knife.

Flowridia had heard of crimes committed to half-elves, murders with method, meant to humiliate as much as send a message: to 'blunt' them, to stump their limbs and face and ears.

Bile welled in Flowridia's stomach, but not so much as the guilt in her heart. Tears pooled in her eyes. In turning this into a massacre—the other bodies surely bore the same half-elven blood—who would think to implicate the small party from Staelash?

And what connection would there be to Lady Ayla of Nox'Kartha?

People hurried to exit, ducking to avoid the blood that dripped from the mutilated body strung with a noose. Frantic priests helped to usher the mass, but silent against the wall, a figure stood perfectly still.

More statue than man, with his shining armor and his hand held out, posed with his sword stuck into the ground, the man truly did hold resemblance to the illustrations in the ancient book. Utterly innocuous among the crowd despite his daunting size, he was ignored by the panicked worshippers, and Flowridia wondered if magic was involved.

She saw him turn his head by a single degree, and from the slits in his helmet, Flowridia swore he stared directly at her.

Flowridia looked back to the archbishop with his orb, thought of Etolié with the orb hidden at her hip, and then spotted Khastra standing with her arms crossed not two rows forward, frowning at the ghastly corpses. She muttered, "Etolié, protect the archbishop. We have to secure the orb."

"Flowers–"

She was cut off by Flowridia handing the Celestial her young wolf pup. "Whatever happens, keep him safe. I'm going to go distract him."

"Who?"

A messy plan, but a plan nonetheless, scrambled together in her head. "Count to ten, then look by the door. If Khastra can strike first, we have a chance." Flowridia darted away, pushing past worshippers and taking care not to set her hair aflame from the many candles.

The man who would claim to be Order watched her movements. Flowridia slid beside him, undaunted though her head barely touched his chest. She spared a glance for Etolié, watching as the Celestial slid toward her half-demon companion in the pews.

"That's you, isn't it?" Flowridia asked, soft enough for only he to hear. "You're Sol Kareena's son."

Flowridia heard him shift, the faint sliding of metal on metal as he turned his armored head to look at her. "A damning assumption," he said, his smooth voice reverberating within the metal helm.

"You bear the same halo," Flowridia said, and between the slits of his helmet, human eyes met her own, the color of earth speckled with sunlight. "And you have the same eyes."

"I am he, in a way. The child my mother birthed is still innocent. But I am granted power by his worshippers."

"How can that be? If you're truly the God of Order, you died ten thousand years ago. Yet, you were born in this era?"

"When true Godhood is achieved, one can exist apart from time."

He said nothing more, looking instead to the statue bearing his face. Sol Kareena and the infant stood serene among the chaos.

Flowridia asked, "What name did your mother give you?"

"It is not a name used in worship; only by those who knew me before I achieved Godhood." He stood silent a moment, this reborn God of Order, stoic among the storm. "My mother named me Soliel," he finally said. "Will you tell me yours?"

Flowridia's mind rifled through every piece of trivia she knew regarding magic and names. Would it harm her for him to know? Finding nothing, she said simply, "Flowridia."

Soliel said nothing, but he did look back down, his brown eyes settling once again on her.

Flowridia spared a glance for the front of the room, to the unveiled statue and for the infant cradled in the Goddess' arms. The room had mostly cleared, aside from the faces she knew.

She realized she still felt his gaze. Flowridia looked back and saw that the man—Soliel, she reminded herself; even monsters claimed names—studied her through the slits in his helm. "Flowridia–"

That was when Khastra's hammer caved into his chest.

Metal crunched, as did bone. The God of Order cracked the cathedral's stone wall, the impact of the hammer sending him flying. The crystal hammer flew back, whirling through the air and into Khastra's readied grasp. The gargantuan woman balanced her hooves atop the pews, eyes glinting at the prospect of a fight. "Tiny one, is he dead? I can hit him again."

Flowridia, frozen from shock, managed to finally breathe. Soliel stirred, grunting as he forced his way out of the caved wall. His armor held a massive indentation, and Flowridia wondered how he breathed. Khastra hefted her crystal hammer high above her head, her entire musculature expanding, nearly doubling as she did. Veins popped, and Khastra flung the hammer forward with a shout.

This time, Soliel held out a hand, a shield of crackling lightning creating a wall between him and the hammer. Flowridia saw the unstable light bend at the hammer's touch, Khastra's will against the supposed-dead God's.

The hammer clattered to the ground, the stonework cracking under the force. It flew back again, into Khastra's grasp.

An armored hand grabbed Flowridia and held her to his ruined breastplate. "Strike me again, and–"

Soliel suddenly cried out. He dropped his sword and Flowridia both, then attempted to tear out the dagger in his neck.

Ayla Darkleaf landed lightly on the ground, fury etched in her face. Planting herself, she stood as a wall between Flowridia and Soliel. "Carry what grudges you will, but Flowra is mine."

Soliel rose to his full height, the dagger clattering to the ground. Ayla suddenly ripped Flowridia away—in time for Khastra to bombard the fallen God, her hammer swinging in tandem with her musculature. Soliel's sword narrowly rose to match it, the metallic clang of metal and rock piercing.

Ayla dragged Flowridia away from the skirmish, protective as she held her to her chest. "Are you hurt?"

"I'm fine."

Etolié, meanwhile, began to shine. Her form morphed, growing, glowing, until not one being, but two coexisted within her body. Flowridia recognized the outline of Eionei and the staff summoned in Etolié's hand. Stars burst through the ruined glass windows, pelting Soliel's helmet.

Soliel warded them away with his summoned lightning, and Flowridia heard clouds gather outside, thunder rolling. But the distraction proved effective, and Khastra managed to strike his face. The entire wall cracked as Soliel hit the stone, his helmet utterly ruined.

He tore it from his head.

Flowridia couldn't say what she expected; perhaps a monster's visage to match his deeds. Instead, Soliel held all the beauty of his mother and his angelic heritage, with hair as radiant a blonde as his halo and a jaw set like steel. But hatred twisted his face, subtly lined with stress and age, cracks in his apparent perfection, the very countenance of one fallen from grace.

He was everything Flowridia had seen in the ancient portrayal, save the enmity in his once benevolent gaze.

Soliel feigned a swing, instead jabbing Khastra in the stomach with the handle of his sword. The blade struck her arm as he shoved past, managing to slide between the carefully constructed plates. Soliel rushed at inhuman speed to the archbishop.

Flowridia saw blood well from the tear in Khastra's armor. In the split second before Soliel stole his prize, Khastra smiled, brought up her arm, and licked the drops of blood.

Flowridia saw her swell and change, this half-demon woman, transformed by her own cursed blood. She stood taller, elongated, her bulk swelling to match, armor shifting to accommodate—as though it were built for this very purpose. Monstrous fangs jutted from her lips. Her nails became claws, and her silver tattoos glowed against skin that threatened to split from her expanding, pulsating musculature.

Bringer of War, indeed. Khastra laughed, and Flowridia swore the shadows rose with it.

Lightning struck the roof of the cathedral, stone falling from the ceiling at the impact, and Ayla tossed Flowridia over her shoulder, expertly dodging the debris. But the distraction proved perfect, and when Flowridia looked up, the archbishop lay disoriented on the floor, and the white orb shone in Soliel's hand.

Eionei, meanwhile, began to glow not only from holy light, but from flame erupting at his feet. The orb shone luminous in his hand. Khastra rushed forward—faster now, wielding the gargantuan weapon as though it were a child's toy—in tandem with an arc of fire from Eionei's staff. Soliel's shield of lightning blocked the flame, but a swift swing of Khastra's hammer knocked the orb back out of his hand.

It flew through the air. Flowridia might have run to claim it, but Ayla's grip on her arms remained strong. Instead, it rolled beneath a pew.

Soliel began to speak. "Lady Darkleaf, I know your legacy–" When Khastra swung, he managed to duck, but Flowridia saw it was a near hit—perhaps a killing blow. "And I know you crave freedom–"

His words were stolen with an 'oomph' when Khastra kicked him in the stomach.

To Flowridia's horror, Ayla perked up, though she clung tight to Flowridia's form.

"Perhaps a deal–" Soliel's cry interrupted his words— Eionei struck with his staff, searing Soliel's body in flame. Though he burned, Khastra grabbed him by the neck, her claws sinking into his flesh. She threw him against the wall, then hefted the hammer for a bone-shattering blow.

When Ayla tried to set Flowridia down, she clung to her dress. "Ayla," Flowridia pled, "don't listen. He's a monster; you know this–"

"A monster, yes, but also a God." Ayla turned, intrigue tugging at her lips. "I want Casvir's head."

With his back to the wall and two behemoths closing in, Soliel cried, "Aid me, and you will have it."

Eionei rushed forward, quarterstaff in hand, blazing wings spreading wide from his form. He stood taller than them all, and when he brought the staff down, Soliel's sword rose to defend it—leaving him vulnerable to Khastra's strike. Flowridia watched him clatter to the ground.

Lips brushed Flowridia's temple as her feet touched the ground. "Ayla, don't do this, please–"

"Our future together does not have to be an idle dream, Flowra," Ayla replied, eyes glistening. Never had Flowridia heard such hope in Ayla's voice. "This is for you."

"Ayla—!" But Ayla disappeared in the shadow of a pillar.

Khastra swung, her hammer glittering under the gold and white glow of Soliel's violent form. Metal crunched as he flew at the window, through the ruined glass and landing beyond the cathedral's bound. With a cry, Khastra burst through the shattered window to follow.

Flowridia dropped to her knees, reaching beneath the pew to grab the faintly glowing white artifact. Upon contact, she felt her senses ignite, the richness of the world increasing ten-fold. Colors sharpened. She saw energy and tendrils of light, waiting to be grasped and harnessed for her bending.

Every shadow flickered under her gaze, including the one that emerged behind Eionei's form. The summoned Drinking God moved to follow Khastra, his nimble feet jumping through the window. As smooth as a dancer before her stage, Ayla appeared for only a moment, leaping to steal the orb from Eionei's grasp and tossing it beyond the bounds of the window, then flickering out as quickly as the flame vanishing from his feet.

Ayla had stolen the orb and gone—all before Eionei touched the ground outside.

Flowridia, white orb in hand, elected to follow them through the front door.

Outside, onlookers screamed at the clash of monstrous figures, of the God of Order—flame now rising at his feet—of Khastra transformed to match her heritage, and of Eionei himself. Soliel's armor, once shining and majestic, had torn and bent, damaged by Khastra's shattering blows. Perhaps this would be it—even without an orb, Eionei made a formidable foe, and though Soliel wielded two orbs of power, what could he do against two heroes of their own realms?

A roar fragmented the clashing of metal and stone. "Look, atop the cathedral!" Flowridia heard someone shout, and from the roof leered a nightmarish creature, familiar aside from a face no longer burned: The Endless Night.

The price of Ayla's freedom grew ever higher.

The monster leapt to the ground, tearing through the crowd, blood spraying as she—it—raked its claws, parting the sea of people. It disappeared in a hazed blink.

A scream—Etolié's—and Flowridia watched in horror as the possessed Celestial was thrown into the air. With her newly attuned vision, Flowridia saw glimmering, seeping liquid well at the deep cut across Eionei's back. Khastra followed Eionei with her glowing eyes; The Endless Night's claw swiped a deep gash across her cheek.

Blood dripped down her face. Khastra's fanged mouth twisted into a rapacious grin as she sneered and taunted in an unknown, guttural tongue. Shadows rose and flickered violently. The words sickened Flowridia's stomach, and she recognized only a single, grating word—*"Izthuni!"*—and heard The Lurker chuckle.

287

When Eionei landed among the crowd, Flowridia ran toward him. She fell to her knees before the prone god, and the voice she heard was neither Etolié nor Eionei, but some mix. "You're Etolié's little one."

Flowridia gave a quick nod. "Let me heal you, please."

Eionei looked at the orb in her hand and made no move to stop her when her hands touched ruined, glowing skin. At Flowridia's beckoning, power drained from the orb, channeled through her body and into the Eionei. He—she, for it was Etolié's voice then—gasped, and at Flowridia's silent command, the skin slowly reformed.

In the shadow of the cathedral, Khastra stood strong, the gash at her cheek soaking her mouth in blood as she valiantly faced the titanic figures. Soliel blasted her with sparks of lightning, his sword clattering against the stone of her hammer, but she swung in an arc, her gargantuan weapon held in perfect control as she batted his elemental blast. Lightning flew from her hammer to the sky, and when flame poured upon her, she laughed, immune to the onslaught.

The Endless Night swung its vicious claws; Khastra beat it away, shattering bones. She brought the hammer down not on Soliel, but on his sword, the great weapon splitting in two beneath her might—

But her form caught in the swing of The Endless Night's claws, throwing her to the ground. Crying out, Khastra fell, skin torn, hammer smashing to the ground. Her hand grasped the hilt—

An elongated claw stabbed through her armor like paper. One shot; through the spine and the heart. A spurt of blood—Khastra's hand fell limp.

Flowridia felt the blow in her own chest, and beside her Eionei cried out and attempted to rise, though his brutalized form was not fully healed. Flowridia tried to touch him again, but Soliel approached.

He held two orbs—one fire and one lightning—and his aura had become the same, a torrent of elemental might. He stopped before the wounded god and looked instead to Flowridia. He extended a hand. "Give me your orb."

Flowridia shook her head, stumbling backwards. Soliel stepped forward, fire steadily rising to cover his lower half, lightning crackling along the smooth curves of his armor. His face lost all semblance of majesty, becoming a nightmarish shadow instead, the illumination casting his fury in macabre colors. "I will ask you again, Flowridia—give me your orb."

Flowridia cowered, fear and duty causing her to clutch the artifact to her chest. She sensed no violent magic inherit in this orb—merely benevolence, divinity, the capacity to heal—and realized it would do nothing to save her. At her wrist, she summoned her energy to expand the shield of maldectine, yet in her fear, it grew no larger than her wrist.

When Soliel rushed her, she screamed, bracing herself for a death of fire and lightning.

But an inhuman shriek nearly deafened her. Flowridia watched The Endless Night swipe the God of Order aside with ease, toppling him to the ground. It stood between them, its nightmarish mouth releasing a roar.

When Soliel stood, weaponless though hardly powerless, even he had to look up to face the deity—The Endless Night in title, but Izthuni, God of Shadows in physical form. Flowridia suddenly felt piercing claws—nearly as large as her body—wrench her from the ground. The touch was cold, each limb deathly thin, the ligaments and bone jutting from sickly, pale skin. The monster held her to its ribs, twisting to stand as a barrier between her and the God of Order.

Izthuni, yes, but also Ayla. The monster held her tenderly, its claws sharp but never breaking skin. It brought a second hand to hold her, to cradle her, as Flowridia held the white orb to her chest.

Soliel stepped back, hands raised in defense. "I would not have harmed her. I only need—"

Again, the monster roared, the sound reverberating against Flowridia's entire body.

"We have a bargain—"

This time, behind the inhuman screech sounded a single word, one that held the rumbling threat of a god, but with it the fury of its undead hostess, their voices combining in an abominable, ear-splitting sound: *"Leave!"*

Soliel stepped back, fear in his human eyes. A God he might be, Flowridia realized, but he had yet to attain his true power. When Izthuni leered forward, Flowridia tucked safe against its form, Soliel nearly fell back. "I will leave—"

Flowridia felt the roar more than heard it and curled into Izthuni's grip to cover her ears. When she looked up again, she saw the last vestiges of flame as the God of Order disappeared—to where, she did not know.

Then, light.

Blinding light touched The Endless Night. From the cathedral, Meira emerged.

Not Meira. Meira's sightless eyes glowed with holy light, her entire form lit from within by divinity. Her figure swelled and grew, glowing from every pore as Sol Kareena's form emerged. The Goddess pulled aside the cowl covering her face, and her hair, as golden as the rest of her sunlit features, flowed behind. A spear appeared in her hand, the other cradling something unknown.

Those in the crowd gasped. Some bowed. Eionei stumbled to his feet, then knelt on one knee. Ayla—Izthuni—actively shrieked as the Goddess stepped closer, and Flowridia saw its skin begin to burn before Sol Kareena's light.

Sol Kareena stepped forward, standing twice the height of the godly interloper. Spear aloft, she threw it forward.

Perhaps to Ayla and her demonic possessor, it was a fleeting moment—Flowridia felt herself wrenched as The Endless Night twisted, standing between Flowridia and the Goddess of Light. But to Flowridia, the seconds grew long, feeling the tension in her capturer's form as it curled to protect her.

The spear pierced through the monster, driving straight through Ayla and through Flowridia. Flowridia felt nothing, the weapon passing harmlessly, but realized the spear had thrust out the possessing demon. She saw Izthuni fade in tandem with the weapon, returning to his realm with nothing to anchor his form to this world.

Flowridia fell to the ground, the orb kept tight to her chest and saw Ayla, only Ayla, but infused with holy light. She burned from within, the elven woman's skin cracking, divinity shining out. The unholy scream tearing from her throat spoke of agony, every piece of her bursting as light shattered her undead form.

The Goddess turned her sights onto Flowridia, but she barely felt it. Instead, she ran to Ayla, the light fading and leaving only a blackened husk. Ayla withered before her eyes, mummified and stiff, the thousand-year-old monster returned to her natural age.

She fell forward; Flowridia caught her and, oh, she was cold. Colder than Flowridia had ever felt.

Flowridia screamed. In her hand, the white orb glowed, blinding even to her, but she screamed, anguish escaping her throat. Yet, she heard nothing. Her throat burned, but the world turned grey, like the demonic realm from whence Ayla had come.

The white orb sang, and from far away she felt something dark resonate, some other half yearning to be joined, a manifest destiny beckoning her to come.

Ayla felt so cold.

The world ruptured into sound and color. Flowridia curled around the corpse of her love, weeping amidst the chaos.

Sol Kareena's voice—Meira's voice—boomed above all. "This body burns from within. My time is short." In her arms, she set down her precious cargo—a body.

Sora's body.

The half-elf began to glow, more blinding than the Goddess looming before her. "Sora Fireborn," the Goddess said, "you will not die this day. Rise, and be my new champion."

When the light faded, perched on Sora's chest was a small bird, one that rose and fell with her gasping breaths.

Then, the Goddess knelt before the prone, still body of Khastra—returned to her natural state in death. "There is a place among mine for De'Sindai. For her sacrifice, Khastra's soul will–"

"Sol Kareena, please," came the reply, and Flowridia saw Etolié, returned to her natural form, fall to her knees. "You can save her."

Sol Kareena turned her searing gaze onto Etolié, whose tear-stained visage dared to face the Goddess. "The cost is one you cannot pay, Daughter of Staella. Sora's life is repaid in Meira's sacrifice. Khastra has pledged to no one, but she has given her life for my people. If she will accept me in her afterlife, I will care for her soul like my own child."

Flowridia clutched the stiff corpse to her body, flinching when Sol Kareena set her gaze to her. Like staring into the sun itself, yet Flowridia couldn't look away.

"Your fate is a thousand tangled strings, Child of Odessa, but you were mine first. Pledge to me, and I will unravel them for you."

Flowridia cowered and clutched the withered corpse, her tears evaporating under the Goddess' light. When she hesitated, the Goddess said, "Be careful, lest you become no

291

different than the monsters you seek to tame." Sol Kareena pulled her cowl back over her head. Light faded. She began to shrink.

Meira deShamira fell to the earth, utterly still.

Then, a wave of nausea struck her. Dizzy, she realized everyone had been hit by the same vertigo. Flowridia held tight to the body, ignoring the wolf pup who desperately licked at her feet.

It began as a sizzling in the air, then it pulled into a line. A rip in space, one that opened wide like a door.

A demon stepped out of the portal. Sickly blue, like a drowned corpse, colored nearly eight feet of monster, a monster wearing a frightening ensemble of jagged, blackened armor. White hair pulled back into a tail accentuated his sweeping horns, and familiar red eyes surveyed the scene.

They landed on Flowridia. Heavy, armored steps echoed against stone.

Somewhere, Flowridia heard the crowd whisper. "Imperator Casvir—?" "The Tyrant of Nox'Kartha—?"

Enormous claws reached out to snatch her from the ground.

He lifted her up. Demitri snarled. Flowridia clung tight to Ayla's body, unwilling to leave her behind but with no will to resist the arms that stole her. She stared down, vision blurred by misted eyes.

The demon was gentle as he cradled her to his chest. The crowd stared wide-eyed as he stepped back toward the portal.

Until Etolié rushed forward, standing with her small body between he and the rift in space. Her swollen eyes conveyed desperation, tears still streaming as the Celestial said, "Set her down."

The demon—Imperator Casvir—spoke with reserve, yet despite his quiet words, Flowridia heard unquestionable menace. "The girl's soul is mine. I gave her all she has."

The flicker of confusion in Etolié's demeanor was enough for Casvir to step beyond her, but Flowridia saw, in the seconds before the portal ate them whole, realization on the Celestial's tear-streaked face.

And fear.

Then, Flowridia covered her eyes, prepared to face whatever hell had been prepared for her.

Fresh vertigo struck. The world grew black and dotted with stars.

Then, a hallway, well-lit and lined with stone and pillars of swirling black sand. Imperator Casvir pushed open a door before them.

He set her on her feet, helping steady her as she surveyed the dark room, one lit by globes of light. Flowridia trembled as she stepped forward, clutching the cold and withered form of Ayla in her arms. The globes were not pure light, she realized, but glass orbs covering nearly every surface of the room—a bedroom by appearances, but with no bed.

Protected within each globe lay some odd object. Flowers, so many flowers, but also a sliver of soap, a teacup painted with lavender buds, the queen from a chess set, and so much more. A white tulip, small pastel buds—she gasped at the large, yellow blossom centered on a vanity. She had worn this to Marielle's ball.

Flowridia realized she knew every flower—most from her hair.

On the walls were drawings illustrating a story Flowridia had lived—portraits of her face, her smile, her blush. Some with Demitri, the pup lifelike as he leapt to kiss her, and others alone but surrounded by floral life, her garden, every individual lock of her hair meticulously drawn and braided with flowers.

There was one, unfinished, lying on a desk beside a lock of black hair, preserved in glass and braided with icy blue flowers. In it, the couple danced, Flowridia's eyes practically shining with adoration but her small companion was unfinished, her dress a mere sketch, her hair unshaded. Yet, brilliant, vibrant eyes looked back at the drawn Flowridia, pure joy in her gaze.

A voice met Flowridia's ears. "Her spirit lingers. I can feel it."

The gasping breath that tore from her throat could hardly be called that, but Flowridia managed to turn and face the demonic figure watching from the doorway. She clutched the blackened corpse to her body.

Her demon from the woods—one with an offer she hadn't refused.

"Ayla is dead, but she is not gone. Save your tears; perhaps you can save her, in time." His relentless gaze left hers. Imperator Casvir cast his eyes around the room. "All

293

that was hers is now yours. I will leave you to collect what you would keep." She let him leave, tears streaming freely. The door clicked shut.

Flowridia sank to her knees, the weight in her arms the heaviest she had ever carried. Ayla's face, blackened and mummified, held no semblance of her vibrant self—a shell with no vessel. Empty.

Flowridia set the corpse upon the floor, and as she leaned over it, what dangled from her ruined shirt fell out— the ear, still chained, and as withered and decayed as the rest of Ayla's body.

Two earrings pierced the dead skin, shattered and cracked. The last shone a vivid blue—the final reminder of Ayla's eyes.

Whisper with intent . . .

"Ayla," she said, more a sob than words, "I wish . . . I wish . . ." She stopped, gasping for breath amidst her cries. Broken words spilled from her mouth. "Ayla, come home. Come back to me."

The earring cracked. All three shone a dull grey, ruined like their mistress. In the ensuing silence, Flowridia felt something dark caress the hollow of her heart.

She let the ear fall back to her chest, tears overwhelming the lingering shambles of her strength.

Flowridia cried herself to sleep.

"Flower Child, your tears make a terrible mop."

Flowridia clung to the wooden handle, vision blurred by her swollen eyes. She trembled, pushing the mop through the dripping puddle of blood, vain in her attempts to clear the floor of gore. Her mother's blood, and that of the infant boy, mingled together and stained the dark wood.

Even through her tear-stained vision, she saw the small, mutilated body on the table.

The woolen cloth slunk across the absorbent floor. Her mind already glossed over what cleaning spell it would take to remove the rust-colored stains. Had she grown so calloused? To think of blood as simply another substance to remove from clothing and walls?

No. The gaping wound in the infant's stomach and the clenching in her own was testament to that.

"Your empathy so often betrays you." Mother, cleaned of blood and other fluids, wore a fresh gown and leaned against the doorframe. Sallow skin, paling from blood-loss, reflected the firelight, a demonic touch to her angelic beauty. "I never thought a protégé of mine could have such a tender heart, but any weakness can be purged."

"It's a weakness to think murdering a newborn is sickening?" Flowridia's tongue trembled, and she regretted the quiet words the moment they tumbled from her lips. She tried to catch them, to stuff them back down her throat, but before she could say more, a sharp slap met her face. Ear ringing, Flowridia merely stumbled, Mother's strength subdued in her post-partum state.

But it held no effect on her words. "Anything that holds power over you is a weakness," Mother spat. "For something so simple as death to cripple you–"

"This child committed no crime!" The mop clattered to the floor. Flowridia stood firm, rage loosening her tongue. "He was minutes old, and you murdered him!"

Mother held a hand to her chest in mock offense. "I'm sorry, but who twisted the knife?"

One blow hadn't done it. Flowridia's own hand had gutted the boy and stopped the painful wailing.

Mother, with care to not stain her fresh clothing, took the corpse in her hands. "We'll feast well tonight; a pitiful reward for nine months of labor, but a reward nonetheless."

Every fiber of Flowridia's being screamed in revolt as she processed Mother's words. Breath seizing, and compelled by a notion she couldn't comprehend, Flowridia ran toward the front door.

Thrown open, the noxious vapors of the swamp bombarded her senses. Daylight filtered through the dense trees, but only just. Phantom figures watched her, ghosts cursed to linger and guard their place of death.

A new one had joined them. An infant boy watched her from the windowsill.

"Running away? And where will you go, Flower Child?"

Flowridia stopped in the doorway, hand gripping the damp wood as she shut her eyes and fought back tears. *"I'm going home,"* she wished she could say, but there was no home to go to.

"I won't stop you. But do you think running away will change the past?"

Ice seeped into Flowridia's veins, each pump of blood growing pained and loud.

"Sometimes, Flower Child, despite all our efforts, all our labor, fate steals what we want through no fault of our own."

The voice held charm and light. When Flowridia turned her head back, she saw Mother's hand resting sweetly on her chest, her demeanor kind, playing the mother Flowridia longed to have.

"So, what do we do?" Mother asked, and she let her hand fall, landing lightly on her womb, now empty and cold. "We make do. We move forward."

Flowridia gazed out into the swamp, felt the damp odors threaten to nauseate her stomach. Should she step forward, the water might drown her. The trees smothered all light. Flowridia reached a hand out, her fingers caressing the invisible wards surrounding the home. Three years ago, she felt nothing. Now, they had become attuned to her being, and she saw the indiscernible cracks.

Alone, she could not run, but if she could reach through the wards, perhaps she might find someone to rescue her. Perhaps she could reach out and bring someone in.

Flowridia let her hand drop and pulled the door shut.

"Good girl," she heard from behind, and then Mother's soft footsteps returned to the kitchen.

Flowridia stooped down to pick up the mop from the floor, silent as a plot formed in her head.

It was as Mother had said: Flowridia would move forward.

Epilogue

Marielle paced. The events of the evening had shaken them all, and Zorlaeus knew that Marielle paced when stressed. Her hand kept coming up to her bosom, to touch the artifact no longer there, and each time he saw her flinch. He longed to comfort her.

The time to steal away his beloved would come soon, but first a meeting. Zorlaeus stood behind the throne, knowing he was the outlier in the room.

Thalmus' hands shook, the only indicator that the half-giant registered the scene.

A visitor stood among them—Empress Alauriel Solviraes sat in Etolié's chair, speaking to a small hand mirror. "I'll be here and awake. Call if there's any sign of Flowridia–"

Zorlaeus couldn't make out the blubbering words spewing from the mirror, but Etolié sobbed. That much he understood.

"At least we know she'll be cared for." Lara's lip quivered, regal as she subdued her own sorrow. "Khastra's mark on this kingdom will never be forgotten–"

Again, Zorlaeus heard crying. Lara continued to try and console her.

Khastra's death weighed heavily upon the room. Meira's too, but her place at Sol Kareena's side was assured. Her life would be celebrated, her end as spectacular as a devoted acolyte could hope for. Khastra would be mourned, beloved by all in her kingdom and others.

Little mention of Ayla, however, beyond a muted delivery of facts. News of her death was, selfishly, a relief, though Zorlaeus feared it would be short-lived.

What was something so petty as death to a creature such as Ayla Darkleaf?

297

The empress put the mirror down, countenance heavy. Thalmus spoke, volcanic in his brewing anger, the threat of eruption constant, inevitable. "None of this explains or justifies Flowra's kidnapping."

"Flowridia's apparent kidnapping is an act of violence against Staelash," Lara said softly, "unless Flowridia herself comes forward to defend him. In the meantime, we must consider retaliation. My kingdom is sworn to act on your behalf."

Zorlaeus saw fear in the young empress' face and understood.

"I'm willing to consider a diplomatic approach," Marielle spat, "if Nox'Kartha will comply." She stopped, fists clenching. Zorlaeus hesitantly reached out to grab one, feeling her hand relax in his. "Zorlaeus, there must be something we can do."

Zorlaeus stepped forward, cringing as the attention shifted to him. "I worked for Viceroy Murishani, but I've had enough interactions with Imperator Casvir to say that he is ruthless above all things. Honorable, yes. He'll bring no harm to Flowridia, but for him to come and steal her–" Zorlaeus' voice hitched, acutely aware of the vengeful half-giant who had stood up beside him. "Imperator Casvir would not have taken her without a purpose."

"What purpose?" Thalmus asked, and Zorlaeus held no doubt that if he misspoke, he would be a puddle beneath the man's feet.

"I don't know," he admitted. "But with as strict an honor code as Casvir holds himself to, it makes me wonder–"

A knock at the door pulled all focus.

The door opened, and Flowridia herself stood between the doorframe, shadowed by the red-eyed Tyrant of Nox'Kartha.

Zorlaeus immediately fell to one knee. Whatever protections granted by his betrothal to a foreign dignitary, it meant nothing if Casvir sensed any level of disrespect from a citizen, former or not.

A tentative voice, one that refused to waver despite the evidence of tears on her face, broke the silence in the room. "Once the funerals have been held, I'll be leaving with Demitri. I've signed a contract with Imperator Casvir."

Zorlaeus' heart seized at the word 'contract.' He kept his head down, but his eyes glanced up and saw the false courage etched into the girl's face as she stepped inside. Casvir remained beyond the doorframe, but he watched.

Marielle dared to ask, "A contract for what?" He saw her stand tall, and it took all of his willpower to not drag her to his side.

"I'll be adventuring with him, for a time, to help him find an artifact."

"Flowridia," the empress said, and with tentative care she took Flowridia's hand in her own, "have you done this by your own choice?"

"He offered. I set the terms."

Before Flowridia could say anything more, Thalmus pulled the girl into a hug. "It doesn't mean you have to do this," he said, and the rumble of his voice spoke of something deep and dangerous.

"I already signed–"

"That means nothing."

"I'm going to do this," Flowridia said as she pulled from his embrace. "This isn't forever."

Zorlaeus heard her uncertainty. He dared to look back, beyond the doorframe, to Imperator Casvir towering in the background. He gave Zorlaeus no mind, instead keeping his stoic, relentless stare on Flowridia.

Something protective steeled his gaze, and something possessive, the willingness to cleave the half-giant in two should he threaten the resolve of the young woman he faced.

And there, in the flickering shadow of a smile threatening to pull at Casvir's lip, shone victory.

Casvir watched. Zorlaeus wondered how long he had been watching.

End

Author's Note:

Thank you so much for reading!

The Sting of Victory has been a labor of love like no other, and being able to share it with the world has been both daunting and infinitely rewarding.

If you loved what you read, I sincerely ask that you leave a review on Amazon and Goodreads, and wherever else you find appropriate. Reviews are a way to spread the word about a good book, as well as qualify for a variety of different services, awards, etc. Plus, it make an author's day to hear that someone enjoyed their writing.

If you want to hear more from me, consider joining my newsletter at sdsimper.com! Currently I'm offering two free prequel novellas to new subscribers—one about Flowridia and her time with Aura, as well as another about everyone's favorite drunk angel and that one time she was blackmailed into running a kingdom (and unknowingly ended up on a date with a certain half-demon).

Keep on turning pages if you want a sneak preview of a short story that lives on my Patreon! Thank you again for all your support. I couldn't be an author if you weren't a reader <3

- SD Simper

Available Now!

"Look at you, as sweet as springtime,
your heart and soul both.
Would you destroy all of that to bring about
your love's return?"

The dead lay gone but not forgotten. War has sparked in the demonic realm of Sha'Demoni, ignited by the wrath of a vengeful goddess seeking recompense for her daughter's death—and she deems Flowridia responsible. Meanwhile, Flowridia embarks on a journey with Imperator Casvir of Nox'Kartha, the mysterious patron of her powers. Casvir's assistance in her kingdom's quest to stop the reborn God of Order could ensure victory, but not without its own costs. After all, he who writes the contracts writes them in his favor.

Flowridia's powers flourish under Casvir's tutelage, manifesting in talents beyond her nightmares and dreams. With the strings of life and death held in her grasp, destiny might come at the cost of her soul.

All the while, Flowridia is plagued by dreams of Ayla Darkleaf, as well as the tantalizing promise of her lost love's return—for a price. But the city of the dead is full of secrets, and those her lover kept were the darkest of all.

Find out more about *Among Gods and Monsters* at
S D Simper's website—sdsimper.com

An excerpt from

Solstice Seduction

A Flowridia/Ayla erotic tale – only on Patreon

Winter howled beyond the shuttered window. A piling of snow reached the edge of the pane, and Flowridia stuffed spare cloth into the spaces exposed to the outdoors. Not their finest accommodations, but it was shelter from the storm.

Snow could be lovely, but when the winds wailed in ghostly tones and the cold cut to the bone, all Flowridia thought of was the warmth of her childhood home. Ilunnes, for all its faults, was far enough south to receive only a light dusting of frost.

A new sort of chill swept through Flowridia at the flickering shadows, unsurprised when Ayla appeared at her side. Her beloved kissed her cheek, a pile of firewood in her arms. "These should help," Ayla said, and she went immediately to the fireplace, to the flame threatening to die.

Flowridia pulled her blanket tighter around her, frankly miserable in the frosty night. Shivering, she paced, hoping motion would stave off the chill, but soon enough a fire blazed, and warmth slowly thawed her pinkish fingertips.

"In Sun Elven culture, the Winter Solstice is a time of a fear," Ayla said, coming to embrace Flowridia, holding the quit around her. "It is the longest night of the year—and we all know what used to emerge in the darkest parts of night." Her ensuing grin bespoke what she thought of that, and a shiver shot down Flowridia's spine—for any mention of Ayla's dark deeds was invigorating in ways not entirely sane.

Ayla stood on her toes, lips coming nearer to Flowridia's. "You might say it's my favorite holiday. A pity, for you to be so miserable. Still frozen?"

"Better now than before," Flowridia replied, but her breath caught when Ayla began removing her dress.

"Perhaps I could help," Ayla cooed, making a show of the motions, chuckling at Flowridia's obvious enamor. "I know how to get you hot."

Ayla moved languorously to the bed, not shy to splay herself across it. Flowridia briefly weighed the proposal against her biological needs—namely, whether or not removing her blanket was worth the prospect of getting her blood properly racing. "Why not."

"Darling, what would you say if I proposed trying something new tonight?"

To read the rest of Solstice Seduction, you can find it at:
https://www.patreon.com/sdsimper or by following the QR
code below:

About the author:

S D Simper has lived in both the hottest place on earth and the coldest, spans the employment spectrum from theatre teacher to professional editor, and plays more instruments than can be counted on one hand. She and her beloved wife share a home with their four cats, a Great Dane, and innumerable bookshelves.

Visit her website at sdsimper.com to see her other works, including *The Fate of Stars,* the story of a mermaid, a human princess, and a love that will shape the future of the world.